CROSS HEIRS

YOUNG ATLANTEANS

T STEDMAN

THE ROYAL FAMILIES
OF ATLANTIS

Dubonnetti
Bonaci
Santalini
Florianna

of Murrtaine
Borge

CHAPTER 1

Camberwell, London

JJ didn't have time to argue before Latitia bundled him into her tiny wardrobe. The door shut, it went black and he fell against the back panel.

'Sssshhh!' Latitia hissed from the other side. 'Don't move!'

Chance would be a fine thing. The slightest muscle flex and he was sure he'd set off the Speak 'n' Spell under his foot, it was so crammed with stuff.

Sneaking out of school during the day seemed a good idea at the time. They never got any privacy; not in the cramped bedroom Latitia shared with her little brothers. Her mum, Valarie, was supposed to be at work and it was just the end of term rubbish and not much to miss. Now here he was, with a feather threatening to make him sneeze, because Valarie had decided to come home from work early. If she found them, she wouldn't be happy, because on top of the obvious truanting, they were supposed to be keeping apart. But that was never going to happen.

He strained to hear if Latitia had been discovered, but

there was no sound at all. He couldn't stand the inactivity, so he moved carefully and poked his head out to see what was happening. At the opposite end of the cluttered room—a lavender shrine to boybands and kids' TV, Latitia had her ear to the door, trying to hear through to the other side.

What is it? JJ projected, straight to her mind, forgetting himself.

Luckily, she was so engrossed, listening, she just flapped her hand for him to stay quiet.

JJ stepped out silently, straightening the collar of his white shirt, at the neck of his navy school sweater and crept up alongside her. She glared at him but didn't say anything and concentrated on listening. She looked so cute in her tiny braids, tumbling into hazel eyes, so unusual against her warm caramel skin. Making even her dull uniform sexy, with her shirt knotted at her waist and filling out the shapeless black pants in all the right places. He pulled her closer to his body while they both kept their ears to the door. He studied her face, wondering how he was ever going to keep his hands off her. He could so easily kill her. Even with her mother just the other side of the thin, plywood door, he almost leaned in for a kiss. Except something stopped him and rocked through his whole body. It went through his limbs, pulsing electricity up his spine, exploding at the back of his mind. He recognised the feeling right away. Like a mental signature. An Atlantean was coming. A very powerful one. Stronger than anyone else he knew. The king. His second father, biological father to his siblings, Alexia and Xavier, was approaching quickly. *Dante.*

There was a light knock on the glass of the front door. Like an expected friend, not using the doorbell.

JJ put his index finger to his lips for Latitia not to make a sound. The front door was opened and Valarie's joyful shriek rang through the flat where she was clearly pleased to see him.

Latitia was staring wide-eyed, straight at him, gauging his reaction for who it might be.

'My father, the king,' he whispered.

Latitia's eyes widened further while her mouth made an 'O'.

There was no point going back in the cupboard, now. He needed to hear what Dante had to say. After Xavier had managed to talk Dante out of pulling them straight out of there, nothing had been said about them all going home to their secret family hideaway for Christmas.

JJ swore under his breath.

After making noise in the kitchen for a few moments, where he guessed Valarie was making Dante a drink, they went into the living room and closed the door. Now they couldn't hear a thing.

JJ cracked the door ajar.

'What are you doing?' Latitia hissed.

'I don't know about you, but I want to hear what they're saying,' JJ said, ignoring her look of terror and already moving out into the large, square hallway. There was nowhere to hide. Just a big magnolia space, with a coat rack that couldn't hold another coat. Only upright by the weight of the wooden chest underneath, overflowing with all different-sized shoes for the five kids and mom that lived there.

Dark shapes moved on the other side of the mottled glazed front door.

Latitia jumped and JJ pulled her down into a crouch with a hand over her mouth. 'My father's guards,' he explained, in a whisper.

They kept low on the dated patterned carpet, until they reached the living room door. Thankfully, it hadn't fully closed and they had about an inch to listen and spy. He didn't care so much about the arrangements; he was more intrigued with what had brought the king all the way here, to a household barely above the breadline, and an insignificant human woman, to explain the trip to her himself. Anyone could have done it for him.

He had a clear view of the familiar tall, black-swathed frame towering over the soft, plump curves of Latitia's mother. She was still wearing her dark-blue nurse's uniform and was an attractive woman, even after five kids. Dante's back was to him, but he saw enough when Valarie's arms went around his waist as he hugged her to him tightly.

JJ was stunned. Even though he knew they had history, it was still a shock to see for himself the obvious feeling they had for each other. The hug went on for several seconds, until he wanted to cough to stop them, it felt so uncomfortable. Latitia seemed as glued to it as he was. She flashed an alarmed glance his way that said, 'What on earth am I witnessing?' It was clear to him that Valarie meant more to Dante than any passing fling.

'It's good to see you again, Val. You look well,' Dante said, releasing her, but keeping a hold on her hands.

'Older. Fatter, maybe,' she said. 'You haven't aged a day.'

'Greyer, and a few more pounds, possibly?'

They both laughed and Dante hugged her again. They were clearly delighted to see each other.

LATITIA WATCHED HER ORDINARY, drab mother, hair scraped back and no makeup, wrapped in the arms of a man – no, a king, she'd only ever imagined in her daydreams. There, he'd been a faceless ghost and now he was here, real and standing in her living room. Tall, athletic build, head to foot in tasteful black, with black hair that touched the collar of his military-style jacket. She couldn't see his face clearly, but what she could see was startlingly like Xavier. His obvious affection for her mother and his soft Irish voice did not fit the character she'd imagined married to JJ's mother. He'd been cold and cruel, driving JJ's mum into the arms of his gorgeous father, Jay. This man blew that theory out of the water. He was stunning.

'I can't believe you're actually here,' her mother was saying. 'Thanks for the TV, by the way. The kids love it.' She was staring up into the king's eyes with complete adoration. Latitia had never seen her mother act so gooey-eyed over anyone before.

Dante held the sides of her mother's face and planted the gentlest of kisses on her furrowed brow. 'You are such a desirable woman, Val. How do you stay so young?'

Latitia couldn't believe it when her mother dissolved into fits of giggles and gave the king a playful shove. 'Stop it! Still a charmer, Dante.'

He laughed, pulling her back into his body with a groan. 'I don't say that to all the girls, you know.'

Latitia's heart was beating hard, not quite believing what she was seeing. This was clearly a meeting between two people who knew each other very well.

This time when they pulled apart Valarie asked, 'Is everything OK? What brings you to this part of the world?'

'Apart from seeing you, you mean? Excuse me a moment,' Dante said, putting his finger to his lips and turning his body to look straight at them.

Latitia almost didn't hear the summons to come in, she was so struck by the impact of his eyes. That smile. His mischievous expression. He was by far the most striking man she'd ever seen. Not beautiful in the same way as JJ's father, but dark and dangerous, with lively, shrewd eyes that appeared to be laughing. So like Xavier, but sexier, with added years that smoothed out the edges. He had a warmth and charisma that Xavier very definitely did not. He smiled right at her, proving he knew exactly where she was. 'Hello, there. Come out, JJ, and bring Val's daughter with you.'

Latitia felt JJ sag back from the door with a groan. She stood up slowly and followed him as he pushed open the door and went inside.

JJ HAD BEEN stupid to think his father wouldn't sense him the moment he neared the flat. He guessed he'd hoped that his Atlantean presence would be masked by his father's many guards. It had been wishful thinking. Dante was more powerful than anyone he knew and would know him as easy as a wolf catches a scent. At the very least Dante could have kept his cover. But he should have known that he had no problem with big scenes or displays of emotion. He was passionate in all things. Fearless and unapologetic. Always sociable, witty and larger than life. But he was unpredictable and could easily slip into the hard, no-nonsense statesman role and was frighteningly clever.

JJ approached a little sheepishly, allowing Latitia to catch up, and took her hand. He had no idea which Dante he was going to get.

Valarie looked annoyed with Latitia. 'I thought I told you two to keep apart ... and why aren't you at school?' she added, as if it just occurred to her.

Dante did nothing more than pull JJ into a tight hug, surrounding him with his signature cologne and kissing his cheek loudly. JJ was used to it, but it was always a shock to feel that engulfed by someone so open with their feelings. Dante was completely ignoring Valarie's anger. After releasing him just as quickly, he picked up Latitia's hand, cracked his wolfish grin and openly appraised her, sending a crafty wink JJ's way. 'I'm very pleased to meet you,' Dante said, sounding more Irish than ever. 'You are your mother all over again.' Then he pulled her closer by the hand he still held and kissed her gently on the cheek. No doubt taking the opportunity to craftily read her.

Magic, power, influence, whatever Dante had, its results were immediate. Latitia put her hand to her cheek where he'd kissed in bewilderment. She was floored by the effect Dante had on everyone. Maybe because he was an actual king. Possibly because he was charming and accessible, but mainly because he was so enigmatic. He simply eradiated power.

It made JJ's heart sink. He and Xavier had a long way to go to have half of what Dante had to be king.

'Ah, leave 'em. They're grand,' Dante said, dismissing it as a trifle, still grinning at Latitia. He looked at Valarie sardonically. 'Can't you see, they're gonna see each other whatever?'

LATITIA FELT DIZZY, she was so captivated by the man in front of her, who, she noticed, still had hold of her hand. He commanded the sparsely furnished room of tatty leather furniture and ridiculously large TV that he had sent them. She was completely starstruck and marvelled at how smoothly he handled a potentially explosive situation with her mother. He wasn't hardened or aloof. In fact, he was nothing like she imagined the husband of JJ's stunning mother. She didn't have one but two of the most gorgeous men she'd ever seen in her life and, what was more, she managed to keep them in love with her. Her heart ached for just the smallest part of that.

'What about two more cups of tea, Val?' Dante said, smiling, then resting his eyes shrewdly on Latitia again. Valarie got up from her chair with a huff and gave Latitia a dagger look as she went out to the kitchen. Dante finally dropped her hand with his smile and looked sternly at JJ. 'Has she taken the elixir I gave you?'

JJ shrugged moodily. 'Yes … well no. We couldn't complete the course because of her getting ill and everything,' he said, flashing his eyes at her, guiltily.

Latitia was vaguely reminded of the disgusting drink JJ had given her, but she was more fascinated by the family dynamic. She'd never seen JJ so subdued.

Dante simply nodded and pulled out three vials from the breast pocket of his stylish jacket. 'Here, take them.' He raised his eyebrows to indicate, quickly.

JJ leaned forward and snatched them, stowing them quickly in his trouser pocket before Valarie came back.

JJ HATED that Dante had known exactly what situation he was going to find. So much so that he'd even come prepared with elixir. He let out a weary sigh as Valarie walked back in with the teas, none the wiser. She gave Latitia hers with another sharp look and JJ's without any eye contact at all and went and sat back down in the armchair. It was clear she was really angry with the both of them.

Dante hadn't missed a thing and leaned forward and gave Valarie's hand a squeeze. On the surface, it was showing affectionate support, so much a part of Dante's character, but to those who knew him, he was affecting her psyche; scanning and calming her telepathically, gently putting her at ease. He did it constantly with everyone, without their knowledge. Even getting away with it with most Atlanteans. He affected the course of every meeting like that, socially or in business.

JJ had to hand it to him; if he'd honed his skill with presidents and prime ministers, poor Valarie didn't stand a chance. It had never really occurred to JJ before, but he was witnessing a masterclass in kingship right here. Every kiss, every squeeze of a hand got him whatever he wanted.

JJ let out a slow, steady breath. He and Xavier had so much to learn. All these years, they'd wasted their time on aggression when all it needed was a light touch or brush of skin.

Dante smiled knowingly as if he'd followed JJ's inner thoughts. He gave Valarie's hand a last pat and let it go as if he'd made his point. 'Now I have you all together, it makes things easier.'

Dante looked directly into Valarie's eyes and JJ wondered if Dante was actually entering her mind. Although something in the way he was with her told him that he wouldn't do that. He seemed to have real regard for Latitia's mother. Latitia flashed her eyes at JJ nervously as if she wasn't sure what was happening.

'I don't think separation is going to work with them, Val, do you?' he said, looking back at them.

Valarie huffed and looked at them begrudgingly. 'What are we supposed to do with them, then, Dante?' Her volume was rising and so was her pitch. 'My kids haven't been the same since your kids came. They're lovely kids, but—'

Dante leaned forward, cutting across her before she got too emotional and picked up both her hands again. He nodded sympathetically as if he agreed with everything she said. 'And you have every right to be upset, but they're all doing so well. I hear your boys are celebrities around here. They're happy. Their grades are good at school.'

Valarie looked away in frustration. Then, with a huff, she shrugged a little, forced to give him that.

'I tell you what. Why don't you all come to my home for the holidays? I have a little island retreat. A great doctor that can give the kids the once-over to put your mind at rest and we'll have a lovely time into the bargain. You can meet Tia and the family. What do you say?'

Valarie just stared at him while she absorbed what he'd said, obviously searching for reasons to say no. 'What, all of us? I'm not sure … there's work and everything,' she said, shuffling irritably in her seat to face him squarely.

Dante laughed. 'Don't get too excited, it's only a small island.'

JJ rolled his eyes.

'An island?' Valarie repeated, flatly.

Dante tipped his head. 'It's called Filfla. A tiny dot, barely visible on the map.'

LATITIA WATCHED EAGERLY, wanting to jump up like a small child and shout, 'can we?' In the end, she couldn't keep quiet. 'Please, Mum. I want to go.'

Valarie sagged in exasperation with her.

Latitia used all her willpower to rein it in. Her mother knew she was being railroaded and if they weren't careful, she'd say no just to give herself space.

'I know you want to, baby, but you have to think about your brothers.' She turned her attention back to Dante. 'It's Dwayne … he and Alexia had a thing …' She fidgeted. 'It'd be awkward.'

Dante clasped her hand in both of his and nodded, sympathetically. 'I know. And I wished heartily that that were still the case. My mind would rest easier than with the guy she's chosen, that's for sure. But here's the thing. Kids get their hearts broken every day. They cry. It's the end of the world, then they move on and they forget quickly.' He sat back in his seat and let out a chuff of laughter. 'Plus, there'll be a hundred bloody cousins descending on me for Christmas, half of which will be female. So I don't think he will be brooding for long,' he finished, sardonically.

Latitia held her breath as her mother appeared to be teetering, but something was still stopping her being sold.

'Argh, come on, Val. Let me repay you a little for all the things you've done for me in the past. Let me do this small thing for you,' Dante said, looking into her eyes intently.

CHAPTER 2

Valarie got to her feet so quickly that JJ thought she would storm out, but instead she wandered over to the window. He knew that view of Camberwell: a sea of haphazard box houses, dumpsters and old cars. Overgrown gardens, dumped furniture and the two huge gasholders just behind. However, that wasn't why she'd taken herself there. She didn't know it, but she was escaping Dante's hold. Rubbing away the pain on her forehead, disguising it as thinking.

Intrigued, JJ watched the master at work. All Atlanteans had certain mental powers by varying degrees, but Dante was the strongest. Mostly bestowed on him when he'd married his mother and took the throne. Some said it was unnatural to hold that much power and was what made him crazy and unpredictable. But most understood it was how he held the crown, and many had tried to take it. He was an exceptional male. Human leaders respected him and Atlanteans loved him. And, most importantly, the fates had chosen him.

Dante rose fluidly from his seat and came up behind

Valarie to look out over London. He gently held the tops of her arms and spoke softly into her ear. 'Please don't worry, Val. I would never let anything happen to you. Your kids are now like my own. I'll see to it that they want for nothing.'

It was so intimate. JJ glanced quickly at Latitia, who seemed mesmerised. Her mother turned in Dante's arms and looked up adoringly, eyes dewy with tears. With that fatal mistake, she'd already lost whatever internal battle she was waging. He almost felt sorry for her and half expected Dante to come straight out with the truth of who they were. 'A hey, no need to worry about a thing. We're just a harmless, separate species, living alongside you clueless humans for thousands of years.' He was that confident in his power to achieve his desired outcome. But with Latitia right there, it felt wrong. Uncomfortable. Like the spell needed to be broken.

However, JJ had to admit that Valarie was right to be concerned. After months of trying his hardest not to get involved with Latitia, for all kinds of reasons, not the least of which was causing her death, he'd only ever brought her more trouble and pain. It was hopeless to fight it. The more he fought, the more fall-out he created, until he was forced to give in and admit he wanted Latitia in his world.

But what then? 'What about after, Father?' It would be pointless for all concerned to go through the mind bend of learning the truth, that a hidden hybrid race had ingratiated themselves into their lives, only to have a meltdown and have their memories taken afterwards. 'What then? Will we be able to come back to school?' he said, not able to keep quiet any longer.

Dante released Valarie and let out a slow breath, as if he was getting a hold of his emotions.

Valarie immediately went to walk away, but Dante caught her and turned her to face him again. 'That all depends on Val.' He picked up her hands and looked deeply into her eyes.

'If she sees who we are and still thinks it's best for you not to mix with her kids, then that will be your answer.'

JJ couldn't believe he'd batted the decision so easily to Valarie. He was soon on his feet, on Dante's heels, walking Valarie towards the door. It wasn't that simple. He couldn't lose everything he'd built there, and he sure as hell knew that Latitia couldn't deal with that kind of trauma. Once was enough to send her out of her mind. He was already racing over a hundred scenarios that could happen while they were there, none of which were good. How crafty Dante had been to extricate himself from blame. There were hundreds of cousins. Loads of kids of similar ages. Fear gnawed at his ribs as he thought of the many Santalinis with teeth, Florianna with mad telekinetic skills and water breathing Murrs that stepped right out of the fountain in the middle of their home. His heart twisted and plummeted. Valarie would never accept it, even if Latitia did, she would surely have a breakdown.

Valarie opened the front door and Dante came to a standstill next to his two huge guards and turned back to face them. He smiled and picked up Valarie's hands for the last time. JJ sensed Latitia right behind him and reached for hers. There seemed no point in hiding their relationship any longer.

'Give us just two weeks, Val.'

JJ's eyes dropped to the king's thumb, gently rubbing the soft skin on the back of Valarie's hands. 'Let me show you who we really are at last and what we can do for you and your family. I promise, you won't regret it.'

Something from long ago passed between them, JJ wasn't sure what, but Valarie swallowed and nodded as if emotion rode her hard.

Dante leaned in and kissed her cheek lovingly, lingering a moment longer than he should.

'It's been lovely seeing you, Dante,' Valarie said in a cracked voice.

Dante seemed reluctant as he let her hands go and walked away, looking back over his shoulder, smiling and shaking his head as if she held some power over him.

JJ was left with a *be ready* from Dante, projected directly to his mind and his heart full of conflicting emotions at what it could all mean. His parting words left a dread-filled hole in his stomach. Latitia would see the Murr of her night terrors with no room for half-truths or excuses. Everything would be laid bare.

He guessed they'd stop once everything was revealed, anyway, but he couldn't stop the fear building inside him. Dante was about to throw them all in the deep end, in his confident, larger-than-life way. Taking for granted that they would all somehow swim and, no doubt, just as ready to teach them the lesson of their lives if they couldn't.

JJ couldn't be so confident. Dante hadn't seen the look on Latitia's face when he'd revealed his true form to her, before he'd scrambled her memories.

Whichever way he turned it over in his head, his father made no sense. JJ thought all the secrecy was meant to protect humans like the Johnsons. Dante was about to rip the band-aid off and JJ knew without any shadow of a doubt that if Valarie reacted badly to it then him and Latitia, their new life at the school, their businesses, everything they'd built, would be over.

The thought terrified him.

XAVIER'S HEART was fluttering up into his mouth, all the way in the car, through Paige's run-down, litter-covered estate. Then it turned somersaults as he parked his sleek little Mazda MX5 and sat, like it was a silver bubble of calm, shielding him from the run-down world outside. He took a breath, opened the door and after putting an expensive Italian loafer out onto the gum-splatted tarmac, he stood and smelled the dishwater air. It was now or never. So, clicking his key-fob over his shoulder and hearing the comforting pip of the car lock, he set off, taking long, purposeful strides. Blind to the path lined with overflowing rubbish bins, urine-smelling stairwell and gangway of cigarette butts. The whole way to the front door of the second-floor maisonette where his girlfriend, Paige, lived.

His nerves were completely irrational because he had no doubt he could make her mother agree to anything he wanted her to. He guessed it was more to do with how Paige would take it when she knew what he was. After all, it had backfired on JJ, which had driven them to this situation in the first place. That bad decision had almost destroyed their life when he'd had to wipe Latitia's memories.

Xavier suppressed his fears and trampled them right down into the pit of his stomach. It wouldn't happen to him. What he and Paige had was real. It wasn't some high school infatuation.

That was enough to send his butterflies into freefall.

He hurriedly knocked the door before he wimped out completely. Xavier Dubonnetti, crown prince of the Atlantean nation, never cowered away from anything. He was a leader already and he always got what he wanted.

'Hey!' Paige said. Her face brightened the moment she opened the door. He gathered her up and kissed her. He couldn't help himself. Her warm, soap-scented skin tantalised his senses, making him crush her to him.

'Zav-yay … Zav-yay,' her young brother and sister shrieked, bounding out.

Xavier bent down and produced the customary chocolate bars.

'Yay!' they cheered, grabbing one each and running off with them. 'Thanks, Zav-yay.'

'Check you can eat them before dinner, guys.'

He knew they'd start on them as soon as they were out of sight.

Linda, Paige's mother, came out from the kitchen drying her hands on a tea towel, while Paige closed the door behind him. 'Hi, Xav. Are you staying for dinner?'

His eyes immediately went to Paige's. Her eyebrows went up, willing him to say yes and melting his heart. But he couldn't succumb. He still had stuff to arrange for his Murr drug business before they all left for Filfla at the end of the week. 'Can I have a rain check on that, Linda?' he said, smiling an apology. 'I've a hundred things to do before I go home for Christmas.' He was secretly pleased with the immediate look of disappointment on Paige's face. 'That's what I want to talk to you both about, actually,' he said, holding eye contact with Paige the whole time. 'Do you have five minutes?' he said, switching his attention back to Linda.

Paige's aura brightened to deepest indigo as she looked pleadingly at her mother to say yes.

'OK, let me just take the pots off the heat,' her mother said.

Paige kissed him on the mouth, quickly, as soon as her mother disappeared back into the kitchen, then led him into the sparsely furnished living room.

Xavier barely noticed the tatty black leather three-piece suite and bare magnolia walls, anymore. There was so much more to the little house than stuff. Paige's little brother and sister briefly glanced their way. They were intent on watching TV and eating their chocolate, which was already a smear at the corners of their mouths.

Linda breezed in and took them straight out of their

hands, to their shrieks of complaint. 'After dinner!' she said with a glare at them both.

Xavier grinned. He'd have done exactly the same at their age. Then he frowned as a thought struck him. JJ would have hidden his and produced it when Xavier's had been confiscated by the nanny. It wasn't the clever move that plucked his heart strings, it was that he would have shared his.

He squashed the unpleasant feeling when he realised that Linda had sat down in the leather armchair and was waiting for him to speak. Paige squeezed his hand as if she sensed he was far away and pulled him to sit with her on the sofa.

He angled himself to face them both and scratched his head, not really knowing how to start now he'd got their attention. He guessed it didn't really matter as no wasn't an option, but a natural yes would be nicer. He frowned, running a finger and thumb against his forehead.

'What is it?' Paige said, sitting forward a little, immediately concerned.

'Nothing,' he said. 'Honestly.' He couldn't believe how hard this was. Paige meant so much to him already. He looked across at Linda, who was beginning to look puzzled, but momentarily distracted by Paige's sister scrambling up into her lap. 'Linda, there is something I wanted to ask you.'

Linda smiled and nodded while she arranged the girl on her lap more comfortably.

'You know I'm going home for Christmas?' He felt Paige immediately sag with disappointment next to him. 'Well, I wondered, my mother and father wondered, if you would all like to join us. I mean, it would be different... We have a large, unconventional family, but...' He tried to stop himself rambling, but couldn't help it as no one had said a word.

Linda looked stunned.

Paige was gripping the life out of his hand and looking wide-eyed at her mother in an expression of pleading and wonder. Her little sister got down from her mother's lap to jump and chant with her brother, 'Father Christmas, Father Christmas!'

Xavier wanted to shout for them to say something. Anything, as neither Linda nor Paige had moved. He couldn't tell if it was shock or whether she was trying to find a reason to say no, even though there wasn't one. He wouldn't allow it. She would be panicking at being caught off guard. He could just imagine. No presents. The difference between the two families to buy them. Feeling different in their company. It made him smile. Nothing would even come close to what she should be concerned about.

Then, of course, she hit on the clincher: 'Don't you live in Ireland? I have a passport that might still be in date, but none of the kids have one.'

Xavier turned his head in time to see the hope drain out of Paige's face. The problem seemed insurmountable to her. It gave him the courage to reply to Linda straight and to the point. 'My father is very influential. As long as he has their full names and dates of birth, he will be able to sort that out.'

Hope returned to Paige's face as she looked intently into his eyes. He had already told her he was royal. The cogs in her mind were already turning as the truth of it now clicked into place. He decided to hit them with both barrels as he didn't want to bat away any more excuses. Linda had already used up her one and only valid reason. 'We're not going to Ireland. We're going to my father's hideaway retreat of Filfla. You will be very privileged as literally no one outside our trusted circle has ever gone there.'

'Fli-fla, Fli-fla,' Paige's little brother, Luke, began to chant. 'I want to go to Fli-fla.'

His cute mispronunciation made Xavier chuckle. Then he took in the stunned look on Linda's face. 'There'll be loads of kids there of all ages. I literally have hundreds of cousins.

You'll hardly be noticed.' That wasn't strictly true. Very few outsiders ever got to see their world, let alone humans.

He turned to Paige expecting her to be thrilled, only to see red cheeks of embarrassment. He had no idea why. 'It will be lovely, I promise you,' he continued, now worried he'd lost them. He was suddenly envious of JJ. He bet he was finding this a lot easier with his father, Dante's, connection already with Valarie.

His gaze went back to Linda, who looked more uncomfortable than pleased. It was exasperating when he was only trying to do something nice.

'I think you might have to explain where Filfla is and who you are,' Paige said, quietly.

None of it was what he was expecting.

Linda was looking between them now, a little alarmed. 'What? What does she mean? Who are you, Xavier?'

Xavier wished he could go back in time and repeat this after thinking it out better, but he'd started now, so he pushed on. 'Filfla is a tiny island off the coast of Malta.'

When he still got no response, 'In the Mediterranean.'

Linda still looked confused.

'Xavier is a prince, Mum,' Paige said.

Xavier raised his eyebrows and smiled at Linda, but her confused look was changing from horror to disbelief and even a bit angry. This was not how he saw any of this going. He simply nodded and ploughed on, the conversation now feeling like a quagmire. 'That's true, but you wouldn't have heard of us, we are a very secretive nation. My father would very much appreciate it if you kept it that way.'

Paige looked worried as she studied her mother's reaction. She did look traumatised. Heaven knew how she'd react to the full story. He got to his feet; the inactivity was killing him. Even the little ones were quiet, looking at each of them to see if they should be scared. He needed to get out of there.

'Look, I'll leave that to sink in, but a car will come for you all on Saturday morning at eight.'

Paige stood with him. He hated that she was so worried and he gripped her hands. 'Can you get a passport photo from everyone and get them to me as soon as possible? My father will sort out the rest.' She nodded and smiled weakly. He wished he could comfort her and tell her it would be alright, but that would have to come later, when they were alone. He turned back to Linda, getting to her feet in a daze. He had no patience left for sugar-coating anything after seeing the effect it was having on Paige. 'Pack for winter. It's warmer than here, but windy and the palace can be draughty this time of year. We'll be flying out of Biggin Hill airfield and it will take around three hours to get to Malta.' He shrugged moodily when he remembered. 'Unfortunately, the Johnsons are coming.' That seemed to bring her back to the room as if it added authenticity to what he was saying. These humans were insufferable at times. 'Don't worry about presents, just your own for each other. Believe me, when you see my lot, you'll understand. There's just too many of them.' He nodded, leaving it at that and made his way out to the hallway.

It was Paige's hand that beat him to the handle of the front door. She didn't make eye contact right away. It troubled him more than anything. He turned her chin to look at him, not willing to leave on a bad note.

'Why, Xav? Why all of us there?'

That wasn't the response he'd expected. Maybe he'd played the whole thing completely wrong. When he looked into Paige's eyes, he didn't see happiness and excitement, only worry and hurt. He was normally so calm and strong about all his decisions. Instead, his mind was scrambling and his heart pumped out of rhythm. For the first time in his life, he felt unsure about himself. All he could say was the truth. 'I thought you'd be pleased.'

'Yes, but my whole family, Xav? How is my mum supposed to feel?'

It didn't seem that odd. People spent Christmas together all the time. His heart began to sink. Maybe not in her world. Perhaps they didn't do that kind of thing at all. When he really thought about it, they didn't even go round each other's houses for dinner. He couldn't think of a single dinner party happening since he'd been there. He felt so stupid now. No one had any money to cater for whole families.

Xavier cupped the side of Paige's face with his hand. 'I'm sorry, I'm a complete arse. I didn't realise it would make you and your mother so uncomfortable.' He leaned in and kissed her tenderly on the lips. It felt the natural thing to do.

Paige melted instantly. Forgiving him for his lack of sense immediately. He loved her all the more for that. He pulled out of the kiss and studied her face intently. It was open and completely trusting. He swore if they'd been alone, he would have ravished her there in the hallway. Sweat was already gathering on his brow. He gathered himself together, 'Look, Paige, you already know who I am. Please understand that although I've made a hash of it, all this comes from the best intentions.'

Paige was already nodding, trying to close the gap so she could kiss him again. But he had to get across his point. 'But, Paige, you don't know everything and your whole family needs to know as it will affect you all. And the same goes for the Johnsons.'

Paige finally stopped trying to dismiss his worries with distracting kisses and gave him her full attention. 'What do you mean?'

Xavier rested wearily on a hip and held onto her hands.

'After Christmas, everything at school will change. Who I am … what I am, affects everyone. You need to know for your protection. I can't say more than that.'

'Because of kidnap, or something like that?'

He bobbed his head. 'Possibly, yes. When you come to my home, it will all make sense. I promise. But please understand that I want you to know me. I need you to accept me for what I am if we're ever going to go the distance.' He wasn't sure where the speech came from, but he meant every word. It mixed him up inside that she meant so much to him. He couldn't even bear to think of the consequences of rejection. He and JJ would simply disappear from all their lives like they'd never been.

Paige seemed to understand as the look she gave him was one of love and wonder.

'You're not a placeholder, OK.' With that reminder of an earlier conversation, he crushed her to him and gave her one blistering, all-consuming kiss. His temperature rose dangerously and he felt Linda approaching. With that, he had the last word. 'You will all be coming on Saturday.' Then, in the next breath he left, the door shut behind him and he was gasping the cool London air.

J felt a strange mix of emotions as he rode up in the cage lift. Despite an excruciatingly long week at school, where he'd been trapped doing stupid, inane things, while his life hung in the balance, everyone was coming and everything was set. He should feel great.

If he was honest, most of it stemmed from a very real fear after his last disastrous attempt at revealing his true self to Latitia. That had led to her almost losing her mind. Now he was taking her home to weirdo central to introduce her to his whole secret world. Where the cute little island retreat his father had pitched so eloquently, was in fact, a WWII bunker, made over to a palatial homage to their home planet and gifted to them by the prime minister of Malta himself. There would be hundreds of relatives, with all kinds of abilities, not to mention those coming and going from their underwater city through a gateway to the sea. *Bloody hell.*

The lift reached the top. He took a moment to gather his composure. He didn't do meltdowns. That was Xavier's department. He had to think practically, one catastrophe at a time. He'd left Latitia in her usual family chaos to pack and was back to the peace of the penthouse loft he shared with Xavier. No stressful packing for them. Just laptops and phones, everything they needed was at home. He felt immediately better.

He stepped out, still amazed and proud that the penthouse was theirs. They'd changed so much. He and Xavier had grown up since they'd been there and accomplished a lot in a short period of time. Despite their father cutting them off, they'd found their loft and ways to fund their lifestyle themselves. He, with his already thriving B2H social media platform and Xavier with his sell-out Murr performance drug business. Now they had their work cut out convincing their father to let them keep it. And it all boiled down to their girlfriends. Ironic really, when they'd been forced to use Dante's team of virtual assistants for the day-to-day running of it all, just to go. Without it, their little trip home that could ruin everything would be impossible. It was enough to blow his mind.

JJ certainly didn't expect to walk in and find Xavier sitting on one of their large leather sofas, the night before they were supposed to leave, with his head in his hands. He assumed he would have railroaded Paige and her family, in his own inimitable style and found it easy. He walked past the kitchen and threw down his keys on the burnished metal countertop. 'What's the matter?' JJ asked. For a moment, his heart spiked, that everything had been cancelled.

Xavier let his hands drop, leaving his hair an uncharacteristic black mess. 'It's bloody Alexia. I just got off the phone to Dad and he said she's refusing to come home for Christmas unless the Russian godfather of Atlanteans is invited too.'

JJ frowned. He didn't usually agree with Xavier's attitude

towards his sister, but on this occasion, he had a point. Yaro Demidov, or Rasputin, as he was known on the street, was a powerful underground Atlantean, as shady as they come. They knew almost nothing about him, except he came from a hitherto unknown, disregarded, branch of the Santalini royal family. That meant a dangerous, disgruntled, vampire. The thought of that in the centre of court, where all his aunties, young children and Latitia would be, gave him the shivers too. 'What does Dad say?'

'Nothing yet,' Xavier said, looking a little relieved. 'He's meeting with him tonight before he gives her his answer.' Xavier looked him dead in the eye. 'We need to get there first.'

JJ was already shaking his head. He totally got Xavier's frustration, but this was not something they could get in the middle of. 'Don't jump the gun,' he said, patting the air for him to chill out. 'Dad won't go in blind. Let's give him a chance.'

Xavier said nothing more, but slapped something small, circular and black on the coffee table and glared at him.

JJ stared at it, frowned, then shrugged at Xavier, confused. 'What?

'Take a closer look. It came out of the remote when I threw it. The TV sound has been playing up for weeks.'

JJ flashed an alarmed glance at Xavier and scooped up the small disc and brought it to his eyeline. It was about the size of a button, but flat and had two thin wires sticking out of it. 'A bug?' His mind was already working on the perfect place it was found. Powered by a battery device used automatically the moment someone cane home. 'Who? Demidov?'

'Has to be. No wonder he's always two steps ahead of us.'

JJ looked up at the ceiling with the mind-crushing thought that he was taking Latitia right into the midst of all that madness.

Xavier was already on his feet, grabbing his keys. 'Come on. We might not have much time to warn Dad before he gets there.'

CHAPTER 4

Alexia rode in the back of Yaro's blacked-out car and gripped his chilled hand. It struck her even after weeks together that he never seemed to warm up. That his family were part of her race but separate. One that had been treated abysmally by her ancestors. They were Santalinis but Ambragio. The immortals. A small off-shoot of elite agents that had been forgotten, dismissed, and written out of the Atlantean history books. Only to appear in human fairy tales as evil blood suckers of the night.

She looked up at his pale, chiselled jaw. He was so serious and deep in thought. She often thought of him as a perfectly contained storm. A pent-up tempest of emotion that was barely visible on the surface, that only she saw at night. Alone, when the lights were doused and his brilliant-white aura broke through.

He sensed her watching him and looked intently down at her. He no longer covered his crimson eyes in front of her. He tipped his head and kissed her without saying a word. He was almost three hundred years old. Older than anyone she knew and yet she could tell a current of nerves ran through him too. Or maybe it was excitement, she wasn't sure.

She was nervous because he was meeting her father, the king, for the first time. She guessed this was huge. A lot was riding on it for them both. Her happiness depended on this one meeting. If her father allowed him home to Filfla, it would mean accepting him as her boyfriend. But for Yaro and his people, it was acknowledging their existence as an Atlantean family. There could be no bigger gesture her father could make than offering his own daughter. Yaro's life's work would be realised. Everything he'd worked for. She couldn't imagine how it must feel to belong to a family that had been eradicated from history.

She calmed down her heart by touching her chest. Her father was fair, but he was also a statesman. Nothing would be straightforward. Yaro would not only want her father's blessing to date her, but he would demand recompense. An apology at the very least and their existence announced to the whole Atlantean world. That would cause a problem with the Santalini royal family. As their closest relatives, they would have to welcome Yaro's people into their fold. Despite her standing firmly with Yaro's cause, she understood what a diplomatic headache all this was going to be for her father. However, Yaro's family had been wronged and it had to be put right.

Alexia gazed up at him again and gave his cool hand a squeeze. He brought it to his mouth and kissed it absently. Her heart fluttered. She'd fallen in love with him within days of meeting him. She couldn't believe she'd actually thought she was in love with Dwayne Johnson. What a fool she was. Compared to this, it was a teenage crush. When her brothers had cruelly tampered with his memories to keep them apart, she'd been heartbroken. Then Yaro had swooped in and saved her and changed everything. He was like no one she'd ever known. He was a vampire in the truest sense of the word. So much more even than her cousins, the Santalinis. They were huge, muscular soldiers and only drank blood within their marriage bond. So apart from extraordinarily long canines, they were like any other warm-blooded Atlantean.

Yaro was a different being entirely. He was cold-blooded and had to keep covered from the light and constantly kept warm. His skin was pale, threaded with blue veins, and he had no colour in his irises at all. They were harsh-looking and red from the blood flowing through them. In fact, what completely amazed her was that he was two different people. The one she was looking at now, pale skin, dark soul and effortlessly dangerous. And the other, that thrived in the darkness with light bursting out of him like an angel.

Living with him in his dark world did make her some-times yearn for simple sunlight, but there was so much more to him that it made every sacrifice worth making. He had great powers, most of which she still didn't know their extent. He could move faster than she could see and half of London was terrified of him. Urban myths had grown up around him. He was a ruthless businessman that no one dared cross. He was proud, strong, and, of course, he drank blood. For him and his family, it was the food that sustained them and they consumed little else. They were the Ambragio, the immortals of the race, because of their long lives. She had begun to crave the sting of his fangs and what it was to be completely his.

She dropped her gaze to the pale hand that held hers. The blackened talons for nails that pitted her skin. The many tiny glyph tattoos that went up the length of his fingers, all the way up his pale arms. It sent cold shivers of excitement all over her.

Today, he wore a beautifully tailored black suit and black

shirt, with a perfectly narrow black tie, whose pattern was only visible in the weave of the black silk. He was always impeccably dressed. Maybe not with the flare of JJ's dad, Jay, but with equal class and finesse. The monochrome look against his pale skin made his eyes and lips a perfectly contrasting red.

She noticed the light-cancelling wraparound sunglasses gripped in his other hand. She felt a pang of sadness that he felt the need to wear them in front of her father, but she understood why. Today was all about their similarities, not their differences. His blue-veined forehead crinkled with worry as he ran through everything in his mind as if to make her point.

She pulled her hand from his and ran her fingers through his black, tousled hair. He closed his eyes briefly, welcoming the soothing touch. He was as utterly terrifying as he was beautiful. Like a wild animal straining against its bonds. No other being could even come close to his magnificence. His fangs distended past his lips at the proximity of her wrist, compelling her to bring it to his mouth. Her hand began to shake as she courted death. She was under no illusion how dangerous he was. Nevertheless, she longed for him to drink from her completely, to be his only sustenance, and not just to taste her as he'd done on that one terrifyingly beautiful, nerve-awakening time.

Love was a gnawing, biting thing, in the centre of her chest. Something that would need to be satisfied soon. Her eighteenth birthday would eventually come and he would no longer hold himself back. She felt it growing inside him. Straining in the corded muscle of his shoulders and the clench of his jaw. And she longed for that day. She needed it. But at the same time, she was petrified of it. For now, she was satisfied with his attentiveness. The way he cared for her. Cherished her. Catered for her every need. Like no one ever had before. Making her feel like an adult – a grown woman.

Although she never truly forgot he was wild. A creature that allowed her near, that could cancel her existence in a second. But that just heightened the intrigue. He was a powerful magnet. Drawing her to him. She was hopeless. Helpless. Addicted to every expression, every movement he made. Completely fascinated by his beauty. The way he paid her careful attention, while keeping his coiled restraint; she was playing with a tiger. Longing for every spine-tingling moment. Losing her breath in anticipation for the leash to snap.

She'd fallen out with her brothers over him. Even JJ, who was her favourite person in the world, who she'd adored since birth. But both he and Xavier did not approve of her choices. Well, it wasn't their call to make. It wasn't even her father's, because with a love like this, no one got a choice. It slammed into you like a freight train and took all your sanity with it. That's what they didn't understand. The fact they thought Yaro only wanted her because she was the daughter of an Atlantean king didn't come into it. Of course it had occurred to her in the beginning. A niggling doubt at the back of her mind. She was perfectly aware she was a prize to a man like Yaro. One whose deepest desire was validation. But when they were alone. When there was no one around to witness the gentle way he cared for her. Not taking advantage of her youth for her blood or her body; nothing in this world would convince her he didn't care. Even when she'd pleaded with him to treat her like an adult, all he'd done was nick her skin at the wrist and sample the smallest drop.

That had been right at the beginning. 'To create a link,' he'd explained. Leaving her panting and yearning for more. But he'd gone on to explain, 'I will always know where you are now, even in the daylight.' She hadn't missed the way his chest heaved with the effort and his brow furrowed when he tried to withdraw his fangs.

He'd wanted her. Even then. It made her angry and confused. He'd behaved like a perfect gentlemen. Seeing to it that she had her own room and could come and go as she pleased. Then she'd relaxed into this growing crush, that soon bloomed into outright adoration. Knowing absolutely that he was fighting his impulses, ready to snap, to have her.

So she'd relaxed a little more. Satisfied with having the best possible place to live for her brothers to sweat. She'd spent her days moping around the house, searching and rummaging whenever she could, to find out more about Yaro. The male who pulled her more and more to him every day, without lifting a finger. He was a captor without chains. She'd become his willing slave, eager to do anything for him within days.

He sat with her every evening for meals, even though he didn't eat at all. He studied her, watching her every movement with low-lidded eyes.

They talked often. He, posing seemingly insignificant questions and then listening closely while she talked for hours. About her brothers and all her siren aunts. Their partners and her father's council at which they all took a seat. The other Atlantean family houses and from where they all came. Their children, her many cousins, he listened to it all. He seemed particularly fascinated with the unconventional family she grew up in, with Jay being JJ's biological father and, of course, the wonders of the underwater city of Murrtaine where she'd spent much of her childhood.

'Do you swim?' she'd asked, suddenly. He was descended from one of the purest bloodlines, but she'd never met an Atlantean more suited to the earth. There was no pool in his house. In fact, he literally never mentioned water.

He'd just smiled and nodded slowly in that knowing way

he had about him. 'It is not something one forgets,' he'd said, his smile growing, slightly mocking her.

She'd eventually ventured out to school to see her brothers, but they soon annoyed her by treating her as the child she no longer was. She ran back to Yaro, upset and revelled in him taking her into his arms. He smoothed it all away. Caressing her with his wonderful scent that she knew contained his magical, luring power. She wasn't a fool. She knew he exuded it a lot whenever he was around her.

Sometimes, when she awoke with a start in her room, she was sure it had reached out to her in his sleep. It felt like a soft, seeking frond that travelled up from the vault where she knew he slept in the basement. It went up through the house, opening her door where it wrapped itself around her. After a few days, she'd begun to expect it. She lay awake waiting, and it always came. Until she couldn't sleep without it. She understood then what it was: an extension of him, that sought her out from his subconscious.

Then one night, she got out of bed and decided to follow it. It became a trail of black mist, graceful and beckoning. Doors opened miraculously, right up to the huge, three-feet thick, circular vault door in the basement that clanked and opened for her to enter.

She walked in cautiously, her skin prickling in fear. Until she came across Yaro's sleeping body, reposed and deathly pale against the black satin sheets of his huge, canopied bed. A soft glow from a single bloodred candle lit him perfectly and dramatically like an old painting. He really did look like a sleeping vampire. Her breathing stopped. Except for the sheet that only covered his lower half, he appeared to be perfectly naked.

She knew she should go, but she found that she couldn't and stood for several minutes admiring him. Simply watching the slow rise and fall of his chest. He looked so peaceful, his usually tense brow now totally smooth. The only hint to the danger within was the tiny glyph tattoos that appeared to cover his entire body. She'd only ever seen them from the tips of his fingers to the cuffs of his expensive shirt.

Something told her that if she doused the candle, his aura would burst through like a spectacular angel, even while he slept. But she didn't want to wake him and reveal herself to be trespassing into his personal space. Even though he had drawn her to him, whether he was aware of it or not. At this moment, he was innocent. There was no criminal mastermind while he slept.

She guessed it was at that point she'd known she would never leave him. She instinctively knew there would be no one else who could satisfy her. He was perfect. A strong Atlantean. A royal that none of the alpha males in her family could intimidate. She knew he could hold his own with them all. He would never be diminished by a living soul. Not even her father.

That night, in the vault, as she went to turn away, something gently stopped her, making her turn back. The wonderful smell grew and filled the place where he slept. Somewhere inside him, he must have wanted her there. No one got to see him this vulnerable. Not unless he wanted them to.

She didn't want to sleep alone, so squashing down the voice that whispered it was a bad idea, she silently crawled onto the bed and slipped under the oily sheet. The bed was firm, but it still dipped. She kept her eyes on him and held her breath. He didn't stir.

She was shaking. It was freezing and her body was alive with anticipation. She tried to stop shivering. She knew his blood needed it this cold to sleep, so she curled into a ball and wished she'd brought a quilt, or at least a throw with her. She was never going to be able to sleep. Her heart was beating too fast with her own daring for a start. She barely knew him. He was a stranger who was a self-confessed, dangerous criminal. She was a young girl who'd just got into bed, without permission, with a male fifteen times her age. She must be mad.

He, on the other hand, continued to sleep peacefully.

She was about to turn and creep out the way she came, when the feeling of soft plumes of smoke crept over her again. It began to stroke down her bare arms, warming and bringing her skin alive, everywhere it touched. The smell she associated with him grew, until it clouded all her senses. Somehow, she knew it was his inner magic, enticing, winding itself around her, crushing her resolve. He hadn't moved a muscle, but it felt like a snake constricting, holding her in place, ready for him to eat.

By this point, she could no longer move, even if she wanted to, which she didn't. Something deep down wanted this. To follow it to see where it ended. Her heart hammered and she didn't even feel him move.

Until he struck.

CHAPTER 5

There was no time to scream. Alexia's hair was out of the way and Yaro's teeth pierced the side of her neck and clamped down hard. A low growl reverberated next to her ear and his strong arms that had moved so fast, crushed her. One around her back, the other around her waist and she was facing the other way. She was nestled perfectly against his taut body as he curved around her in one fluid manoeuvre.

She only attempted to move once and he growled and gripped her harder.

Then she felt the pulls. Huge, heavenly drags at her neck that seemed to reach down to her groin. He was drinking, but it felt like the pull of harp strings with butterflies going outwards from her chest to the extremities of her whole body. She should have been repulsed, or at the very least scared, but she wasn't. She didn't struggle. She submitted completely. It all made sense. He called in his sleep and she came. For this, she now realised.

He had warned her on that first night. He'd said if she lived in his house, he would drink her blood and this was it.

And it was heavenly. She felt warm and safe and her whole body felt alive to his touch. She'd never experienced anything like it, nor would she again. It was the being held so completely that melted her. All without being hurt, in a dangerous predator's arms, taken so near to death.

The feeling was bizarre. Delirious. Happy. Dazed. Drugged. She could sense the end and yet she wanted it. Yearned for it. Willed him to take it all. She was so comfortably warm and drowsy. Her eyelids began to close as his pulls slowed. His teeth retracted and he kissed her neck, holding it a long moment in his lips. Then she felt his arms travel and he turned her around easily to face him.

He was fully awake now and his face looked hard in the warm light, but he was utterly beautiful. His deep, carmine eyes bore intently into hers. Obsessively. As if he were looking directly for her soul. Then he drew closer and kissed her for one all-consuming moment. It sealed them both. He engulfed her. Even if she was dying, there would never be another like that. A pact that there would never be anyone else for her.

Her eyelids fluttered closed. 'Thank you,' became an echo, that she wasn't sure came from him or from her. Then, the next thing she knew, she was in her own bed, in her room.

Her hand went to her neck. A small plaster was there and it ached a little. Heat bloomed between her legs as she remembered the feeling. She knew now that she wanted him. In every way. She wanted to own him as completely as he now owned her.

ALEXIA SWALLOWED at the strength of the memory. They'd made good time as it was late and pulled into the underground carpark of Jay's hotel in Soho. The Bluebell. The tyres screeched on the tarmac as they entered the electric gate and went downwards.

Alexia wasn't sure how she felt about meeting here. It was her favourite place to come when she was a child, and she didn't want her memories mixed or tarnished if today didn't go well.

Yaro hadn't said a word during the whole journey. She guessed he wouldn't have brought her along at all unless her father had insisted on it. She couldn't believe her father had the situation so wrong.

They turned a sweeping circle and pulled up at the furthest point, near the stairwell, where she realised another car had been following behind them. Nerves buzzed and fluttered in her chest. The driver held the door open for her and she got out and counted at least five of Yaro's closest men. Ambragio, all of them. She could tell by their identical black hair, pale skin and sunglasses. They were all extremely tall, too, and very slim and athletic-looking. With the driver, that was six.

Alexia looked at Yaro nervously as he got out of the car on the other side. It meant that despite his power and reputation, he was taking no chances. This wasn't how she wanted it to go. She wanted a simple, friendly chat, where her father's worries got put to rest and he gave them his blessing. This was fast becoming like some diplomatic summit. If her father had a similar show of strength, then there could be trouble. 'Please be careful,' she whispered, picking up Yaro's hand. 'Please don't lose your temper ... for me,' she added, gazing up into his strange, hypnotic eyes.

She knew he could barely see her as he was almost blind in the light, but he would hear the plea in her voice and feel the anxiety in her blood. He put on his sunglasses and leaned down to kiss the centre of her forehead. 'Do not worry,' he whispered back. 'I have come to make history, not to fight.'

She'd rather hoped it was to make a good impression on her father for her sake, but she guessed she was being naïve. She was scared for him if her father had his huge Santalini guards with him. Scared for her two fathers, she sensed waiting upstairs, and, most of all, she was scared how this would leave them as a couple after all this was over. Her life would literally be over if this went badly.

Yaro felt it all and kissed her again on the lips. Then he brought her hand to his mouth and kissed the back of it. 'Ready?' he asked.

She nodded, but she didn't think she'd ever truly be ready for this. However, as soon as they began to walk, her thoughts were swept away as two huge Santalini guards stepped out of the opening lift. The welcoming committee. She recognised them instantly. Her uncle Keenan, married to her mother's sister and his cousin Reeve. Her two favourite Santalinis. She didn't know whether to be happy or terrified. Everything seemed so much easier when none of her worlds mixed.

Keenan took an instant visual sweep of her for damage and gave her the smallest smile, then directed his sole attention to Yaro. 'Leave your men here, you have nothing to fear.'

Alexia felt Yaro's grip on her hand tighten. It was the only clue to the escalating tension. He was getting angry and her heart sped up in case he erupted. She'd never seen it herself, but she always suspected it would be terrible. However, she needn't have worried. As usual, he was the perfectly contained storm. 'Very well, but two of my closest brothers is the etiquette, is it not?'

Yaro's Russian accent sounded very strong in the present company and her heart fluttered as her gaze shifted from Yaro to Keenan for his answer. Keenan surveyed the wall of testosterone as if he was making up his mind and then reluctantly nodded.

Yaro smiled a little and held out an arm for Keenan to lead the way. Alexia hadn't seen much of Yaro's dealings, but she was starting to think that he was more formidable than even she imagined. She guessed he would have to be after three hundred years of dragging himself up from nothing, through a world that grew to fear him. Suddenly she felt more uneasy for her fathers. If this wasn't handled carefully, someone she loved a great deal would be hurt.

The six of them rode up in the lift in silence. All with their backs to the wall, she noticed, in case of trouble. It made her want to scream how ridiculous it was. She was tiny in comparison to any single one of them and they were all in a confined space. She didn't know what they thought either side would do. It felt like two American football line-backers facing off against three NBA basketball players. With her in the middle, barely coming up to their chests. Ludicrous. She huffed loudly, making all eyes switch to her. This was a terrible idea. But how else was she going to make Yaro and her father meet? She wanted Yaro accepted into the family and his family acknowledged and welcomed into the race.

At last, the lift stopped, pinged and the doors opened. They were hit with warmth and the sound of the soft piano jazz that Jay loved. Keenan and Reeve immediately stepped out, but Yaro and his men paused, scanning the panelled hallway.

'It's OK,' Alexia said, quietly.

Yaro wasn't listening. He nodded to his two men, who ventured out next. Not budging until they gave the signal it was safe. It was all so unnecessary. Sending her blood racing, driving her crazy, already.

They trooped in behind Keenan and Reeve. Through the open double doors, to the main bar and restaurant. Alexia was surprised to find the place had been emptied of guests. It was late Friday evening, but it was always busy till at least 2 a.m. Jay must have closed early. The staff were finishing up behind the bar.

Jay was busy with them. He said something quietly and the barman took off his apron and left.

Alexia let go of Yaro's hand for the first time and ran to Jay, who scooped her up and kissed her cheek. Slowly, releasing her down to her feet, he nodded cautiously at Yaro as if getting the size of him and shooting a glance at the two Ambragio standing with him. 'Hang back, Keenan. It's OK,' Jay said, tipping his head for him to stand by the door.

Keenan swapped a look with Reeve, a little unsure, but Yaro spoke something quickly in Russian and his two guards nodded and went over to the door. Satisfied the odds were even, Keenan and Reeve immediately followed. They stood and eyed the opposition suspiciously.

'Drink?' Jay said, bringing their attention back to him. 'No!' Yaro said abruptly. Then, 'Thank you.'

Alexia added, 'He doesn't eat or drink.'

Jay's eyes lit with sudden understanding and he tipped his head. Alexia could literally hear the cogs whirring. Comparing differences between the Santalinis, who didn't drink blood to survive and realising they must be vampires in the truest sense of the word. His gaze shot to hers, as the thought of him feeding on her dropped. Her heart sank a little.

Thankfully he didn't say anything and held out his arm. 'Follow me, then.' Jay turned and they left the bar area and went into the restaurant where she spotted her father, Dante, in the furthest corner, hunched over the tomes and paper-work in front of him. He was with his human adviser, Max, who was the world's leading expert on all things Atlantean. He'd been a constant fixture in her father's court for many years and was now very old. She didn't know whether to be pleased or not. It meant he was taking her seriously, but it also meant he was checking Yaro out.

Max's eyes widened the minute he saw them and he was on his feet. Her father looked up but remained seated.

Alexia couldn't help herself. She ran the last few feet and flew into her father's arms. He held her in his lap and she buried her nose in his shoulder. He smelled of comfort and home. It had been so long since she'd seen him. A lifetime, it felt.

He kissed the top of her head but then she remembered herself. Yaro was looking on, a little unsure. She quickly stood up and took her place again, holding Yaro's hand. 'Sorry … this is Yaro, Dad.'

Dante's gaze went from their joined hands, taking in the glyphs and talons for nails, and then up to the smart suit until he reached Yaro's face.

Alexia anxiously looked between them to see their reaction. Yaro seemed unfazed and still while Dante studied the contrast of his overlong black hair and white skin. But then Yaro did something she wasn't expecting. He pulled the wraparound sunglasses off his face with his free hand and bowed his head. 'Your Majesty.'

Alexia wasn't just shocked at the deference Yaro was showing, but that he had revealed his face to her father so quickly. He straightened and looked defiantly at the king. She looked at her father, fearful of his reaction. If he was shocked, he didn't show it. Just the minutest pause. It made her wonder if Yaro's initial shyness had been simply not to scare her. It made sense as she was convinced Yaro was not scared of anything.

Alexia's heart beat hard in her chest as her father slowly rose to his feet. He came around from behind the table and stood directly in front of Yaro. He was studying Yaro's eyes like a scientist, in fascination. Yaro showed no discomfort, but Alexia froze, frightened to breathe. Her father was tall, but Yaro was easily another head taller at almost Murr height. However her father didn't seem perturbed at all. He stood a full minute, just getting the measure of the male who dared take his daughter. Everyone else remained still, holding their breath. Watching. Waiting.

Yaro didn't back down either. He stared back, his senses alert, even though she knew he could barely see. She knew her father. There was no animosity; he was simply studying, logging away the differences of this apparent new specimen of Atlantean male.

Then, as if he'd simply snapped out of a daydream, he held out a hand and said, 'Take a seat.'

Alexia finally remembered to breathe and watched in a daze as Yaro sat in the chair offered and her father returned to his own seat on the other side of the table. 'Jay?' Dante said to her second father just behind her. It was their own weird brand of telepathy they'd always shared. Where they knew what the other meant with the minimum of words. Today it annoyed the hell out of her because it was dad-speak for 'can you take Alexia somewhere and give us some privacy'? Her blood rose and she went to stamp her foot and whine, but the look Jay gave her silenced her immediately. He put his hand at the small of her back and moved her along in the direction of the kitchen. Every time she dragged her feet, he gave her a firm push. He nodded at Keenan, watching from the door in another brand of unspoken guy-speak. Then pushed her inside the kitchen, where she instantly whirled around on him. 'I should be out there, Jay. It's my life. It concerns me.'

Jay ignored her and went to the freezer. She went to go straight back out the door but Keenan's big, befanged smile greeted her. She stamped and huffed and turned back around, letting the door spring shut again.

Jay pulled out a big catering tub of ice cream, two spoons

and indicated for her to sit at the stool next to the island. 'This isn't about you, Alexia.' He slid the tub closer to her and held out a spoon.

She snatched the spoon and ripped off the plastic lid, moodily. She wanted to argue, but she knew what he said was at least partly true.

'This guy has come from nowhere, claiming to be from a new, pure bloodline. We know nothing about him except his somewhat shady business dealings.'

She dug deep with her spoon into the ice cream in frustration.

Jay slid over a bowl. 'Don't eat straight from the tub.'

It made her crack a smile. She couldn't help it. He must have said it to her a thousand times over the years. She would sneak down when she should be in bed to steal some since she was little.

When she looked into his eyes, they were serious and soulful. He wasn't laughing. 'I love him, Jay.' The words tumbled out before she could stop them. She dropped the spoon on the counter with a clatter and ran into his arms. She burst out crying and she didn't even understand why. He held her close, just like she remembered. A little stiffly, like he wanted to be there, but wasn't sure how.

'Has he been good to you?' Jay said eventually, with his mouth in her ruffled hair.

She sniffed in a lungful of air and pulled apart from him, nodding. Then she walked back around the counter and began digging into the ice cream again. This was the real issue and she recognised she had to be careful what she said. This was the two cops' routine, splitting the witnesses to get a truer picture. 'He's all I want, Jay,' she said, simply.

She was glad she'd got Jay. If it had been her father, she would be screaming at him by now and not having her side listened to at all.

Jay remained silent for a minute, watching her closely. 'Has he … ?'

Her eyes shot to his, but there was no apology in them. They were strong and direct. Only he could get away with asking her a question like that. Her father was cleverly leaving it down to him, knowing he could never be objective about it. She supposed, for that, she should be grateful. She shook her head and watched as Jay visibly relaxed. 'But I want to, Jay, I want to.'

Jay frowned and shifted awkwardly. 'He's a much older male,' Jay said, stressing his last word carefully. 'None of us know yet what he's capable of.'

Alexia bit down on her spoonful of ice cream to get a hold on her temper. 'You think I'm a child. You don't think I know that? He's a true vampire, Jay. Lightning fast, sleeps underground, can't bear sunlight … exists solely on blood.' She said the last bit spitefully, landing it like a blow that registered immediately on Jay's face as he made the association to her. 'Straight out of everyone's nightmares.'

'And you want that?' Jay asked, his blood rising too, as his face creased in disgust.

That's what hurt the most. That people just couldn't see Yaro in the way she did. Past all that stuff. 'Yes, I do, Jay. Because he cares for me. He's strong and he makes me feel safe.'

'And he will never let you go. You realise that, right?' Jay said, raising his eyebrows in a question.

Like it could possibly be a passing phase she could change her mind about. Nothing could be more ridiculous. No one would get over this kind of love. 'Yes! I do,' Alexia said, defiantly. She wasn't angry; her spirits soared that even Jay could recognise it. 'I'm glad, Jay. That's exactly what I want.'

Jay's face hardened. 'That he sees you as the king's

daughter before he ever thinks of you as a woman. He's ambitious, Alexia. Can't you see that?'

His words were the knife that twisted in the centre of her chest. He was right, but he wasn't. Yes, Yaro wanted advancement for his family, but all the bloody princes in all the families had done the self-same thing with her aunts. Her own father had done it with her mother. Her heart ached and then it sank. *What was the use?* None of the males would ever get past that. 'For his family, Jay,' she said on a weary exhale. 'A family that was obliterated from history after they literally founded the world for us. He's supposed to stay quiet about that?'

Jay didn't respond and let out a weary breath, too. He nodded eventually, probably thinking this wasn't an argument he was ever going to win with her. She hoped a little of what she'd said had sunk in. Yaro did have a genuine grievance. However, she also understood that who she was did factor into this, but she was sure it didn't define them as a couple.

Then they heard a commotion outside.

CHAPTER 6

*D*ante studied Yaro for a full minute across the table while Jay steered Alexia off for the other half of the interrogation. Yaro seemed to remain cool and stared right back.

What the hell is he? He was a creature right out of a horror film. Weird and pale and those eyes that fixed on you like a hawk. 'You know you didn't have to trap my children to get my attention,' he said as an opener. 'I would have granted an audience through the proper channels.'

Dante felt Max push up his glasses on his nose and shuffle uncomfortably next to him.

'I didn't seek to trap anyone. Your boys came in a round-about way to me, remember? A happy coincidence. They went to an associate of mine for a property and I happened to have one in the area. Of course, I knew who they were immediately. It seemed to come at an opportune moment and the fates favoured me … and you, it seems. South London can be a very dangerous place for young princes, alone.'

Dante's blood rose at his inference that he'd stepped in to

look after his boys in his place. However, he'd been a king a long time and he recognised when someone was deliberately trying to rile him, so he changed tack. 'And Alexia, did she arrive at an opportune moment?'

Yaro registered the touché with a spiteful smile, revealing a deadly set of heavy-duty dentistry. 'I offered her my driver when she appeared to be unprotected.'

'But you knew who she was.'

'Of course. I am a prince. Your children were in my area. I make it my business to know any new Atlantean faces that enter it. As would any royal. It couldn't be ignored.'

Dante nodded slowly. He needed to treat this meeting for what it was: a political meeting of diplomacy and not some personal jab at his parenting responsibilities. The guy was right, all Atlanteans sensed when others were around. He had always known there would be a high chance they were conspicuous there. That was why he'd sent Santalinis to guard them. He just hadn't banked on a secret family. 'Had I known of your existence there, I would have forewarned you,' Dante countered, watching his reaction closely 'I thank you for your protection.'

Yaro regally inclined his head.

Just when Dante thought they were getting on some sort of diplomatic footing, Yaro added, 'It has been my pleasure,' and smiled dangerously again. He swore if he'd been in his youth, he would have jumped up and punched the guy in the face at that point. Being king or not would have been straight out of the window. He hadn't met anyone who had pressed his buttons like this for years. The guy was much older and a shrewd leader, he had to keep telling himself that. He'd known exactly what he was doing with his kids.

'So, happy coincidences aside, what are your intentions with my daughter?' Dante asked, no longer able to keep the edge out of his voice. Jay was so much better at navigating this emotional stuff than he was. Mainly because it never got to him; always remaining detached. He just wanted to smack the smile off the arsehole's face.

'Much the same as it has been with your sons. Patronage. Guidance … vindication,' he said, dropping the last word in slyly. Neatly steering them back to the real point of the meeting.

In another life, Dante might even admire him for it. It *was* the point if Alexia wasn't such a major part of it. He had to force himself to look at the same scenario as if she wasn't. What would he think of him then? He had to concede, pretty much the same. An outlaw who'd clawed and scraped his way out of obscurity to the top tier of the underworld, using every advantage his genetics had given him. What other choice did the guy have? 'What do you want?' Dante said, finally.

'You deciphered and read the document I previously sent you?' Yaro asked, casually crossing his leg at the knee.

Dante looked at Max next to him, following the conversation avidly. Yaro had sent the ancient document through his sons and he'd quickly given it to Max for authentication. 'Max did … he's an expert in the field.'

Yaro tipped his head at the small, frail man, sitting next to him. 'And what does Max think?'

Max looked at Dante for permission to speak.

Dante answered by tipping his head in Yaro's direction to answer him.

'Well …' Max started nervously, producing the letter from the box in his briefcase. 'It is clearly authentic. A decree from Artaxerxses II of Atlas, that you would be the specially revered secret agents of the race and would make first contact with the humans already genetically seeded on this planet.'

Dante watched Yaro's reaction. He nodded as he followed

along like he knew every word. 'And what does our exalted king think about this?' Yaro said, switching his attention back to Dante.

'You have to understand that this was news to us all,' Dante said, honestly.

Yaro inclined his head as if he was giving him that. 'But what do you intend to do about it? You must also understand that my whole family has been disowned by its people and reviled and vilified by humans for millennia.'

Despite the outwardly calm exterior, Dante caught a glimpse of the anger carefully contained below the surface in this male. Strangely, he appeared to have no aura at all. However, whatever plans he had for Alexia, he was sure this was what burned in the guy's heart. 'What would you like to happen? There is more I still need to learn.' Dante was watching his every movement carefully as he was so intense and almost as still as the Murrs.

'I would have my family re-written correctly into the history books of Atlantis to claim our rightful place. An announcement to be proclaimed worldwide to all Atlanteans of our existence and to vindicate us as elite guards.'

That last statement threw up a whole other shit-storm of worry. Not only would there be chaos in the Santalini family, who were his current elite guards, but even if they allowed it, could they be trusted that close to everything he loved and held dear? 'And ...' he said flatly, sensing that he hadn't finished.

'And to show true commitment to putting right the wrong done to my family, marriage to the eldest daughter of the king, cementing our bond.'

Dante frowned while his heart thrashed at that. *His little girl.* She wasn't yet eighteen and had led a charmed and sheltered life. He would probably have given him most of his demands, but that? *Could he? Would he?* He didn't think he'd ever felt so exposed and vulnerable in his life. Not only could he not bear the thought of Alexia close with a male like that – any male – but it meant that this guy would be right in the centre of court life. There would be uproar with the other families. 'So what you're saying is that despite me considering all your demands, it won't count unless I let you marry my daughter?' He shook his head in exasperation. 'She is so young. She has her whole life to choose a mate?' The more Dante said it out loud, the more it felt an impossible thing to even contemplate. Everyone would be against it. He was against it.

'I think you will find that it is she who has chosen,' Yaro said, looking him insolently in the eye.

Anger shot through Dante's chest like a rod of fire and he was on his feet. Yaro was on his feet in a second, too and they were nose to nose. Dante didn't care about any of the weird shit he could do. Right then, he was growling in his face. He was also aware that Yaro's men were right there the second after, soon followed by Keenan, Reeve and then Jay.

Then, like a splash of cold water, Alexia came running in, screaming. 'Dad ... stop it, please.'

'He dares to take you like that?' Dante's voice dropped, guttural like a snarl.

Jay was there, talking quietly in his ear. 'He hasn't, Dant— Nothing's happened yet.'

'Dad,' Alexia pleaded, being held back by Reeve. 'I just want to bring him home for Christmas so you can get to know each other. Please, Dad. Is that too much to ask?'

The ridiculous naivety in the request, dwarfed completely by the reality of the situation, almost made him laugh. Dante relaxed down a little, tempered by the upset in Alexia's voice and suddenly aware of the stand-off all around them. There were knives and firearms pointed everywhere. He had to concede that this guy was no pretender, he was a capable and well-protected leader. A huge threat should he want to be. This required much more serious consideration.

Was it possible to take the chance of revealing his family's secret location? *Should he?* Could he ever trust this guy like that? *Was it the kingdom he was after?* Up till today, this family were lowlife base dwellers. At least on Atlas. Who's to say the document wasn't some elaborate forgery, conjured up after they stowed away on the journey to Earth? They were lowlifes on Atlas and they are lowlifes here. Maybe that's why they were never in the ancient tomes.

Dante looked at his daughter properly for the first time. She was crying and pleading with her eyes. This guy had done a real number getting her so into him, that was for sure. But the girl standing crying in front of him was no longer a girl, it was clear she was a woman, with very clear ideas of what she wanted.

The guy was right about one thing. It was obvious that Alexia thought she loved him. He'd been clever about that. He was in no doubt if he went up against him, he would lose her to him forever. Perhaps, for the time being, he needed to keep his enemies close.

He let out a slow breath. 'Let me think on it. I need to decide how much I'm willing to trust on mere words and parchment.'

Dante was forced to watch as his only daughter left with the formidable, much older male he didn't trust. His little girl. He couldn't speak until she disappeared from view, out through the bar and into the lift.

Jay was at his side and knew him well enough not to speak until then. 'The boys came by earlier. They were kicking up a fuss to see you, so I couldn't let them in.'

The image of Xavier and JJ broke through his fixation on

Yaro Demidov. He turned to look at his old friend. 'They were here?'

'Yeah,' Jay said, scratching his head. 'Their timing was terrible. I didn't see them, but Keenan and Reeve intercepted them. They left this.' Jay held out a closed fist and dropped the small black disc into Dante's hand.

He frowned and examined it, holding it up between his thumb and forefinger. 'Where?'

'TV remote in their loft.'

Dante swore under his breath. 'Demidov?'

Jay shrugged. 'Probably.'

'We swept it before, though, right?'

Jay nodded. 'Whoever did it, did it after they moved in.'

Dante looked off into space while he thought. Demidov was the likely culprit. It was his property and he would have easy access to it. He looked over at Jay. 'Keep it to yourself for now. As soon as the girlfriends' families leave, have their houses swept too. We need to know how far this goes.'

Jay nodded.

CHAPTER 7

Xavier went straight back to the loft with JJ in stony silence, more disturbed than when they left. It was a bachelor pad any boy their age would dream of. An open-plan space of exposed brick, dotted with tasteful furniture, foosball table and expensive art they'd long since taken for granted. Now it just reeked of Demidov.

He was fuming. They hadn't been allowed into the *big* meeting to confront him. All they'd been told was that it was about to start, and their fathers had issued instructions not to be disturbed on any account. Then they were patted on the head like good little boys and sent on their way. Even when he'd slapped the device in Keenan's hand. 'Present from Demidov.'

He'd merely nodded. Thanked them for the new intel and told them to stick with their plans. Nothing had really been resolved. Both of them were still worried about their girl-friends' reaction when they got to Filfla, and they still had no idea whether their discovery made any difference to Yaro coming or not.

'Father would be insane to let him come,' Xavier said,

throwing his keys down on the burnished metal countertop. He couldn't shake the feeling that he wasn't being treated like some pretender. More like some powerful, visiting dignitary. This was obviously far bigger than either of them realised.

JJ NODDED THOUGHTFULLY, wandering over to their juke-box and pressing the button to one of his favourite tracks. He flopped down, exhausted, into the nearest black leather sofa with his forearm over his eyes. 'He hasn't said yes yet. Knowing Dad, he's looking for the best way to get out of it, so Alexia still goes.'

Xavier shrugged and sat on the white leather sofa across the room. 'I don't think he will this time.'

JJ allowed his arm to drop so he could see his brother clearly. 'You think Yaro is a match for Father?'

Xavier nodded, leaning forward with his elbows on his knees. 'I do. Think about it. He's treated like a prince round here. He has super speed and God knows what mental powers.'

JJ had never seen Xavier look so worried. 'You think he could best a Santalini?' JJ asked sceptically.

Xavier bobbed his head. 'Probably. Santalinis are strong but Yaro could stab one of them before they even knew he'd moved.'

JJ sat up and looked ahead of him, shocked. Xavier was right. 'Stronger than a Murr?' JJ said, looking across at Xavier.

Xavier shrugged letting out a loud exhale. 'I dunno. Maybe. Possibly Darres could beat him. I really don't know. But would you want to take the risk of him anywhere near Latitia and Paige, completely ignorant of everything?'

JJ closed his eyes and shook his head. He was right. Darres could scramble a male's brain to a pulp from a distance of more than fifty feet, but did he want Latitia in the middle of that? 'I guess we just have to pray Father finds a legitimate reason for Yaro not to go.' Then there were all their cousins. 'At least we will be on home turf,' JJ said, smiling, but not really feeling it.

Xavier laughed derisively. 'A real bevvy of beauty, ambition and mental powers. I feel safer already.'

JJ chuckled genuinely at that, but it really wasn't funny. The whole thing was becoming a worse idea by the minute.

SATURDAY MORNING CAME AFTER VERY little sleep, Xavier arrived at the garages behind Paige's building. He was in the usual Santalini-driven, blacked-out SUV his father always used to ferry them all around in, followed by a large grey van to transport their luggage. There were going to be a lot of people on this trip; plus all the stuff they had to take with them.

One Santalini came up with him to the second-floor maisonette where Paige's family lived, and the other stayed with the vehicles.

Xavier took a deep breath to calm his beating heart and knocked on the door. It was unusual for him to be this nervous about anything. Over the last twenty-four hours, he'd been a wreck. He hadn't pinpointed why exactly; probably a multitude of things: the Alexia/Demidov thing, what Paige would think, whether it would all go horribly wrong, or simply having responsibility for someone other than just himself for a change. Whatever it was, he didn't like the feeling.

He looked at his watch – 08.45 – and knocked. Squeals of delight pealed through the front door. Paige's little brother and sister. *At least somebody was excited.* It helped him get his head on straight. It was Christmas. It would be a lovely trip, where he could get closer to Paige while their families met and they absorbed he was from a master alien race. *Oh, Bloody hell.*

Before his anxiety completely stumbled his resolve, the door opened and there was Paige, standing there looking beautiful in a simple grey jogging suit and trainers, hair up out of the way and smelling great, as always. 'Ready?' he said on an exhale.

She grinned, put her arms around his neck and simply kissed him. It was exactly what he needed, dispelling his fears instantly. There was no way he wanted to spend Christmas without her. 'Mum's still trying to shut the case,' she said, shaking her head. She stepped aside and Xavier saw Linda, red-faced and flustered, sitting on the corner of a case last seen in the 1970s, closing the zipper one inch at a time.

Xavier looked up at the guard next to him, who nodded, and stepped straight inside. 'May I, Mam?' he said, immediately.

Xavier followed him into the square hallway and was met by two bouncing under-fives. 'Zav-yay … Zav-yay.'

'Have you got all your stuff?' Xavier asked, keeping an eye on the guard, helping Linda to her feet and making short work of the case.

'Yes!' both children shouted, twisting their little bodies so he could see their backpacks on their backs.

Paige disappeared to her room and came back out with an overnight bag.

The guard was finishing tightening two leather straps around the bulging mustard faux-leather case, while Linda looked on, still red in the face. She grabbed another backpack and her handbag and keys off the side and put her hand out towards the door to say she was ready.

The guard exchanged a look with Xavier and picked up the case that had no rollers, communicating what Xavier was already processing. That this was it. One case for all of them for ten days. They'd brought a whole van just for luggage. 'Let's go then,' Xavier said before the silence got too weird.

By the time they got down to the two waiting cars, Xavier's heart was flipping at how awkward it all felt. Paige hadn't said a word, and she was huddled together with her mum and the little ones, even more so when they caught sight of the waiting cars, now joined by the security detail as well. Xavier's eyes went Heavenward. Keenan put up a hand of greeting from the steering wheel of the new car. *For god's sake, now his father decides they need protection.* They'd been fending for themselves for months.

'Who are they?' Paige asked, as Xavier came up alongside her.

Xavier glanced anxiously at the guard, seeing that Paige was fast becoming a flight risk, and he opened the rear door for them. 'Miss?'

'Just security … don't worry.'

Paige and her mother exchanged a worried look and they both got in with her little brother and sister between them. Xavier quickly sat next to the driver. 'We've got to make another stop for the Johnsons,' he explained.

Linda looked doubtfully at the seats.

'They'll have their own car. We've got the luggage van, that's all.'

Paige smiled at him a little. He loved her for that. Even though she was almost as apprehensive as her mother, she was trying to make him feel better.

They pulled away and he faced front, but before he could finally relax, a silver-grey van passed them with a 'Lightning Speed Broadband' logo on the side, and swung into their newly vacated space. He tried not to crane his neck round to look at it, but there were Atlantean signatures bursting out in every direction.

He angled himself to check the wing mirror just as five guys in matching grey overalls and baseball caps, jumped out of it and walked quickly in the direction of Paige's building.

His eyes shot to the driver, who couldn't have missed it. *Ours?* he quickly projected.

The Santalini smiled benignly, which he took as a yes. His mind scrambling to the obvious answer of what it must be. A surveillance team. The question was, was his father sweeping to take one out, or taking the opportunity to put one in? He honestly didn't know. Nor if he should be angry or pleased. Mixing his two worlds was so much harder than he thought. He silently prayed that everything worked out, but the fears crowded in. The further they got, the more it felt like a terrible idea. He just told himself over and over that he wanted Paige. She was his and this was the only way to keep her.

CHAPTER 8

When JJ arrived, there were three holdalls, one big case and a pile of toys, heaped up in the middle of the Johnsons' hallway. Not a lot really for one adult, three teenagers and two little kids.

The two little ones, Marcus and Joseph, were squealing and zooming around, pretending to be planes. Valarie was switching off the timer on the boiler and closing all the windows – not that anyone was likely to climb up six floors. Richie and Latitia were standing, looking bewildered, next to the bags. 'Where's Dwayne?' JJ asked.

Latitia and Richie shrugged. 'In our room, I think,' Richie said.

JJ looked at his watch. It was nine on the dot. The car horn would honk soon. He went over to the room Richie shared with Dwayne, knocked and put his head inside. He was shocked to see that the top bunks had gone from when he and Xavier lived there. He wondered where Valarie had put them.

Dwayne was sitting sullenly on his bed, scrolling his phone. 'Room looks bigger,' JJ said.

Dwayne flashed him a look, nodded and returned to what he was doing.

JJ went over and sat on the bed opposite. 'Not into it then?'

Dwayne just flashed him another glance.

'The trip I mean,' JJ persisted.

Dwayne just looked at him deadpan. 'Do I want to miss all the DJing work at the busiest time of year to watch your sister getting cosy with her new bloke, then no, I'm not that into it.' He went back to scrolling, shaking his head.

JJ let out a deep sigh and nodded. He totally got where Dwayne was coming from. 'You'll have a great time, you know. And we don't even know whether her bloke has been given the OK to come.' JJ watched Dwayne absorb what he said, with the only clue being the set of his jaw. 'For what it's worth, me and Xavier would much rather it be you.'

Dwayne rolled his eyes at that. 'I find that very hard to believe.'

'But true,' JJ said, smiling and getting to his feet. 'Come on. My dad will make it more than worth your while missing the DJing gigs. You'll probably even get a chance to play. I know my mum will want you to.'

Dwayne's eyes widened at that. 'Oh yeah, I forgot your mum was a superstar DJ.'

JJ bobbed his head. 'Back in the day … she'll love you. Come on, the others are coming,' he said, getting back to his feet.

Dwayne shook his head as he stood up too. 'No one's knocked the door yet. You're a bloody weirdo, JJ.'

JJ grinned, already on his way out of Dwayne's room, just as there was a light knock on the front door. Valarie let the two big Santalini guards straight into the square hallway and they both smiled and shook JJ's hand. 'This it?' one of them said.

'And me … I'm coming,' little Marcus said, jumping up and down and craning his neck to look up at his full six feet five in height.

'Well, OK then,' the guard said, laughing, showing his impressive canines. 'Two more for the baggage van.' He stooped and picked both small boys up, holding them both around the middle, under his arms. 'Grab a bag, JJ,' he said, proceeding to walk out of the front door, to fits of squeals and giggles.

Valarie looked at JJ warily. 'After you!' he said, holding out his hand for her to lead the way.

He, Dwayne and Richie each picked up a holdall and the other guard made easy work of Valarie's case.

The first guard carried Joseph and Marcus all the way down to the large blacked-out seven-seater. Keenan got straight out of the escort car to open the sliding doors for him. The guard released the excited little boys who immediately tried to run. He caught them by the collars and went to throw them in with the bags. He relented and only let them go when they climbed in with their mother in the SUV. JJ got in the front, with Dwayne and Richie at the very back, he guessed Xavier was already in the other SUV with Paige's family. He hated that the only place for Latitia to sit was in the rear of Xavier's car with Paige. *It wasn't far to the airfield,* he told himself to calm his nerves.

Then the three cars and the van slowly pulled away.

'Won't be long. About half hour to Biggin Hill,' the driver said, smiling. JJ looked behind him and everyone was looking out of the side windows with worried expressions. He shuddered at what he could be getting them all into. *What were he and Xavier thinking?*

Xavier didn't seem to care as long as he kept Paige with him. If only it was all that simple.

'Has my father made a decision on Alexia yet?' he asked

the Santalini driving. He wanted to see Alexia, of course he did, but he certainly didn't want a guy like that in the centre of his family. The guard nodded. 'I believe so.'

JJ stared at him, waiting for him to carry on speaking, but he continued driving, silently. 'So, what is it?' JJ prompted, losing patience.

'I can't say,' the guard said, flashing him a serious, no-nonsense, look. 'What I can say is that extra security has been flying in from New York all week.'

JJ looked out of the front screen and his blood pumped. *Bloody hell!* That wasn't good. New York was where the Santalini family were based and more security meant his father had said yes. *Was his father losing his touch?*

CHAPTER 9

'This is an insult!' Pavel said.

Alexia looked on at the heated discussion between the brothers from the dainty armchair next to the fire, as Yaro's younger brother threw up his hands and went to walk off. He was so like Yaro, just a much less contained version.

'Calm down … it's a victory,' Yaro reasoned.

'A victory? Asking a prince of the pure line of Ambragio to go alone and unprotected to a place where we have no control. You would never allow this in the human world.'

Yaro tipped his head conceding that point. 'But this is not the human world, Pavel.' He smiled faintly, conveying it was the price they must pay.

'You could be imprisoned as soon as you get there. Or worse, assassinated and the king's problems immediately solved.'

Alexia was straight on her feet, no longer able to stay silent. 'My father is an honourable man. He wouldn't do that.'

Yaro pulled his brother into his body by the side of his neck, but his eyes remained fiercely on Alexia.

'He wouldn't need to, someone could work for him from the shadows,' Pavel persisted.

Yaro put him away from him and held him by the shoulders, forcing him to look him in the eyes. 'Think about it,' Yaro said, without raising his voice from his usual soft tone. 'He has shortened the trip to four days to make it manageable. He wouldn't need to do that if he simply wanted me out of the way. I am an unknown quantity, living in the grey area of human law. He must accommodate me in the bosom of his cherished family. It is exactly what I would do.'

'But completely alone, Brother, with no protection?' Pavel groaned.

Yaro let out a weary sigh and noticed Alexia watching the exchange closely. He pulled her into his side and inhaled her scent at her neck. 'You insult me if you think I can't look after myself.'

Alexia's heart was still skipping from the speed of his actions and she shivered as he planted the gentlest of kisses on her throat. She relaxed a little in disappointment. He did that a lot. He said the smell of her blood drove him wild.

He was still visiting one of his familiars to feed. She hated that and longed for him to stop. He'd explained that it wasn't seemly for him to get his sustenance from her until she was an adult and as a princess, very definitely married. He had sampled her and that had to be enough for now. Still, her heart fluttered in his arms, waiting for the day the straining leash on his willpower finally broke.

It occurred to her then that he would be away from his family and familiars for four whole days. Surely he would weaken and drink from her then.

CHAPTER 10

The three cars and luggage van were whisked straight through the gates of Biggin Hill airfield, along a winding road and straight to the private hangers where the royal Dubonnetti plane waited for them.

Xavier wished he was sitting next to Paige when she first saw the Dubonnetti crest on its tail that matched the tattoo above his heart exactly. His name was emblazoned – Dubonnetti Industries – along the fuselage, in black and white for the world to see. His heart never ceased to lift when he saw it.

They finally pulled up and everyone began to get out of the vehicles. The Johnson boys looked up in awe at it. None of them would have seen a private jet outside of a film. His eyes locked with JJ's as he moved closer to him. 'We need to talk,' JJ said, immediately.

Xavier nerves bristled as JJ went to move past him and brushed arms to make a psychic connection. *He's coming,* JJ projected straight to his mind.

Xavier's anger burned so quickly that he forgot and spoke aloud. 'You're joking … They told you that?'

'Sshh!' *You'll frighten the girls,* JJ said, switching back to projected speech. *Not exactly. They just said a decision had been made and that extra security had been flying in from New York all week.*

'Bloody hell,' Xavier spat. It was his worst nightmare come true. *Whatever happens, we need to protect the families,* Xavier projected, looking intensely into JJ's eyes.

JJ nodded. *All of them.*

And there's something else, Xavier said, before JJ could move away. *A surveillance team went into Paige's right after we left.*

JJ looked off into the distance while he ran the same thought process as him. *Do we know—*

Xavier shook his head, not able to answer that question. *Only that Latitia's house would definitely be next.*

JJ TRIED to put on a smile and look enthusiastic for Latitia. He took her hand and followed her brothers who ran up the steps and dispersed the moment they reached the cabin inside. Laughing. 'Whoa' and 'Sweet ride!' as they bagsied seats at opposite ends of the plush cream leather seating.

'Sit together,' Valarie hissed, her eyes widening as she took in the luxurious surroundings. 'Stop showing me up!'

Dwayne's whole body sagged before he got to his feet and went and sat nearer to where Valarie had chosen with the little ones. The seating was arranged; four chairs around a table. The little ones bounced in their seats as Valarie struggled to strap them in. Dwayne and Richie sat in the ones behind. JJ sat with Latitia opposite them.

'It's a lot bigger than I imagined,' Dwayne said.

JJ squeezed Latitia's hand, resting on the arm of the seat. 'It's a Bowing 747, not an executive jet.' JJ's interest shifted to Xavier walking in with a much-less rowdy Paige and family. They seemed quiet and timid compared to the Johnsons.

Paige's mum was gripping the little one's hands as if they'd be sucked back out of the door while she looked around her fearfully.

The six Santalini guards were coming too and took their seats at the back of the plane. They were soon ordering drinks, spreading themselves out and making themselves at home.

JJ looked across at Latitia taking everything in next to him. 'You OK?' he asked.

She took in a ragged breath and nodded. He could feel her nerves from where he was sitting.

The engines revved and hissed and the cabin crew began doing security checks and closing the doors. Then a thought struck him, 'You've never flown?'

She shook her head. 'I bet you do it all the time.'

He nodded, thoughtfully. 'My father has homes all over the world.' It felt weird. He was no longer hiding anything. It was liberating and so easy. But he was conscious of the way Latitia was looking at him.

'You really are a prince, aren't you?' she said as a statement.

He nodded again, with a wan smile. 'Don't worry, it will be normal for you too after today.'

The plane began to taxi to the runway. Valarie's little ones squealed in excitement, prompting Paige's little brother and sister to whine to look out of the window. JJ smiled as Paige's mum whispered loudly for them to sit still, although both families craned to look.

JJ found himself watching Paige across the gangway. He tried to see what bound Xavier to her so tightly. She had an innocent purity about her, he guessed.

A weird feeling stirred in his gut as Xavier leaned across the arms of their chair to kiss her, which she met easily. In fact, everything between them seemed to be fluid and natural. Linda had her eyes screwed shut and the kids were trying to kneel up in their seats to see.

The engines roared louder.

"ere we go,' Dwayne said, grinning.

The plane moved off. Faster and faster, pinning them back in their seats, until the nose lifted and the wheels left the tarmac. JJ's stomach rolled and the plane slowly climbed.

After a few minutes a bell dinged signalling the seat belt sign going dark and they could move around the plane. 'No! Keep them on,' Linda said, fearfully.

Keenan was walking through and heard her. He leaned down and whispered something directly in her ear.

Linda smiled reluctantly and the two little ones bounced with glee when she said, 'OK, but no running around.' They wanted to scoot across and see what Valarie's little boys had, as they were pulling pens and colouring books out of their backpacks.

Keenan straightened up and faced the rest of the plane. 'Listen up! Just thought I'd introduce myself properly. 'I'm Keenan, JJ and Xavier's uncle. Their father wanted me to go through a few things before we get to Malta. First off: no phones. You will need to hand them to me for safekeeping.'

JJ's gaze shot straight to the Johnson boys. 'We can't!' Richie said immediately. 'The show!' he said, appealing to his mother in protest.

'Do as you're told,' she said right back.

'Sorry, guys,' Keenan said. 'Where you're going is top secret. There are only a handful of people in the world, outside of the family, who know where it is.'

JJ studied all the anxious faces. He glanced at Xavier, thinking the same thing. That this whole trip was going to be hard. Dwayne and Richie slumped back moodily in their chairs.

Keenan ploughed on, regardless. 'When we get there,

you'll be shown to your rooms to freshen up, then you will meet the king in the great hall. It will be informal. You can call him Dante. He wants you to be able to relax and make yourself at home. Please don't wander off. The place is a maze, so there's an army of staff to get you what you need.'

'When is Alexia getting there?' JJ couldn't resist calling out.

If he wanted to make Keenan uncomfortable, then it didn't work, because after a shrewd glance, he simply answered, 'The day before Christmas Eve.' He didn't elaborate. He knew what they really wanted to know but he'd obviously had orders for what he could give away. He couldn't be any happier about this than they were.

They settled down after that. The stewardess brought around drinks and snacks that the kids thought was the best thing ever and the journey passed quickly. Three hours and they were beginning their descent into Malta.

Despite his nerves, the loving look Latitia gave him cut right through it, making it all worthwhile. He studied her beautiful heart-shaped face and hoped to keep that look in his memory for ever. Terror was always lurking in the pit of his stomach. That once she knew what he was, she would reject him like she did before. Except this time, there would be no do-overs after memory wipes. He wanted to stay like this, with her looking at him as if he was the best boyfriend in the world.

XAVIER WATCHED Paige the whole time after they transferred to the cavalcade of air-conditioned Jeeps. This time he managed to sit next to her. They soon drove the short distance through a private barrier on the far side of Luqa airport, where they pulled up right next to the helipad where three shiny black helicopters waited.

Linda almost wobbled and ran the other way, when one of the heavily accented ground crew told her to get in first with the kids. Her eyes looked wide with panic and she held both children in her arms.

Xavier took the little girl and grounded her with his eyes. 'It's OK, I'm right here,' he said soothingly.

Paige held onto his arm as her steadying rock and he loved the feeling of strength it gave him. He led the way and helped everyone inside the first helicopter. Five of them in total, one Santalini guard and the pilot made seven.

They strapped in, the engine started and the blades began to whip above them. The little ones squealed excitedly. Linda closed her eyes and gripped the edges of her seat and Paige squeezed his hand. He kissed her forehead just as they left the ground like a nose-heavy bumble bee and headed west. He didn't look back to see how JJ was faring. The Johnsons would be split between the two remaining helicopters with the guards and JJ would make sure he was with Latitia.

They cleared the airport and climbed higher. Xavier held Paige closely so she could see the dusty yellow-stone streets below, crammed with people and impatient cars. High above, hearing nothing but the rhythmic, loud engine, it felt like they were looking down on ants, competing for space on a postage stamp island. They swept over bleached flat- roofed buildings. Crowded roads gave way to stonewalled fields, dotted with little huts and tiny shrines to the catholic church. Avenues became lined with palms and their walls with prickly pears, until they finally reached the sheer cliff side of the island and flew over cobalt blue sea.

It took no time at all for the flat-topped island to come into view. He watched Paige's enraptured profile the whole time. 'There it is,' he said, waiting for her response.

He laughed as she looked shocked. It was just a yellow, sheer-sided table covered in grass. There was nothing else visible at all. It had been granted nature reserve status and was the perfect place for a secret underground bunker.

'What … that's it?' she said, making him laugh.

The little ones were struggling to see it too and Linda was trying to keep them in their seats.

'Just wait and see,' Xavier said, chuckling to himself. He was tuning in to the Maltese pilot requesting clearance for landing. 'Watch!' he said, taking in every line of her expectant face.

JJ's STOMACH churned with dread as they hovered over the table mountain that rose straight out of turquoise sea. The Johnson boys whistled in amazement. 'We're landing on that?' Richie asked.

The grass top, the size of a football pitch, began to open in a slowly turning octagon, to reveal a huge black hole. 'Not on, inside,' JJ said with a ragged breath. *Show time.*

Latitia's eyes shot to his to see if he was joking, then switched to alarm. 'Think James Bond film,' JJ said, tipping his head for her to continue to watch. He studied her fear slowly turning to wonder and then amazement. He hugged her closer, the scent at her neck tantalising him in the heat. 'It used to be an old World War Two bunker,' he said, clearing his throat. 'The Maltese prime minister had it turned into a palace and gifted it to my father.'

Latitia's eyes widened, but she remained riveted to the cavernous hole they were slowly descending into and didn't say anything else.

Inside was like a huge grey hanger of pipes and metal staircases. The noise was deafening as they slowly settled next to Xavier's and another hovered above them to come down next.

JJ helped Latitia out. He looked across straight into

Keenan's eyes, who nodded and tipped his head to go to the exit. He wanted them all clear of the blades while he unloaded their kit. The third helicopter landed and the first took off to return to the airport.

Valarie and the boys joined them at the meeting point and the remaining engines were cut, whirred down and the rotors gradually slowed.

The lessening noise was a relief, but they were still a fidgety group. JJ was itching to get going, but they had to wait for their luggage to be loaded onto a trolley. Most he recognised, but some were long, oblong, suspicious-looking cases. *Guns.* He didn't know if he should be pleased or worried they were taking no chances.

When both loaded trolleys were finally wheeled off, Keenan came and stood in front of them. 'I just want to go through a few last-minute things with you. You'll be shown to your rooms right away. You're all near each other, so don't worry. Someone will knock for you shortly and take you to meet the king and then to the great hall. Please don't be alarmed if you see anything you don't understand. All your questions will be answered during your stay. The king asked me to welcome you and wish you a merry Christmas.'

JJ raised his hand.

Keenan nodded for him to go ahead.

'What about us? Are we staying near them?'

Keenan grinned knowingly. 'No … you will be in the royal apartments, near your parents.'

JJ flashed a glance at Xavier, who shook his head wearily. Their father didn't want any bedhopping, which was ridiculous. If they were going to do it, they certainly didn't need a bed. 'Don't you think we should tell them something before they go down?' JJ could just imagine Linda and Valarie's reaction to their Murr cousins stepping out of the fountain after spewing the water out of their lungs. His blood was rising with every new thought and Latitia's face, when she saw his true form the first time.

No! Are you mad? Xavier hissed, straight to his mind. *Everything strictly on a need-to-know basis. Are we clear?*

Keenan indicated for them to get moving with an annoying smirk. 'Your father said leave all that to the adults.'

JJ went ahead first, tutting and shaking his head at what a bad idea that was. He pushed through the steel doors and stopped dead. He would have turned and scrambled back if Xavier hadn't stepped right into the back of him.

'Shit! I think they're gonna need to know as soon as possible,' Xavier said, over his shoulder.

It was no use. There, at the bottom of the steps, waiting to meet them, were his cousins, Keefa and Dannon, with their adopted cousin Loki. They were the same age as them, waving goofily and making their mad clicking sounds like a pod of dolphins. In other words, clearly a species very different to present company. JJ wanted to be furious with them, but it was very difficult with them so pleased to see them. They were beaming huge human-like smiles; they'd obviously been practicing, already six feet seven in height, looking very like stripy basketball players, still in their long shorts.

Keenan swore for him, when he saw why he'd stopped.

'I guess this is the proverbial deep end,' Xavier sighed. 'Meet the family.'

Everyone stopped and stared, dumb struck. Except the little Johnsons, who appeared by JJ's legs, inched closer and craned their necks up to look at them. 'Wow … Giant avatars,' Joseph said, pointing.

Before Valarie could pull them back, Dannon stooped and picked up the little five-year-old and held him out in front of him. *Hello, little human,* Dannon projected, so everyone heard, but his lips never moved.

Valarie gulped and swayed, like she would faint.

JJ's legs refused to move, while he lived his nightmare.

Thankfully, Xavier had it together and stepped forward. 'These are our cousins, Keefa, Dannon and Loki.' Then he proceeded to introduce their party to them one by one, but JJ was frozen. He watched Xavier's lips move, but didn't hear what he was saying until the cousins bowed low.

Paige bravely held out a hand for Keefa to shake. The rest of them simply looked on shocked. JJ included. All he could do was look from them to Latitia's dazed face.

Paige let out a tiny squeal of surprise when he pulled her close to his face and placed his forehead against hers. They each did the same thing, as was the Murr custom of greeting close friends and family. By the time it was Loki, she'd got quite used to it and closed her eyes as they did. JJ got the first glimpse of what Xavier saw in her.

'Right, shall we?' Keenan said, wanting to move things along while the situation was stable.

'Yes,' JJ muttered, grateful for the interruption before the barrage of questions could begin. He finally got his legs to move but felt irritable with guilt. He was being rude towards his cousins, who were completely innocent in wanting to say hello. But he couldn't help himself. He was panicking inside. He was relieved when Keenan added, 'Tell everyone to give them some space until they've settled in, can you?' as he passed the cousins, with wide eyes, for urgency.

Keefa just grinned and nodded, innocently, which made JJ feel worse. *Your girlfriends have beauty like ocean flowers,* Dannon projected loudly.

I should like to take a human girlfriend, Keefa called.

Loki remained quiet and thoughtful.

JJ felt hot with embarrassment as they rounded a corner and they were out of sight at last. He could hear Dwayne and

Richie discussing their size and the little ones calling them giants and asking if they eat boys for dinner.

He caught Keenan watching him with a look of sympathy. He clenched his jaw in temper. This was going to be emotional carnage. If either of them came out of this still with a girlfriend, it would be a miracle. Paige looked thoughtful and Latitia looked blank and said nothing at all.

CHAPTER 11

Xavier breathed a little easier when they came to the first of their rooms. Paige had handled the first hurdle brilliantly, but she remained quiet.

'Ms Johnson, you're in here with your two little boys,' Keenan said, pushing the door wide. 'Your other two sons are next door.' He tipped his head and pointed to a door next to the bed. 'Bathroom's through there.'

Valarie walked slowly into the room holding the little one's hands and turned suddenly. 'What about Latitia?' she asked, looking straight at JJ as if he'd manoeuvred this in some way.

Keenan spoke quietly into his headset and then nodded, with a 'Roger that.' Then he smiled. 'Bear with us, Ms Johnson. Latitia and Paige are sharing the next room after your boys. Then it's Linda and her small two.'

She flashed JJ a mildly annoyed glance, with no apology, as if it was his fault they were in this in the first place.

'Your bags will arrive as soon as they've been security checked. Get comfortable. Someone will be back for you soon,' Keenan was saying as he moved on to the next rooms.

Xavier flashed JJ a satisfied look. He understood immediately. It was perfect that the girls were on their own. They both went to follow them in when Keenan put out an arm to stop them. 'Not you two. Your father wants you in his study, now.'

Xavier swore under his breath and leaned inside the room. 'We'll see you shortly. We've just got to go and get the "keep it in your pants" lecture.'

Paige grinned. Latitia looked quiet and thoughtful. Xavier felt a nudge from JJ to get it over with.

JJ WALKED shoulder to shoulder with Xavier through the WWII bunker that now had a white space age feel, with colour-coded lights dotted in the ceiling to show your way through the maze of semi-circular tunnels. He mentally logged the girls were in green. Red was the main thoroughfare that led straight to the great hall, purple was the king's study and the royal quarters.

They came to a standstill at the double oak doors, to a grin and a nod from the Santalini guard, Reeve, who'd been with Keenan in London. They knew most of the elite guards well. He pushed the door open and ushered them inside. 'Boys.'

'Sit!' their father said immediately.

They sat on the orange sofa, directly opposite the king's heavy oak desk. Cesaré, prince of the Florianna royal family, sat in the leather armchair next to him. 'Where's Dad?' JJ asked, seeing him in his father's place.

'He's coming in a couple of days. He'll be coming in around the same time as your sister.'

JJ let out a breath and sagged a little. Of course. Dante wouldn't delegate such a delicate task to anyone else.

'He's coming, isn't he?' Xavier said, flatly. He shook his

head and could no longer hide his disgust. 'Didn't you get the listening bug we left you? Have you all lost your mind?'

Dante leaned back in his chair, widening his eyes and letting him rant.

Xavier went on and on. 'You have no idea who this guy really is … You're giving away our secret location … Everyone we love will be vulnerable to attack … You have no idea the full extent of his power.'

Dante let him peter out without biting. It was an excellent lesson in handling Xavier's temper. But in this instance, he had to agree with Xavier. Everything he said was true.

'Well, it's a good job I have my seventeen-year-old son to remind me of all these things I hadn't thought of, eh, Ches?' he said, winking at the prince next to him.

Xavier scowled at his father for making fun of him. 'Why then?' Xavier said, looking like every emotion had been wrung out of him.

'Because that is the business of kingship, Xavier. Sometimes you must cover *all* your bases. Some several moves ahead.' Dante seemed to relent and smiled at his son a little regretfully. 'Whether you believe everything he has told us, or not, it is clear he is an Atlantean. It is also clear he is from a branch of a family we have never come across. So that in itself gives weight to his story. He is a prince with a family that feels justified in their beef with us. A king does not simply brush all that aside unless he wants trouble down the line. He is angry enough, without me adding fuel to it.'

JJ couldn't argue with the wisdom in that.

Xavier huffed in frustration, begrudgingly seeing it too. 'But here … at Christmas, with our loved ones?'

Dante nodded indulgently. 'And what better way of showing we are reasonable and not connected to the decisions made by our ancestors, who very clearly wronged him.'

Xavier continued, even though it was obvious it was an

argument he was never going to win. 'You could at least let us have rooms near Paige and Latitia to protect them.'

Dante burst out laughing and Cesaré grinned and said something too quick for JJ to catch in Italian. 'Oh, you think so, do you?' Dante said, still unable to help his amusement. Then he let the smile drop from his face. 'Let me remind you of the diplomatic nightmare that you yourself have created. We have humans at Filfla that know nothing of our existence. *You* now have the challenging task of finding a way of educating them without them losing their minds.'

JJ felt his cheeks heat as Dante flashed a glance at him.

'This is your once and only chance to do that before you return to school, otherwise it is over.'

Xavier went to cut across him, but Dante put up his hand. 'Do you understand me?'

Xavier exchanged a dark look with JJ. They both got the message that this was a one-time gig. If it didn't work, they wouldn't be returning to Camberwell and the people they now knew and loved would never even know they'd been. 'How do you suggest we do that?' JJ asked.

'Yes, bloody Keefa, Loki and Dannon already formed a welcoming committee as we arrived.' Xavier said, his anger rearing up all over again.

'What did you expect when you suggested this, Xav? Everyone hides what they truly are? *You* wanted to bring them home.' Dante pointed at him, his own anger rising for the first time. 'With no forethought at all. These are the things that you will come up against.'

Xavier deflated back into the sofa, finally admitting defeat. Dante was right. They'd been so preoccupied with Alexia and what was going on with her life, that they hadn't come prepared for their own.

'Where would you start?' JJ asked, feeling a little sorry for Xavier.

Dante let out a sigh and eyed them both sternly. Then he appeared to soften as if he'd given them a hard enough time. 'I'll start them off with a history lesson. Then the rest is up to you.'

Xavier looked at JJ. They were both relieved. It was a start. It should come a lot easier after that.

'But what I want you to remember is that unless the two families respond favourably and are happy to be onboard by the end of their stay, then it's over. Do you understand?'

JJ felt Xavier nod along with him.

They'd had all these things they'd planned to say to their father. About when they went back, Demidov and the surveillance, but it all paled into insignificance with that.

'Call 'em in,' Dante said to Cesaré.

JJ's heart thumped as Cesaré got up and went to the door. He opened it and said something to Reeve, too quiet for him to hear. Then he went and sat back down. Cesaré continued to chat in hushed tones in Italian with Dante, and JJ and Xavier sat in silence.

JJ's mouth had gone completely dry and all he could think of were the hundred things that could go wrong. The look of horror on Latitia's face and how he would have to take it on the chin.

Minutes passed until there was finally a soft knock at the door.

'Come in,' Dante said.

The door opened and Valarie, Linda, Dwayne, Richie, Paige and Latitia all slowly entered, looking around at all the shelves filled with books that lined the king's study. 'Where are the kids?' Xavier asked, suddenly looking alarmed.

JJ looked at his brother as if he truly was an alien. It had been the last thing on his mind.

'At the crèche. Can you believe they actually have a crèche here?' Linda said, eyes wide with amazement.

Chairs were brought nearer by Reeve and JJ faced front as they all found their seats. Cesaré stood and stepped closer to kiss the mums' cheeks and shake the teenagers' hands.

Valarie's eyes widened in wonder as she received hers and looked cheekily at Dante. He immediately softened with the soft spot he had for her. 'My cousin Cesaré,' Dante said by way of introduction.

'Are they all this pretty?' Valarie asked with a giggle, while Latitia rolled her eyes.

'Yes!' Dante said, as a matter of fact, making both women laugh. Paige and Latitia looked bemused, as if everyone had gone mad.

XAVIER SWAPPED another look with JJ as Dante walked around his desk and leaned back against it. 'First of all, let me say, welcome. I thought here was a little cosier to meet than the great hall,' he said, smiling widely. 'I would say to my humble abode, but we all know that it's not. It's a huge rabbit warren of tunnels that you can easily get lost in. You noticed the lights in the ceiling?'

Each of the guests nodded, hanging on his every word.

'Well, that is your route to places. Rather like the London underground. One of my staff will give you each a colour-coded map. I want you to enjoy your stay here, so just be aware there are over one hundred rooms, so it's easy to take a wrong turn. Just remember it is the red lights that take you all the way to the great hall, where we all get together and relax… Now to business,' he said, wandering back around to sit at his desk. 'I wanted to have a chat with you before you went down to the great hall, because you're going to see some pretty unusual and wonderful things that maybe won't make a lot of sense to you.'

Xavier scanned the room and everyone was completely riveted to his father.

'Please know that nothing will hurt you and I will happily answer any questions should they come up while you're here.'

'You're starting to scare me now, Dante,' Valarie said, laughing. 'You'll be telling us next you are some evil genius, mastermind, with ambitions to take over the world.'

Richie and Dwayne laughed. 'Yeah, Dr Evil,' Dwayne said.

Xavier looked at JJ frustrated, as he couldn't help smiling. Dante pointed at Dwayne and said, 'Close,' making everyone laugh.

'At the moment, family are arriving all the time, from air and sea,' he said, flashing a look at Xavier and JJ. 'Five families make up our nation. I am the head of the Dubonnettis and Cesaré here is head of the Florianna.'

Cesaré tipped his head and smiled his dazzling smile at Valarie and Linda, who grinned back.

Valarie dragged her eyes from Cesaré to ask, 'What made you choose an underground bunker, Dante?'

'Great question, Val. What I'm about to tell you now is an official secret, known only to prime ministers, presidents and a few select individuals. From this moment, you will be one of these. Before you leave, you will be asked to sign a Non-Disclosure Agreement that you won't divulge any of the official secrets you witness here. Are you ready to know what it is?' He looked at each of them, one by one, keeping the weight of his seriousness. The air went still as he allowed them to absorb what he was saying.

When they realised that he expected them to answer, each of them looked around at the others and nodded. Xavier looked straight into Paige's eyes and gave her a reassuring nod.

'OK,' Dante said, satisfied. 'We are a very rare bloodline that dates back to before the building of Atlantis.'

Xavier's heart was pumping as he looked between his father and the rapt faces.

'We've done well in industry and commerce. You could say we are a successful nation. But there are those who would try to take what we have away from us. The green-eyed monster, so to speak.'

Valarie and Linda shared a puzzled look. Paige put up her hand.

Xavier turned in his seat to watch her, fascinated.

'Isn't Atlantis a myth?'

'Some do think that,' Dante said with a nod and a glance Xavier's way, as if she had impressed him. 'We kind of like to perpetuate that idea.' He sat back in his seat and addressed everyone again. 'The truth is that Atlantis was not a myth. This is why there is enormous trust in extending this invitation to you. If you keep our secrets, then I'll do all in my power to see to it that you are looked after, even when you return to London.'

'And if we don't?'

'Richie!' Valarie hissed. 'Don't be rude.'

Dante tipped his head in Valarie's direction. 'No, it's a very good question.' Then he fixed Richie with a hard glare. 'You will never see any of us again. It will be as though we never existed.'

Ritchie was instantly shocked and sobered as if it was the last thing he'd been expecting. They all looked at each other, aghast.

Xavier watched them nervously. It was obvious that had unsettled them. Thankfully, Valarie got them back on track, looking around at the others furtively. 'What do you mean, looked after?'

Dante smiled at Valarie indulgently, 'Forgive me, I've known Val for a long time, so I will be perfectly frank with you. I will be taking over the board of governors for the school. When the children return, it will no longer be a state school.'

Dwayne and Richie looked at each other and then their mother, startled.

Dante put up his hand. 'Please don't worry. All students will have full scholarships to go there and your children will have a first-class education,' he said, letting his eyes fall on Paige.

Xavier read the excitement building in her aura as the pink blush entered her cheeks. How proud he was of her at that moment. Opportunity was what she'd homed in on, not the possible riches his father could bring.

However, Linda looked serious and worried as if something had been pulled out from under her. 'That's really generous, but—'

Dante read the woman's concern immediately and quickly brought the meeting to a close by getting to his feet. 'Remember, I'm here to answer your questions at any time.'

Xavier looked at JJ with a frown and he looked just as confused. He hadn't really told them anything.

'Who were those weird, tall blokes we saw when we first got here?' Dwayne blurted.

'Dwayne!' Valarie scolded with a hard glare.

Dante looked at Xavier, who shrugged. *What did you expect?* he projected irritably.

Small drips at a time, Son. They can't handle it in one go.

'That was Keefa, Dannon and Loki, my nephews,' Dante said brightening as if he'd been saved by the knock at the door. 'Come, meet my wife. The boys' mother. It's time to take you down to the great hall to meet everyone.'

Xavier closed his eyes. This would not be a small drip. He

looked at JJ, who looked back just as terrified. *When it doesn't rain it pours.*

JJ's HEART was beating so hard he could barely breathe and one of the things he always prided himself on was his calmness under pressure. Introducing someone he cared about to the real him laid him wide open and he didn't like it. He didn't do vulnerable. But he and Xavier were on a runaway train now, impossible to get off and say they'd changed their minds about the whole thing.

Instead, they went along with everyone to congregate in the great hall. Like humans promenading on the sea front to get the sea air, Atlantean royals came and got their fix of ancestral culture, by spending time with the king and his family several hundred feet below sea level.

Trouble was, some lived ninety percent of the time underwater. Like his cousins, Keefa, Loki and Dannon. He wasn't sure what he expected to happen. He guessed he hoped they wouldn't go straight to the shocking part first. 'Are you alright?' he asked Latitia. She'd barely spoken since they got there. 'Sure you don't want to go for a rest first?' he said, forcing a smile.

The corners of her eyes creased with a fake smile. 'Nice try. I'm wide awake. It's all so exciting.'

Xavier grinned at him. He wished he could wipe the smug look off his face. Just because Paige had handled everything well so far, didn't mean she could accept everything.

JJ checked on Valarie next, with Richie and Dwayne walking next to her. None of them looked worried or asked the right questions, but they should. This trip would change their lives forever. It had been selfish of him and Xavier to bring them here.

He felt the burn of Dante's eyes on him as he followed his

thought process, exactly. The intended lesson had come through loud and clear. However, there was no getting off the roundabout now and the happier their little party looked, the more JJ worried. He brushed Xavier's arm. *Shall we sit as far away from the fountain as possible?* he projected, straight to Xavier's mind.

Xavier hooked his arm around Paige's neck and kissed her temple, his eyes on JJ the whole time. *Why? It's all going to come out in the end.*

JJ would have launched himself at Xavier and pummelled his head had his mother not come around the corner at that exact moment. Instead, he gripped Latitia's hand as if she would fly away there and then. He'd forgotten they'd met before – the night everything had gone wrong. He prayed it didn't trigger anything in her.

His mother swept in and made a beeline to kiss her first, greeting her as an old friend. His younger brothers, Roman and Zander, were with her and were shaking Paige's hand. The world suddenly became muted, like being under water. He felt detached as his mother introduced herself to everyone else as Tia and kissed and hugged them all in turn.

Linda and Valarie openly stared at her, mesmerised by her ethereal beauty.

Before he knew what was happening, he was engulfed in her arms. Her warmth thawed him and he woke from his daze. There weren't that many people he loved so intensely. Perhaps Alexia and now Latitia. He found he wanted to bury his nose and cry into the crook of her neck as he'd done as a small child, whispering, 'Mother, make it all go away.' His eyes went to Latitia, enraptured.

His mother finally pulled apart, holding the tops of his arms to look into his eyes. The softness in her face told him she understood. *It will all be OK, darling. You'll see. I promise. Just be yourself.*

Then, keeping a hold of one of his hands, they came out into the great hall. Its magnificence struck the whole party dumb.

*L*atitia came into the hall holding JJ's hand from a tunnel under a staircase to a room so large it more resembled the concourse of a London railway station. A great pyramid staircase was behind them and Tia called excitedly for them all to climb it. 'Come on, you'll see everything much better from up here.'

Latitia looked up into JJ's eyes and he smiled back haplessly. He was doing it a lot lately as if he was worried about her reaction. She didn't want to dwell on why that was and happily sped up to follow his mother.

They all climbed the angled sandstone to a platform easily thirty, forty, fifty feet high. She couldn't tell. They arrived to face two shiny lift doors.

'Turn around,' JJ whispered.

She turned around and the sight before her took her breath away. Everyone exhaled and felt the same thing, letting out an audible sigh, murmuring words of wonder and amazement. The room was spectacular. A huge circular dome cut out of the sandstone rock with a curved window to an aquarium the size of three Imax screens. The glass made up the walls of at least a third of the room. Calming, luminous, blue crystal water was behind it. Fish swam past. Sun rays filtering down.

Then it struck her. She pointed weakly. 'The sea.'

JJ nodded. 'We're about two hundred metres below sea level.'

She ran her eyes over the huge expanse as a small shoal of brightly coloured fish zig-zagged excitedly past. Then she took in the rest of the vast room. Huge, twisted trees seemed to make up the pillars that held up the vaulted ceiling of rock. Each one like braided vines intermingled with sparkling gem-like yellow lights. Polished white marble floors were covered in clusters of sofas, armchairs and low tables in soft tones of blue and green. But the centrepiece, the whole focal point of the room, was a great marble fountain with at least five tiers that almost reached the ceiling. The illuminated water shone like tumbling blue sapphires, cascading down into a turquoise pool below. Then, as if that wasn't enough, the intricately carved wall surrounding it had cushions with beautiful people sitting on them, casually chatting. Gorgeous people. As her eyes darted around, she could see that all the people were beautiful, even the children who ran around, giggling and excited to be there.

Latitia felt someone squeeze her hand. She turned her head and looked directly into JJ's eyes. Stunning eyes the same colour as the fountain pool. They were curious eyes. Unsure. Not proud of the magnificent room as she would have expected. 'Are you OK?' he asked, frowning. *Why did he keep on asking her that?*

She nodded, puzzled by his reaction. 'It's amazing.' Her eyes went back to the fountain, just as two incredibly tall people stood up right in the middle of the water. Her first instinct was to laugh, as they appeared to have been swimming in it. Then they looked straight up at her. It stopped her heart in her chest. She couldn't make out their features, but they knew the moment she looked at them. They were so strange-looking. Hair so black and so were their eyes. Their skin was ash-grey and covered in vivid tiger-like stripes. Joseph had been right. They were like Avatar people. Except, while they were strange, they were still startlingly good-looking. Like proud Native Americans in full war paint and very few clothes. Their lower halves were barely covered in just a thin, shiny material that captured the light of the room. One nodded slowly and put up a hand.

Then everything felt weird. Heat surged through her from her toes. 'Are you OK?' echoed through her mind for the hundredth time.

The world span.

Then tilted on its axis.

And everything faded away.

'Wow,' Dwayne said.

Richie swore.

'Oh my god,' said Valarie.

Paige looked across at her mother to her right. She hadn't said a word at all. Just enthralled by the scene. Like standing on a hill looking down on a small town below. At least she wasn't freaking out, she supposed.

She felt Xavier kiss her cheek and turned into it, just as the commotion broke out.

Latitia appeared to have fainted.

'Bloody hell,' Xavier whispered. 'Stay here.' He went forward to help JJ and his mother, who had taken charge.

Two of the huge guards came from nowhere and several servants ran up the stairs to help. Latitia appeared to be waking up as they all carried her down the many steps, then behind them and out of sight.

It left Dwayne and Richie with her family. The tall, beautiful guy, Cesaré, from the king's study, came up behind them. Paige caught a glimpse of the lift doors closing. He came and stood with them, taking Xavier's mother's place. 'Come on, it's just a faint. Come and make yourselves comfortable,' he said in his melodic Italian accent. He went forward and jogged down the steps. When they didn't immediately follow, he stopped and turned. 'Come, don't worry, she will be fine.'

Paige swapped a look with her mother, nervously, and they followed Dwayne and Richie down the steps.

Cesaré took them over to a vacant group of sofas and comfy chairs arranged around a table. Then he asked them all what they wanted to drink. He gave orders to one of the servants, who went off quickly to get them.

Paige was relieved when Xavier returned from helping with Latitia and squeezed into the same chair as her. 'Is Latitia OK?' she asked quietly in Xavier's ear.

He turned his head and kissed her on the mouth. 'She'll be fine. Low blood sugar and feeling a bit overwhelmed, the doctor says.'

Paige let out a ragged breath, relieved. It sounded reasonable. She had been unwell a lot over the last few weeks. She wondered how nice it must be to have your own doctor on call. Xavier's family were more rich and powerful than she ever imagined.

A dark-skinned woman, around her fifties, arrived holding her brother and sister's hands. They broke away and ran to her mother. 'They wanted Mama,' she said, smiling.

After climbing up and hugging her mother they scrambled to get down. 'Can we play?' her little sister whined.

'No, stay here,' her mother ordered, a little too forcefully.

Two boys of similar ages came over dragging a large box.

Her brother and sister were soon chatting away to them and had their hands in it, pulling out cars and trucks.

'They will be fine,' Cesaré said with his gorgeous smile, completely affecting her mother.

She blushed and relaxed back into her chair, satisfied that they weren't too far away. The woman, who must have been a nanny from the crèche, curtseyed and left after a wave goodbye to the children.

Paige felt a warm glow inside and allowed herself to look around her in wonder. The place was amazing. Spectacular. But still wrong somehow. Maybe too good. Something was niggling at the back of her mind. 'What is all this?' she said to no one in particular. Her stomach was suddenly tight and knotted. She turned her head to look deeply into Xavier's stunning, exceptionally green eyes.

As he said the words, 'You know what it is', the answer echoed around her skull, but she couldn't articulate it. It was too outlandish. Or maybe she didn't want to admit it to herself. No wonder it was too much for Latitia. It was too much for anyone. Try as she might, something was growing at the back of her mind. She closed her eyes for a second, refusing to acknowledge it.

Paige felt the seat lighten and opened her eyes to see that Xavier had stood up. He was holding out his hand for her to get up with him. She welcomed the distraction and used it to pull herself out of the chair. He said something to Cesaré, which he understood and began to talk to her mother. Xavier used the opportunity to lead Paige off towards the large window.

It did the trick. She was immediately enraptured by the size and magnificence of it. 'Wow,' she said. 'Is it really the sea?'

'It is,' Xavier replied, standing close, still holding her hand.

A particularly beautiful iridescent fish, that looked like someone had painted tiger stripes down its back, bumped its nose on the glass like a pecking bird. It made her laugh but made her think of the strange-looking people around the fountain. 'Everything here is so … I dunno, different. It's like a book, or a film. Like forty thousand leagues under the sea.'

Inevitably she searched and found the striped strangers sitting on the wall of the fountain and Xavier pulled her head around to look at him. His look was intense, boring right into her. 'The sea is fundamental to my people,' Xavier said, still gauging her expression, like he was conveying some kind of deeper message.

All she could do was stare up at him bemused. When she didn't say anything after a few seconds, he picked up her hand and kissed the back of it. Then he led her over to the fountain.

At first she didn't want to go, but he gave her a little tug and she went and sat with him on the wall like all the others. A few looked over at her with strange blank faces. Her attention was quickly taken by delightful small children, splashing in the water and having a great time. Their skins were pale and covered in grey stripes like their parents. Their eyes were very black and their hair pure white. They were strange and like no children she'd ever seen.

She looked back at Xavier, startled. He remained quiet and was watching her closely. Something moved behind her and she turned and looked up at two of the boys they'd met earlier. They were really tall and had the same stripes as the small children in the pool. She looked between them, spotting the only difference was that their hair was long and black.

Her eyes shot back to Xavier's. He was still watching her, allowing her to come to her own conclusions.

A loud slosh in the water brought her attention back to

the children. But something else was happening. Something big. She wanted to stand up and get out of the way. But Xavier covered her hand. 'It's OK. Don't be scared.' The water was bubbling and coming up in the centre, but she found she couldn't move.

Two heads breached the water, one huge male with long black hair and another; a small, ethereal woman, delicate, small-boned and blonde. They were both vividly striped. Stripes that covered their shimmering skin completely. They rose up out of the water slowly. She couldn't take her eyes off them. Particularly the male. He was the biggest, tallest, scariest person she'd ever seen.

She felt a squeeze and looked down at Xavier's tanned fingers gripping her hand. She looked up into his eyes. 'Breathe ... stay calm. It is my aunt and uncle, that's all.'

Paige felt herself nod, but she wasn't taking in anything at all. She was grounding herself in Xavier's steady gaze. *Do you want to get out of here?* became an echo in her mind.

The next thing she knew, he was leading her away.

'Nice to meet you, Paige,' came from behind her. She craned her neck around to see the two boys from earlier, grinning widely and giving her a child-like wave.

'Come on,' Xavier said, pulling her away with him.

She sluggishly allowed it, feeling like everything was a dream.

CHAPTER 13

*L*atitia woke in a bed in a room she didn't recognise. 'It's OK. you're in the infirmary,' JJ's voice came from next to her. She turned her head and he was immediately in her eyeline, looking concerned.

Another face loomed over her. Strange, pale, wearing black goggles, with impossibly white hair.

She went to shrink away, but JJ steadied her with a hand. 'It's OK. It's only Rune. He's a doctor.'

Her mother was there next. 'Are you OK, love? You fainted. Scared me half to death. Have a drink of water,' she said, holding out a tumbler.

Latitia took a few sips and felt her head rise to an easier angle, as her upper body was smoothly adjusted by the mechanism of the bed.

JJ's beautiful mother was there looking as stunning as she remembered.

'I think we should go home and get some tests,' her mother was saying.

'We've taken a full blood profile. You'll get the results much more quickly here,' JJ's mother was saying. 'Our doctor seemed to think it is low blood pressure. It's quite common in girls her age.'

Latitia caught the stern look on her mother's face. She was angry. She was a nurse, but thankfully she kept her mouth shut and just tipped her head. 'Thank you.'

Her eyes went back to JJ's, riveted to her. Large, dilated and fearful. There was something else going on here. Something big and scary, below the surface, that she just couldn't reach. JJ knew it too and he was scared and waiting for her to get there.

Then, as if she knew, too, JJ's mother went to the door. 'Come on, Valarie. Let me get you a coffee.'

She went to put her hand up with an excuse to stay, when Latitia smiled. 'It's OK, Mum. Go. I'm fine.' Latitia knew she stood a lot more chance of getting to the bottom of things without her mother there. 'I'll rest for a bit and come and find you.'

Valarie reluctantly allowed herself to be led by JJ's mum, until she was left with JJ and the weirdest-looking doctor she'd ever seen. He hadn't said a word but looked across the bed at JJ and nodded. He moved the goggles up high on his forehead and she was struck again by how white his hair and skin were. Then he looked right at her and she was pulled into the darkest black pools for eyes. *That's right. Look directly at me,* the soft male voice said, without moving his lips.

A deep, tightening fear was crawling up from her stomach to her throat, making it harder and harder for her to breathe. The blood was draining from her face again, leaving her lips tingling.

A grip on her hand broke her gaze and she turned her head to look at JJ. He seemed so worried. 'It's OK. He's going to help you remember.'

She swallowed, now terrified. 'Remember what?' *What was happening?*

The strange man was right in her eyeline again. Looking at her intently. An overwhelming feeling of warmth and contentment began to wind itself around her. His eyes were so black. So deep. So inviting. She was falling into them. Falling. *Falling.*

She was at a pool. Steam was rising from the water. She remembered it. London. JJ's dad's hotel. She was watching JJ swim because she was too self-conscious to get in. *No,* she was worried. Terrified JJ hadn't come up to breathe. The same scared feeling reared up in her now. She pleaded for him to get out. He climbed up the steps and stood right in front of her. Taller. Different. Striped. *Just like those boys in the fountain.*

Her mouth opened to form the scream. The same scream as last time. Someone was shaking her. *JJ.* 'Please, Latitia. It's me. See? I'm right here. I'm nothing to fear. I love you. I would never hurt you.'

His words slowly broke through and the fear slipped away. She blinked and the doctor nodded and smiled strangely. Then he pulled the goggles back over his eyes. *You have full recall now. Your memory is restored.* She heard him distinctly, but his lips never moved. He bowed his head at JJ and seemed to glide away from the bed and out of the room. JJ was now in his place on the edge of the bed, still holding her hand and looking concerned. She continued to stare at him, then down at the tingle his fingers left as he absently rubbed the back of her hand. He gave her a nervous smile.

'You're not ... not ...'

'Exactly human?' he finished for her. 'Not completely, but genetically very close. We're from the same gene pool at some point in the distant past. There are just a few evolutionary differences.'

'Like breathing underwater?' she said, seriously wondering if she was having this conversation in delirium.

He bobbed his head a little. 'Some of us … not all. But yeah, if you like.'

'And stripy skin?' she asked, feeling a little braver.

He was smiling widely at her now. 'Yeah … and stripy skin.'

THE SENSE of relief and elation flooding JJ's body almost brought him to tears. He wanted to crush her to him and whoop for joy, he was that damned relieved. He imagined her screaming and cowering away from him and it all being over between them, because she would have been scrubbed of all knowledge of him and packed off back to London. Her delightfully oversimplified questions were perfect. He could totally work with that. For the first time since he'd met her, he felt a glimmer of hope. A tiny slither that made him think they might actually work and get past all the differences between them.

'Who are you then?' she asked.

It was the question that was always going to come up one day and, strangely, it didn't terrify him nearly so much anymore now she'd accepted what he looked like. He patted her hand and shuffled on the bed as he attempted to get straight what he wanted to say. 'Everything I told you before was the truth. I am royal. I come from a very rich and powerful family.'

'Why do you look different when …' she trailed off with what she really wanted to ask.

'I'm in water?' he finished for her. He took a deep breath and just said the most logical thing he could think of. 'Our genetic makeup makes us suited to being underwater. We are five families, but one of us is the purest bloodline of all.'

'The tall boys we saw.'

JJ was thrilled she was following along without freaking

out. He nodded, smiling happily. 'Yes, that's right. We are the descendants of a great civilisation. Atlantis; the one my father mentioned earlier. Have you heard of it?'

She nodded. 'Kind of.'

This was so much easier than he expected. He had to really concentrate on not overwhelming her with too much, so he decided to leave it there for now. He took a leaf out of Xavier's book, letting out small snippets only when it is needed. Telling her they'd crossed galaxies to come here, or the Murr cousins she'd seen live underwater permanently, could tip the balance, and he didn't want to try his luck. He leaned down and kissed her on the mouth. 'I'm still the same me.' He sat back up. 'So if you see anything you don't understand, just talk to me about it and I'll explain. Don't freak out, OK?'

Her smile seemed so fragile. 'That's why you have those weird mental powers,' she said more to herself.

He leaned forward and tickled her ribs. She was remembering him felling one of the debt collectors who came to her house, right in the middle of her hallway. She laughed into him and he was kissing her again.

The bonding urge shifted and rose dangerously in his chest. He pulled back instantly. The last thing he wanted was to put her in danger with that.

LATITIA DREW BACK from the kiss and studied his beautiful face in wonder. She could scarcely believe it. But somewhere deep down, she'd always known he was different, in more than just a privileged, rich kid kind of way.

He seemed relieved and leaned into her hand as she gently traced the side of his face. She couldn't help remembering the stripes that appeared there on that terrible night. The night that had blurred to a haze just before her illness.

The strange illness that had lasted for weeks, that she could barely remember at the time and could now remember perfectly. No wonder her mother had changed overnight. She'd loved JJ at the beginning and had become so hostile towards him. Now it all made sense.

Even more confusing was the feelings of chronic déjà vu. Like she'd lived this before. *She has full recall now,* the weird doctor had said. Those terrifying eyes, hidden by goggles. They'd done something to her when she looked into them, and it wasn't the first time. *Headaches. Pain.* Then JJ had moved out and kept his distance. *Would he have done that to her if he cared?* It just proved something had been hidden from her in the first place.

A weight of disappointment hit the bottom of her stomach. *How could he?*

These people. JJ. *Had mixed up her thoughts. Tampered with her mind.* She'd been so ill. For weeks. Lost. Barely knowing who she was and what she was meant to feel, and he'd abandoned her once. He could do it again. Then cover it up with the man with the goggle eyes.

A cold icy finger trailed down her spine. She'd been used and, worse still, treated like a fool, by the very person she'd allowed to get close and fallen in love with.

'Is everything OK?' JJ asked.

The frown dropped from her face, immediately, at his concerned expression and she quickly replaced it with a smile. She pulled him to her to give herself time to think. 'I'm fine … Just scared. I could have pushed you away for ever.' She didn't recognise the words leaving her own mouth. They were so alien to her. Only that she needed time. To sort it all out in her mind. How much of all this was a knee-jerk reaction at the hopeless way JJ had handled things and what she should be genuinely angry about. She needed to decide whether JJ really loved her. And more importantly, whether this had changed how she felt about him.

She pulled apart to check his face that looked so handsome and gorgeously insecure. She immediately leaned in and kissed him. For now, she would wait and see. It could be just the weight of everything. She might just need to get back some sort of control.

CHAPTER 14

*P*aige had to get out of there. The two tall boys' interest in her was the last straw. Suddenly, there were just too many inquisitive eyes. Too many people. *People? Could she even call them that?*

Finally, she gave herself permission to acknowledge the words knocking around the back of her mind. *Strange. Abnormal. Alien!*

Paige began to walk faster. She felt Xavier match her steps next to her, continually watching her expression. He was scared. Terrified she'd reject the whole thing.

They entered the tunnels under the pyramid steps. *Red lights,* she remembered. Then she went left into blue. Right into yellow. Left. Right. Left. Right. Faster and faster, until she finally halted with a stamp of her foot. 'Oh, where the bloody hell are we, Xavier?'

He pulled her into his body and rested his chin on her head. She allowed it stiffly, determined not to give in to his pull so easily. 'I want to go to my room, please, I'm tired.'

Xavier pulled her round to look at her and gently pushed back the tendrils of her hair with a finger. 'Don't push me away,' he said, sounding heartbreakingly vulnerable. It affected her as it was the only time she'd ever seen him anything other than supremely confident.

'I'm not,' she said, sagging wearily. 'I just need to process all this, OK?'

He searched her face to make sure she was being honest.

'Can you tell Mum I've just gone for a nap?'

Xavier nodded after a beat of indecision. 'Sure.' He turned and walked away and left her, looking over his shoulder at her a couple of times. 'Your room is just down there,' he said pointing.

As soon as he was out of sight, she went further down the green corridor and followed it as it veered to the right. 'Guest 4' was on the first door she came to. She hurriedly went inside and sat down on the bed.

Her mind was racing. She looked around the whole room for the first time. It really was lovely. *But underground?* The walls were made of the same large blocks of bumpy cream stone that seemed to make up the place, but all the soft furnishings were a deep red. The quilt, the comforter and the cushions on the dainty little armchair. All the wood was dark and highly polished. The dressing table and chest were beautifully ornate and matched everything else perfectly. The door to the bathroom was closed, she'd check that out in a minute.

Paige allowed herself to sink back into the soft downy quilt that felt like it wrapped itself around her as the air dispersed perfectly. This place was for rich people. Comfortable and luxurious. It was so comfy that her eyelids became heavy and she let herself drift for a few minutes. A long day, mixed with the excitement of a new place and the magnitude of what she absolutely knew she was avoiding, was enough to send anyone to sleep.

. . .

SHE BLINKED RAPIDLY, realising she must have fallen asleep. She sat up quickly and looked at the digital clock next to the bed. It said, 16:30. *15:30 at home.*

Paige breathed normally and lay there for a few minutes. Xavier must have respected her wishes to give her some time. She'd had enough now and slid off the bed and went over to the door that went into the bathroom. A light automatically came on to reveal a perfectly white, serviceable bathroom. It looked brand new. Everything pristine and no mould between the tiles. There was a huge tub, which she promised herself to use at some point. For now, she'd use the walk-in shower for quickness.

She was soon enjoying the pummelling spray at the perfect temperature and began to lather her body. She was acutely aware that she hadn't given the headspace to what was clearly going on here. She was avoiding it. A separate species of people, living alongside humans and had been for a very long time. Of which Xavier, the boy she'd fallen for, was one of.

She shook the disturbing thoughts away and turned the faucet off with a squeak. She wasn't ready to face him or anything else yet. She dried quickly and pulled some slouchy grey track pants out of her bag and a white T-shirt. She scraped a comb through her hair and decided to let it dry naturally. Then, pulling on her white trainers, she sneaked out of the door.

AFTER THE DOCTOR gave Latitia the 'all-clear', JJ kept his arm around her all the way back to the great hall. He wasn't entirely sure whether the extra protectiveness was because he thought she would fall over or run off screaming. All he knew was he didn't want to let her go. She had taken the information so well; maybe too well. He guessed he was still a little in denial. Then, after a few minutes, when she hadn't freaked out, he allowed his hold to loosen and his spirits to rise. He didn't want to jinx it, but it made him so happy. He had to keep touching her, constantly reading her surface thoughts, aura and body language just to make sure. 'Where do you want to go?' he whispered in her ear. He was already imagining kissing her in a quiet corner somewhere.

'I just want to say hello to my mum, so she knows I'm OK, and then I want to explore.'

JJ was a little unsettled at the pulse of anxiety in her aura but brushed it aside as perfectly normal to want to check in with her mother. He guessed his misgivings were mainly due to worry that Valarie might put unnecessary fears in her head. *Think positively.* He should be pleased she was brave enough to explore the unknown. He looped his arm around her neck and kissed her forehead. *This girl was sending him crazy.*

Her mother was with the rest of their group in a cluster of sofas at the foot of the pyramid. They were chatting to more of his cousins. His heart sped up a little, but he had to learn to relax, or he would transfer it to Latitia. He took a deep, measured breath and exhaled to bring down his heartrate. Otherwise, this was going to be a very long, stressful trip. Although on closer inspection, Valarie seemed relaxed, talking easily to Reeve Santalini, one of the guards. He was a great guy and close friends with his uncle Keenan. He'd been on security detail with them in London, so she would kind of know him. However, something about their interaction was too easy. Like they were more than just acquaintances. He hadn't noticed any familiarity or hint of becoming friends at home, but he guessed he hadn't lived with the Johnsons for a while. They certainly looked friendly now. He glanced sideways at Latitia to check, and she hadn't appeared to notice. No kid wanted to see their mother loved up with a new guy. *Oh well,* it could only be a good thing if she was occupied and off his back.

Valarie was out of her seat as soon as she spotted them approach. 'Oh, honey, you're up. Come and sit down.'

JJ looked straight at Reeve, who simply nodded and moved away. The no-nonsense look made JJ even more suspicious. There was definitely something going on there.

Valarie had her arms around Latitia in a vice-like grip. 'It's OK, Mum. Just wanted you to see I'm fine. JJ's going to show me around. Where's Paige?' she asked, having to pat her back to let go, as the air was being squeezed out of her. She managed to extricate herself from her grip to look around her.

'She went off with Xavier a while ago.'

Xavier was nowhere nearby. He would feel him. A stab of envy punched his insides. He'd already sloped off to be alone. 'Where to first?' JJ said, brightening up with a smile.

'The big window. Can we take a look?'

She looked so innocently excited that he felt ashamed at the direction his thoughts had taken. 'Sure,' he said, his eyes catching Valarie's.

She mouthed the words, 'Watch her.'

He nodded discreetly and steered Latitia away from the group and through the many sofas and tables. They were all starting to fill up with relatives saying hi to them and each other. Sending greetings from other royals who couldn't be there. He inwardly cringed and watched for Latitia's reaction the whole way, until she finally had her hands on the super-thick glass of the panoramic window.

This is all real. It's actually happening. Everyone here is an alien. Was a constant ticker tape monologue going through her head. The window to the sea and the pretty little fish happily swimming across it was a tiny piece of normal in a world of madness going on all around her. She would spin it out as long as possible

She would have stayed longer with her mother to at least acclimatise to it all, but she knew it would have come off as weird to JJ. He was super perceptive. She just hoped she just came off as excited, which to a large extent was true. She guessed she was still at the 'pinch herself' phase. Not to mention her discovery that her boyfriend, although insanely hot, was a very controlling alien, which she wasn't sure how she felt about yet. To think she'd thought that was just Xavier. It was a hard lesson to come to terms with. She guessed it boiled down to what she was prepared to take.

PAIGE MANAGED to direct herself to the main thoroughfare of red lights. They gently pulsed in one direction, so she guessed that meant towards the great hall.

She stopped, undecided, and looked the other way. She wasn't ready to face Xavier and everyone yet. She wanted more time to get her head together before she did that. More precisely, she wanted to examine how she felt about it. Whether it changed how she felt about Xavier.

She began to walk in the opposite direction. Figuring as long as she didn't veer too far from the red lights, then she wouldn't get lost.

Her thoughts inevitably drifted back to Xavier and what he had revealed to her. It had been a huge shock, *but should she have been so surprised, really?* She had always known there was something very different about him and his siblings. It hadn't just been that he was extraordinarily good-looking and into ordinary, drab her, but that he seemed to know so much about everything. He felt things. Sensed things. That alone always made him seem so clever and confident. She'd never met anyone like that.

The red lights went on forever. It was starting to sink in just how vast this place was. Corridors of lights in all different colours went left and right, all the way along. Until she heard a cheer. Then what sounded like clapping. There were stamps of feet and squeaks that sounded really familiar. *The gym at school.* It was trainers on a smooth surface. People were playing a game.

Paige came to a cross junction in the tunnel where white lights crossed over the red. She faced one way and then the other, just as there was another cheer. *That way,* she thought with a prickle of excitement, and she directed her steps to follow the noise.

It wasn't long before she came across a pair of grey double doors. She put her ear to the cool metal. It sounded like there were a lot of people behind them.

'Can I help?' a rich American voice said, making her jump and turn around. She must have looked as guilty as hell as all the moisture seemed to go out of her mouth and she couldn't think of a coherent thing to say. Coming up with nothing, her cheeks ignited and exposed her as completely busted.

Not only had she been caught snooping and listening at doors, but by a boy she'd never met, who happened to be staggeringly good-looking. He was not quite as tall as Xavier, but he was darker-skinned, almost Asian-looking, except he had the deepest-blue eyes she'd ever seen. Like deep ocean blue. His hair was black and wavy to his shoulders. She found her eyes wandering down his body to check out what he was wearing. A lab coat. *Yes, it was definitely a lab coat,* over an old grey T-shirt, battered jeans and flip-flops. She couldn't stop staring. He was surfer dude meets chemistry student. The two just didn't mix.

'Are you mute?' he asked.

She looked back at his face in shock. Not necessarily because she was insulted, but that she'd only just realised she hadn't uttered a word. 'No … no I'm not. I'm just new here.'

She was expecting him to tell her off for trespassing, so when he just bowed his head and said, 'I meant no offence. Many of the people here have no vocal cords and so they speak telepathically.'

It completely threw her off balance.

Her eyes went wide when she fell in with what he meant. It was all so overwhelming. She felt herself blush again. She just couldn't get over the hurdle that she was talking to someone who was at the very least part alien. 'I'm sorry … you are perfectly within your rights. I shouldn't be here. I wandered off,' she trailed off, looking around her doubtfully.

'I get you; I hate these kinds of get-togethers.' His face beamed into the most gorgeous smile. 'I escape down here to get away from everyone, to my lab.' He bowed low. 'Forgive me. My name is Hunter.' He straightened and offered her his hand.

'Paige,' she answered, stunned, touching the tips of his fingers and drawing her hand back sharply. Suddenly the white coat over scruffy clothes made sense and conversation possibilities move far closer to comfortable territory. 'You have your own lab?' came out more like a squeak, which she hated herself for. 'What are you working on,' she said coughing her voice deeper.

He half frowned and half smiled. Then his eyebrows went up in surprise. 'Forgive me,' he said, shaking his head. 'I don't often meet people here not into sports, surfing or music. It really is a pleasant change.'

He looked at her appreciatively for a long, laden moment. Her heart quickened and she had to remind herself she was with Xavier. He immediately snapped himself out of it, so she had to wonder whether it had been there at all. 'Would you like to see it? My lab, I mean?' he said laughing, making her cheeks burn all over again. She'd been confused and overwhelmed when she'd needed space from Xavier. Self-conscious and nervous among all the strangers. Meeting Hunter, a fellow lover of science, could be the perfect anti-dote. It was so nice to meet someone who spoke her language.

He was looking at her curiously. As if he was following her thought process, until he held out an arm and said, 'Shall we?' and they walked further into the bunker and away from Xavier and the red lights.

JJ DIDN'T KNOW how he felt as Latitia marvelled at all the beautiful fish. He was all over the place and not at all how he expected. On the one hand he felt elated, relieved, excited, but now there was a gut-wrenching fear for another reason. The last roadblock to a proper relationship had been taken away. Now Latitia seemed to have accepted him, there was no reason why she couldn't be his girlfriend. She was fully aware of who he was and in the inner circle of his family and that was, he realised, the most terrifying thing of all. The finality and inevitability of what was to come. The problem was him. Because now the only thing to keep them apart was his willpower and where Latitia was concerned, it was shaky at best.

Latitia's eyes went wide and she pointed through the glass. 'There's … there's two … two … girls? … swimming out there.' Her voice went squeaky and high-pitched.

JJ immediately followed the line of her arm and saw two of his cousins: Flame and Rochelle, or Rock as they all called her. They were the daughters of Keenan Santalini and his mother's sister, Lacy. He loved them dearly, but he could have murdered them at that moment. They were happily swimming in their shimmering, iridescent, Murr outfits. They reminded him of figure skaters in fish scales. Their black hair fanned out all around them, their pupils were wide and dilated and their skin displayed very vivid tiger-like stripes. In other words, looking very otherworldly. He looked up at an imaginary sky for strength. 'It's just my cousins who I'm going to kill.'

Latitia was studying his reaction. He shook his head wearily and she looked back at the girls.

JJ, is that you? Rock mentally blasted through the glass. She was pointing right at them. Flame looked over and waved. *We'll come in.*

JJ's heart beat faster. He was panicking. He wanted to tell them not to, but Latitia was already watching him strangely. He was going to have to give in to this some time, because the whole week was going to be one weirder thing for her to cope with after another. *Scratch that. For him to cope with.* It was like holding back a tide that was always going to come in no matter how strong you were. *OK,* he blasted wearily, but they had already dove down for the tunnel.

JJ began to lead Latitia towards the fountain, but she kept looking back over her shoulder. 'Where have they gone?' she asked.

He pulled her to a couple of armchairs right next to the fountain. 'Let's sit here. They're coming out.'

She sat down reluctantly, still looking back at the glass.

JJ kept his eyes on the fountain. 'Don't worry. You can meet them.' He took a deep breath. 'They won't be able to talk for a while, so don't be scared when they talk in your head.'

He felt her eyes burning a hole in the side of his face. She was assessing whether to believe him. He blinked slowly summoning strength. 'Well, you wanted to know all about me. Now you do.' He turned and looked her squarely in the eyes and saw the bewildered look in them. He reached out and took her hand. He never thought he'd wish to go back to London. It was so much harder here than he thought. *Don't be scared,* he projected to emphasise his point.

Latitia stared at JJ's face, now very pink in the cheeks, like he was hot or something. His pupils had expanded too, making them almost black. At first she thought he might be going through one of his scary changes. Now she was beginning to wonder if he was scared. Worse still, panicking. And he'd been weird like this since they'd got there.

She looked back at the window, but the girls had gone, and he didn't seem OK at all that she was about to meet them. *Was that all it was? A fear that she would know everything about him?* He'd been cagy about himself before they got there. Then there was the mind-bending. The stealing her thoughts. Making her believe she was losing her mind. *Just to protect the secret of who he was?* That wouldn't necessarily mean he didn't love her. *Or maybe it did.*

It was a troubling idea. He was no longer the self-assured, mysterious boy she'd met in London. He was an alien she didn't really know, nervous about what she'd find out. *What else was he hiding?*

CHAPTER 15

aige walked a little hesitantly with Hunter along one long corridor after another. With each step further away from the red light corridor, she became more conscious of how alone they were. He seemed nice, but she didn't know him at all. It made her continually look over her shoulder to try to memorise small markers, like fire extinguishers or 'In case of emergency' signs, but pretty soon one looked pretty much like another and it became obvious that she would never find her way back on her own.

'Don't be nervous,' he said, snapping her out of her thoughts. 'There is nothing to fear. I will see to it that you get back to the great hall.'

He didn't look at her, as if he sensed everything. She continued to gaze at him long after he finished speaking, until she resigned herself to relax a little. There was nothing she could do right then, but there was still something about him that made her feel wary and a little on edge.

She frowned to herself. She was being paranoid. He had only been polite and friendly. Perhaps it was because he was insanely good-looking and she felt disloyal to Xavier. She certainly wasn't unaffected by him. She couldn't imagine any girl not being. She hadn't done anything wrong, so she made a concerted effort to snap herself out of it. 'So, what are you working on?' she asked to break the silence.

He looked at her curiously.

'In your lab,' she added, embarrassed, that her comment had come from nowhere.

His face relaxed into the most stunning smile. 'Transcendental levitation, or particle levitation, as I like to call it.'

She widened her eyes at just how advanced and out there that was. She was expecting something more on par with what they did at school, like testing and sorting elements, or something.

'It starts with that,' Hunter said.

'Starts with what?' she said, still distracted by her thoughts.

'I began with testing and sorting elements when I was eight years old.'

She swallowed and halted her steps, so he was forced to stop with her. 'Wait! I never said that.' Then her eyes went wide with understanding. 'You read my mind?'

He shrugged and went to continue walking. 'You humans are easy to read. Your thoughts are so loud and erratic.'

Her heart was beating hard as she jogged to catch up with him. This was something she couldn't ignore or run away from, no matter how much space she put between her and Xavier. It probably meant he had the ability too and did it to her all the time. She had to face this head on. 'What are *you*, then?'

Hunter continued his purposeful strides but narrowed his eyes on her, suspiciously. 'What, Xavier brought you to Filfla and hasn't told you anything?' His mocking tone made her irritable and feel even more disloyal to Xavier. She knew she should be talking to him directly about it, but she guessed she needed an independent party to corroborate what she already knew. 'Bits and pieces. More when I got here ... Am I different to you, then? How do you know? What are you to Xavier?' she spurted, knowing she was coming across as prickly.

Hunter shook his head, smiling in disbelief and continued walking. Paige ran to catch up again. She recognised then that Hunter could be a good source of information. 'Come on, what are you then?'

He looked Heavenward and let out a sigh. 'I don't see why I should do all this for Xavier, we're not exactly close.'

'Oh, really?' Paige said, pouncing on his words.

'We're first cousins,' Hunter said, wearily. 'My mother and his mother are sisters. And before you ask again, I know you're human because the whole island knew you were coming. Few humans apart from presidents come here. You have no mental blocks and you leak emotions like a rusty bucket, so you are exceptionally easy to read ... that enough for you?' he finished, flashing a single, irritable glance her way.

Paige felt her temper rising to match his, with his shortness and insinuations that she belonged to a lesser species. 'So? What are you then?' she said in the same mocking tone. 'Because all I see is a moody arsehole, in a lab coat, with questionable taste in footwear.'

He laughed loudly at that and stopped and looked at her squarely. He continued to grin and nod as if she impressed him or took the last of his patience. She couldn't decide which. She hoped it was the first one. He let out a weary sigh. 'I can see what Xavier sees in you and I don't normally go for humans.'

She frowned at the weird non-compliment.

'You're not like ordinary girls.' He sagged a little as if she'd worn him down. 'Look, I'm Atlantean—a descendant of the civilisation of Atlantis. Everyone you see here are the same. Hybrid descendants of the Atlasians that came here from a world called Atlas, ten thousand years ago.' He shrugged, 'Except the tall stripy guys. They're the purebreds with no human DNA.' He allowed that to sink in, watching her closely.

Paige absorbed it all. Sifting through it, ticking and crossing off what fitted in with what she'd already seen and the little Xavier had told her. She tried to use the analytical side of her and not dismiss it out of hand as too far-fetched. She had to face the proof that was all around her. *The stripy people around the fountain.*

'The Murrs, Our Borge cousins,' he filled in for her without her even asking. He shrugged again. 'But we all kind of look like that to varying degrees when we get in the water.' He walked on a little further, leaving her staring after him. Then he stopped in front of a door that appeared to click open without him even touching it. 'Are you coming?'

She shook herself out of her shock and quickly caught up. There was no way she was finished with him yet. She followed him inside. The darkness soon changed to ambient light with their footfalls, then all her previous thoughts simply dropped away. There, in front of her, from floor to ceiling and all around her, was science geek heaven. Everywhere she looked, on every table and shelf, were books, glass flasks, tubes, burners and scopes. She even spotted a spectrophotometer, a centrifuge and an autoclave. This was a set-up worthy of a top pharmaceutical company, but with a hint of something antique or ancient, like—

'Merlin?' Hunter said, before the word solidified in her mind.

She couldn't even tell him off for being in her head again. All she could do was sigh and nod. That was exactly it. It was something more alchemic than mere chemistry. 'Wow,' was all she could say as she turned a slow circle. Taking in an impressive set up of flasks and tubes bubbling away, distilling a thick green liquid.

When her eyes finally landed on his, he was watching her strangely with a look of awe. 'You really are different, aren't you,' he said, chuckling lightly. 'I just told you everyone here is from another planet and you're more impressed by my lab set-up. I think I'm in love,' he said, laughing.

She frowned, dismissing the awkward comment with a wave of her hand. 'So, explain what you're doing here?' she said, going closer to the interconnected glassware, following it with her eyes to see where it all went to.

She felt him come very close to her shoulder. 'OK, I'll show you.'

Latitia shelved her misgivings for a while and waited seated with JJ for the two girls to come out of the sea. Everything was so fascinating; she wanted to watch JJ a bit longer before she challenged him about his behaviour.

JJ indicated with a nod of his head that they would come out of the fountain. *Amazing.* It made sense why so many people appeared to be paddling in it. They weren't using it as a strange way to cool off, which was ridiculous now she thought about it. It was all so incredible, that she was forced to suspend reality for a while. She'd entered a dream or a film plot, where everything was strange and kind of wonderful. Where it was easy to bench the truth about JJ, the dark cloud hovering at the edge of it all.

JJ was squeezing her hand so hard and now she knew why. He was terrified she'd run away. He needed to relax because he was making it worse. It was a relief when the girls finally stood up in the fountain. They were tall, slim and stunning, with their long black hair now plastered flat to their shoulders and their weird black and grey skin glistening with water.

JJ stood up, stiffly, pulling her with him. He grabbed two towels from a pile on a table and handed them to the girls who sat down on the wall and began to dry themselves off. She'd never seen him so uncomfortable.

Latitia took in every difference while they rubbed their hair dry. The large, dilated eyes and the lower legs that appeared longer. *Like JJ in the pool.* Except he'd been bigger. Taller. Scarier. It was strange, because now she was confronted with it all, she was starting to suspect that it wasn't simply the physical changes that had scared her about JJ.

She was forced to snap herself out of it before she appeared rude. They were smiling expectantly at her, like any other teenager she was meeting for the first time. However, when they switched their gaze to JJ, it became obvious they were communicating in some way. 'Can you include me?' Latitia said, a little irritated, after a few soundless nods and gestures.

'Of course. Sorry,' JJ said, immediately. 'We're all so used to talking this way.' He pulled her into the side of his body.

It was weird how a simple move like pulling her close could immediately dispel her fears. She guessed it was the naturalness of it. Nothing contrived. Completely subconscious.

'These are my favourite cousins, Rock and Flame,' he said, pointing to each of the girls. They smiled beautifully, showing perfect white teeth with particularly pointy canines. 'This is Latitia, my ...'

Her heart stopped. Waiting. Burning her stare into the side of his face.

JJ paused for a long moment, while he thought what she was to him. 'Girlfriend,' he said, eventually. 'From school.'

His cheeks went pink and she got the first true response that he wasn't exactly comfortable saying it. It was lukewarm to say the least and hurt.

The girls, however, were looking at her with wonder.

'Pleased to meet you,' she was forced to say, to break the uncomfortable silence.

Wow, so you're the one. Came directly to her mind from the one called Flame. Her stunning blue eyes widened and she nodded while she said it. JJ went on to talk about where they lived in South London and she couldn't help study the interaction between them. They were just like any close cousins, she guessed, but she couldn't help wondering how different that made JJ under the surface. How he thought. *How he felt.*

What are you doing here this early? JJ asked, looking at his large watch. *I wasn't expecting you until evening meal.*

It felt a strange conversation that was clearly very comfortable to them. All little hints to a completely different culture. *Haven't you heard, Loki and Dannon have demanded a rematch of last year's surf and turf basketball game.*

JJ laughed, but his eyes shot to hers a little cautiously.

'What?' she asked. 'What's a surf and turf?'

The girls giggled, seeming to revel in JJ's discomfort as he'd paused before he answered, obviously unsure what to tell her. 'Come on, tell me,' Latitia said, nudging into him. It was good to see he was acting strangely, even to them.

Oh, come on, JJ. You thought enough of her to bring her here. Rock said.

It is the best way to introduce her to all the cousins, Flame added, grinning.

Yeah, throw her straight in the deep end. They continued to bat to-and-fro.

Or are you scared she'll see us get thrashed by the fish? They really seemed to be enjoying themselves, digging him out, just like she would do with her brothers. *And who were the fish?*

You wuss. Rock walloped him in the stomach as she stood up, making him double over with an, 'oomph!'. Then she ran off across the huge hall with shrieks of laughter, with Flame running after her, to catch up.

Latitia put her hand over her mouth to disguise her smile as JJ straightened up, frowning. 'Well?' she asked, not able to keep the grin off her face. She liked the girls already. Seeing JJ off his 'Mr Perfect' pedestal was refreshing.

He let out a long breath and gave her a hapless smile, still rubbing his stomach. 'You sure you're ready for this? It isn't exactly NBA rules. They fight dirty.'

She studied his face, the laughter seeping out of hers. Along with an underlying, much deeper question. 'Do you want me to be?'

The lines of worry on his face disappeared and were replaced by amazement. Then a real smile that made him extraordinarily handsome. 'Yeah, I think I do. I actually do,' he said, laughing, like he'd surprised himself.

She would take that for now. Her focus was quickly taken from JJ to her two brothers coming up behind him. 'Hey! Can we hang with you?'

'We're bored and weirded out by mum acting all girly and giggly with that bloke with the teeth.'

It made them both laugh. Latitia looked at JJ with her eyebrows up. 'In the deep end,' she said, reminding him. 'Course … We're going to a family basketball game.'

'Sweet!' they both said, shuffling their feet and beaming smiles.

JJ smiled back, not looking so enthused. 'You play?' he asked.

Dwayne tutted and looked at him deadpan. 'Is the Pope catholic?'

Richie laughed. 'Of course we can play.'

JJ nodded once and moved her off by the small of her back. She looked up at him, spotting his brow was furrowed again. Her brothers were unaware, talking animatedly behind them, about past games and hoping the tall blokes they'd seen were on their side. This was going to be a test on so many levels.

CHAPTER 16

*P*aige had lost track of time with Hunter. She was watching him closely while he put powdered elements into a mixing flask with a solution; heating and distilling it through his complicated set-up of glass tubes and receptacles. Until it finally came out the other end in a black, viscous goo, resembling molasses.

'What do we do now?' she asked, enthralled.

'We take out the last of the moisture,' Hunter said, holding it up to his eyeline, rolling it slowly around in the beaker.

'To leave us with what?'

Hunter walked up to a heavy door and opened it, revealing what was some sort of kiln. Then he swapped the beaker he was holding for a large flask. He held it up so she could see what looked like glitter. Except it wouldn't stay still. Everything in the flask was moving constantly and colliding. 'What is that?' As she asked the question, she already felt a bubbling excitement inside her.

Hunter held it closer to his eyeline to watch the particles. 'This, my page-turner, is Elemental Gold ... the stuff of legend.'

She looked at him for a long moment, allowing the flattering pet name he'd decided to call her to sink in. Being a geek made her an outcast at school. *Did that mean he found her interesting? Intriguing?* She snapped herself out of it to look back at the flask. 'Gold?' she repeated, frowning. Convinced she couldn't have heard right. 'You've made gold.'

He nodded, completely distracted by its hypnotic movement. 'The goal of all alchemists.'

When she realised he was being deadly serious, she was astonished. 'You realise how rich you could be with this?'

Hunter shrugged. 'We are already rich. What you have to understand is this isn't ordinary gold found buried in the rock. This has a secret ingredient held sacred by our society for millennia.'

She remembered she'd read somewhere how great alchemists had always looked for the recipe for making gold. Now she understood why.

'Watch,' Hunter said. He picked up a green apple from a bowl of fruit on the counter and placed it on a metal tray on the bench in front of him. Then he took a small pipette and pulled up a little of the swirling gold solution. Come to think of it, she wasn't sure if it was a solid, liquid, or a gas. It was ridiculously hard to tell. He proceeded to place a couple of drops on top of the apple and watched as it slowly slid down its skin like oil, until it completely coated it. It was weird because two drops didn't seem enough. It was like it grew until it engulfed it.

'Now hold out your hand,' Hunter said.

Paige looked at him, alarmed.

'Go on. I won't hurt you ... I promise.' His look was intense, as if he was conveying so much more than the experiment. He tipped his head to prompt her.

She gingerly held her hand out flat. Hunter proceeded to hover his over the apple on the silver plate and mumble words she didn't understand, like a chant or a spell. It almost made her laugh after all the logical science stuff. She thought he was joking. But the gold began to shiver and then slowly circle around the apple. She looked at Hunter, shocked, wanting to ask how he was doing it, but he was transfixed on the apple, still mumbling the strange words.

Her eyes went to the apple again. The gold began to shake and circle it more and more quickly, making a bigger and bigger ring around it until she could no longer see the apple at all. She blinked in astonishment, wanting to get closer to him to see what was happening.

'Stay still!' Hunter barked, continuing to chant as if he hadn't been interrupted.

She straightened, chastised, with her hand out, rigid. Then she began to feel pins and needles in the centre of her hand. At first, she thought it was from loss of blood flow from being so tense. Then she let out a small yelp of alarm as the gold began to leave in a steady stream from Hunter's hand, holding the silver plate, all the way to her hand. Her eyes went so wide, it took all her willpower not to pull her hand away and let it drop onto the floor. It was forming a shape. Buzzing and vibrating in her palm until Hunter stopped chanting and she felt the weight of a ball in her hand. The particles dropped into simple glitter, leaving a perfectly crisp green apple, with a soft white mist clearing around it.

She looked at Hunter, dumbfounded.

'Go on, bite it. It isn't an illusion,' Hunter said, grinning.

She must have looked completely gobsmacked as Hunter began to laugh. It brought her to her senses and she closed her hand and brought the apple to her mouth. It smelled slightly of sulphur, but then she bit into it and felt the soft apple zest hit her face and smelled the wonderful subtle green apple smell. It tasted of pure sweet apple. Her eyes went to his as she chewed, in awe. 'You realise what this is. What you've achieved.'

'Transcendental particle levitation,' Hunter said with a small bob of his head. 'Except I haven't perfected it to move anything larger or further than a few feet.'

'You're a genius,' she said, shaking her head in wonder. 'You should win a Nobel prize or something for this.'

'It's not all my research,' he said, his face clouding. 'My father belonged to an ancient mystical order of alchemists. He was said to be a master practitioner.'

She couldn't help registering the past tense and felt immediately sorry for him. She didn't push to ask whether he ever saw him. She never saw her father. He hadn't stuck around much past her third birthday. 'Wow,' she said, simply, directing the conversation back to his fantastic experiment.

She was shaking and looked around her for somewhere to sit. She couldn't help trying to remember anyone that resembled Hunter from the people she'd met.

Hunter looked relieved and put his arm out towards an old, brown, sagging sofa in the corner. A lamp miraculously came on next to it. It occurred to her for the first time, how much was technology and how much was telekinesis with him.

'Soda?' he asked, going to a big silver fridge. 'I have coke, orange, lemon?'

She nodded, still looking all around her a little dazed. 'Orange, please.'

Paige smiled as he took one of the cans next to racks of samples in test tubes. 'Hope there isn't anything nasty in there,' she said, smiling, taking the can offered and popping it with a hiss.

Hunter cracked his can and flopped into the seat next to her. 'To be honest, I can't guarantee it.'

It made her laugh and she watched as he slipped out of

the lab coat and let it fall behind him. She couldn't help raking her eyes over him. He was such a contradiction. The pure white lab coat and the grungy, cool casual clothes underneath.

'What?' he said, proving her point with his slow, gorgeous smile. He eased back into his seat, taking his can back against his lips. 'Don't I look like a science geek?'

She took a gulp of her own drink and shook her head. 'No … actually, you don't.' She laughed, thinking of the guys she knew from her science club. It'd be putting it mildly to say he looked nothing like them. 'I know I shouldn't generalise, but you'd look more at home …' She couldn't put her finger on exactly where he best fitted. 'I dunno, a skate park.'

'Beach?' he added for her.

'Yes!' she agreed, like a bolt of inspiration. 'Sorry.' Even she couldn't work out whether that was an insult or not.

He bobbed his head graciously. 'You're not far off. I spend a lot of time in Southern California. My dad is a musician and a keen surfer.'

Dad? She thought he was out of the picture. Now she was confused. She must have given it away on her face because he immediately shook his head.

'He's great but he isn't my biological father.' Despite his words, his look darkened.

She felt instantly sorry for bringing it up. 'Yeah,' she said, back peddling madly. 'It happens a lot around our way. People split up all the time. Get together with someone else and have more kids.'

She felt her cheeks burn as he just stared at her for a long moment. She thought she must have put her foot in it again as his expression was so weird. It began to feel really uncomfortable when he hadn't looked away for a full minute.

'Forgive me,' he said, seeming to shake himself out of it. 'I can't help feeling how fortunate Xavier is to have found you.'

Her cheeks prickled yet again. It was all she seemed to do around him. 'I'm sure there are loads of stunning girls in your world – especially California,' she said, hurriedly, attempting to get up out of the sofa, swallowing her down. She wasn't sure if it was his inappropriate comment making her feel uncomfortable, or her deep-down reaction to it.

Hunter leaned forward and stilled her by the arm. 'Relax … Finish your soda first and I'll walk you back. You'll get lost.'

Paige eased back down into the seat and looked at him cautiously. He was such a confusing boy; he unsettled her even more than Xavier did right at the beginning. She felt an instant longing to see him. 'A guy like you must have a girl-friend somewhere,' she stated, dropping her eyes away from his.

'A guy like me?' he said, smiling into his soda can.

She was getting tired of feeling on the back foot with him. She looked back at him flatly with a huff. 'Look, you seem a lot cooler than the guys I'm used to in my science club, OK?' She shrugged and took a sip from her can to hide her embar-rassment.

He laughed. 'And what are they like?'

She frowned at his playfulness. 'They don't look above the age of thirteen because they have pasty, spotty skin that never sees the light of day, because they stay in their bedrooms on their computers.'

He grinned throughout her whole speech, raising his eyebrows and following every word. 'And is that what you do?' he asked, laughing.

She scowled, which turned into a frown. 'Well, yeah. I suppose so.' She ended laughing along with him. 'You look like you spend a lot of time in the sun.'

Hunter sobered a little and her heart stopped at yet another blunder. He let out a sigh. 'We were all put on a board and learned to surf before we were three.' His eyelids lowered. 'But my skin is pretty much always this colour.' He put his can down on the table and went to stand. Paige's heart went up into her mouth. *What a complete idiot.*

'I'm so sorry,' she said, getting to her feet with him. 'I didn't mean to offend you. Far from it. I thought it was a tan … I mean … I'm not a racist … God.' The more she said, the more stupid she sounded. Stammering, following him all the way to the bench where he picked up his keys and then went on to the door.

Hunter whirled around suddenly on her, taking her breath as she bumped onto his chest. She smelled whatever soap he was wearing and a masculine strength inside him that shifted something in her insides. It was then she realised how completely dangerous he was to her and her relationship with Xavier, who she definitely loved. *She did. She definitely did.*

'Little Paige,' he said with low-lidded eyes, dropping to her mouth.

She was acutely aware that she was right up against him. His arms now circling around her.

'You are a little sparrow taking shelter in a viper's den.'

Seeing the spite enter his eyes, she pushed him in the chest and he let go of her instantly.

'Go back to your falcon,' he said. His smile now nasty.

She hurried past him towards the door. She put her hand on the handle and paused at his last words.

'Beware, little sparrow. Everyone is a snake or a bird of prey here. Any one of us could easily devour you.'

She looked over her shoulder and glared at him. To think she actually liked him.

He put up his hands in surrender. 'I'm just saying, don't trust anyone.'

She stared at him, deciphering the genuine warning from

the digs. Despite the good looks, his face held an undercurrent of anger and resentment and very definitely hurt. Instead of scaring her, she found she wanted to cry for him. It was a defence mechanism. 'I'm sorry if I upset you. Thanks for showing me your experiment.' Then she opened the door and went out, breathing for the first time.

Hunter was soon at the door behind her. 'Don't be caught in the fight between those two,' he called after her.

Her steps slowed a little while she listened, then she sped up and began to run.

LATITIA FOLLOWED JJ through the double grey-painted doors into the large space that was a fully functioning basketball court. Perfectly sprung wooden floor, scoreboards, hoops fixed to the wall and everything. It was also full of young spectators on both sides. Then, when an older guy with enviable long dark curly hair blew his whistle, everyone on the court stopped and turned to look at them. She wanted to quickly exit the way she came, except her brother Richie was right behind her and she bashed right into him. He took no notice and just said, 'Sweet!' looking at the room, completely impressed.

It gave JJ time to pick up her hand and stop any further attempt. 'Don't be scared,' JJ said.

She looked up into his incredible aquamarine eyes and saw how much he needed her there and to be OK with it. The truth was, she didn't know if she was or wasn't but the fact that he cared was a huge point in his favour. Everything was so strange and out of whack. It felt unreal, like she was dreaming. She could only deal with it if he truly allowed her in.

'Please, Latitia. Everyone here is just cousins.'

She looked at him a long moment, her heart thundering

inside, gauging his face. He didn't realise it, but she'd just had a major eureka moment. Explaining why his changes had hit her with such shock back in his dad's hotel in London. It was because he'd lured her in with all his confidence and mystery and yet kept her at a distance. He was rich, handsome and like no one she'd ever known. Caught easily in his gravitational pull, sucking slowly and irrevocably any kind of strength or resistance. Then before she could get close to any real part of *who* he was, he hit her with *what* he was, and that had shocked her to her core. *No wonder.*

Before she could analyse her self-discovery more deeply, the whistle blew, taking her attention away from her thoughts.

The players' trainers squeaked as the game continued and the guy with the hair jogged over. Xavier appeared next to them and the guy clapped hands and hugged him. 'Are you two playing?' he asked with a rich American accent she wasn't expecting.

Xavier shook his head. 'Not me. I'm going to check on Paige.' He put his hand up to someone on the other side of the court and disappeared back out of the doors. The guy's gaze then fell on her and then her brothers. 'And who do we have here, JJ?' He put out his hand for her to shake, then Richie's and Dwayne's. He man-hugged JJ. 'This is Richie, Dwayne and my …' JJ looked her dead in the eye this time. 'Girlfriend, Latitia.'

It felt like a victory after the direction her thoughts had been taking, but he wasn't off the hook. She accepted it as her due and switched her stern gaze to the guy and smiled,

The guy tipped his head in her direction as if he was impressed. 'So, you all go to the same London school, I hear,' he said, nodding.

He was extremely good-looking in a rock-star kind of way. Long hair and startling blue eyes. Latitia wondered at the gene pool that produced such handsome men. 'I'm Drew,' he said. 'I keep most of this band of delinquents out of trouble.'

A large group of boys and girls had abandoned the game and gathered around them. Rock and Flame, she recognised. The three boys from earlier, too, now looking ridiculously tall in their yellow and grey basketball uniform. There were a few others a little shorter and several of regular height.

'These guys are from my school. They're mostly human too,' Drew said, nodding towards the motley-looking group of boys. If it weren't for his look of absolute pride, his use of the word human would have struck her a lot more. Instead, it bounced over her. She was suspending reality more and more today. 'Can you play?' Drew asked, looking directly at her.

He threw her for a moment. 'Can I watch?' she asked, quickly. She played all the time at school, but she wanted to decompress what she'd seen. The surroundings. The people. How she felt about everything. She was sure she wouldn't keep her mind on the game at all.

Dwayne was already pulling his T-shirt over his head. 'I'll play,' he said, immediately stepping forward. 'As long as I'm on the tall blokes' team.'

'And me,' Richie said, following.

Drew laughed. 'Come, meet everyone.' His eyes rested finally on JJ.

'I'll sit this one out,' he said, tipping his head in Latitia's direction.

Latitia knew he was just worried about her reaction, but she needed time to simply observe. She gave him a gentle shove towards her brothers. 'No … it's OK. Go ahead and play. I'd like to watch. I'll be fine.'

After a moment of indecisiveness, he smiled reluctantly and walked off towards the others who were now huddling in the middle. After one last reassuring smile, Drew blew his whistle and jogged over to them too. 'Right! Listen up!' Drew shouted. 'Two teams. Humans and Murrs against Atlanteans.'

Several of the players groaned or grumbled. She guessed they were the Atlanteans as Drew's human boys grinned. The only ones who remained silent and expressionless were the exceptionally tall ones. *The Murrs.* They fascinated her the most.

She held her breath as one went and towered over her brothers. At first she thought he was trying to intimidate them, but Richie nodded and she realised he was talking to them with their weird telepathy. Her brothers then high-fived and Richie looked over at her and grinned. 'In the bag,' he mouthed, making her laugh, as he nodded his head at the group of tall ones. They looked really odd standing next to the regular human boys, some of whom barely came past their waists.

Drew blew his whistle and they all went to their positions on the court. Another blow and they were off.

The space she'd given herself to think was soon forgotten, because it went on to be the most funny, entertaining, free-for-all farce of a game she'd ever watched in her life. The tension and worry simply drained away and she didn't stop laughing. The Murrs were scoring basket after basket with minimal effort, sometimes bouncing the ball off the Atlanteans' heads, catching it and scoring with a tiny hop, making it look so easy. Her brothers were dribbling the ball low, running rings around everyone. The Atlanteans were forced to stage fouls, where they bent to tie their shoe laces and Flame or Rock came along pushing the tall ones over. They were shoving, diving, distracting. JJ even shot between Loki's legs. Drew was blowing his whistle and pointing to the Murr/Human end constantly for them to get a free shot.

Latitia's sides ached, she laughed so much. But her eyes

followed JJ most of the time. He hated losing, she realised. All his Atlantean cousins seemed to. He was a natural athlete, even managing to score two baskets despite the Murrs bending right over him to stop him. But it wasn't enough to make any kind of dent in the score. The Murrs were exceptional – their long gait eating up the court and dunking the ball in the net easily. By the time the Atlanteans began scrambling on the floor with the human boys, Drew blew the final whistle before anyone got hurt.

The human boys cheered. Even the tall ones bounced chests. Only JJ's team grumbled and blamed each other for poor position and play. It was still entertaining how seriously they all took it. 'Christmas Day rematch, bean-poles,' Flame was shouting.

Drew turned and grinned at Latitia and shrugged exaggeratedly. Then he winked at her and pointed. 'You! ... Next time.' he shouted like an order.

She nodded shyly. He was so nice. She guessed it wouldn't hurt. *Was it enough to forgive JJ?* She wasn't sure.

CHAPTER 17

Xavier knocked on Paige's room. There was no answer. He tried twice more, looked left and right along the corridor and turned the handle. It wasn't locked. He closed his eyes, his mind creeping forward to see if he could sense her. Maybe hear her heartbeat. Slow if she was asleep, fast if she was ignoring him, but nothing came back.

His mind scrambled at where she might be. He opened the door. Checking he was alone in the corridor again, he slipped inside. The bed was rumpled but empty and the quilt cold. She hadn't been there for a while. Her scent was all over the bedding but no longer hung in the air. He poked his head into the small bathroom and it was the same: used, but not recently. *Where the hell had she gone? Had she found her way back to the great hall while he was at the game? Was she lost?*

He marched for the door. Sudden rage mixed with panic seared his chest as it began frantically beating. His mind churned. Which of his cousins should he worry about her coming across without him? *All of them.* He swore to himself.

He stomped down the corridor wondering where she would possibly go in a massive underground bunker where she didn't know anyone. All he could do was anxiously search the tunnels, going left and right, praying she hadn't strayed too far. Sticking as close to the main corridor as possible, hoping her good sense would make her do the same. Spreading out his senses like a net, he prayed he would feel her.

He'd almost given up, thinking he'd have to go to the guards and report her missing so they'd look at the CCTV, when she rounded a corner and they almost bumped right into each other. She said, 'Oh sorry!' before she realised who he was.

'There you are,' came out more moodily than he intended. He toned it down immediately at the wary look that entered her eyes. 'I was so worried when I went to check on you and you weren't in your room.'

She frowned a little. 'I went for a walk to clear my head and got a bit lost, sorry.'

He sobered, realising how insane he sounded. Then he gave her his best smile and linked arms with her and steered her back in the direction of the great hall. He cursed himself for revealing how anxious he'd been. 'Are you OK?' he asked, once he was breathing more evenly. He had to remember how hard all this was for anyone to digest.

It wasn't made any easier by a psychic blast they could both hear from his Murr grandmother. *Visit me, Xavier, in my quarters.*

Xavier muttered, 'Bloody hell.'

Paige was looking around her for the source of the voice.

I am with my girlfriend, Grandmama, Xavier blasted back.

Paige looked at his face in amazement.

I want to speak to you both, privately. Come now, child.

Xavier let out a loud sigh and looked at Paige, deadpan. 'We have to go and visit my grandmother. Do you mind?'

There was no avoiding it. No sugar-coating it. His alienness was about to be laid bare and it was pointless fighting it.

She gave a tiny shake of her head, looking so small and vulnerable, like a deer stunned by a headlight. She seemed to gather herself and coughed. 'Of course. I'd like to meet all your family.'

He nodded curtly and nudged her irritably to keep walking. He wanted to get her back to her mother where he felt he could control the situation more effectively, but he knew no matter where he took her, questions would need to be answered and Paige was too clever to be fobbed off with half-truths. He closed his eyes and blasted, *Coming, Grandmama,* to get her off his case and steered Paige in her direction.

PAIGE WATCHED Xavier a little nervously as he knocked the door and they walked into his grandmother's room. She had no idea who or what she would find.

When they got inside, she realised it was fairly ordinary, but posh. A suite of rooms, more like an apartment. The older woman was sitting on an elaborate day bed, covered in a peach and cream brocade with soft curtains tied at the corner posts in the same colours. The sort she'd only ever seen in stately homes in films or magazines. The rest of the room was full of paintings of the ocean, with little touches of blue in little figurines of mermaids and beautiful blown glassware. There were no windows, which was something she was growing used to down there.

Sit, children, the grandmother said, indicating two dainty powder-blue armchairs facing where she sat.

Paige felt Xavier's eyes on her the whole time as she walked forward and sat down. She refused to look at him as she was still a little disturbed by his outburst in the corridor.

He had to release his hold, as it had started to feel stifling. He had to understand that he couldn't control her. Instead, she looked around at all the fine furnishings and then at the strange woman who sat so still but seemed aware of her every move.

The woman seemed too young to be a grandmother of someone Xavier's age. She had smooth skin and wore a deep-blue floaty gown that left her long, sinewy arms bare. They were covered in the faint stripes that she recognised from the tall boys of earlier and her fingers seemed very long, too. She was tall, even sitting down. Her hair was blond and almost touched the bed behind her and her brown eyes were deep-set and her cheekbones high and angled. She guessed she would have made a great fashion model in her day, but for the fact that it was clear that she wasn't human. She seemed all angles and her eyes were too large. Even if you overlooked her stripes, she sat way too still.

Xavier's gaze was still burning the side of her face.

I'm going to talk to you in the way of our people, directly to your mind. I am Naomi, Xavier's grandmother. Please don't be alarmed.

Paige swallowed, but found her mouth had gone dry. 'I'm not,' she said, not entirely sure if that was true. 'I'm Paige.'

She felt her hand squeezed. She looked down and followed the arm to Xavier's concerned face. She softened and gave him a smile. Her heart was hammering the walls of her chest, but she kept it under control.

XAVIER COULD SEE the blood pumping at Paige's temple. His grandmother would undoubtably hear it. He was proud and sad at the same time at the effort she was taking to cover it up.

So you believe you have chosen, Naomi projected, directly at him.

He tutted in exasperation. 'No, Grandmama. We are still at school. We're too young for mates.'

And yet you bring her whole family here and expose them to the dangers of knowing us. Do not delude yourself, Xavier. Kings must mate early as responsibility will soon weigh on you greatly. Do not ignore the bonding urge.

Xavier felt his cheeks heat up under her knowing look. Murr senses were more acute than even Atlanteans'. She probably scented it on him or saw it in his aura. He hated that he was so transparent. She was right, but he was right too. He and Paige *were* too young for a decision like that, but a pain stabbed his heart when he had to concede that they were too far along for him ever to let her go.

There it is ... the real reason. You and JJ are rutting stags, just like your fathers. The girls will be collateral damage if you do not face up to what this is. Naomi turned her attention back to Paige, who'd been looking between them curiously.

Xavier fumed. This was supposed to be a nice holiday, where he revealed a little about himself to a girl for the first time. A milestone in his life. And here she was, his own grandmother, turning everything into a diplomatic incident.

Are you in love with my grandson? Naomi asked.

Xavier's stomach fell into his bowel. He went to protest but Naomi put up a restraining hand. He was nonplussed with frustration. She had always been so wise and now she was behaving like a blunt, impulsive old woman.

Paige went red and stuttered. 'I—' She flashed a look at him fearfully. 'I believe I do.' Her cheeks were now scarlet and he couldn't blame her.

Naomi nodded slowly, accepting the answer as the truth.

Xavier jumped to his feet. 'Enough… Come on, Paige. I'm sorry, Grandmama, we have to go.'

Goodbye, child. You have told me everything I needed to know.

Xavier was beyond angry as he strode to the door and held it open for Paige. He was embarrassed.

Paige held up a hand weakly and wandered, bewildered, towards him.

Xavier! his grandmother blasted. He was already pushing Paige through the door by the small of her back. *Remember she is not a chattel.*

Xavier rolled his eyes and went to go.

And she is not as neatly in your pocket as you think.

Xavier huffed and shut the door loudly behind them.

Latitia's sides ached from laughing at all the antics of both teams by the time Drew blew his whistle to break up the last of the arguments. He shook his head indulgently. It was all in good fun. He grinned and called over to her. 'It gets worse every year.'

She found herself thawing to everything, despite her misgivings. Everyone seemed so nice. It felt more like going to another country, than another world, which she had to keep reminding herself, this was. It felt so real. So normal.

'How much did we win by coach?' one of the human boys said, grinning at some of the others.

Drew blew his whistle at some the girls hovering by the scoreboard. They instantly understood and forty to two hundred and ten came up. But what really made Latitia laugh was the names they'd called the teams: The Filfla Dream Team versus the Marlin Shoal Stoppers. There was a lot of exaggerated grumbling coming from JJ's team and a few, *Dream on Dreamers,* called out by a few of the tall guys.

Drew looked blandly at the human boy as if it was obvious.

Some of the other boys were pulling out soft gym mats

for everyone to sit on. Drew began putting out bottled water and energy drinks onto a table for everyone to help themselves.

JJ came jogging over and picked up her hand, making her heart quicken. She looked down at it briefly and wondered at the power he held over her. She immediately swept away the dip that followed, disguising it with a sympathetic smile. He shrugged. 'Not our best game.' He didn't seem too disappointed. 'Because of all the cheaters!' he said a little too loudly over his shoulder.

'Boo. Sore loser,' someone said to a few giggles.

He laughed and looked gorgeously flushed from running around. 'Do you want a drink, or shall we go?'

She was quite happy there and studied him for any tells that he might be embarrassed mixing her too long with close family. But she didn't spot any. There *was* something bothering him though.

I just want you to feel OK, he said directly to her mind.

'I am,' she said, still a little alarmed he could do that. 'I'd like a drink.' She said it quickly, with a nervous smile. Desperately hoping he couldn't read the monologue of dark thoughts she'd been having since she woke up.

He smiled, looking pleasantly surprised. Even impressed. Such a walking contradiction. 'Get us two cokes while you're up there,' he said as Rock went past them.

'Get them yourself, lover boy.' Rock said, without breaking stride, which made Latitia laugh. She decided she liked the relationship he had with his cousins. In fact, she had to admit, she liked everyone she'd met so far.

JJ grabbed them a drink and they went and lounged on the mats with the others. She faced JJ with one of the three tall guys who'd greeted them earlier, next to her. She looked up at him, not able to help herself. He nodded, and *Keefa* filtered through to her mind. She couldn't help gazing a trail down the full length of his long body and measuring her outstretched leg against his. Her eyes widened when she realised her whole leg only came to just past his knee. Everything about him was in proportion, just bigger, longer.

He was still staring at her by the time she followed his torso back up to his face. She heard his laughter as he attempted a strange smile. His eyes shot to JJ, opposite. *I think your human finds me attractive. You'd better watch yourself. Tell her I'm even bigger in the water,* he projected with a sly wink.

Latitia blasted red and looked at JJ, alarmed. 'I don't … I mean, you're perfectly fine.' JJ rolled his eyes and Keefa's two brothers rolled over with laughter without moving their lips. She ended up putting her head in her hands to hide her embarrassment.

JJ slid in beside her and put his arm around her shoulders, protectively. She hated that she almost dissolved into his smell, warmth, magnetism, or whatever it was that radiated out of him. Only saved from her sinkhole of addiction, by a hefty shove flying over her head making Keefa fall sideways, laughing. Nothing like teenage bants to pull a girl back from the brink.

The next thing she knew, JJ's breath was at her ear, setting her butterflies alight. 'Hey! Don't take any notice of that shark bait,' then he punched Keefa in the arm right across her. She let her hands drop. No one was really focused on her. They'd moved on, too busy laughing at Keefa rubbing his arm, grumbling he'd been assaulted. Drew slapped him playfully around the head as he walked past, too. JJ looked at her apologetically. *Gorgeously.* 'I ought to warn you that all my cousins are going to hit on you.' He looked sideways at Keefa, still watching them fascinated. 'Some of them rarely get to interact with human girls and so they are very inexperienced.'

The jab caused a chorus of raucous laughter that quickly turned into a scrum. Latitia had to scramble out of the way as Keefa lunged and grabbed JJ in a head lock. *I am prince of hearts in Murrtaine, you genetically challenged runt,* he said, rubbing his hair until it stuck up and JJ managed to get free and kick him.

Keefa didn't seem perturbed, he just faced her deadpan and said, *Let me know when you're ready for a real mate.* That made everyone laugh.

Latitia was amazed by how normal it all felt. Just like human-style ribbing. Like with her brothers. Or her friends. It could have happened anywhere in the world, in any bunch of teenagers. She *was* OK with it, she realised. The alien thing was beside the point. The question mark was over JJ.

JJ sat back down next to her, smoothed down his hair and put his protective arm back around her. Her two brothers came over and bumped cans with Keefa and Dannon and sat opposite them. 'So you and him are related?' Dwayne asked. Trust him to be so direct.

First cousins, Keefa answered.

'His mum and my mum are sisters,' JJ added.

It means I do have some human DNA in me, Keefa said, with a weird wink. *Do you have any Atlantean in you?*

Latitia shook her head solemnly. 'No, I don't think so.'

JJ closed his eyes.

Do you want some?

Keefa and Dannon doubled over laughing.

Dwayne swapped a mock angry look with Richie next to him. 'Don't make me have to punch you in the kneecap.'

Everyone fell about laughing at that.

'So, where you come from, is everyone like you?' Dwayne asked, getting more comfortable on the mat.

We come from Murrtaine, not far from here.

'It's an underwater city,' JJ added.

'So you can all breathe underwater?' Dwayne asked, looking wide-eyed at his brother.

'You saw them all getting out of the fountain, dummy,' Latitia said, kicking Dwayne's foot.

She turned her head to JJ. 'Can you do that? Breathe underwater, I mean?' Her lids were low as she asked the direct question. Testing him. Knowing the answer full well. A sharp pain burrowing into her frontal lobe at the memory of his dripping striped form, getting out of a mist-covered pool and stalking purposely towards her.

JJ looked at Dwayne for a second, as if he wasn't sure if he should say. He nodded eventually. 'All us kids can because we were born there and kept the ability. Most Atlanteans can't do it anymore. It's been bred out of them.'

Latitia breathed, letting him off the hook and switching her gaze to Drew, sitting in conversation nearby with a group of kids. 'What's their story? I thought we were the only humans here. Are they relatives?' she asked, nodding her head in their direction.

'Kind of. Drew rescues kids from the streets, whatever their DNA. He runs an academy where he trains them ready for the world,' Flame said, earwigging her question.

'Wow,' Latitia said wistfully, genuinely impressed.

'Yeah. He's a really great guy. He's married to another of my mum's sisters.'

'Wow, how many has she got?' Latitia asked.

'She has four sisters and two brothers.'

'God, your family is so big.'

JJ nodded. Then looked right into her in a laden moment. One that made her swallow and didn't need words. *How did he manage that?* He took her from wanting to tear him apart for how he'd tricked her—for how weak he made her feel. To wanting him to do anything he liked to her. To exert all that power on her just to see where it led to. She took in the incredible shade of his aquamarine eyes, smouldering with unanswered questions. 'You really are an alien, aren't you?' she said it quietly, but as a statement, not meaning to say it aloud at all. He simply nodded, taking no offence, then his hooded eyes dropped to her mouth. He always made everything feel so natural and sexy. She thought he would lean in for a kiss, when Flame walked past behind him and ruffled his hair up again. 'No snogging, lover boy,' making the others laugh.

He let out a long, weary breath while he slowly shook his head. 'Let me know when you wanna get out of here.'

CHAPTER 18

*X*avier accompanied Paige back to her mum in the great hall and said he was going for a shower. She had already had hers so was quite happy to sit there and people watch.

Valarie Johnson seemed to know one of the big guards, she recognised from back in London, and went off with him somewhere on a guided tour. Her mother still hadn't relaxed, hovering over her brother and sister playing nearby with some kids with a box of toys. She didn't know what she thought would happen to them.

Paige went over and gripped her mother's hand. 'Try and relax, Mum. This is the first Christmas you get to have a proper rest.'

Her mother gave her the brightest fake smile. 'Did you know about any of this?' She looked around her nervously.

Paige shrugged. 'Not really. I mean, I knew Xavier was rich and not like a regular kid at school. But this?' She slowly shook her head. 'No.' She wasn't sure how she felt about it in all honesty. All she knew was that her mum was hanging on a thread. She squeezed her hand. 'Relax.'

Her mum smiled genuinely then. 'I'll try.'

Just then the beautiful woman that she remembered was Xavier's mother, sat in the chair opposite. She really was the most stunning creature she had ever seen with perfectly proportioned features, long honey-blonde hair and the most unusual dark-green eyes.

Then her attention was taken by huge trellis tables being set up all along the outside of the room. 'They'll be serving food soon. You must be starving,' Xavier's mother said. 'I'm Tia,' she reminded them with the most brilliant smile. 'Hope you like fish or vegetarian. Not many of us can eat meat. But if there is nothing you like, let me know and I'm sure the chefs can rustle you up something.'

Paige looked around at the mountains of food appearing and couldn't imagine not liking something. It was a banquet. They were obviously used to catering for a lot of people.

'They just put it out and everyone helps themselves. It seems to work best.'

'Wow,' her mother said next to her. 'How many people are here?'

Tia shrugged. 'Not everyone is here yet. By Christmas, I guess around two hundred. That includes all the kids, of course,' she said, laughing. 'I just love all the kids here. Dante's having a tree flown in from Norway, especially. The kids are all gonna decorate it tomorrow. Ah, excuse me.' Tia jumped to her feet, leaving the two of them gaping after her, while she ran and hugged another stunning woman who'd appeared, just as gorgeous as she was.

Paige swapped a look with her mother. She couldn't help noticing how tired she looked. Her hair was greying, making her look older than her years and weight loss had left hollowed cheeks and circles under her eyes. She guessed worry and stress would do that to a person. She couldn't imagine JJ's stunning mother ever having to worry about anything.

More people began to drift into the hall, making them feel smaller and more invisible by the minute.

After being introduced to so many teenagers, Latitia was sure she wouldn't remember most of their names.

'Come on, let's get out of here,' JJ said, standing up and holding his hand down to her.

She looked at it like it was some prophetic sign, then used it to pull herself up before she came off as weird. However the quick manoeuvre left her standing right in front of him, closer than expected. 'Where to?' came out on a breath.

His eyes immediately dropped to her mouth and she felt her temperature rise. *Correction.* He was the heat and she was the delicate winged insect caught in the thrall of his flame. She swallowed, not sure what he would do.

JJ looked around to make sure they weren't overheard and looked back at her intently again. 'I could do with a shower,' he said, his voice gone to gravel.

'Me too,' she found herself saying, shocked at her own confidence – foolishness – death wish. Whatever it was, she didn't avert her eyes. The place. All the beautiful, confident people. *He* made her want to throw away any caution. Despite what he'd done, she knew exactly what she wanted. Even though it was emotional suicide. JJ was always going to be her first, she was helpless to fight it, and she would never get a better opportunity.

'Then mine is safer.' He looked death-nell adorable with his slight frown of insecurity. And that, she realised, sealed her fate.

Before she was conscious of what she was doing, she'd gripped JJ's hand. 'Come on then, before anyone notices us.'

Like she had no control of her body, or what came out of her mouth.

JJ wasted no more time and put up a hand to Drew. 'See you at Evening Meal.'

Drew smiled, his eyes flicking to Latitia. 'Don't be late,' he said with a knowing look. 'Stevie, Lana and Cole will be here by then.'

Latitia wanted to ask who that was, but she couldn't take her eyes from the amusement on Drew's face. As if he knew exactly what was on their minds and that she'd go through with it even before she did. Her thoughts and her body were so far apart, it was like an out-of-body experience. JJ led her out through several jibes from the boys and out into the maze of corridors. Her cheeks were hot, while her brain felt numb, wondering how everyone seemed to know. A walk of shame. Not because of what would happen, but that she would lose herself to him if she did. And despite knowing all that, she knew she would do it anyway.

'You emit an aura that everyone can see,' he explained, laughing. 'Yours is pulsing the rainbow.'

She put her hand out in front of her eyes, like an idiot, even though it was impossible for her to see. Then reverted to autopilot, allowing JJ to lead her through the maze of corridors, even jogging in the end to keep up. 'Wait up,' she said breathlessly.

'I don't want anyone to see us,' he said, continuing on, purposefully. He looked up and she followed his line of vision to see a red blinking light on a camera. *CCTV.*

She didn't know why she was so shocked at the level of security in a place like this. Guess it just compounded how important these people were. How in over her head she was.

The next thing she knew, she was pushed into an alcove, behind a pedestal and white marble statue of a naked man. 'Wait here!'

'Where are you going?' she called after him, her voice high-pitched.

'I won't be long,' he called back over his shoulder. 'I'm just going to do something about the cameras.'

Latitia watched him jog off and disappear out of sight. It was so incredibly quiet and lonely that it was inevitable that she would ask herself whether she was mad. She could slip off in the other direction and all it would mean would be an embarrassing conversation when she had to face JJ later. But when she imagined actually doing it, or simply saying she'd changed her mind, a sharp pain twisted in her chest making it impossible. It was always going to happen. If not today, then tomorrow, or the next day, or the next. It *was* going to happen. Because deep down, she wanted it. It was never going to be anyone else. She'd been ruined for other guys without him needing to do a thing. It had to be him. Not some random guy. She trusted JJ with something so huge as her first time, she just didn't trust there to be anything left of her at the end of it. Yet she was still helplessly walking into the sun that would inevitably swallow her whole. So many doubts.

She peered out into the corridor and looked up and down.

She might know him enough for them to have sex, but did she really know him? He'd held so much back from her already. But who really knew anyone completely? Which she knew was absolutely skating around the bigger issue of species. Random guys couldn't control her with their mental energy alone. *Oh god.* She was doomed.

It was an agonising five minutes of mental toing and froing, like that, before she heard running footsteps coming towards her.

'Come on,' JJ said, slowing to a walk and gesturing with

his arm for her to come out and follow. 'Let's get you into my room before anyone realises they're off.'

Her feet were already moving while her heart was jumping out if her chest. From excitement, nerves, to abject terror. He pulled her along so fast, turning into the last corridor, before she had any more time to think. Then a huge oak door was in front of them.

She tried to slow everything down by dragging her feet, but JJ pushed the door open and pulled her with him inside. The light came on and a latch miraculously flipped behind her. Before she could form a word or express her amazement at his room, he held up a finger for her to wait a moment. Then he went over and leaned into a heavy chest, and with several hefts, pushed it in front of the door. She guessed he wasn't the only one who could open locks with his mind. Then in a second, his mouth was on hers and she was lifted so her legs clamped easily around his waist. Doubts dissolved and her thoughts became as automatic and as fluid as the manoeuvre. As if they'd been doing it their whole lives. The truth was she couldn't believe it was happening. After weeks of illness and confusion. Of them being off and on again, of will they, won't they. From living like brother and sister, to maybe, girlfriend and boyfriend, to right then, where he was real and tangible under her fingers. This wasn't the dream she'd been fantasising about for months. It was better. She almost gave herself over and completely lost herself, not caring if she ever breathed again, when panic cut a chasm through the whole thing. She stopped and slammed her hands on his chest between them.

JJ pulled back immediately and eased her down onto her feet. He was frowning, searching her eyes while they both still breathed heavily. 'I'm sorry, did I hurt you? It's the first time we've been alone.'

She melted a little. It had overtaken them both and she

was equally to blame. She just needed to slow things down before she gave him everything. She was so grateful he looked more concerned and hadn't taken it as rejection. 'How long do we have?' she asked, now hoping she hadn't killed the hot moment.

JJ smiled his gorgeous, crafty smile, picked up her hand and led her further into the room, which was nice to finally take the time to see. It was at least four times the size of hers. More like a suite, with a bed and seating area and everything. It was grown up and masculine, with huge dark-wood furniture and bedding and cushions in earth tones. There was even a desk with a computer and a huge TV. 'You get a signal down here?' she asked, pointing at it. Feeling strange having a normal conversation like normal teenagers.

'Cable,' JJ answered and pulled a couple of cokes out of a fridge hidden in a cabinet. He flopped into his large brown leather sofa and patted the space next to him.

Latitia took the coke offered and was still taking in the surroundings when she sat at the opposite end. She kicked off her trainers and put her legs up to face him, keeping the distance between them. She was still shaking after the effects of their last tussle. He stretched his legs out next to hers and absently rubbed her ankles. He took a sip of his drink, with his eyes locked on hers the whole time, then he placed it down deliberately on the low table next to them. It was done in silence and captivating to watch. She had no idea what he would do or say next. Always so damn confident.

He pulled her legs on top of his and got more comfortable. 'Are you afraid of me, Latitia?'

The words and the way he said them did something to her insides. He made everything sound so inviting and tempting. She guessed a part of her *was* scared. But not simply about sex. 'Not you, exactly. All this,' she said, holding out her hand to encompass everything around them. 'I know you won't hurt me—'

'Then what?' he prompted, nudging her to continue with his foot. Smiling, tilting his head, like he was genuinely intrigued.

'You're so … it's all come at me so fast. I mean, I still can't quite believe any of it is true.' *Real,* she amended in her head.

JJ looked down at his hands still rubbing her ankles.

Even that: a foot massage. No one had ever done that for her before.

'You're right to be scared,' he said with a rueful smile.

Latitia studied his face, slightly pink with embarrassment. He looked almost sad. 'What do you mean?' she asked, putting her own drink down, sensing this was going to be one of those rare times he opened up to her. Her breathing went shallow as she slowly sat back in her seat and waited.

When he looked her in the eye, his were so dark and dilated – as if he had no irises at all. It made him look vulnerable and serious. 'When we do it, it will be different than with other guys.'

She swallowed at his smouldering look that seemed to burn right through her. She was still hung up on the words 'when we do it' not if, or maybe. 'I've never done it,' she found herself saying, feeling her cheeks blast hot, as she was pulled ever closer, knowing there would soon be no way back. 'What's different?' Her reedy voice, barely audible through parched lips.

He continued to study her closely.

She put her chin up defiantly, despite herself, not even sure why. She guessed he was assessing whether she could handle any of it. The judgement. Of not being worthy. Or old enough. Strong enough. It all made her more determined about the whole thing. Despite being terrified of how much of her would be left.

He looked down at her ankles again and then stopped and looked straight at her. 'There is something extra … something more, with me.' He stared at her to let that sink in and when she didn't shy away, he continued. 'Royals, purer-blooded Atlanteans, have something in them that can kill a human.'

Her heart was thumping, but not out of fear. Not for what he was thinking, anyway. She dreaded he would stop what they'd started almost as much as the consequences of if they just did it. But she had to hear him out; she'd be a fool of she didn't. 'The nasty medicine?' she said, her voice gone to a rasp. She had to cough, remembering how insistent he'd been that she drank all three vials.

He seemed impressed, nodding slowly. 'That's right.'

'What happens then? What's so dangerous?' Her heart was now a painful irregular thud in her chest, watching his every move.

He picked up his can and took a huge gulp, she mirrored him and did the same. 'Well, for starters … with someone we really like, we're a lot more territorial than humans.'

That didn't sound so bad. She relaxed a little, thinking that maybe he was blowing it out of proportion.

'And we have something – an energy – that builds inside us.' His hand went to the centre of his chest where he absently rubbed it.

'OK,' she said in a steady voice.

He seemed lost in his thoughts, as if he was trying to remember every detail. 'It gets really painful, until it comes out with our breath. It's supposed to go into our intended's body.'

Latitia frowned, trying to imagine it. It sounded strange, not really scary. And so hot butterflies flipped in her stomach. 'And you've done it before?'

JJ was already shaking his head. 'Nooo.' He straightened

in his seat. 'I have done the sex part,' he said, flashing her a wary glance.

That was obvious. She'd never assumed otherwise and continued to watch him steadily.

He picked at the ring on his can. 'Just the bonding urge part … I've never had that before. I didn't realise it could happen with me.'

She didn't fully understand what he was saying. Her mind was stuck on the bonding part. 'Wait … back up. What's a bonding urge.' Heat, flushing through her cheeks.

He looked her dead in the eye. 'That's the serious part. With that, it's not just sex. It does something to you where you're tied to me for life. I've seen how it's affected my mother and father. It can never be broken… No matter how much you might want it to.'

Latitia couldn't help herself. Her heart was beating wildly. Even though she could see he'd gone to some dark memory in his past, she loved the sound of that. It sounded so romantic and she already knew it would be him. The fragile edges of her resistance were already being singed by him.

He looked at her sternly as if he'd followed her thought process. 'You don't understand, Latitia. I wouldn't just be your first. I would be your last. There would be no others. It's that huge a decision. And that's assuming you survived.'

She should have been more shocked that he'd just read her so accurately, but all she saw was his sadness. While her barriers had burned to the ground, he'd already given up on them. He didn't get to do that when it was her life at stake. Maybe she should have been relieved that she'd dodged a bullet, but she wasn't. She felt angry with panic. That something that belonged to her was now slipping away. Somewhere deep down she understood that if he truly gave up, it would be over between them. And that, ironically, destroyed the last of her will-power. Everything wonderful and exciting he'd introduced her to, saving her from her boring life of before, would completely disappear. 'You don't get to decide that for both of us, JJ.' They were already on that trajectory. She was burning and going to Hell and he was sure as damn coming with her.

He went to move his legs to get up, but she trapped them, now furious. 'What about if I wanted it? I decided. You can't just come into my life in London, smash through it like a bulldozer and just leave me there for ever.' It wasn't until that moment she realised how much she really wanted to escape. She wanted to be different. She wanted an extraordinary life. Tears were now in her eyes. 'Can't we at least try? Take it slowly? See how we go?' Even then she knew how completely irrational and crazy she was sounding. She'd gone from not trusting him, keeping him at arm's length, to wanting nothing more than his arms, breath, anything he could give her, around her, in her. As long as he gave it all, freely, completely and wanted her as much as she wanted him.

His eyebrows drew together and then went up in surprise, but he looked as flushed and red as she was. Then he smiled a little sardonically. 'I'm flattered, but I still don't think you fully understand what's at stake.'

She tutted and pushed his leg off hers angrily. He laughed. Infuriating. Sitting up straighter, he held onto hers. 'Your DNA would be spliced to mine for life, Latitia. Think about that for a second. Your life would never be normal. You'd be in danger from all our enemies. And I know myself around you. I would never let you go after that.'

Despite hearing everything he just said to her, and every part of it hitting her skull like a wake-up alarm hammer, her heart pounded and she was bowled over by the absolute romantic notion of it. While a sweet pain bore and twisted into her gut. To experience a love like that. To be joined. Never to part. Forever. 'Surely that's up to me,' she said, her voice now reduced to a husky whisper. 'Aren't you taking that away from me?'

He threw his hands up in exasperation with her and flopped back into the cushions.

She pulled her legs out of his grip and began to crawl to his end of the sofa. 'Can't you just try a little bit to see if I can take it?' she whispered, slowly smiling.

His eyes rolled and he began shaking his head. But the closer she got, the more he was focused on her mouth. His words said one thing and his body another. His hands were already tightening around her thighs. His expression was pained, like he was fighting internally. His eyes were now red and bloodshot as he switched suddenly to anger. 'It doesn't work like that. Once my spirit is inside you, it doesn't matter how little or how much. We're joined!' He tried to shrink back, away from her, but there was nowhere left to go,

Latitia let out a deep breath she hadn't realised she'd been holding, then moved in fast and put her lips to his.

He sat rigid, lips pursed, eyes screwed shut, but not pushing her away.

Her knees were now either side of his torso, clamping him down. 'Maybe it's exactly what I want.'

CHAPTER 19

'Yes, but, there's more … much more,' JJ attempted to say against Latitia's lips, already crushing and moving against his. Until the last of his strength was beaten away and he could no longer resist. He didn't care. With the safety now off, he devoured her. Huge gulping kisses, where his hands found the hem of her top and it was over her head. Her bra loosened and his face incinerated.

He was dangerously overheating and had to get to water. 'I need the shower,' he gasped.

But she wasn't listening. He struggled, fighting to get to his feet and stand up. He just about managed it, staggering, but she was fused to his mouth. A short hop and her legs clamped around his waist too. There was no prising her off. He tottered and backed up unsteadily, crashing his hip into a chest, then a lamp, in a desperate attempt to get to the bathroom.

Her tongue was battling his in his mouth. There was no breathing. Despite him holding her weight, she was driving them. The pain in his chest was steadily rising. If he didn't get cool quickly something bad would happen. But if he stepped under the water it was game over with Latitia. He would lose control and unleash whatever was threatening to come out of him.

His feet were still edging backwards and he was still matching kiss for blistering kiss. The ball of fire in his chest rose higher, until it was a painful knot at the back of his throat. He had to do something. Anything. He had to let some out. That's all he could think to do that could possibly save the situation. But it felt so good to be this with her. To be natural. To finally let things go.

He struggled to pull apart.

Groaned and gave in to another volley of biting kisses.

Tried again.

Harder.

She tightened her grip around him.

Then the lever was finally pulled down, past the point of no return.

A jolt – a sudden rod of panic shot through him. There would be no regulating it. It was coming. Rising. Higher. Brimming. More painful. Scraping his insides, from the walls of his chest, through his oesophagus, throat. Tongue.

They bashed through the shower room door, too quickly and not quickly enough. He slammed backwards heavily into the cold tile wall. She was in control, roughly pulling up his T-shirt. The cold ceramic was a welcome shock, but it soon warmed. He fumbled with his right hand, found the dial and turned it quickly. A squeak and the glorious cooling spray covered them from the overhead waterfall. He put his head back and finally broke the seal, opening his mouth and taking in the soothing water. Free. Bathing in relief.

Then he lowered his head and took in her stunning heart-shaped face. She was watching him. Lust-filled eyes, lowered. Rosebud lips swollen from rough kissing. The blessed cold of the water was making her perfect little teeth chatter and with a final groan of helplessness, his leash snapped.

For a moment reality disappeared and he became an animal. Moving on instinct. Allowing his genetics to take control. Twisting and trapping her against the shower wall with his heavier body. The ball of fire rose into his mouth and he had no restraint. No conscience. He simply grabbed her chin and poured himself into her. Everything streamed from his mouth, in a single breath, into her. Completely. Utterly. Emptying his soul. Blind. Not even able to make sure if she welcomed it, found it pleasant, or could even breathe. Everything was so far gone and too late. His lungs heaved, driving his living essence out until it filled her. And all he could think of over and over was *Mine. You're mine.* Everything else disappeared, until he finally registered a loud pounding at the door.

CHAPTER 20

*I*t was over anyway. JJ crumpled to the floor, dragging Latitia down with him. They were naked from the waist up and both still in their sopping wet jeans. JJ was trapped and unable to move, because Latitia was limp and in complete disarray, on top of him.

He had to drag himself out of his afterglow stupor, now conscious of how bad it would look. He struggled and managed to reach up with the tips of his fingers and pull down a towel from a rail to cover them. Just as an almighty bang and splintering sound signalled that his bedroom door and chest had been bashed in. He couldn't do anything about the position they were in. Latitia was covered and breathing against his neck at least. Then he closed his eyes and held his hot forehead in his shaking hand.

In just a few seconds, he felt them in the doorway of his bathroom. *Shit!* Unmistakably Keenan.

He tried to move but it was hopeless, until large hands appeared, the water shut off, and Latitia's weight was lifted from him.

JJ finally squinted up at them and saw his father, Jay, calmly assessing the situation. Keenan was holding Latitia, who seemed to be stirring in his arms. All JJ could think of was that she was only half dressed, in another male's arms. A guttural growl echoed around the tiled room.

'Easy tiger,' Keenan said, laughing. 'Just getting her to the doc, that's all.'

It was only then he realised the sound came from him. Completely disorientated, his gaze shifted from Keenan to his father. He was still immobile, taking in the scene as if he still couldn't quite believe his eyes.

'Is she still alive?' Jay finally asked Keenan in hushed tones.

He nodded. 'She's running a temperature though.'

For some reason, his father didn't seem nearly as furious as he imagined. A little broadsided, maybe. He was known for his coolness under pressure, but he thought this might at least chink the armour. He simply put his phone to his ear and with his eyes still on him, spoke clearly and calmly. 'Sick bay? Yeah, it's Jay. The human girl is on her way back to you. Get an elixir shot ready.'

'Is she going to be OK?' JJ asked, swallowing hard. Knowing he needed to get up, but his legs just wouldn't work. His knees buckled and his voice broke in panic.

His father caught him. 'Easy.'

'I didn't mean to give her all that.'

'Let's just get you both to the doc to check you over,' his father said, not sounding angry at all. It made JJ look at him, to check the calmness was real and not just suppressed anger.

However, his balance took all his attention. His legs felt disjointed and wobbly on the walk towards the door. He could only worry about one thing at a time. Latitia seemed barely conscious in Keenan's arms. It was the second time she'd be visiting the infirmary in one day. And it was all his fault.

In the corridor, they were met by a porter with a gurney. JJ's legs felt a little more solid, so his father could let him go. He held onto the side and they made quicker progress. They were soon back in the white, sanitised room.

The team of tall Murrs conferred like strange monks in their long white tunics. It was a stark contrast to their sleek raven hair and pale skin.

Latitia was transferred from the gurney to the hospital bed and a drip inserted into her arm. JJ's mouth filled with saliva and he thought he was going to be sick.

His father looked at him strangely. 'Alright?' he asked.

JJ managed to swallow, steady himself and nod. He felt wretched. Just when things had started to look up between them, he had to do this to her. The Murrs began to pull a machine down over her, but before JJ could protest, his father pulled him outside the room. 'Let them do their job.'

JJ immediately wilted and slid down the wall next to the door. Still in his wet jeans and bare feet, he sat on his haunches. Water droplets dripped to the floor either side of him. He was a mess.

Jay crouched in his eyeline in front of him. 'Don't beat yourself up, this was always going to happen at some time.'

JJ stared his father in the eyes and saw heartfelt sincerity in them. A rare peek at how he felt. He should be happy. But the deep, intense look only made tears prickle and fall down his cheeks. He wasn't angry, he was sad. He shouldn't be crying, he should be strong, as a prince and as a man. The fundamental example his father had always set him. Instead, he was showing him just how weak and pathetic he was, and that just made him bitter. 'I'm a curse, Dad. I turn everything to shit.' He went to get up to get away from his father's concerned look, but he held him still.

'Don't be silly, Son. You're a much loved prince with extraordinary abilities.'

A sob escaped him. He wasn't even totally sure of the reason. Mainly how hopeless his existence was. How he could never have anything like Latitia, as he would ruin her, like he'd done twice now already.

'Come on, now, JJ. Her mother will be here in a minute. You have to be strong for her. If she survives the next twenty-four hours, she will be fine.'

JJ shot his father a dark look. Like that was supposed to make him feel better, but it did make him get back up on his feet. He was right about being strong in front of Valarie. It was the least he could do. He hadn't even thought about facing Latitia's mother. Another relationship he'd ruined. She hated him enough already. He shook his head in misery. 'What can I possibly say?'

Keenan appeared and handed Jay a navy bundle of cloth.

Jay took it from Keenan and handed it to him. 'For now, put this on. We'll stick with what we know and that is she fainted again, but this time in the shower.' Jay smiled haplessly. 'It's a stretch, but you are both wet.'

JJ wasn't convinced it would work but pulled the t-shirt over his head, anyway. He almost felt better when Dante arrived with a very flustered Valarie. She shot past him in a gust of wind and went straight into the room. At least she wasn't launching straight into questions. Dante just looked blankly at Jay. 'Do I need to ask?'

Jay's sad, almost imperceptible, shake of his head said so much more than words. It wasn't anger, or even disappointment, it was the inevitability it conveyed. As if there was some weird déjà vu stuff going on he knew nothing about.

'Sorry, Father,' JJ said in a hopeless voice, cracking with emotion. He was barely holding himself together.

Then his mother was there, wrapping him in love and smelling of spring flowers. 'It's OK, my darling. Everything will be alright, you'll see.'

JJ couldn't hold back his tears and sobbed in her arms. But as he blinked and caught a glimpse of Dante, his look was grave – as if something had already died.

CHAPTER 21

$\mathcal{P}$aige ate lunch with her mother, brother and sister in a tight little group while the hall filled with lively, chattering people.

The food was amazing. A mixture of hot and cold seafood, pasta, salads and round crusty loaves the size of bowling balls. It was a banquet meant to be a light lunch, but she just picked at it, not able to take her eyes off all the beautiful people of varying skin colour and ages, some with stripes and some without. The lift seemed to open constantly with more people pouring down the pyramid steps and more extraordinary water-breathers rising out of the fountain by the window.

The latest was a couple she simply couldn't take her eyes from; they were so powerful and enigmatic. They had the same white-blond/jet-black hair, stripes and stature she was becoming accustomed to in the pure-bloods, and they were dressed in the same clingy, iridescent clothes, but they seemed to rise out of the water like an apparition. Gracefully accepting towels from an army of servants that appeared from everywhere, proving they were definitely VIPs. A slightly smaller boy and girl were with them.

'That's Vionne and Ashaya.' She was surprised and turned her head to see Xavier sitting down beside her.

She looked back in awe. 'They're so stunning. All of them.'

Xavier put up a hand to the youths. 'That's their kids, Quin and Brodie. Loki you've already met.'

She dragged her eyes away to look at Xavier more closely. He looked and smelled great. Freshly showered, looking as if he stepped straight out of a magazine in his subtle white t-shirt and dark-blue jeans. Almost human. The VIP family sat down quietly on the fountain wall and she focused back on Xavier. He had that same charisma. Utterly beautiful, but emitting something else. Something otherworldly. Now she knew why. He wasn't really human at all. Hardly anyone in this whole room was. Some were just able to hide it more than others. Maybe that's what had attracted her right from the beginning. He exuded something more. Magnetising her with his raw power. *Was that what it was?*

For some strange reason, Hunter came to mind. She looked around and caught sight of him over Xavier's shoulder. He was just disappearing behind the pyramid with a plate piled high with food. He still looked scruffy and intent on leaving right away, simply nodding at a couple of people as he walked quickly past them.

'What are you looking at?' Xavier asked, turning in his seat, trying to follow what had caught her attention.

Paige felt her cheeks go red, as if she'd been caught doing something wrong and straightened in her seat immediately. 'Oh nothing,' she said, going back to nibbling her food. 'Just a guy I bumped into in the corridor. He showed me the way when I got lost.' She didn't meet Xavier's eyes, but she felt them burning into her. She wasn't sure why she felt so guilty that she missed off the part about visiting Hunter's lab.

'Oh? Who was that?' Xavier asked.

She sensed him coiling and bracing himself for her answer. She couldn't look at him and continued to push her food around her plate. 'Oh, I don't know ... what was it? Er, Hunter, I think.' She dared a quick glance when Xavier hadn't said anything. What she saw in his face shocked her. In a micro-expression, a storm of hatred entered his eyes and then was banished. But she couldn't unsee it. It had gone, but his expression remained tight.

'Don't go near him again. He's dangerous,' Xavier said, his face so controlled, his lips barely moved.

Paige stared at him, stunned and forgot to be cagey. 'I thought you were first cousins. He didn't seem dangerous.'

Xavier's eyebrows rose in surprise. 'Oh, didn't he? ... And what in the five minutes of knowing him imparted all that?'

Paige shrank inside at his mocking tone and spiteful eyes, instantly realising her mistake. Anger slowly rose up her spine. Why was she making light of the meeting? She shouldn't have to feel she needed to. 'Actually, it wasn't five minutes. It was the best part of an hour. He showed me his lab.'

Xavier's eyelids lowered as he visibly closed off and all she saw was hatred. It was the first time she'd ever been uncomfortable around him. Something felt gravely wrong, but for the life of her she didn't know why. Surely it was something more than immature possessiveness. This was just silly and had somehow spiralled out of control.

She put out a hand and covered his. He looked down at it and snatched his away as if she'd burned him. She wanted to cry. 'Please, Xav. Don't be angry. I was lost. We got talking and he showed me his lab and what he was working on. Hey! Science geek,' she said, ending with a silly, pointy finger dance in her seat to make light of it.

When he still stared at her as if she'd sprouted another

head, she let out an exasperated breath. 'Strange as it might sound, in all the madness, talking science with a fellow geek made it all feel more normal.' She felt a pang of guilt at the understatement. Hunter's ground-breaking, molecular transportation experiment with the apple, was worthy of a Nobel prize. But right then, she was settling for damage limitation. She had no idea Xavier was so possessive. He'd always seemed so self-assured.

He did seem to relax a little and her breathing returned to normal. But there was still an edge of anger in him, hidden beneath the surface. She had to get to the bottom of it and reached for his hand again. This time he allowed it. 'Why was that wrong though, Xav? I thought everyone here was a relative of yours. Isn't your mother his mother's sister?'

Another flash of annoyance made her flinch inside. She'd given away how much they must have talked. Xavier finally nodded, rolled his eyes and let out a heavy breath. 'That's true, but his father was dangerous, OK? He's a bit of a loner here.'

Just then two incredibly tanned kids, a girl and a boy, wandered up to the regal family sitting on the fountain. It immediately captured her attention as they couldn't look more opposite in colouring and size.

Xavier nodded his head in their direction. 'That's Kali and Kai over there, talking to Quin and Brodie Borge.'

Paige frowned at Xavier, not understanding what that was to do with anything. 'Kali and Kai are Hunter's half brother and sister.'

She looked back and recognised the same effortless beach look, but their hair was light brown and singed from the sun. Hunter's hair was far darker. Somehow she couldn't see him venturing out of his lab, much less topping up his tan with surfing.

A beautiful, unusual-looking woman with dark, curly hair

and a handsome blonde guy joined them. He had the same cool, effortless look as the kids. They shook hands and bumped foreheads with the two parents sitting on the wall.

She looked back at Xavier and he nodded. 'Yeah, Hunter's mum and stepdad, Lily and Lance.' Paige instantly saw the family resemblance in the kids and then felt sad for Hunter. Apart from fashion sense, he didn't appear to share anything with them. 'They don't look like Hunter.' She couldn't help a lump coming up into her throat.

Xavier let out a breath of derisive laughter that puzzled her. 'Lance is human. Hunter's dad was Florianna. Royal, mixed with human, and an enemy of most of the people here.'

How Xavier felt about Hunter was starting to make a little more sense. She couldn't help risking Xavier's anger again when she just had to ask, 'What happened to Hunter's dad then?'

'He's dead,' Xavier said with a little too much relish, getting to his feet. He held out his hand to her. 'Enough about Hunter. You will not go near him again. Come and meet the prince and princess of Murrtaine.'

Paige rose slowly, smarting from his direct order. She went along with him, not sure how to react. Except that it had the opposite effect. She couldn't stop thinking about Hunter. How awful it must be if everyone here thought like Xavier. How alone he must feel with only his work to keep him company. She felt sad and a little disappointed in Xavier.

Before she knew it, she was in front of the strange aristocratic-looking family. Xavier leaned in and appeared to touch foreheads with the huge male and then his incredibly beautiful wife. He bumped fists with the youths and straightened, grinning. 'This is Lord and Lady of Murrtaine and my cousins Quin and Brodie.'

Paige nodded, not knowing whether she should attempt

the strange greeting or curtsy. She was thankful when the woman held out her delicate hand for her to shake. She smiled, letting a blast of air out in relief, making the woman laugh. It was obvious they were all from the same family as Xavier's grandmother, but more approachable. Although they still seemed a little too still. As if they only moved if directly addressed by someone else. And, of course, their sheer size. Despite their obvious similarities to humans, their eyes were so black it was impossible to think of them as anything other than alien. *Call us Vionne and Ashaya. I'm so pleased to meet you,* Ashaya said, directly to her mind.

It was always a shock when they did that. Paige tried not to show it and tried to remember what a privilege it was to see any of this. 'Hello.'

Ashaya smiled, making her think she knew what she was thinking.

The huge male reached out his arm but instead of shaking her hand, playfully ruffled Xavier's hair at the last minute.

It broke any tension and made her laugh.

You will have to grow up now you've taken a mate, Vionne said with a chuckle that reverberated through her head. *No more silly competitions with your brother.*

It seemed an odd thing to say. *Mate?* She took that as differences in culture or language, or something. It conjured up such a feeling of permanence. *She was crazy about him, but did she see herself as Xavier's mate? Like, for a lifetime? Did Xavier?* It left her troubled.

Xavier's eyes darted to hers and he laughed. 'Of course, Uncle. Please don't scare her off, we haven't known each other that long.'

Paige looked down at the tingle she felt go up her arm and realised Ashaya had picked up her hand. *Don't be scared. It is daunting to be here for the first time. I myself felt it. I too came from very far away.*

Paige didn't know if she was the only one who heard what she said, but she looked deeply into the blackness of her eyes and realised there was nothing human there at all. Somehow she knew that this woman was the purest of her race. It was an astonishing feeling. Like it oozed from every part of her. The way she phrased her words. The way she moved and carried herself and the way she seemed to look right into her soul. It made her shiver and pull her hand out of her grip. The tingle from her touch was her way of reading her. It jarred that it was what she'd been doing all along. She felt tricked.

She looked pleadingly at Xavier, who was catching Vionne up on everything at the school. He seemed oblivious and went on to laugh about the ridiculous yearly basketball match that JJ had subjected Latitia to.

She was grateful when Xavier looked at her. 'Come on, let's get some food before it all goes.'

Paige nodded, bewildered, even though she wasn't hungry. She put up a weak hand of goodbye as Xavier pulled her away. It was now sinking in just how far out of her comfort zone this trip actually was.

CHAPTER 22

The executive car was already waiting for Alexia and Yaro. Alexia got in and peered out through the tinted window as Yaro locked forearms with his brother Pavel. It was an impassioned farewell where they looked deeply into each other's blood-clouded eyes. Alexia wasn't sure if they were choked with emotion or speaking telepathically to each other. The moment was so charged and went on for so long she got back out of the car.

They snapped out of their trance and finally let go of each other. Then, in a gust of wind and a flash, she was thrown up into the air and down heavily onto the car bonnet. The air was slammed out of her and sharp pain bore into her wrist all at the same time. For a moment she went limp and felt completely disorientated. Just a snarl and a deafening growl and she was free again.

Dazed, she slowly sat up. Yaro had his brother by the neck against the wall. It had all happened so fast all she could do was straighten up and wait for her brain to catch up with the rest of her. She rubbed her wrist, looked down and saw torn skin oozing blood. Then back at the two brothers.

Blood was still on Pavel's lips and Yaro was bearing down on him to submit. They were two wild animals, locked together, neither willing to step down.

Her wrist was stinging. She looked more closely and saw there were two puncture wounds. Pavel had bitten her. She gazed back at the scene, now in shock. The driver came forward and offered her a handkerchief to wrap around it. 'Please, Yaro,' she said, wanting to cry. She always thought Yaro's family liked her. It made no sense.

Pavel was trying to speak, but Yaro looked like he would kill the brother he couldn't bear to let go of a moment ago. Another of his family came up to his arm. 'At least let him speak, Brother.'

Yaro's crazed expression gradually faded as his words sank in. Then he shoved Pavel away with a forbidding growl and finally released him. He was then at her side in a blur, removing the make-shift bandage to examine her wrist.

Pavel was coughing and rubbing his throat. 'If we don't hear from you at the appointed hour, there is nowhere in the world they can hide her that I won't find her.' His voice was cracked and unrecognisable.

Yaro pointed at his brother, incandescent with rage. 'You insult me.' Then, as if the anger never happened, he opened the car door and gently eased Alexia back into the seat. She meekly allowed it, still deeply in shock. He slid in next to her and the car moved off, leaving an argument going on in Russian between the men they'd left behind.

Alexia was shaking now and remembered very little of the car journey. Only the kiss Yaro placed on her wrist and the cool tongue that miraculously sealed the wounds. They soon joined the private jet that was not one of her father's. It had gold film over the windows, so she guessed it belonged to Yaro.

She began to feel a little better. The shaking had stopped,

but she was left feeling bone-achingly tired. She looked up at Yaro a few times as they strapped into their soft leather seats and hoped he could shake himself out of his anger before they reached Filfla.

Her wrist was now just a scratch and would heal quickly. She let out a ragged breath as they taxied and the plane lumbered along faster and faster until it took off.

Yaro continued to simmer, his brow furrowed where he was obviously running things over and over in his head.

They passed a silent journey, arriving in Malta at dusk, which she guessed had been deliberate. The harsh sun was less than ideal for Yaro; burning easily, with no natural protection. He'd also be able to keep its unnatural glow covered, travelling at night. Then they would be away from human eyes and underground when they reached Filfla.

The air was as humid and fragrant as a greenhouse as they descended the metal airstairs from the plane. Her spirits rose a little as she inhaled it, reminding her of good times and home.

Yaro did the same, but his keener night vision scanned the darkness for a very different reason. Mapping angles, escape routes, sensing danger on vibrations carried on air currents. Always on high alert. She wished he could relax, just a little.

He was still ridiculously overdressed with a high collar and long sleeves, but he'd swapped the long black coat for a jacket and a baseball cap for his large fedora hat. He looked young and sexy, like some sort of incognito emo rock-star. She gripped his hand and smiled up at him. After one last look around them, he helped her slide into another sleek car for the short journey across the airport and he finally started to relax. 'Have you been to Malta before?' she asked, intrigued. It still astounded her how long he'd lived.

'Not for many years. And certainly not by plane,' he said

with the smallest of smiles that warmed her insides. 'I was fortunate to see it while it was still governed by The Order of St John. Back then it was a jewel of art and architecture.' Then he shook his head bitterly. 'But the French took it shortly after and then the English. It was never really the same again.'

Alexia looked up at his handsome profile. What things he must have seen in his long lifetime. He was utterly amazing.

He looked down at her, his eyes obsidian beneath the peak of his cap. 'You would have looked beautiful in that era. A time of sailboats and horses, silk brocades and masques,' he said, touching her cheek with his gloved hand.

She leaned into it, wishing she could feel his cool skin. But they had reached the helipad where a fleet of her father's helicopters were on permanent standby to take VIPs to Filfla. They found their seats and her stomach rolled as it slowly lifted into the air.

They went west over rows of yellow-stone, flat-roofed blocks and dusty streets, already alight for night-time. Then trees and tiny, walled fields. Until only dark, moody sea chopped beneath them. She suddenly felt excited and alive. This was it, the beginning of the whole rest of her life. And from this day, Yaro would always be in it. He would never have been invited if not.

Yaro remained thoughtful, looking out to sea. 'Quicker than sailboats though, eh?' she said.

He turned to look at her.

'The sooner we'll be in our bed.' Her eyes dropped to his dark-red lips. She'd become quite adept at goading him, knowing he knew exactly what she was doing, but always remaining so damned restrained. She loved doing it just to watch the tempest of passion in his eyes that he contained and repressed so efficiently. She giggled, always finding it funny.

Yaro let out a weary breath and looked back out of the window. She gave up trying to talk to him after that. He was intent and focused on what was to come. She had to remember how important this trip was to him. It went far deeper than it ever would for her. For her it was taking a boyfriend home for the first time and having him accepted by her father. For Yaro it was a momentous occasion. He would be the first of his family accepted at the Atlantean court for ten thousand years and acknowledged by the reigning king.

The closer they got, the more her anxiety bubbled. After all, this was her life too. All her happiness rested on this going well and there were so many things that could go wrong. So many variables. Cousins. Uncles. Some already determined not to give Yaro a chance and that was apart from her father, himself.

She took some deep slow breaths and decided to concentrate on one thing at a time. Her father was the important one who could determine her future. For now, nothing else really mattered. They were nearly there.

The dark table of Filfla loomed, like a giant flat pebble in the distance. Yaro was already studying it closely, his eyes now working in the darkness. He seemed riveted. There were no lights or fanfare to guide them in. To the outside world it was simply a remote nature reserve. The skilled pilot would have to negotiate a tricky landing in the darkness.

'Ready to claim our future?' Alexia whispered.

He swallowed and gave her one small nod.

CHAPTER 23

JJ sat so long in the sick bay his jeans dried on him. Across from Latitia's comatose form, Valarie held her hand, dozing with her head cradled in her arms on the bed next to her. For the first three hours they'd sat in silence with Valarie shooting daggers with her eyes every time she opened them.

She should have saved her energy. He blamed himself enough for the both of them. He'd never worried like this. Not even when Latitia had seen his true form and rejected him. He prayed to whatever deity was up there to spare her. Even offering to walk away, if only she woke up.

Valarie shifted irritably in her chair, proving she was really awake. She didn't understand that he could see by the pulse of her aura and hear that her heartrate was far too fast for sleep. She opened her eyes and flashed him another hate-filled look, as if she felt his gaze on her. Then she finally cracked under the silence. 'I know you had something to do with this, JJ.' Then she put her forearm across her eyes to cover her misery.

He wanted to shout that she didn't need to throw barbs at

him. He felt wretched enough, crushed in self-loathing. 'You're right. If I could go back in time I would.'

Valarie's arm dropped from her eyes and she sat up straight in her chair to glare at him. 'So you admit it,' she said, flatly.

JJ just stared back at her, already too emotionally battered and bruised to fight.

'What did you bloody do, JJ? Tell me now!' she said, getting louder and until she stood up shouting over the bed.

JJ looked around the room in a long sweep of misery and rested his eyes back on Valarie. Resigned. Her face now a picture of contorted anger and hurt.

He hated her. Hated himself. But most of all he hated the life he'd been born to that was determined to drive him someday to this. If not with Latitia, someone. Everyone else got to have someone special. Even Valarie had Reeve, who got to play the simple part of hero.

But not JJ. He was the bringer of shit. The Darkly Begotten, who was doomed to hurt anyone who remotely got close to him. The will or inclination for any kind of resistance had long drained out of him. 'You want to know?' he said, now exhausted.

'I deserve to know what you bloody did, JJ. I'm her mother.' Her voice quavered as she held back tears.

JJ let out a long sigh and pushed his fingers up through his already messy hair while he thought how to put it. He toyed with softening the blow with some cotton-padded bullshit, but she was right. She deserved better. And what was the point? If by some stroke of luck Latitia came out of this, he'd mess it up, anyway. He was programmed to. So he dragged his sorry eyes up to look straight at Valarie, while hers brimmed with tears and gave it to her straight. 'I breathed my life's essence into her because I couldn't help myself. Because I'm pathetic and weak.

I bonded myself to her at a genetic level, so she is with me for life. If she survives the next twenty-four hours, she will be fine. Stronger, even. But she will need medication to stop her getting ill if she is ever separated from me for any length of time.' He held her gaze, insolently, while everything made a slow journey through her anatomical nurse's mind. He admired that her first response was not hysteria.

'So you're saying there's a high chance she might die?' she asked, her voice going high, cracked with emotion. She grabbed her mouth to stop a sob.

'There's an equally strong chance she won't,' JJ lied. He had no idea really. All he kept telling himself was that she was young and strong. 'I gave her elixir to drink days ago. It should help the process.'

He could no longer look Valarie in the eye, he felt so guilty, so he looked down at Latitia's flushed and sweaty face. 'Her immune system is simply fighting the process. Once it loses, she will be fine. My dad went through the same thing after my mother—' He stopped, realising he wasn't helping and looked up at the ceiling for strength. 'Look, he was fine, wasn't he?'

Valarie just stared at him, blinking in shock, as if he'd slapped her round the face. 'So you're telling me you knew this could happen and you did it anyway.' She looked off into the middle distance while it all began to sink in. 'Dante knew this could happen and still sent you all to stay with me.' She shook her head slowly as if she'd made some kind of damning decision. She bent and smoothed back the strands of damp hair from Latitia's brow. 'I swear to God, I will kill that man if anything happens to her.'

JJ felt the level of panic in his stomach rising. 'It won't. She'll be OK. You'll see. Then Dante will see to it that you never have to worry again in your life.'

Her eyes flashed angrily to his. 'Yes, he will. Because you won't be going anywhere near her after this.'

JJ swallowed. There was no point in arguing with her now. The cold reality meant that none of them would ever escape their world. By one selfish act, he'd bound the whole family to it forever. Even if Latitia died, which made him close his eyes in pain just thinking about it. The Johnsons could never escape. *What on earth had he done?*

XAVIER DIDN'T KNOW exactly how he felt about Latitia's collapse. Paige was worried so he took her to sit with her mother and offered to go and find out more. The truth was, he was glad to escape. To process what had clearly gone on between JJ and Latitia and the H bomb Paige had dropped earlier. How could she have made a friend of the worst possible person in the whole bunker.

He seethed and couldn't trust himself around her to hold his volatile temper.

Hunter would not get away with toying with him like this. So he made his way to the furthest-most point of Filfla and his tucked-away lab. Just the effort it took to get there bugged the hell out of him. He would have had to lead Paige away from everywhere she knew. It could have only been deliberate.

As he navigated the labyrinth of tunnels, his mind drifted back to the situation with Latitia and JJ. The other source of his disquiet.

So, he'd actually gone there with her. The bond. He must have.

The most closed-off person emotionally he knew, after his father Jay, had gone all-in and sealed his fate with Latitia. He couldn't believe it. Part of him wanted to laugh. He'd destroyed both their lives. There was no way he could be sure she was the one. No one could. Not at seventeen. It was history repeating itself. Their mother had done the same thing with JJ's father, but it happened because she was a Siren and fulfilled prophesy. If Latitia's body couldn't take his essence and it killed her, JJ would become a raging bull and a danger to everyone. It was the fate of all grieving mates.

His steps ate up the ground and his eyes darted. He would need to box clever from now on. As much as his own bonding urge pushed him to do the same, he must resist it. He must not bond with Paige. That would give him a distinct advantage to inherit the kingdom from his father. JJ had proved he was not thinking straight. He'd been foolhardy and weak.

That thought made Xavier's mood lighten considerably. Now he just had to make Hunter aware that his territory was very definitely marked with Paige.

He turned into the last corridor that was a dead end of jagged yellow rock and turned to face the grey metal door. He knocked twice, not sure exactly what he would find. He'd never been inside. He'd never had the slightest interest to go there.

He knocked again more loudly. Rattling the handle, unable to penetrate the lock with his mind.

Go away, Xavier. I am busy sticking pins in my eyes.

Xavier laughed derisively. The feeling was mutual. He just wanted to give him a message. 'If you don't open this door, I will see to it that the sprinklers come on in this quadrant, so all your papers get ruined.'

There was an immediate clank of a bolt and Hunter opened the door a few inches. He looked him up and down and settled on his face, blankly. 'What?'

'I need to speak with you,' Xavier said, evenly, trying to keep the menace out of his voice.

Hunter stepped out and closed the door behind him. 'Forgive me if I don't trust you around my private things.'

Xavier quirked a brow and let out a derisive blast of air. 'Well that makes two of us.'

Hunter looked up for strength and faced him squarely. 'You are referring to a certain human girl, I'm guessing. Paige, I believe? Yes. A very rare and brilliant mind,' he finished with a spiteful glint in his eye. 'I can see why you might feel insecure with her.'

Xavier flew to grab his cousin around the throat, but Hunter was too fast and batted his hands away with telekinetic energy. He was thrown to the right, where he recovered quickly. He roared and ran at him like a charging bull, seeing only red.

When he was sent hurtling in the other direction, he stood back up, shook his head and snarled his frustration. He had to calm down. He hadn't lost his temper like this since he was a child, fighting with JJ. But JJ he knew. And he guessed there was always a small part of them that never really wanted to hurt each other. Hunter was different. He was an unknown force and it was quickly becoming apparent that despite being a year or so younger, he was an extremely strong adversary.

After a moment of catching his breath and luring Hunter to believe his anger was subsiding, he charged again and this time the two of them grappled. He managed to pull him down and the two of them rolled around, locked together on the floor.

Time slowed down until all he heard was his own breathing and Hunter's clear voice. 'If you want to tangle with me, crown prince, then strengthen your mental blocks. I was not interested in your romantic partner, but after this, I think I am. I must see what all the fuss is about.'

Before the red mist of rage could descend again, he was

propelled backwards so he slid along the polished marble floor. He smacked against the wall and the air was knocked out of him. He groaned and slowly attempted to get up. He'd grossly underestimated Hunter. He was indeed his real father's son.

Hunter was standing, straightening out his clothes. Xavier scrambled to his feet, stopping halfway to regain his breath and pointed. 'You'd better keep away from me and what is mine, or I will end you.'

Hunter seemed unruffled by the threat and walked closer until he loomed over him. 'I'd be more troubled about your inheritance than a girl, Xavier Dubonnetti,' he said, drawing out the surname of the royal family. 'You already have one crown prince to fight.'

Xavier looked up fiercely into Hunter's spiteful smile, which turned into a grin, as he turned and opened his door with his mind. 'Now if you excuse me, I have better things to plan.' His grin widened. Then he slipped into his room and the door snicked closed.

Xavier got to his feet and was left reeling. *What did he mean by that?* His mind scrambled over his last words. Everyone knew that he was the true crown prince. JJ was only in the mix as the Darkly Begotten because his father, Jay, had assumed the crown briefly to save it for Dante. Who'd had it taken by Malleven.

Malleven Mancini.

Hunter's true father.

Another king.

Xavier stared at the closed door to Hunter's lab in shock. He was right. If the old ways were strictly adhered to, then there were three princes with fathers who'd been king. Didn't that mean three were eligible for the crown?

Xavier strode off, not sure where he was going.

CHAPTER 24

*L*atitia was in an inferno. She was hopelessly lost, screaming, screaming, pleading herself hoarse. One minute she'd been blissfully happy with JJ and the next she found herself in Hell.

She couldn't breathe, she couldn't swallow, she couldn't think. Her mind was scattered. Loose memories rebounded of what went on before. The cool shower. The kiss. A feeling of floating. Or falling. Flying. Soaring. Then here. In literal Hell. Where breathing was like inhaling ashes from a bonfire. Clothes sawed her skin raw and she couldn't pull them off. They felt tied like bindings, squeezing the life out of her. She couldn't breathe. She couldn't. *Couldn't.* She was about to scream out what little breath was left in her shredded lungs, when a cooling breeze gently stroked her flayed arms. Then ice-cold balm on her forehead. 'Thank you. Thank you,' she rasped.

A reedy voice filtered through to her. Male. No one she knew. It broke up and then became stronger. *Where was she?* 'Help me … please?' she croaked.

'It's OK. I'm here now. JJ's father.'

Her mind shot to the beautiful blond man she'd met in London, but the voices didn't match. Then it became clearer. The strong accent. Irish. The king. 'Can you help me?' she asked again, her voice barely a whisper. Panic rose in her that she was imagining him.

'It's OK.'

She felt the wonderful breeze on her again.

'Put another fan over there.'

It was the first time she became aware there might be others there with them. But she bathed in a wash of cool air and she didn't care. Only that she felt relief.

'Just lie still and accept the feeling. Try not to fight it and all will go well for you.'

She relaxed a little. 'What's happening to me?'

'You took JJ's breath, darlin'. Your body just needs to adjust, that's all. Don't worry. Rest, and it will pass and you will feel stronger and maybe a little different. You'll see.'

Latitia tried to rack her brains to remember the last moments before this. All she could remember was the mind-blowing kiss. The rush of air that took her breath and then she was here. In agony. 'What was it? What does it mean?' Her mind was muddled. She couldn't think straight. But even she knew it as a strange conversation for a teenager to be having with her boyfriend's father.

Then an image of JJ, striped like the huge men she'd seen at the fountain. Tall, savage and strangely beautiful. 'Are you really aliens?' Somehow, feeling so tired and sick gave her the courage to ask such a direct question. Before she knew it the words were out there and she didn't care. They were all told the truth as soon as they'd got there but her mind still hadn't faced it. That was until this.

'You know it is, Latitia. Somewhere inside you've always known it.'

'Am I becoming one of you?'

A light chuckle like wind chimes went drifting through her mind. 'Maybe a little. We have human genes in the mix too. Especially JJ.'

The mental picture of his powerful striped body pulling himself out of the swimming pool made her doubt that very much. The feeling that she'd been losing herself to JJ, slowly but surely, ever since the moment she'd met him, never felt more real. Like the quicksand of everything about him was swallowing her whole. His beauty. His strength. How different he was. What he was. What he could do. All of it had pulled her in and was absorbing her until nothing of her was left. And what's more, he knew he would do it. Right from the very beginning, when he'd climbed up onto her bunkbed.

'I'm disappearing,' she whispered. 'Will I die?'

'I don't think so,' was the king's straight answer. 'You're strong. It's what JJ sees in you. When you wake, you'll be stronger.'

A fresh coolness landed on her forehead and she did feel more comfortable.

'You've no need to be afraid. Because of what's happened today, JJ will take care of you the whole of his life. We all will. You and your family. Today, you gained a mate and more family than you can handle.'

A feeling of ease made its way through her. It was warm, but not the searing heat she'd felt before, but the soothing warmth that blanketed you in sleep.

'That's it. Sleep, Daughter. Because you mean a lot to my son and so you will be very important to me and my race.'

'I feel so tired, Mr... Er, your highness.' She struggled to stay awake, to think about what the king had told her, but the weight was too heavy.

'Call me Dante. Sleep now and know that I am here for

you whenever you need it. I'll send JJ's mother to have a chat with you when you're feeling up to it.'

'Thank you. I don't remember my father.'

'Now you have two. You are one of ours now.'

Latitia breathed a long, contented sigh. She no longer wanted to fight; it was too hard work, and the flames seemed a long way off. They were slowly, bit by bit, being doused. Until she finally felt herself sinking into soft, feathery sleep.

DANTE RELEASED Latitia's hand and broke the connection with her mind. He and Jay had entered the sickbay moments earlier to find Valarie and JJ sitting vigil either side of Latitia's bed. Valarie was glaring at JJ. He'd eased between the stand-off to assess the damage by slipping into Latitia's mind. Something he'd become quite skilled at over the years.

He'd closed Valarie's mouth with a flick of his hand before she could launch into threats and recriminations. She didn't need to. It pulsed in her flashing aura. Somewhere in the periphery of his mind he'd heard Jay explaining what he was doing. Calming some of Valarie's fears by explaining how he went through something similar and ended up just fine.

Dante left Latitia and turned his full attention to JJ and Valarie, who were now watching him closely. 'The fever has left her. She will sleep peacefully now.'

The air left Valarie as she collapsed back in relief in her chair. But she was soon sitting back up to attention. 'Well why doesn't she wake up, then? This isn't right. What did he do to her?' she said, pointing an accusatory finger at JJ.

JJ put his head in his hands. The guilt was already breaking him to pieces.

Instead of answering Valarie, Dante projected straight to

JJ's mind, *You did a foolish thing, but she will live and you have gained a responsibility above all others. You understand that, right?*

JJ dropped his hands and looked up at him with a red and anguished face. This kind of thing took a while to sink in for anyone. Dante hoped he never grew to regret it. In the end, all he could say to comfort him was, *Trust in the fates. Things such as these rarely happen for no reason.* Then he turned back to Valarie, growing exasperated that he hadn't answered her question.

'For God's sake, Dante. Tell me what's going on.'

Dante let out a long breath and looked at Jay. He tipped his head towards the door, indicating for him to take JJ outside to give them some space. JJ scraped his chair and went, leaving his chair vacant for Dante to walk around and sit down.

Valarie followed him with her eyes the whole time. 'Well?' she prompted. 'JJ told me some old rubbish. Are you actually going to tell me the truth now?'

Dante smiled at Valarie and despite the worry and tiredness in her eyes, she really was still a handsome woman. 'So Reeve, then.'

She frowned at the sudden change in subject, not completely following him at first. Then she tutted and rolled her eyes. 'I'm not talking about my friends here, Dante, I'm talking about my daughter's health. Let's keep it relevant, eh?'

Dante chuckled at her naivete and narrowed his eyes. 'It is relevant, Val. Don't you see? How long have you been seeing each other?'

Valarie let out an impatient sigh. 'A couple of months, I suppose. I don't see how—'

'And you haven't noticed any biological differences in him to other men?'

Despite her dark skin, it was gratifying to see it go a deep red under the surface.

Dante nodded once when he saw that she'd got it. 'So you know Val. You push reality under the rug because you don't want to face it, but you know he's different. You know we're different.'

'I don't understand what any of that has to do with my daughter and JJ.' Then her face changed to horror. 'Does JJ have the— ' Her hand went up to touch her own teeth.

Dante quickly shook his head before she could really panic. 'No, he doesn't. But he is special, even in our race. He is a prince and princes still have the gift of what we call the breath.'

She suddenly looked pained and hopeless.

'Look, Val, it's not a bad thing. It's astoundingly beautiful for those who share it. It's the giving of oneself, utterly and completely.' His mind went to his own wonderful memories of being with Tia, JJ's mother. It quickly clouded when he also remembered all the trouble that came with it. 'It's an extension of lovemaking that humans don't have. One that Reeve may want to share with you one day.'

'Don't say that, Dante,' she said, shaking her head like it would make it all go away.

Dante walked around the bed and pulled Valarie up by the hand to stand with him. Then he rubbed her cheek with the pad of his thumb. 'What? That you are human and we are another species. That we are Alien, Val? Because you must face this. We are. You and your children are now in our world and we would kill to protect you. So, I'm going to give it to you straight. JJ and Latitia got in the water today and he breathed for her. It was an instinct. What she is suffering are the effects of her body fighting elements of his DNA binding to hers. When she wakes, her DNA will be slightly altered.'

Valarie's face looked horror-struck and she went to pull away, but Dante held her to him. 'She's changing into one of you.' she said, bitterly, barely able to get out the words.

Dante shook his head indulgently and resisted the urge to laugh. 'No, never that, but she will always be bound to JJ. She will be his for life, and he will have to breathe for her regularly for her to stay healthy.'

Valarie was crying now as she shook her head. 'But she is so young. For God's sake, Dante, they're still at school.'

Dante had to concede that with a nod of his head. 'Not ideal, I grant you, but she is one of us now and so are you and your family. That does come with a few perks,' he said, waggling her chin and trying to get her to smile.

She wasn't convinced so easily. 'And you're sure she will be fine?'

'Ah, she'll be grand. Better than fine. You'll see. She'll be stronger in a lot of ways. Senses. Immune system. Stuff like that.'

Valarie nodded as if she was parking it all away, one by one, in her mind. Then her eyes shot to his. 'Did you know this would happen when we came here?'

'Noooo,' Dante said, rubbing the back of his neck and walking back around to his seat. It was true, he should have. He felt a little guilty he hadn't been more on the ball. His mind had been solely on the debacle of his daughter's romantic choices. 'I will be speaking sternly to Xavier after this, don't you worry. I won't want the two of them making this mistake.'

'Mistake?' Valarie said in a shrill voice, throwing her hands up all over again.

Dante swore under his breath at his poor word choice. 'Only in the timing, Val. I promise you. This is more binding than marriage. One that JJ should have given more consideration.'

Valarie looked him deeply in the eyes until she finally accepted the truth in what he was saying.

'Wouldn't we have been having a similar conversation if they'd eloped, or he got her pregnant?'

She sagged in her seat, proving she accepted that. 'It wouldn't kill her, though, Dante.'

Dante conceded that point and put up both his hands. 'That's not going to happen, I promise you… I have this bond with my own wife.' He smiled ruefully to himself. Then he scratched his head. 'And so does Jay, which has been a real pain in the arse, I can tell you.'

She did smile a little at that. She would have remembered all the shenanigans that went on when they were young. Dante stood and looked down at Latitia, now sleeping peacefully. 'She'll be more than OK, you'll see.' He wandered slowly towards the door, where he stopped and turned.

Valarie picked up Latitia's hand, let out a ragged breath and looked right at him. 'I guess I should thank you for being brutally honest with me.'

Dante inclined his head, taking the compliment, but then he narrowed his eyes and pointed a reprimanding finger at her. 'I'm not sure I like this budding romance with my cousin, though.'

She finally laughed and he knew his job was done. 'Be careful. That one bites.'

She laughed louder. 'We're just friends. Nothing more than that.'

There was no harm in it. It made good sense for their safety. Now Latitia was bound, it made sense to tie the rest of them in more firmly for everyone's sake. 'Reeve is a lucky male,' he said, pulling open the door. 'Send him to come see me though, OK?'

She let out a sigh and shook her head. 'OK,' she said, wearily.

'And go easy on JJ, eh?'

Her face clouded at that. He could tell that was easier said than done.

'He's in bits over it. He has to face far bigger implications over the bonding than just Latitia's health.'

'Mmm,' she murmured, not sounding convinced.

He closed the door, taking that as a yes.

JAY PASSED JJ a bottle of water which he took, cracked and sipped. He felt a little better now his clothes had dried and he'd been sent out of the room of blame and shame. Now it was just the wait.

They'd left Dante to work his charm on Valarie. He hoped it worked because he hated himself enough. All that kept going around in his head was how he could have been so weak. He was usually so strong, emotionally. Nothing got through his hard exterior.

'She'll be OK,' Jay said, watching him closely.

He knew the score here. Dante was on clean up and Jay was babysitting him, in their usual tag-team method of parenting. JJ smiled bitterly and nodded, taking a glug of his water to control the hard lump that kept on coming up in his throat. He guessed it worked, because he swore, if he'd been alone, he'd have been a complete mess. 'Did that happen to you?' JJ asked, tipping his head towards the sickbay door.

His father nodded. 'Exactly the same. Except your mother was a Siren and had no idea how strong her breath was or how it would affect me. I was out fighting it for a long time. Days, I think.'

That made JJ feel slightly better. Latitia's fever had broken after a few hours. 'Her mother hates me.' JJ said, feeling a new flood of misery flow over him.

'Not a great start. Probably up there with getting her pregnant,' his dad said, with a small smile that went just as quickly. 'She won't when she comes round. I promise you. Latitia will be stronger than she ever was before.'

JJ took another large gulp of his water, not so sure. He was right about the first part. It was just as much a stupid, juvenile mistake as knocking her up. He shook his head; he was so dumb.

'You will need to think and act differently towards Latitia from now on. Everything will change.'

JJ searched his father's face intently. 'Like a grown up, you mean,' he stated, flatly. As if he didn't know that.

Jay bobbed his head a little. 'Yeah … kind of. More that she's yours for life now, JJ. Things are going to get a bit hairy around here.'

JJ didn't have time for further questions because Dante strode out of the room. 'Alexia just landed.'

CHAPTER 25

*D*ante glanced at JJ and continued walking. 'Latitia will wake soon. She'll be OK, but a bit shaky for a while. I'll catch up with you later.'

JJ got slowly to his feet and watched his two fathers stride off down the corridor together. One catastrophe averted, replaced immediately by another in the guise of his wayward sister. However, he felt the vice on his chest loosen and he could finally breathe again. Dante had worked his magic and now he would have to face it, whatever it was. Change he supposed. A hard lesson for any seventeen-year-old, but for him, it included a fast track to what it was to be king.

He thought more clearly about what his father, Jay, had shared. He had been right; this was so much more. It would never be as simple as merely walking away from her. That was impossible. He saw that now. He was no longer just responsible for himself. Not even for just Latitia, but the whole of her family. And, by association, the whole school.

He walked back towards the door and turned the handle. Something had shifted inside him. He would have to win the battle with Xavier to do that effectively. For everyone in this bunker, who relied on the king, as they do Dante right now.

He had to grow up.

He had to be ready.

ALEXIA GRIPPED Yaro's cold hand and let her eyes sweep over him. He was entirely swathed in black with a bandana right up to his sunglasses. His baseball cap was pulled right down over his forehead. Apart from their linked hands, not an inch of bare skin showed at all.

'You know, you don't need to worry. The whole palace is underground. You'll be able to relax.'

He continued to look out at the cobalt sea that he could never experience in daylight. 'Will I?' he said absently.

'Look, we're here.' Alexia said, pointing.

'The pilot said something into his radio in Maltese.'

Alexia's stomach flipped with nerves as they approached the tabletop islet and hovered above it.

Yaro strained to see what was happening below them.

'It opens,' Alexia explained.

The octagonal hole appeared below them and widened into a huge circle and the helicopter slowly descended into the depths of the island.

It felt strange because the journey she'd taken for granted hundreds of times now took on new significance. She was experiencing it through Yaro's eyes for the first time. The loud clanking noises of the mechanism. The darkness engulfing them. Even how the signs changed from English to ancient runic Atlantean. By the time they left the sky behind, Yaro's mask was pulled down, his hat was off and so were his glasses. She felt the wonder and excitement building in him. His grip tightened around her hand and his eyes seemed glassy. 'Welcome home,' she couldn't help saying.

He turned his head to look at her, bewildered, and she saw raw emotion there. He was gauging whether she understood what this meant to him and she got it. She really did. He swallowed and gave her the smallest of nods and kissed her chastely on the forehead.

The helicopter settled with a small bump and several guards appeared at the doors to open them. They were helped down and escorted quickly under the blades. All the while she never let go of Yaro's hand. Even when they patted him down expertly for weapons, she clung to him. He seemed in a daze, still looking around him, even though the lights meant he couldn't see.

It was her Uncle Keenan who came forward and went nose to nose with him after he was given the 'all-clear' for concealed weapons. It really brought home how serious all this was. She wanted to whine in her little girl voice to leave Yaro alone, but Keenan was very much in work mode. Especially when Yaro smiled back spitefully, revealing his teeth and mirroring his threat.

'Uncle Keenan,' she said, a little too high-pitched. 'He's my guest, don't forget.'

Keenan finally took a step back and his eyes fell on hers. 'Welcome home, darlin',' he said, smiling, but the aura of threat still hung over him.

He turned on his heel. 'Come on, I'll escort you down. Your father wants you both in the study before you go to your rooms.'

'Rooms?' Alexia repeated with a huff. 'Oh my god! He knows I live with him.'

Yaro squeezed her hand, still in his. 'He is your father, Alexia … I would be exactly the same.'

She looked up at him, suddenly curious. She'd never imagined him as a father. He was certainly old enough. Keenan flashed him a glance, but didn't say anything.

They entered the lift and went down until it opened at the top of the pyramid staircase in the great hall. They stepped out and Alexia remained silent, watching Yaro's face intently. She knew he couldn't see, but his senses were super-heightened. He would be bouncing sonar-like signals off all over the place to map it. She allowed him to take it all in and vowed to bring him back in the dead of night for him to see it with his eyes, properly.

She'd never seen him amazed. He was infuriating like that. He'd been everywhere and seen everything in his almost three hundred years of living. But that was his expression right then. Sheer wonderment. Moved.

The room never failed to affect anyone who saw it, but for Yaro it meant so much more. He was the first of his family ever to come this close to Atlas since his ancestors left it. They'd been cruelly cut off and today they got to see a glimpse of their homeland again.

His chest was moving up and down while he processed it all. The panoramic window, the fountain, the vines, the sheer scale of it. He was taking it in. Then, eventually, that the room was far from empty. It was full of Atlanteans. Her whole extended family were seated below. And of course the Murrs, which she doubted he'd ever seen in the flesh, even as old as he was.

Keenan completely missed the importance of the moment and was already walking down the steps. 'Come on. Don't keep your father waiting. You'll be introduced to everyone later.'

Yaro looked startled and turned to look at her. As if he'd been suddenly woken from a dream he didn't want to leave. She wished they were alone so she could just hold him. To let it sink in and let his suppressed emotion out. Because when it finally came, it would be devastating. She'd never witnessed him so lost. With an almost child-like wonder, that she never thought possible in a hardened male like him. And she loved him all the more for it. She adored him.

Alexia pulled Yaro with her down the steps and he allowed her to lead, as if he accepted this was her world, which was heart-breaking.

They followed Keenan down the steps, turned left, and into the maze of tunnels. She prattled on about the light system that was like an underground map to find your way around. Even though it was light that blinded him, she knew he could make out some shapes and colours. He listened avidly to how red was the main thoroughfare and purple led to the royal family's apartments. Until they came to the carved oak doors of her father's study.

Reeve was stationed outside and after a brief nod to Keenan, he knocked and spoke into his headset. Alexia took advantage of the lull to give Yaro's hand a squeeze. It was weird because, for a moment, she was struck by Reeve's size. Someone she'd known her whole life. She guessed it was in comparison to Yaro. Everyone was compared to Yaro. He was just as tall, but with an athlete's physique. Reeve smiled down at her. At six feet five, he was a wall of protective muscle that dwarfed her.

The door was pushed open and she led the way inside. The room felt alarmingly crowded. Her father was seated behind the huge oak desk, Cesaré was seated in the corner to his right and Alfonzo and Sebastian, her grandfather and great-uncle, to his left. Only Jay appeared to be missing. Her father immediately stood and held out his hand for Yaro to shake. It allowed her to let out a breath she hadn't realised she'd been holding.

Yaro still held his sunglasses in his left hand and took the hand offered with his right. His expression seemed cautious. As if he hadn't been expecting it. Her father looked deeply into his exposed carmine eyes and indicated for them both to sit on the orange sofa, opposite. 'Welcome,' Dante said, finally breaking a silence that stretched out uncomfortably. Then he sat back down behind his desk. 'Drink?' he asked and frowned as if he was suddenly unsure.

Yaro shook his head. 'Perhaps a little water.'

Her father's eyes shot straight to hers, totally giving away his train of thought.

Yaro read it too. 'I drank from my familiar right before I left. This will sustain me for many days before I need to drink again. You have nothing to fear,' Yaro explained.

A pain hit Alexia's chest while her mind whirred on when that must have been. She hated that he had to do that.

Her father, despite being completely busted on assuming his guest had been blood-sucking on his daughter, relaxed back into his chair. Although he still looked troubled. 'And you eat nothing else at all?'

'Nothing,' Yaro repeated, with a small smile. 'I am a cheap guest, shall we say.'

Her father was mentally logging the information away. The super-quick, analytical brain would be finding it interesting. She found herself longing for them to just chat together, like normal people, and not go through all this standoffish state, crap.

Dante looked at Cesaré next to him to make sure he'd got it and looked seriously at Yaro again. 'Thank you for making the trip and complying with all our demands. I know it all rests on trust and our nation has not given your family much cause for that.'

Yaro inclined his head graciously. 'I hope this signals the beginning of closer ties with my family.' A smile crossed his face. 'And yours.'

Alexia was looking between them, knowing the words were polite but there was an undercurrent of tension. Like a tight wire of threat between them. She wanted to shout at them to stop it, but her father spoke first.

'OK, I want you to make yourself at home here. You are free to go anywhere, except each other's rooms. That is out of bounds.'

Yaro raised his eyebrows and for the first time looked mildly amused. 'Of course.'

'My guards will show you to your suite in a moment. Freshen up and then I will introduce you to the other families. We can start here.' Dante turned to his right. 'This is Prince Cesaré Florianna, head of the mighty Florianna royal family.'

Yaro immediately stood up and shook hands with Cesaré.

'And this is Sebastian and Alfonzo Bonaci, Alexia's grandfather and great-uncle, heads of the great Bonaci royal family and personal friends and advisers of mine. I of course lead the nation and the Dubonnetti royal family. Everyone, meet Yaro Demidov, head of the Ambragio, the hitherto lost line of Santalini.'

Yaro shook Sebastian and Alfonzo's hands. 'I look forward to many conversations,' Yaro said. 'I understand you have one of the most extensive book collections outside of Atlas itself.'

Alexia swelled with pride at how well Yaro was coming across and how it was all going. Everyone seemed genuinely enthused and welcoming to him. 'Thank you,' she mouthed to her father.

Dante winked and held open his arms for her. She ran straight into them and he held her for a full minute, talking over her head. 'Keenan, show Yaro to his rooms, please.'

Alexia went to pull apart, but her father held her while Yaro left the room separately. She went to grumble, but he released her and caught her by the tops of her arms. He looked searchingly into her eyes. 'Are you well?'

She ached to catch up with Yaro but realised there was no escaping this. She nodded, quickly.

'I mean it, Alexia. As I've already said to the boys, you sleep in your own rooms in the royal corridor. Are we clear?'

She huffed and rolled her eyes. 'OK,' she repeated after him, wearily. Then something in him made her pause before she broke away. 'What is it, Dad?'

'There is another problem you need to know about. JJ has breathed for Latitia.'

All thoughts of arguing evaporated and her hand shot to her mouth with a sharp intake of breath. 'Oh my god!' She wasn't sure if she felt jealous or scared for him. Either way, she was shocked. 'Is she OK?'

Dante shrugged a little, then nodded. Then drew her into his body again. 'She's sleeping it off in the sick bay. It was touch and go for a while, but she should be OK. Not sure about JJ though. I think he's more in shock than she is.'

Alexia ran over all the ramifications. This was huge. She loved JJ. After Yaro, he was her favourite person in the world. They were all growing up, but she never in a million years expected JJ to be the first. 'I need to go to him.'

Her father reluctantly let her go. 'Go on then … You can help me introduce Yaro to everyone after.'

She gave him a last tight hug, with a muffled thank you into his chest.

'Please be careful with Yaro. Promise me. Remember he is a relative unknown to everyone.'

She simply nodded quickly, wanting to get away to find out how JJ was doing. There was no way she wanted to be trapped into a long, pointless conversation about Yaro. They didn't know him.

.   .   .

Dante let Alexia rush from the room, knowing she was successfully preoccupied with JJ. It wouldn't hurt for her to see her brother in the mess he'd created.

'Jay is on his way,' Cesaré prompted.

Dante let out a breath of relief. Alexia hadn't seemed to notice that he was absent from her escort detail. He'd been waylaid by everything going on with JJ. But not before his network of agents was in place. They'd been the real welcoming committee in Malta. Humans, perfectly hidden, and undetectable by strong Atlantean senses. He smiled to himself. Except, of course, Jay's. He'd know his closest friend's presence anywhere. By the time he walked back around his desk and sat down, there was a soft knock at the door.

'Come in, Jay,' Dante said, right away.

Jay walked in casually and nodded to everyone present.

'Everything went to plan?' Dante asked.

Jay flopped onto the sofa and shrugged. 'All seemed well. My source said there was some sort of altercation with his brother before they left. Just a driver who dropped them at the airfield right before take-off. They arrived alone and remained alone at the airport at Malta.'

'You're sure no one followed?' Dante asked, sceptical that Yaro had no contingencies in place.

Jay let out a deep breath as he shook his head. 'Yeah, we had eyes on him the whole time, till the helicopters lifted off. I had the helipad watched, twenty-four hours prior. The choppers were combed for any GPS devices several times. They were cleared minutes before Alexia and Yaro boarded. He's clean.'

'And they didn't suspect?'

Jay shook his head. 'Can't guarantee they didn't feel anything, but some sort of security would be expected, anyway.'

'What about the girlfriends' homes? Any news there?'

Jay nodded, thoughtfully. 'Yeah. Both had similar listening devices to the boys in the TV remote.'

That wasn't good. 'Why on earth would he be interested in them?'

'Did you remove them?'

Jay shook his head. 'I wanted to check in with you first.'

Dante let out a ragged breath and nodded. 'Remove them. Whoever's listening, knows the places are empty. Have them watch closely for who comes back.'

Jay nodded. 'And then what?'

'I'll be having a chat with our resident vampire.'

Jay was watching him closely. Thinking what he was thinking. There was something far more troubling than Demidov watching the kids. It could be someone else they didn't see coming at all.

CHAPTER 26

When Alexia reached the sick bay, Latitia was sitting up and JJ and Valarie were standing up and glaring at each other across the bed.

She had to cough to get their attention. 'Do I need to get Father?'

It was JJ who broke the stare off first. 'Hey,' he said in a cracked voice. He relaxed a little and looked genuinely pleased to see her, but he looked awful. Like he hadn't slept for a week.

'It's OK, Mum. I feel fine. More than fine, actually.' Latitia pushed the covers back off her legs and went to turn. 'I think I can get up.'

'No!' both JJ and Valarie said at the same time, stopping Latitia swinging her legs over the bed.

Valarie tutted. 'This is all your fault, JJ. I'm not going to allow—'

'You don't get to make that decision anymore,' JJ said, evenly.

Alexia rushed forward before Valarie could erupt and

moved Latitia's slippers under her feet. 'What JJ means, Mrs Johnson, is that we're all one big family now. Isn't that right, JJ?'

Latitia slipped straight into the slippers and stood up shakily. Her mother got under her arm and took most of her weight. 'We're going back to *our* room, where we will get our stuff together and leave,' Valarie said, not able to hide the spite in her voice.

Alexia watched JJ's face darken, knowing full well that nothing was Valarie's decision anymore.

'No,' JJ said, low and deliberately, almost like a growl.

Alexi immediately butted in. 'What JJ means is, it's best for you all to stay so that Latitia can be monitored for a few days,' she finished, widening her eyes in warning at JJ.

'Please, Mum. Stop it,' Latitia said, wriggling out of her hold. 'I need to be here.'

Alexia came a little closer and pointed her in the direction of the door. 'Everything will be fine. Go with your mum and we'll catch up with you in a minute,' she said, as if she was talking to a child and glaring again at JJ to let them go. It would give Valarie time to calm down and her time to talk to JJ, alone.

Valarie immediately took the opportunity and helped Latitia towards the door, who was already much steadier on her feet. She was looking over her shoulder at JJ the whole time.

'Go on,' JJ said, with a nod, and she finally left with her mother, leaving Alexia alone with her brother.

'What the hell are you doing, JJ,' she said, immediately whirling around on him. 'Have you lost your mind?'

JJ was red in the cheeks with emotion as he shook his head. 'Honestly, I don't know. I guess I wasn't thinking.'

'Not with your head, anyway,' Alexia said, taking in the

state of him. She'd never seen him so unravelled. She sat down heavily on the messy bed. 'You're going to have to let her breathe, JJ. No pun intended. Give it time to sink in.'

JJ sat down on the opposite side and angled himself to face her. Alexia raised her eyes to look directly in his. He looked exhausted and scruffy. Two things she'd never seen in him. 'Out of all of us, I never dreamed you'd be the first.'

He let out a deep sigh. 'Me neither. I mean, we haven't actually … you know,' he said, going red and rubbing the back of his neck in embarrassment.

All she could do was study him in amazement.

'So, you're here with Demidov?'

She let out an impatient breath and nodded, deciding not to pick him up on using his surname. She straightened to get up. 'I've got to go to him now before Dad reads him the riot act.'

JJ laughed on a single blast of air, but he looked far from OK.

She wished she could stay longer with him.

'Everything is changing, Lexie,' he said, looking achingly lost. 'Be careful not to end up as collateral damage.'

It was very hard to get angry with him in his present state, but she was not prepared to allow JJ to dismiss her very real relationship with Yaro. 'And you too, JJ. Xavier will feel he has a very real advantage over you now.' She felt guilty at how her words hit and sent a wave of bewilderment right through him. But they were a slap of truth. Xavier could be extremely driven when he wanted something and above all things he wanted to beat JJ.

She gave him a wan smile of sympathy. 'I'm going to go,' she said sadly, getting to her feet.

'Don't rush headlong into things,' JJ said, not looking her in the eye.

She ambled to the door, finishing his sentence, *like he had,* in her head. She opened it and turned and looked back at him. He looked so like the little boy she remembered. She smiled, knowing she would always love him. 'I won't, I promise. But I have made up my mind, JJ.' She took in the lost resigned look in his eyes and swiftly left the room.

YARO WASN'T sure how he felt exactly. In all his nearly three hundred years of living, he'd never felt so exultant, but also fearful. Yes, there was definitely an element of fear. It was a most disconcerting feeling. All he'd ever wanted was to stand where he stood now. On the hallowed ground of his ancestors as an equal. Here he was on the edge of the great room, a replica of the splendour of Atlantis, amongst its royal family where he belonged. For so long he'd been a stranger looking in. It would take time to accept it was real.

Alexia surprised him by slipping her hand into his. But looking into her gently pulsing aura, trusting him implicitly, only served to fuel his sense of confusion and disquiet.

Even in his blindness, he could see that her eyes were a perfect shade of green. Perfectly ripe apples, staring adoringly up into his. Youthful. Innocent. He never expected to feel the way he did about her. He never expected to feel the way he did about anything. The fear came, he guessed, from reaching the summit of all his desires so easily. His ambition had been fulfilled, not by smashing, killing and taking, as it had often been in the past, but because of this one royal child. Because that was what she was. A naïve child, who held his hand simply because she wanted to go with him.

He felt suddenly unworthy, as he looked out again at the room filled with Atlantean auras. Royals. Family. His family, he was yet to meet. Of course, he'd met many royals over the years. Ones that had no idea who they were dealing with. Only that he was Atlantean and a strong one. Now they must see him without his worldly disguise and know who he truly was. It was this level of exposure that made him feel vulnerable.

His empty gaze went straight to the family congregating around the fountain. Despite them only being a bedtime story for him most of his life, he knew exactly who they were. The fabled Murrmen. The only other purebloods in the room. Untainted by this world. The permanent water-breathers of the race. The ones who lived unchanged since their shared forefathers left Atlas. He was enraptured by their size, the strength of aura, highlighting the prominence of their stripes and their absolute stillness.

His family had no need of stripes. Their speed and competence in the darkest reaches where few reeds grew, rendered them pointless. His mind wandered to whether they would surface on his skin if he spent any real time in water, which, of course, he never had.

His attention was suddenly captured by the king clinking his heavy glass with a spoon and urging him forward into the room. Cesaré and the Bonaci brothers were clustered around him. He called him to his side and Alexia squeezed his hand, smiling her encouragement up at him. He swallowed, raised his head and walked purposely to the king's side.

'Family … Friends,' Dante said, clinking his glass again, until the last of the chatter died down. People soon noticed him as a stranger and began to straighten to listen. 'Fellow sons and daughters of Atlas. I have a guest with me today that I would like you all to meet. May I introduce Prince Yaro Demidov,' Dante said, holding out his hand. The room had grown silent. He nodded, looking around at them all. 'Yes, you heard me right. He is royal. From a branch of the Santalini royal family that up to recently, we never knew existed. His claim has been authenticated and recognised. His family has been greatly wronged by our ancestors and I seek to put that right by welcoming him and his great family back into Atlantean society.'

Yaro felt the amazement and unrest ripple through the room as the realisation spread. He couldn't see individual faces, but auras burst and pulsated and emotions went taut like piano wires. He stood straighter. Alexia gripped his hand tighter, but he was too intent on the scene in front of him.

'From this day, the name Demidov, ancient family of Ambragio, will be added to the history books as the sixth family of Atlas.'

There were audible intakes of breath. He almost laughed in amazement at the clever move by the king. By separating them from the Santalinis, his family's closest relatives, he was removing the threat to their role as elite guards to the crown. Creating a new line and possibly a role of their own. For what, remained to be seen. But he was impressed, none-theless.

Someone called out, 'Not six. Five! There has always been five!'

Yaro homed in on the source. There was always going to be a certain amount of opposition, but Dante carried on regardless. 'And to prove my sincerity and commitment to putting right this great injustice, as king and head of the Atlantean government, I offer Yaro Demidov my own daughter in betrothal. Which, as issue of a siren's mate, quali-fies him for a seat on the council of Atlantis, after their wedding.' Then a little more quietly, 'After the standard period of courtship has concluded, of course.'

Yaro's unseeing eyes shot to Dante. His pulsing grey and silver aura was almost as bright as his own and impossible to read. Nevertheless, it was more than he could have hoped for.

After a brief moment of silence, the room erupted into

excited chatter. Some angry and protesting, others just venting their shock.

'Thank you,' Dante concluded with his hand raised. 'I am sure you are eager to speak to Yaro to congratulate and welcome him… Oh yes, and the happy couple. There will be a celebration on Orbstice Day to celebrate the engagement. We are happy to answer any of your questions.'

Yaro knew what Orbstice Day was. It coincided directly with the day after Christmas. It was the day the Orb stood still and chose the earth as its home. He was told the stories from when he was a small child. He was stunned. All his demands had been met.

Alexia burrowed into his side. 'I'm so happy,' she said through muffled tears, into his jacket. He put an arm around her stiffly, still numb with shock. It had all happened so quickly. He was at least expecting some sort of negotiation. He was elated. Everything exceeded his expectations, except the courtship period.

He rubbed Alexia's back while he absorbed that. The standard courtship period was clever wording, as everyone knew it could be set by the king in royal weddings. So in other words, as short or as long as the king liked.

He let out a ragged breath and tapped Alexia's back to release him. He smiled down into her trusting green eyes, still marvelling at the doubly clever move the king had just pulled. Because despite a public reinstatement and apology, in reality, he had given him nothing. Not yet. Dante's hands were tied and he'd given himself the time for Yaro to prove himself trustworthy. The Santalinis were placated for the time being and Dante would have time to assess him as the man who would marry his daughter and have a hand in government. He had heard of the council and thought he would have to fight to be on it.

He felt Dante's shrewd eyes on him and tipped his head.

Credit where it was due, despite his age, he was an able and clever king. He acknowledged it with a low bow to him for the whole assembly to see.

Alexia was openly crying with joy next to him, but his eyes were locked with Dante, knowing he'd effectively set the bar for him to win over a very difficult crowd. That would be his real fight.

CHAPTER 27

lexia ran to her father and hugged him. He caught her and burrowed his nose in her hair. 'He still has to prove himself, Alexia,' Dante said next to her skin.

For her it was the happiest moment of her life and a rare win. She'd come there for Yaro to be accepted. To be engaged was beyond her wildest dreams. 'Thank you… Thank you, Father. I'm so happy.' He put her away from him and held the top of her shoulders. 'You are so grown up. I can't believe it.'

Tears were soaking her cheeks. 'You'll love him, Dad. I promise… just like I do.'

Dante looked past her and she followed his eyes to Yaro, shaking a line of people's hands. She wasn't sure how he felt, exactly. Right then he looked bemused. She knew it hadn't really sunk in with him. She understood, perfectly. He'd spent his life fighting in the streets and now he was cata-pulted into a different fight. One of smiles and politeness. The world of the Atlanteans, that he'd only ever glimpsed from the outside.

'You really love him, don't you?' her father stated, next to her.

She nodded, drinking Yaro in, receiving pats on the back and bows from his peers. 'I do, Dad. More than you'll ever know.'

XAVIER STOOD shoulder to shoulder with JJ. He'd just joined him with a fragile-looking Latitia and a bewildered-looking Valarie. The latter looked like she'd cut down anyone who approached her at that moment with a look alone.

'I can't believe it. Father has given him everything,' Xavier said, so only JJ could hear.

JJ turned to face him. 'He's keeping his enemies close.'

Xavier's gaze flicked to Latitia next to him. She was a lost fawn who'd suddenly found herself in a pride of lions and was desperately trying to adjust to her new reality. 'So you did it, Brother,' Xavier said, with a slow, wolfish, smile. 'Was it as good as I imagine?'

JJ shifted uncomfortably. 'We didn't go all the way, but enough.' His eyes only rested on him for a split second. He didn't seem pleased or elated and that strangely made Xavier very happy.

'Come on ...' Xavier said, giving him a friendly nudge. 'You're a bonded male now. How does it feel?' Xavier was goading him and could barely contain his laughter.

JJ did not see the joke and his face heated, so he knew he was baiting the tiger. JJ's eyes pierced his with a real warning. 'Heavy ... it feels heavy,' JJ said in a deadly low tone. 'And you will know for yourself soon enough, won't you?' JJ tipped his head towards something past his shoulder.

Xavier glanced and saw Paige a little way off with her family and laughed loudly at that. 'No, I will not! I will never be as stupid and rash as that.' Nothing had been clearer in his mind, watching the realisation spread over JJ's face. 'Seeing you like this … I will never make the same mistake. I will not bind Paige to me.'

JJ did not react, which surprised him. Instead, he looked past him again.

Then he leaned in and finished in his head with relish, *not until I am king.*

JJ's attention remained annoyingly on whatever was behind him.

Then the reality seeped through with an inward flinch of dread, as Xavier turned slowly to see what JJ was looking at. He could already feel who it was. Paige was standing right behind him.

For a moment, he prayed she hadn't heard, but it was easy to read the hurt on her face, in the red cheeks that looked as though he'd slapped them. He forgot everything else and went to take a step towards her, but she ducked away from him and ran from the room. He took a step to go after her, but JJ put out a hand to stop him. 'You can't talk your way out of that one, Xav. Give her chance to cool down.'

CHAPTER 28

*A*lexia worked the room on Yaro's arm, the proudest and happiest she'd ever been. It was like a dream. Everyone wanted to greet and talk to Yaro and congratulate them on their engagement. It was like he was a visiting superstar that everyone had a rare chance to speak to.

Alexia watched him, starstruck too. She studied his every movement. How he answered every question intelligently, actively listened and answered with real charm. She'd never witnessed him in this setting before. She'd only ever seen him with close family or dealing with the underworld at his clubs and that was only rarely. It hit home, then, his years of experience. The clever, sophisticated male she was engaged to. *Engaged.* She said it in her head over and over, she could scarcely believe it. Her heart leaped every time.

They moved on to cousin after cousin, getting nearer and nearer to the Borge family assembled around the fountain. Yaro's eyes continually strayed to them while he was in conversation with others. She could see he was edging closer, to reach the person he was keen to meet.

Eventually, her father approached Vionne, Lord Advocate

of Murrtaine and his brother, Darres, the biggest and scariest of all the Murrs and married to her Aunt Isla. The Murrs and Yaro were a stark contrast. Cultured Vionne, with his white-blond hair and striped features that had become quite expressive since he'd spent long periods with Atlanteans. And mysterious Darres, with long straight black hair to his waist, who barely spoke and watched his loved ones fiercely, like some great panther.

Isla immediately broke her thoughts with a crushing hug. She congratulated them both. 'I too married my great love,' she whispered in her ear, always understanding perfectly what was really going on, which she loved her for.

Vionne's wife, Ashaya, bowed gracefully from the waist. *Mighty prince ... welcome,* she projected so they could all hear, setting herself apart immediately as the true Atlasian she was.

Yaro seemed to instinctively know and bowed dramatically over her hand, as if she was the queen instead of her mother.

'Ashaya was one of the legal delegates sent from Atlas to judge us. She decided to marry and make Earth her home,' Dante explained, winking kindly at Vionne.

'I had heard rumours there was such a being living among us,' Yaro said, looking a little starstruck himself. 'Forgive me, but I have never met anyone outside of my own family genetically intact from our home planet.'

Alexia watched him curiously. It had never occurred to her before. He would have met Atlanteans in his dealings from time to time. They were everywhere and he would sense them, but a Murr, or someone directly from their home planet like Ashaya, would rarely have crossed his path. It blew her mind.

Yaro seemed genuinely impressed. Catching the wary look exchanged between her father and Vionne, she felt a small tentacle of fear. It wasn't that she felt there was a need to feel jealous. More concern for his strange reaction to them. As if they were the only ones that really mattered. Like everyone else in the room was somehow lacking.

Alexia checked her father's response to the conversation and he gave nothing away. She hoped Yaro had just forgotten himself in his excitement. However, composure was usually his strong suit, so she doubted that very much.

The male Murrs were taller than him, but not by much. Maybe by two or three inches at almost seven feet tall. What made them seem bigger was that they were a little thicker set and muscular. Yaro's family were tall and lean. It made sense now that they were built for speed. It occurred to her that it may include speed under water.

'So the great city of Murrtaine truly does exist,' Yaro was saying, staring directly at Vionne and Darres, as if he was mapping all their differences and not intimidated by them in the slightest.

It does and not too far from here, Vionne's strong mental voice projected back. His eyes never left Yaro's as if he was doing the same.

'I should like to go there and see it one day. It would be one of my greatest ambitions realised.'

And yet your eyes fill with blood rendering you blind, Vionne replied, still studying Yaro, uncomfortably closely. She hoped Yaro understood that it was not an action of aggression, but merely that Murrs did not have the boundaries that humans and Atlanteans had.

Yaro stiffened and she watched his jaw clench and quickly said, 'Yaro's other senses are heightened and far superior to ours. The Ambragio are built for the deepest ocean trenches, where they can see clearly and withstand far greater pressure than us.' All the while she looked between Yaro and Vionne and was grateful when she saw Yaro relax down again. Her heart bloomed when she was rewarded with the look of gratitude that Yaro gave her and the small, genuine smile, that followed.

He returned his unseeing gaze to Vionne and Darres, insolently, with an eyebrow up, which almost made her giggle. She had to remember how supremely confident he was, being the only one of his age here, except maybe Ashaya, and she'd spent most of her three hundred plus years in suspended sleep on a spaceship.

'We were once known as the base dwellers,' Yaro said, his eyes resting on Ashaya, as if he'd followed her thoughts. 'Maybe they still speak of us on the home planet and you have heard of us?'

Indeed I have, Ashaya said, bowing her head demurely. *Artaxerxes' elite forces were world renowned and those that still carried the Ambragio gene were sought after as bodyguards and secret service because of their unique abilities.*

Vionne and her father both turned to look at her in amazement.

Even Yaro looked stunned.

'You never thought to mention that earlier?' Dante asked, flabbergasted.

Ashaya shrugged in a very Atlantean way. *Well, nobody asked and it slipped my mind. There was rather a lot going on at the time, if you remember. You'd just been deposed and a new king sat on the throne.* She looked at Vionne cautiously. *You'd just lost your father.* She turned to them all, slightly exasperated. *My commander updated the digital files of the Orb in the great library. It was no secret. It was part of the audit.* She was beginning to look perplexed, like she'd made some huge blunder.

Strangely, it was Yaro who calmed the situation down. 'I expect it held no relevance to anything back then.'

Ashaya smiled gratefully.

Alexia looked up at her father. He looked like he didn't

know what to make of the whole thing and was completely broadsided. 'There's your proof then,' she said, directing her gaze to Vionne. But he seemed more troubled than pleased.

Alexia was observing the shared understanding that passed between Yaro and Ashaya. It felt a little weird, like everyone else was intruding.

Thankfully, it was her father who shook them all out of it. 'Well, today we move forward and repair a great wrong done to the Demidov family many millennia ago.'

The weird, uncomfortable silence went on for a few more excruciating moments, until her mother bounded up to the party. 'Sorry I'm late. I was caught up with Roman. An urgent wardrobe malfunction.'

It was a welcome breeze of normality that cut through the tension. Relief showed on her father's face when he drew her into his side and kissed the top of her head. She kissed him back on the mouth and turned her attention to Alexia, holding open her arms for her to come to them. Alexia couldn't remember being so pleased to see her and was soon engulfed in tight arms and warm perfume. 'How are you, baby girl?' her mother whispered against her hair. Then she straightened and said immediately, 'Is this him? How handsome.'

Vionne had used the distraction to gently steer Ashaya away with a parting, *Your highnesses... We wish you a pleasant stay, Prince.*

Yaro bowed low, with far more deference than he'd shown her father and hadn't seemed to even notice her mother. It threw her a bit. As he rose, he was still looking after Ashaya. 'I look forward to visiting your great city and viewing those great tomes myself,' he called.

Ashaya looked over her shoulder as Vionne had already led her off. Alexia couldn't help finishing in her head, *not if I can help it.* And then prayed that Yaro hadn't tuned into her thoughts. She looked at her father, fearfully, hoping that whatever had just gone on there, hadn't changed anything between them. He was difficult to read.

Yaro turned back to them and appeared surprised to see her mother standing there, holding out a hand for him to shake. He seemed on the back foot for a moment and that never happened.

At first Alexia thought her mother had bowled him over with her beauty. It was a usual reaction, but the way he studied her mother was very different to the way he looked at her, and certainly nothing like the way he'd just looked at Ashaya. He was taking in who she was. Or rather, *what* she was.

Yaro clicked his heels together and bowed dramatically over her hand, touching it to his forehead. 'Forgive my rudeness, Your Majesty. I had no idea I was in the presence of such a rare creature.'

'Call me Tia … please,' her mother said, giggling. She shot her a 'where did you find this one' look, and went in swiftly for the hug. It happened so fast, she didn't have enough time to dissuade her. It was still unclear if Yaro could bear anyone that close to him for blood reasons.

He just held her, jaw flexing and looking bewildered at her father. Her mother, unaware at what she'd just done, released Yaro and hugged back into her father's side. At least it seemed to make them all forget how he'd acted around the Murrs. She told herself that he was just weird because he was meeting all his fairy tales in the flesh. She should cut him a little slack for that.

Her father held out his arm and steered them to an area of vacant seating, where he left them with her mother and his apologies of pressing matters. She hoped that was all it was, but she knew her father well. Yaro's meeting with Vionne had unsettled him as much as it had her and he needed to process it. However, it didn't stop him from whispering to a Santalini, who moved in closer and hovered nearby.

Her mother seemed so excited that it soon dispelled her worry. She reached over and squeezed her hand. 'I can't believe it. My daughter, engaged.'

Yaro was still studying her mother closely, probably trying to sense any differences to regular Atlanteans. 'So they tell me you're some Russian mafia godfather with fangs,' her mother said with her usual directness. 'You'd better not mess her about.'

Yaro's eyes widened and a blast of laughter left him.

Alexia covered her eyes with her hand. 'Mother,' she said, wearily.

'What?' Tia said, innocently. 'It's true, isn't it?' she looked at Yaro to back her up, who was still smiling.

'I do my best not to disappoint,' he said, making her mother shriek with laughter.

'I like him, he will definitely be able to look after you.' She got to her feet, giving him a wink. 'I'll leave you two to it. I need to see what your brothers are up to.'

Yaro was shaking his head as if he was amazed as well as amused. 'So that is the famous Tia Storm I have heard so much about.'

'In the flesh,' Alexia said, watching her mother hug several people on her way out of the hall.

Yaro was already surveying the room. Even though she knew he saw very little, he was taking it all in. Like a bat mapping hard surfaces and warm bodies. 'What was that?' she asked, not able to help herself.

'What was what?' Yaro said, resting his hawk-like gaze directly on her. 'I like your mother.'

'Not my mother … before that …This is the greatest day of our lives. My father has accepted us. We are engaged and everyone has welcomed you, so why did you behave so weirdly with my Uncle Vionne and his wife?'

His gaze appeared to search her face as if he could see her. Maybe he could in his strange, heat-seeking way. Then he disarmed her by leaning in for a soft, lingering kiss on her lips. 'There are more powers at play here than you realise, Alexia.'

'Please don't patronise me, Yaro. I know a face-off when I see it. And what was all that with Ashaya?'

Yaro laughed and tried to school his features. 'Forgive me, I forget how worldly wise you are.' He ended up grinning at her indulgently, making her want to smack him for making fun of her. 'I might not be an ancient old fogey like you, but I know what I saw … what I felt.'

He bobbed his head and conceded that. Then he turned in his seat and picked up both her hands. He looked around him to make sure no one was nearby to hear and then spoke in hushed tones. 'All your life your father has been accepted on the Atlantean throne. He appears to be a much-loved and able king. He rules with good sense and knowledge of humans, with advisers on his council and by good relations with the Murr king. Because that is a necessary fact, to remain close to the underwater city and the power it holds.'

All the while he spoke, he gently rubbed the backs of her hands with his and looked her directly in the eyes, as she sifted through what he was saying. Everything came across fine until she landed on his reference to Vionne being a king. 'But he's not a k—'

'Not in name, maybe,' Yaro cut in. 'But that is what he is. In his domain, that is how his people see him. He knows this and so does your father. Atlanteans are not able to rule a people like the Borge. Not effectively. Not and live. And so he has always done this by Vionne's cooperation and pledge of fealty.'

Alexia frowned. Everything Yaro was saying was true. That was how it worked and why her father was such a beloved king. He didn't keep everything tightly to himself. He and Vionne had always been close friends. 'Then I don't get it.'

Yaro looked around him again and relaxed back into his chair. She leaned forward and picked up his hands again. 'Please tell me, Yaro. I need to understand. Whatever it was, my father saw it too.'

Yaro gripped one of her hands but looked disturbed. He brought it to his mouth and kissed the back of it. 'Remember me telling you the story, how right back at the beginning we were known as the base dwellers on Atlas?'

She nodded eagerly. 'Because you could survive in the deepest ocean pressure and see where there was no light.'

Yaro let out a slow breath. 'You have forgotten the bit about the deep-sea caves, my love. We could also breathe in the oxygen pockets. It was where we made our homes.'

She nodded. 'Yes, I remember.' Not really seeing what he was driving at. 'It was why you were chosen to come here. It was your family that went ashore first and founded the earth for the Atlanteans, not the Santalini soldiers. It was the great wrong that was put right today, Yaro,' she said, smiling, giving his hand a little shake.

But he wasn't snapping out of it. He continued to watch her face as if she would somehow join the dots and fall in with what he was saying. She had always understood the hurt in no one ever recognising that. She got why he would be upset by the likes of Vionne and Darres, perhaps looking down on him as a monster, or a lowlife base-dweller. When he still didn't elaborate, she sagged in her seat. 'I'm sorry, I still don't get it.'

Yaro dropped his voice an octave lower and leaned towards her, so his mouth was next to her ear. 'I can't talk in depth with you about it here but know that I have no such designs on your uncle's city.'

She frowned and looked at him aghast. It was the very last thing she'd suspected. She was more bothered by how interested he was in Ashaya.

He rolled his eyes and pulled her back in. 'Look, Atlanteans are many and Ambragio are few. But we can survive anywhere. In water or on land. Atlanteans are effective on land and weak in the water. Murrs are weak on land and effective under water. Ambragio…' he left his last word floating.

Alexia hitched a breath, falling in immediately. 'Are strong in both,' she finished for him, sitting back with her hand to her mouth. 'Oh, my God. They see you as a threat to the kingdom.' Her heart stopped in her chest and her eyes were wide with fright.

'We have to go. We have to explain to my father it's not true.'

CHAPTER 29

*O*f course Xavier wouldn't want her long term. *How stupid she'd been,* Paige thought, fighting back tears, turning left and right in the tunnels, blindly. She was just a young girl from a deprived area of London. She'd always known that. But what really hurt was Xavier's constant denial of it. It was him who had constantly convinced her that she wasn't a placeholder and she'd started to believe it. Why was he so cruel, to do that?

Tears were now streaming down her face as she let out a sob. She finally looked up at the lights in the ceiling and they were yellow. She had no clue where she was in the warren of tunnels. She spun around to try to get her bearings and it was hopeless. She was lost. It was the last straw and she slid down a wall to sit on the floor and bawled. She hit the heel of her hand against her forehead over and over. *How stupid she'd been, stupid, stupid.* She held her head in her hands and cried until she petered out to listless silence.

She wasn't sure how long she stayed like that, with her eyes closed. When a noise, a flip flip flip of sandals got louder as they neared, until they stopped and she knew they were right in front of her.

'Are you OK? You shouldn't be here, you know.'

She opened her bleary, sore eyes and saw the brown bare feet in flip-flops and travelled up the scruffy jean-covered legs to the hem of a lab coat. Then straight up to the handsome brown face. Outrageously handsome, she realised. Framed by black, overlong, unkempt hair. 'Here!' Hunter said, producing a tissue from his pocket. 'I can't promise it doesn't have some sort of corrosive agent on it.'

She laughed, in spite of herself, took it from him and blew her nose loudly. 'I think it will be overridden by the 80/20 rule,' she said, nasally through the tissue.

When she looked up at him, he was grinning. 'So what brings you to my neck of the woods? You know I got a visit from your boyfriend, warning me off, after your last visit.'

Paige sank against the wall and scrambled onto her feet, her disbelief quickly turning to anger. 'He's got a bloody cheek!' she said, flashing her eyes at Hunter.

Hunter didn't react. He tipped his head in the direction of the way he came. 'Do you want to come with me and calm down?' He looked around him. 'I don't want to leave you here.'

She nodded and dabbed her eyes with the tissue, but didn't move her feet. 'I don't want to cause you any trouble.'

He studied her face for a moment. 'No worries … honestly.' He smiled and held out his arm. She walked along with him, knowing she shouldn't, really. It would aggravate an already fraught situation with Xavier, but he had no right telling her what to do, especially now.

The next thing she knew, they were standing in front of the familiar grey door. Hunter looked at the door handle and, without a key, the lock turned. 'After you?' he said, pushing the door open.

The black cavern turned to the soft green light she remembered, revealing the set-up worthy of Merlin, and Hunter hadn't touched a light switch. She didn't ask how. Instead, she checked out the old books, bottles and equipment, stacked right up to the rough ceiling, while Hunter filled up a glass flask and put it on a burner. 'Tea?'

The normality of it made her relax and she nodded.

He grabbed cups from a cupboard and dropped a teabag in each.

She felt strangely at home here, considering she hardly knew him. It occurred to her that with Latitia and Alexia completely preoccupied, he was her only friend and she wasn't even sure she had a right to call him that yet. She felt instantly bad for the trouble she'd put him in. 'What did Xavier say to you?'

He shrugged, stirring a cup. 'You know ... the usual stuff: keep away from my girlfriend or else I'll kill you.'

She let out a blast of laughter, partly in amusement, partly in exasperation with him. He should be scared of Xavier but, clearly, he wasn't.

He passed her a cup. 'I take it not all is well in paradise.'

For a moment she warred with what to tell him out of some confusing loyalty to Xavier. She quickly shook the misplaced thought away. It was the least she could do for someone who was literally the only one who cared. She swallowed and just blurted, 'I overheard him say to JJ that he would never bind me to him.' She looked away in embarrassment, sure he wouldn't be surprised. She was a nobody after all and these were all princes.

'What?' he said, drawing her eyes straight back to him. 'He said those exact words?'

She studied his face, amazed he looked so surprised, even a little angry. 'I was standing right behind him. JJ had just bound Latitia and was talking to him about it. It's like a marriage, apparently.' A lump came up in her throat again.

Hunter walked around the counter to stand in front of her. 'That explains all the increased activity around the infirmary earlier today. And you want that with him? Have you actually thought about it?'

Paige studied his face, all serious, with his eyebrows up in a question. She did, well she thought she did and, no, she probably hadn't really thought about it more than a rejection. She shuffled uncomfortably. 'I guess it's the principle of the thing. You don't know what he's like.'

Hunter's eyebrows went up again. 'I do know Xavier. Probably better than you, I think.'

She batted his comment away with her hand. 'You know what I mean. He said a lot of things. Been great with my family and brought us here and everything.' Saying it out loud, it had to mean something. Her eyes stung with new tears.

Hunter didn't say anything, thankfully. Only looked thoughtful for a minute. 'You know, he is the lawful crown prince. That means the heir, Paige.'

She nodded sadly, looking down at her fingers. 'So is JJ. His dad was king once too, apparently. They're locked in this pointless battle between them, or something. I don't really understand it. In a lot of ways, they're so close.'

When her eyes rested on Hunter again, he seemed bored, impatient even. 'My father was too, Paige. There was a lot of it going around.'

She stared at him, shocked. She had no idea. He seemed almost a recluse here.

'Don't worry, I'm almost forgotten,' he said, laughing derisively. He sighed and walked over to the huge centre table, where one of his complicated experiments was fermenting away. 'I don't want it anyway.'

She wasn't sure whether he was talking to her or himself.

Then he looked right at her. 'But Xavier does, very much. It will always come first for him. You will always come second. Even if he binds you. It will make no difference. You want that?'

Hunter looked stern and direct, as if he was telling her off. She wasn't upset. It was the first time anyone had really spoken so directly and honestly about it all. He really was an important person too and hid himself away in his lab. 'I don't know what I want,' she answered, looking up at him, a little startled. 'Is that daft?'

Hunter straightened and let out a long sigh. She realised he thought deeply on most things. 'I don't think you should need to at our age. Forever is a long time to choose a partner.' He closed the gap between them and pushed some bottles back on the counter to tidy them before finally resting his eyes on her again. 'Because it would be forever with one of us.'

She didn't fully understand why the weight of his words made her cheeks heat and her mouth go dry, but they did. His lids were low and his voice was quiet and rasped. 'No divorce when you are physically joined ... except by death.'

He began to sort through an old wooden box of small bottles, but she continued to study him, wondering what he meant. Like he'd disappeared in his memories, to a place a very long way away. There was a weight growing in her lower abdomen when she was around him that she was noticing more and more. A pain that moved to the centre of her chest that she couldn't ignore. She loved Xavier, at least she thought she did. She was hurt, but Hunter had started to mean something to her. Something that she wasn't sure she could give up. 'Can I come here when I need to?' She coughed when her voice cracked. 'You know, escape ...'

Hunter stopped what he was doing to look directly at her.

They seemed to have gravitated closer without her even realising. His face was serious, like he was running calculations in his head, deciding whether he should. Whether she was worth the hassle. 'You know I have always managed to keep out of the squabbles between those two.' Their eyes remain locked. 'Until recently.'

She knew she wasn't being fair, but he seemed so alone and she liked him. There, she'd admitted it. To herself, at least. 'I know it's aggravation for you, but can I? I won't be any trouble.'

He raised his eyebrows and smiled sardonically.

'OK, I'll try not to be.' She was shamelessly pleading and he was so close, she could feel his breath.

He considered it for what felt like a full minute, while his eyes never left hers. Until he eventually looked over her shoulder and tipped his head. 'Pass me one of those slides.'

She twisted and spotted an open cardboard box of microscope slides. Reaching and pulling one out, she passed it back to him.

'Give me your hand,' Hunter said.

Curious where he was going with this, she held out her hand palm up.

Before she knew what was happening, he'd grabbed it and pricked her middle finger. She went to snatch it away, but he held it fast. 'Only if you allow me to study your blood.'

It all happened so fast, she was still reeling when he squashed the tip of her finger against the slide. Vaguely, she was aware that it was to study it under a microscope, but something felt personal and confusing about the whole thing. Nevertheless, she allowed it, surprised when he pricked his own finger and did the same. 'We will compare them,' he said, smiling, warmly. 'I have never had the opportunity. Have you?'

She shook her head like an imbecile, completely captivated by him. Truthfully, it had never occurred to her that they would be different. She let out a ragged breath, determined to get a grip and be as analytical as he was. But she still couldn't shake the feeling that she was embarking on something truly dangerous. Because she would want to be here all the time.

CHAPTER 30

'Come in and sit down, 'Dante said, from his seat behind his desk.

The imposing figures of Vionne and Darres entered and overshadowed the room with Ashaya coming to a standstill on Vionne's other side. Isla was with them and he smiled at the deceptively delicate-looking Siren.

Sebastian, Alfonzo and Cesaré, nodded a greeting while they took their seats on the sofa. Jay had gone to meet his wife, Ruby, flying into Malta, with their young daughter.

Keenan whispered something to Reeve stationed outside and then he closed and stood against the door.

'Thanks for meeting with me so quickly … I wanted to call it before everyone notices we are missing,' Dante explained.

'What's up?' Keenan asked. 'It's quiet and the kids are behaving.'

'It's not the kids I'm worried about … maybe, JJ,' Dante said with a weary shake of his head. That was a brewing problem for the backburner.

Keenan frowned.

Cesaré chuckled, rolling his eyes. 'JJ and his human girl,' he said, as if he couldn't quite believe it. 'He might regret that one.'

Keenan grinned and shook his head along with them.

Dante batted it away with his hand. There were more pressing matters. 'That's not why I called you here. My immediate concern is Yaro and what I witnessed just now.' He rested his eyes on Vionne and Ashaya, seated right in front of him. 'I take it you saw the same threat that I did?'

Vionne nodded and exchanged a look with Ashaya sitting next to him. 'I did,' Vionne said, dragging his gaze from his wife, as if they were in the middle of a telepathic conversation.

He is no match for us, Darres projected, stonily. It sounded all the more ominous as he communicated so rarely.

'I think you are wrong,' Dante said, matching his bluntness. 'You haven't seen his family in action.'

'I have and they're fast,' Keenan said from his place, arms crossed, leaning against the door.

They are puny in comparison to either of us, Darres said.

'When he says fast, he means you don't see them move,' Dante said, cutting between them.

Darres finally started to listen and swapped a look with his brother. *Then we need to see what he can do underwater.*

Only then will we know what we are dealing with, Vionne added.

Dante nodded, relieved they were finally getting it, but it still threw up a problem. 'Do you really want him seeing Murrtaine?'

What better way to test him, Vionne said. *We will present it in such a way that he thinks he is being welcomed by my family. Precautions will be taken should he prove dangerous and we will trap him.*

I did not detect any malicious intent when I read him, my love,

Ashaya said. *Only awe. I don't think he'd ever met anyone like us. Just as he said.*

Vionne put his hand over hers and said something privately, Dante was sure, judging by the smile that followed. However, the whole business filled him with unease. After all, there was Alexia to consider, here. 'You may very well be right,' Dante said. He let out a ragged sigh. 'I don't think we can take that chance.' It was a good a plan as any. 'I will need to know how you intend to trap and hold him, first. There is Alexia to consider. It will be hard enough on her as it is.'

Darres' look darkened. *Fear not, the Ambragio will not be returning from Murrtaine.*

CHAPTER 31

*P*aige finally relaxed and spent a very pleasant couple of hours with Hunter. They drank tea and swapped stories of their very different childhoods. He sounded an accomplished surfer and didn't fit the mould of every other science geek she'd ever known. He was utterly fascinating and she couldn't understand why he locked himself away like he did. Her life seemed drab and boring in comparison. His eyes seemed to mist over when she expressed her wish to be a doctor. He probably felt sorry for her. Like everyone did who knew she didn't have a hope in hell of attaining it. It seemed to kill the mood and they fell silent for a long moment.

'What happens when you bind someone? Is there a ceremony or something?' she asked, to change the direction of conversation.

Hunter shifted in his seat and looked thoughtfully into his cup. Then he shook his head.

She hitched a breath with a sudden thought. 'Have you ever done it?' She'd been so wrapped up in herself that it hadn't occurred to her that he might have a love life of his own.

He looked mischievously sideways at her. 'Why? Do you really want to piss your boyfriend off and try it?'

She burst out laughing, completely scandalised, but she got the impression that he was cleverly deflecting. From what, or rather, who, she was dying to know. 'Oh my god, can you imagine?' she said, playing along.

Hunter's face turned serious and she wondered for a moment where he went. 'We call it breathing. It's a physical act. Ordinary Atlanteans have long lost the ability, but most royals still have the urge.'

She wanted to ask if that included him, but she decided against it, as it already felt weird between them. 'What happens? Physically, I mean.' Her breathing was shallow, her heart sped up and she found she was hanging on his every word.

He seemed relieved, like he was grateful that she'd steered it to practical, scientific territory. 'It's like a kiss where something comes out of one person and into the other. I've never managed to study it. It's hard to capture to quantify. I would like to one day,' he said, with an unsure smile.

'What do you think it is?' she asked, enraptured.

He looked uncomfortable again and looked around the room. 'The books all say it's a part of the person's spirit or soul. I guess. It's everything that makes them who they are. Their essence, if you like.' His eyes ended on hers, then averted again.

She knew he was hiding something very painful and was dying to ask him about it. 'Maybe it's a part of their DNA in a gas form,' she said, keeping them on the scientific track.

He stared at her then and smiled. A small smile as if he was aware of what she was doing and appreciated it. He looked away, then back at her, with eyes that changed to direct and intense. 'There is something else. A more secret way.' He shrugged and narrowed his eyes, smiling craftily. 'A little illegal, maybe. You can have a link to someone that is not so binding.'

She was intrigued. Everything about him was so mysterious and he was so captivating. She couldn't help comparing him to when she'd first met Xavier. They were both different to everything she knew, but equally poles apart from each other. 'What is it?' she found herself whispering.

It felt like his eyes bore into hers as if he was making up his mind. 'Come, I'll show you.' He walked to the end of the counter, to the pretty impressive-looking microscope, she'd envied before. It was expensive. Not at all like the prehistoric ones they used at school.

He reached over and picked up the slide she knew had the smear of her blood on it and slid it under the lens. 'Take a look,' he said, stepping out of the way and without looking at it himself.

She was immediately on her feet, walking over to him. He tipped his head for her to look. 'Your pinprick of blood.'

She put her eye to the eyepiece and turned the little adjustment knob on the side to get the specimen in focus. The round red blood cells reminded her of a slice of something from a deli counter. Nothing remarkable.

'OK?' Hunter asked.

She shrugged, not sure what he was getting at, exactly.

He leaned in and removed the slide from the plate, sending a warm scent from his skin that smelled of some sort of soap. Then he put another one under it. 'That's mine.'

Paige looked at him, surprised he'd made another slide and put her eye over the lens again. What she saw was remarkable. The difference was startling. Nothing was stationary. Everything was moving like living organisms, making her recoil in shock. 'What's in it? A parasite or something?' she asked, alarmed.

Hunter laughed. 'No … Atlantean blood has something else in it. A force, I guess, that humans do not.' He picked up a vial from a wooden stand of what looked like any other blood and a pipette and drew some of the blood from the vial. Then he squeezed a droplet onto her slide and swapped it for the one on the microscope. 'Now, take a look.'

This time when she put her eye over the lens her heart began to beat out of rhythm. Her round red cells where being swarmed by his constantly moving red and purple thistles. Seeking, covering and absorbing her stationary ones until all that was left was a swirling stream of red and blue. Moving slowly as one mass, nothing recognisable was left from before.

'And that is from a sample cut off from its source many hours ago,' Hunter explained. 'Imagine if it came directly from the vein.'

Paige lifted her eyes from the microscope. What she'd learned was staggering. She became absorbed in his eyes, gauging her intently. They looked almost black in this light. They dropped to her mouth. He seemed so close, she became conscious of his breaths. How shallow they'd become, like her own. 'What are you suggesting?' she asked, on a breath, mingling with his.

His lips stretched into a smile and he tilted his head to the side. 'I'm not suggesting anything.' His smile grew into a grin. 'Your mind has leaped to something illegal in my circles.'

In a single moment, embarrassment flashed through her like a furnace. Hunter picked up the slides while she stepped back out of his way and he put them into the sink. She was cursing her stupidity for ever thinking there had been a moment between them, when he said, 'It's never made sense to me. It's allowed for the Santalini and now, evidently this new one as well, and wrong for everyone else.' All the while he rinsed off the slides under the tap. 'I can't see what all the fuss is about. It was a fashion a few years ago. Everyone was doing it. Even my mother and the queen.'

Paige was trying to keep up with what he was saying, guessing they were still talking about blood, but wasn't really sure what he meant about it. She leaned against the countertop watching him, simply grateful the heat appeared to be off her.

Hunter dropped the slides in a tank of solution and looked at her as if he expected an answer.

'What was wrong? … I mean, what did they do with it?' She averted her eyes again. 'Did you do it?'

When he didn't answer right away, she was forced to check his face again. He seemed to be studying her closely. 'They ingested it.'

Her eyes went wide in surprise while she imagined what that must be like. It sounded pretty disgusting.

'It acts like a drug and can be highly addictive… Some say it has certain binding properties, without the full genetic splicing that happens with breathing.'

It was so strange and fascinating, she thought about that for a moment. 'So are you suggesting I could have that with Xavier instead?'

He shrugged and laughed sardonically; his eyelids lowered. 'I guess, if you wanted to accept that as a substitute.' He began to wipe over his countertop. 'Or, you could share it with whoever the hell you wanted to. You're an independent girl. Didn't Xavier himself declare it?'

Paige's heart hammered again at what he was inferring. She felt herself harden and get angry with Xavier all over again. Hunter was right. Xavier had really shown how he felt about her today. She was hurt. 'How will I know whether I will like it?' she asked, not knowing why she was still talking. She should shut the hell up, but out it came.

The atmosphere became thick and balmy around her. Maybe it was the lit Bunsen burner nearby or maybe the electric equipment in a confined space. Her eyes inevitably went to the rack that still contained the test tube of Hunter's blood.

He followed her line of vision, tutted, and opened a drawer. 'That's disgusting,' he said, removing a small scalpel from its sheath.

She held her breath at what he intended to do with it, but he pushed it to his own thumb and made a small nick. 'Shall we carry out our own clinical trial?' he said, squeezing a small bead of blood in the centre of his thumb. 'You're a scientist … try mine,' he said, holding out his thumb to her. 'In a controlled environment.'

She looked at his cheeky smile and then at the ripe bead of blood, alarmed.

'Quick, it will drip,' he said, urging her again, laughing.

'What? … what do you want me to do with it?' she said, grabbing a hold of his hand and beginning to panic.

'Put it on your tongue. It's so small, it can't hurt you… Quick!' he urged her again.

Briefly, she thought of Xavier and how much he'd hate it. Then she got angry and thought he had no right. She thought how attractive Hunter was and then chided herself, as he was simply carrying out an experiment with her. In the end, she grabbed his hand with both of hers and pulled it to her mouth and put her lips around his thumb. In a second, he was right there in front of her. 'That's it,' he said, quietly, while his other hand went around her back.

It seemed strange that he was holding her like she would

fall when nothing appeared to be happening. She was looking up into his eyes as he watched her closely, clinically, fascinated by her reaction.

He withdrew his thumb and put it in his own mouth to seal the wound. She watched him do it, thinking how metallic blood tasted. Then her cheeks went cold as the blood drained out of them and her forehead poured with sweat. A loud whoosh went through her ears. The blood in her veins rushed through her body and her heart started to race. It went harder and harder. Faster and faster. She let out a whimper.

Hunter's arms tightened around her and her feet left the ground. It felt like she floated until the old couch softly met her back. She struggled to sit up, but Hunter firmly eased her down by her shoulders. 'Rest,' he whispered. 'Give it a minute. You fainted. Here,' he said, passing her a hot mug. 'Sweet tea,' he explained.

She hadn't even felt him go to make it. 'What happened?'

He grinned, perching on the sofa next to her. 'You tell me?'

She marvelled at his smiling face and then frowned, as broken snatches of memory came to her. Eclipsed more by how it felt than anything. Overwhelming, heat. Pleasure, so acute, it was too much to handle. Too much to bear. It was unbelievable. 'That was the blood?' It was such a tiny amount.

He nodded. 'Times that by a hundred, and you have an inkling of the breath. It's like a drug ... supposed to be,' he amended, giving her pause for thought.

Paige shook her head in amazement. No wonder Latitia ended up in the sick room. She couldn't imagine anything stronger than what she'd just felt. Despite that, it still gave her a pang of pain that she would never experience it with

Xavier. She realised that she didn't want to shy away from it. She wanted to experience everything.

Hunter was watching her reaction quietly.

She smiled at him, guiltily, that she'd been thinking of Xavier and not the clinical experiment that it was.

'I think I should try yours,' he said, his eyes wide and soulful. 'In the interest of fairness.'

She was already thinking about their blood moving and changing while his smothered hers on the microscope slide.

'It's such a tiny amount,' he said, echoing her exact thoughts of earlier. His eyebrows drew together and then he was smiling to reassure her. He dropped to his knee next to her, all the while her eyes never left his.

She was still a little dazed, but she was with it enough to know she was being unfair and held out her hand to him. 'OK, but I warn you, I am a dreadful wuss.'

He grinned and miraculously produced a pin from his pocket instead of the scary scalpel. Before she even had time to question him further, he'd pricked her finger and drew it to his mouth slowly. She held her breath, glued to his lips as they slowly closed around her thumb. His eyes remained on hers the whole time. She couldn't help herself. It felt strangely erotic, as he gently sucked on her thumb. His lips felt warm and soft and made her stomach clench. He squeezed and drew more blood out across his tongue. She'd never seen anything so seductive in her whole life. She wasn't expecting how it made her feel. After all, this was meant to be his half of the experience. But it didn't feel like that at all. It felt all hers.

Something twisted in her lower abdomen. A sweet pain. A welcome one. Making her swallow hard. By the time he finally drew her hand away from his mouth they were staring at each other. The moment so utterly heavy, without a single syllable being uttered.

Her heart hammered on the walls of her chest and it was no longer anything to do with the blood. It was the intensely charged moment. One so powerful, she'd never experienced anything like it. His eyes held hers so she didn't know what he would do next. Longing. Breathing for something to happen. If it wasn't for the three heavy bangs on the lab door.

CHAPTER 32

'Let me in, Hunter. I know she's in there,' Xavier shouted, giving the door a heavy thump with his fist again.

When no answer came, he gave it a hard kick, which reverberated through the corridor as it was metal. He stepped back and went to run and drop-kick it when the door was snatched open and Hunter stood there.

'Come in,' Hunter said, with a dark look. 'But if you try to smash up my lab, I will put you down.'

Xavier laughed and sauntered past him. 'You can try … where is she?' His eyes took a moment to adjust to the dim light. It reminded him more of a tacky themed bar than a lab, with neon green everywhere. He wrinkled his nose at the rotten egg smell of gas, while he scanned the room. Quickly spotting Paige with her legs up on Hunter's sofa. He was immediately punched with fear and then anger. 'What's the matter?' he asked, walking quickly over to her.

'She fainted,' Hunter said, from behind him.

Xavier turned his head to gauge him for lies and then

dropped down to his knee to speak to her. 'Are you OK?' he asked, softening his tone.

Paige nodded, not willing to look him in the eye.

That scared him more than anything. 'Look, we need to talk. What you heard … Can we at least get out of here?' he said, looking around at the creepy surroundings.

She didn't answer, she just looked over his shoulder to where Hunter was hovering. That really got on his nerves. 'Have you been here the whole time?' His voice pitch beginning to rise.

It was enough to startle her to speak. 'I didn't know where to go.'

Xavier was using every bit of his willpower not to give in to his anger. It was clear Hunter was messing with him after their last conversation, but he recognised he'd made a huge blunder with Paige. He needed to salvage the situation, quickly. 'Please, Paige. Won't you let me explain? You only heard part of the story,' he said, in his quiet, coaxing voice. He went to pick up her hand to make a psychic connection, but she quickly pulled it away.

He turned his head and shot a dagger look at Hunter, who simply raised an eyebrow as if to say, 'what?' He was wasting his time there and faced Paige again. She seemed in a daze, almost as though she was traumatised. He would have accused Hunter of hypnotism, had he not wanted to get her out of there so urgently. He wanted to get her away from Hunter's influence, as if it was tainting her the longer she stayed.

Instead of asking, he simply helped her to her feet and guided her past Hunter with his arm around her waist. She smiled wanly at him as she passed. 'Thank you,' she said, quietly.

Hunter nodded. 'Any time.'

Xavier seethed, wanting to punch the smug look off his face. Instead, he sped up their steps, opened the door and pushed her out into the light.

LATITIA FELT DIFFERENT. Despite knowing she'd been gravely ill, she felt alive. Awake. Strong. Full of energy. She'd had a bunch of crazy dreams and in them the king, of all people, had spoken to her. Weird hazy snippets where she felt like she was being pulled apart until there was nothing left. The delirium, probably exacerbated by all the fears she'd had about JJ. No wonder. She already felt vulnerable and scared at the strength of her feelings for him. Then finding out he'd been taking her memories. How angry she'd been. Scared she was losing her personality; being swallowed up by him. Real or not, what the king had said to her had been right. She couldn't remember feeling this good. She hadn't disappeared and she was thinking more clearly than she ever had.

Xavier had run off somewhere to be with Paige, Alexia was introducing her scary older guy to everyone, so that just left her as referee between her mother and JJ, who were still shooting dark looks at each other.

She let out a deep sigh and surveyed the great hall, still not quite believing that she was now a part of all this.

Her brothers seemed completely at home, laughing and joking with a group of teenagers around the fountain. She looked across at her mother, watching the same thing. 'They're happy, mum,' she said, before her mother could be negative about it. 'We all are.' The words felt inadequate. Like she wanted to dance, or shout it from the roof tops, that she was happy. That she'd grown. Expanded. Become alive. And it had all happened since JJ and his family had come into their lives.

But her mother was closed off and she didn't need to

point it out, because the perfect example came right up behind her and gently put his hands on her shoulders. Reeve, just letting her know he was there. Handsome, protective and *alien*, Reeve.

Her mother immediately turned her head to look up at him. Her initial smile fading, where she didn't know whether to melt or push him away after the way she'd been acting. It was obvious he was a nice guy. Everyone they'd met here was nice. She wanted to shake her out of this glass house she'd built over their genetic differences. Her mother was a hypocrite and she'd had enough. 'I want to move my stuff into JJ's room,' she blurted, without any forethought at all. If ever she wanted to take control of her life, then now was the right time.

Latitia felt JJ's eyes burn into the side of her face. Reeve widened his eyes over her mother's head and her mother turned to face her, sharply.

She finally shot a sideways look at JJ and he didn't look angry. Only stunned. He shrugged and gave her a small smile. 'You like causing trouble, don't you.'

It was all she needed to spur her on. She turned to her mother. 'What will it help, keeping us apart now?'

'Your age … pregnancy.' Her mother put her hand to her forehead, looking exhausted with it all.

'Do you want me to leave and give you some privacy?' Reeve said, quietly next to her ear, but she held onto his hand that was still resting on her shoulder. 'No, don't. Can you help us move her stuff?'

Reeve nodded.

Latitia's heart pounded in pleasant surprise, as he spoke directly to JJ. 'I will have to tell your fathers.'

JJ nodded, not giving much away. Maybe, in shock at the speed things were moving, but not against it.

Latitia was riding a high, still not believing her mother

had caved so easily. She felt elated, dazed, as they got to their feet and made their way to her room as a group.

There was very little to pack as most of it was still crammed in her carry-on bag. So she suspected Reeve had been brought along for moral support. For the first time, it struck her that she was glad her mother had someone. Strangely, it was JJ who concerned her more. Now they were all-in, his whole demeanour was off. He was subdued, like nothing had really sunk in for him and he was just rolling with the punches. 'You sure it's OK?' she asked, while they waited and her mom went into the bathroom to grab her sponge bag.

JJ drew her to him and smiled. *We'll talk when we're alone.* It wasn't the answer she'd hoped for, but it distracted her, as it was said straight to her head. *It's easy now, after the breath.*

The breath, she repeated in her head. The thing that had changed everything. Given her everything. She was determined not to waste it. However, when she studied his concerned face, she felt conflicted. This should be exciting for the both of them. She had liquid energy pumping through her veins. But instead, she was gradually deflating. She was worried because he was sad. That alone should be amazing, that she knew exactly how he was feeling. That he cared about her, but she also knew he was unhappy. Overwhelmingly so and that made her feel terrible. Desperately disappointed, like a stab to the gut. This wasn't what she expected or wanted. She had to get to the bottom of what was going on with him before he ruined everything.

JJ WAS grateful that Reeve and Valarie left them at his door. Valarie hugged Latitia and clung on for far too long. Reeve gave him an amused look and went off in the opposite direction, probably straight to his father's study.

After promising he'd look after Latitia, her mother reluctantly left them, leaving him feeling a backwash of relief. He immediately faced the door and clicked the lock with his mind out of habit. He looked sideways at Latitia who'd witnessed the whole thing with a hapless smile.

She returned it bemused. 'I've got a lot to learn, don't I?'

He nodded on a sigh and pushed open the door for her to go inside. 'Go on, let's get you unpacked.'

JJ had no idea where she could put her things. His room was big, but he'd never had to share his personal space before. In the end, he went to his big bank of wardrobes and pulled out armfuls of shirts and dumped them in the one next to it. 'Here, use this one.' It was the first eye opener to cohabiting that he would have to get used to. Nothing was just his anymore.

He stood back and watched her undo her bag and hang a few things. Her eyes drifted to his, nervously. 'I know it's weird. You don't have to live with me when we go back to London.'

The surprise was on his face before he could control it and his heart plummeted. He hadn't even thought that far ahead. In the end he sagged and opted for honesty. 'Sorry. I didn't think this through. Believe me, you wouldn't want to share with Xavier.'

A cute secretive smile crept over her face, that completely surprised him and pulled him from his gloom. 'I can stay over though sometimes, can't I?'

He sank down on the end of his bed, pulling her into his lap. 'Of course,' he said, breathing into her neck and loosening her many braids with his free hand. They fell charmingly around her face. He brushed his lips against hers, remembering the fierce girl she was when he'd first met her. All moodiness and swagger. That underneath all the crap they'd been through, she was still there, knowing exactly what she wanted, with that delicious hint of naïveté.

The familiar weight shifted painfully in his chest as a reminder. She may have pushed him over the edge, but they'd both wanted it. He had to take responsibility for that. It was remarkable how quickly it came now. Like it had tuned into her and knew its way home. *What had he done?* He felt wretched. Even now, as his life spun out of control, he was tipping her to lay flat on the bed so he could roll on top of her.

Just as he would dissolve into her and let caution blow him away, there was a loud rap at his door. Then his door opened to loud chatter and Alexia marched straight in with Xavier, talking animatedly.

Their steps halted and she stopped talking.

JJ paused, leaning up on his arms and gave them both his blackest look.

Instead of apologising, Alexia said, 'Ew, JJ. Haven't you done enough of all that?'

Xavier rolled his eyes and said, 'Bloody rabbits!' wearily.

They continued their progress into the room and flopped into his brown leather sofa and armchair nearby.

JJ groaned, kissed Latitia's forehead and pushed himself up, pulling her up with him.

It felt wrong—out of kilter, his brother and sister finding them like this and he knew it was very little to do with their lack of boundaries.

Latitia was watching his face closely, feeling everything through their bond. He had to remember she would know everything. It irritated him that he didn't know how to act around her. He wanted to throw his brother and sister out and punch something.

Instead, he took a slow breath and didn't react. He was

rewarded by a squeeze of his hand. 'Is it OK if I take a shower?' Latitia asked.

He relaxed immediately and felt bad at how relieved that made him. She was giving him his much-needed space. He leaned in and kissed her on the lips. 'Of course.'

He watched her disappear and turned to his brother and sister blankly. 'What?'

They were openly staring at him as if he'd spoken a profanity.

He shrugged irritably. 'She's staying here now.' He sank down onto his bed. 'Stable door after horses bolting and all that,' he said with a huff.

Alexia pulled a face and looked across at Xavier. 'Did you hear that? He's allowed and I've got to have a hundred yards between me and Yaro at all bloody times, and we live together,' she finished going up in pitch.

JJ let himself flop back on the bed, with his arm across his eyes. Then he felt the bed dip either side, as his brother and sister sat down on the bed with him.

Alexia gently touched his arm to move it away from his eyes, so he had to look at her. The look of sympathy she gave him felt like a thump to his chest. He sat up when his eyes filled with tears and leaned forward with his hand to his forehead to hide it.

'Are you OK, JJ,' she said, rubbing his back like she did when they were kids. Using the soft coaxing voice, she reserved only for him. He'd be angry and upset and he would turn and sob into her shoulder. He wanted to do that now, so badly.

His brother hadn't said a word and was watching him closely. Always calculating and working things out. He could literally hear his cogs working. Xavier knew him too well and would know how confused he was feeling. 'The truth is, I don't know how I feel. Only confusion, because I do have feelings for her. But I gave it no further thought beyond wanting to own her. None!... Doesn't that make me some kind of monster?' he said, feeling his cheeks going red in anger. 'I don't think I've given anything less thought.'

'I don't believe that?' Alexia was saying, still soothing and rubbing his back.

He turned on her sharply. 'You're wrong Lexie. Instinct just took over.'

Instead of arguing, her face took on a dreamy look. 'Wow, I can't wait to experience that.'

JJ had to spring away from her and the bed. They had no idea what it was like beyond a stupid teenage notion of love.

Xavier shook his head wearily, trying to come off as superior in some way. In reality, he knew no more than Alexia. 'How did you get on with Paige?' JJ threw at him, spitefully.

Xavier's face immediately clouded, receiving the dig loud and clear. But he didn't bite. He just shook his head slowly. 'I could kick myself for saying that out loud.'

JJ registered that he was only sorry that she'd heard, not that he'd said it.

'I had to search the place high and low,' Xavier continued, unperturbed. 'And you never guess where I found her?'

JJ shook his head. Alexia said, 'Where?'

'In Hunter's lab … lounging on his sofa, drinking tea. Completely at home with Sir -nerd-a-lot.'

Alexia giggled.

JJ frowned. He knew he liked science and kept to himself, but he was also a champion surfer, good enough to give his whole family of surfers a run for their money. He was hardly like the science geeks at school. He could totally see why a girl would like him. Still, he and Alexia swapped a look, surprised that she even knew him. Hunter wasn't exactly Mr. Popular.

Luckily, Xavier only read the last part of their thought

process and batted it away with a hand. 'They bumped into each other earlier, when she got lost, or something.' He made little air quotes with his fingers. 'He showed her his experiments.'

Xavier's obvious jealousy made JJ smile, but he schooled his features.

'I'd like to bloody …' Xavier caught onto his anger and pulled himself back together. 'The point is, she says she's alright, but I know she isn't.'

'What did you say to make her like that? She was so into you, Xav,' Alexia asked.

Xavier shuffled uncomfortably.

'He said he would never bind her to him,' JJ said for him. 'He was talking to me, but she was standing right behind him and heard everything.'

Xavier looked in physical pain as JJ recounted the story. Like he'd take it back in a heartbeat.

Alexia simply mouthed, 'Oh,' with wide eyes. What else could you say. Except, with perfect tactlessness, 'Well you've blown it then.'

'Why did you say that?' Xavier said, jumping to his feet. 'I can explain … put things right, if she'd let me.'

Alexia was immediately on her feet too, matching his ferocity. 'Because you've effectively told her she will never be permanent to you!'

They began to scream in each other's faces, neither listening to what the other was saying, until JJ had to shout over both of them. 'No one should feel permanent at our age.'

With JJ's glare, they both stopped shouting and deflated in shock in front of him. 'We're too young,' JJ said more quietly. That was it. The answer to why he felt so bad about his situation. The enormity of it all washed over him, forcing him to sit back down on the bed and filling his eyes with tears.

Alexia's anger crumbled and she sat next to him and picked up his hand. 'You'll be fine. You will, JJ.' Anyone can see you love her.'

JJ swallowed the hard lump in his throat and nodded, but he wasn't a little kid who Alexia could placate with soft words. He was an adult. A very young one who wasn't sure of anything anymore. 'What about you?' he asked, sniffing his own emotion away and staring intensely into Alexia's eyes. 'He's been accepted and you're engaged. If this was going to happen for anyone, it should be you.' His brow furrowed as, for once, he genuinely meant what he said.

'Oh please,' Xavier said, shaking his head and pretending to gag. 'I heard he was getting the royal visit to Murrtaine tomorrow. Dad has truly lost it.'

JJ studied Xavier. He was being a complete arse to Alexia, as always, but he did have a point. Taking him to their secret city that housed their nation's power source, seemed very rash. Too rash for their father.

Alexia didn't look best pleased either. Which didn't feel right. 'What's the matter? This is huge for you?' JJ picked up her hand and gave it a squeeze.

Instead of answering, she turned her head slowly to Xavier. 'For once, I think Xavier is right.'

JJ frowned and Xavier's eyes widened as they both straightened up in shock. She looked uncomfortable. 'What I mean is, Dad doesn't do anything rash.' She looked pained and put her hand to her forehead and began rubbing it. 'I'm scared they've got something else in mind.'

JJ let out a long sigh. What she was saying made much more sense than letting a complete stranger into their sacred city. He gave her arm a squeeze and felt sorry for her. She really had grown up. Her father was no longer an infallible god and her brothers, not her partners in crime. She was not gullible and spoiled. This was real and she saw it for exactly what it was. 'They won't try anything in front of you. Just make sure you stick with Yaro the whole time,' JJ said, with a smile of encouragement.

She wasn't easily convinced. 'Oh, I will. Don't you worry. But I'm scared … really scared,' she said, eying them both, steadily.

CHAPTER 33

*A*lexia spent a troubled night tossing and turning and worrying about the trip to Murrtaine. They were due to assemble after breakfast, at the fountain at nine. She'd clock-watched since five and finally, when it was six, she got up, deciding to shower and choose what she'd wear under her regular clothes to spend the day under water. It was a long time since she'd spent any real time in Murrtaine. She took comfort that her aunt Isla would be there with all her many Murr cousins.

She hadn't seen much of Yaro last night. He'd turned in early after such a ground-breaking day. He was exhausted and this was another huge first for him.

A pain twisted in her heart. She prayed her fears were unfounded and nothing would happen today.

She was ready.

Alexia ventured out into the corridor around 7 o'clock, not able to wait a minute longer. She knew she was early, but figured her fears would be allayed a little around other people.

She came to a stop at Yaro's door in the guest corridor.

Something felt strange. Firstly, there were no staff and more importantly, no guards. They'd been hovering around Yaro the whole time he'd been there. It had irked that her father had him watched all the time.

Her heart was already thrashing when she knocked on Yaro's door. She looked left and right in the hope she'd see someone around.

It remained eerily quiet.

She put her ear to the door to hear any movement inside. There was nothing. Not even a radio. She slowly turned the handle, holding her breath, praying that perhaps Yaro was still asleep.

She cracked it a little. 'Yaro?' she whispered.

Then a little further, putting her head inside. The room was in darkness. Her throat constricted and she sent up a silent prayer before she willed on the bedside lamp. She knew what she would find. Yaro's luminescence would have lit the room in the darkness. Instead, the bed was made. As her thoughts began to scatter in alarm, she remembered he was a night owl. Nocturnal and didn't sleep for long when he did sleep.

Her heart sped up in hope and she retraced her steps out of the room and in the direction of the main thoroughfare. Yaro would be sitting reading some boring Russian novel in the great hall.

As she was nearing it, her father's study came to mind like a bolt from the blue. She altered her steps and was hit with enormous relief to see a guard stationed outside. She smiled a hello and went to go right past him, to open the door.

The guard immediately swung around and gently caught her before she could burst in. 'I just want to ask my father something,' she said, her heart beating right up into her mouth.

'He's not here,' the guard answered, smiling.

Her brain completely seized for a moment and her gaze went from the guard to the door handle. 'Well, where is he then?'

'One moment,' he said, holding up a finger. He straightened up and talked into his headset. 'Control, is the king still on site?'

Her blood pulsed in her temples.

'OK, roger that.' His smile was regretful. 'You just missed him. He just left for Murrtaine.' Her eyes widened in horror as everything clicked into place.

The guard went to steady her, but she ducked under his arm and ran. She continued to run flat out, all the way to the great hall. She wasn't sure what she would do, but she had to see for herself.

Apart from a few servants milling around, arranging stuff for breakfast, it was completely empty. She ran right up to the window to see if anything was visible leaving, which was ridiculous. They would have not left being seen to chance. They'd have left really early. Plus, the sub aqua loading bay was at catacomb level, so it was very unlikely she'd see anything anyway.

Her mind went into freefall. Tears fell involuntarily, flooding her cheeks. She let out a long, ear-piercing scream. She must get there somehow. Wake her brothers. Anything. She turned abruptly and stepped right into the hard chest of her second dad, Jay.

In her deranged state, it took her a moment to realise who it was. She didn't know why she was surprised. Without her father, of course he'd be there. On damage limitation duty. He wasn't a water breather. The king would have asked him to oversee things while he was away. And when he said, things, he meant the kids. More precisely, her. There were others who could manage matters of state. She was suddenly furious with him. He would have known all about this. Her two fathers were in on everything together. 'Get out of my way, Jay.' She screamed his name, rather than Dad to deliberately hurt him.

He blanched a little as he caught her by the arms. She felt instantly guilty. 'Not calling me Dad today?' he said, with his small smile playing on his lips.

It ramped up her anger and she scowled her darkest look. 'Let me go, Dad. I need to get Xavier and JJ.'

He hadn't let go of her arms as he shook his head regretfully. 'That's not going to happen, Alexia. You need to let your father do his work today.'

She burst into tears and attempted to struggle out of his arms. But he simply pulled her into his body for a hug. 'Come on. Have some breakfast and we'll have a talk.'

She dropped to the floor screaming. Not caring that she was resorting to a complete tantrum. 'Let me go, Jay. Let me go. I hate you all. They're going to do something to him. LET ME GO!' she screamed, punching and kicking.

Continuing her meltdown, she felt herself lifted. Legs and arms still flailing, she was hauled across a shoulder, knocking the air out of her.

Jay was talking. Issuing orders. People were running around him and she continued to fight. Everything was out of control. Nothing was fair. She hated everything. Until finally, the energy just got used up in her.

When she went limp, Jay put her down gently onto her own bed. JJ was there, followed swiftly by Xavier. She groaned and went to turn away as Jay sat on the end of the bed. 'I don't care about whatever it is you're going to say.'

Jay pointed at the jug of water by the bed and JJ quickly poured it and passed it to him. 'What's happened?' JJ asked.

'They've taken him and they're going to hurt him,' Alexia said, leaning up on her elbows, her voice now just a croak. Her anger and hysteria rose just as ferociously as before. 'We should never have come here,' she said, directing all her venom at Jay.

Jay sighed and looked at her sadly. 'Shh. Calm down and drink this,' he said, passing her the glass of water.

She snatched it and guzzled it down. Her throat was far too sore to ignore it.

'What's happened?' Xavier prompted again.

She threw him a dark look, not knowing why he was even there. But as she had the spiteful thought, she knew it was none of their faults and they would have just sensed her distress.

'Your father has taken Yaro to Murrtaine for a meeting with Vionne and the Borge. It's no big deal,' Jay explained.

'Well, if it's no big deal, then why didn't they want me there?' She flashed her eyes at JJ, knowing he was thinking the same thing.

'Finally,' Xavier said on an exhale. 'At least Dad isn't taking any chances.'

Alexia threw her glass and the remainder of its contents at Xavier. 'Get out!' she screamed.

Xavier twisted his body so it bounced off his arm and looked outraged, as if it was totally uncalled for.

'Not helping, Xav,' JJ sighed, while Xavier brushed the water droplets off his fine knit sleeve.

'Bloody idiot,' Xavier said, glaring at Alexia. 'I am still your brother you know.' He seemed genuinely hurt by her reaction, which was laughable. He switched his glare to Jay. 'Just because I'm not pandering to her doesn't mean I don't care.' Then he scowled back at her and pointed. 'You've got to grow up and realise the world doesn't revolve around you.'

Jay attempted to steer him away, but he shook him off.

'Dad has to think about a whole nation, not just you.' He tutted, gave Jay a last glare and stomped off and slammed the door as he left.

Alexia couldn't believe Xavier could be so mean and burst into tears. She was soon pulled into Jay's chest as he sat back down next to her. She revelled in the softness of his shirt and the warm familiar smell.

'What are they planning to do in Murrtaine?' she heard JJ ask, while her nose was still buried in Jay's arms. She pulled apart to listen properly to Jay's reply.

He gave her an uneasy glance, but she knew he had to give them something. 'Nothing … just talks, I think. And to see how he behaves in the water.'

JJ was studying his father strangely as if he was sifting between the lines. She didn't like the sound of it either. 'What do you mean, how he behaves in the water?'

Jay shrugged a little. 'Nothing untoward, I don't think. Have you ever seen him swim?'

Alexia frowned, not fully understanding. She thought back over the whole time she'd known Yaro. 'No, but I don't get—'

'But you've seen he has extraordinary abilities on land?' Jay continued.

She still didn't get it. 'Well, yes, but – ' She looked at JJ for help.

He shifted uncomfortably.

'What? What is it, JJ? Can someone please tell me straight?'

'They need to know what he can do under the water.'

She widened her eyes at Jay in horror. 'They can't do that.' She went to scramble off the bed, but Jay grabbed her to stop her. 'They aren't going to hurt him,' Jay said, pulling her back.

'He's not some lab rat, Jay,' she said, sobbing all over again.

Jay gave her a little shake to get her to look at him. He had that no-nonsense look she knew so well. The one where there was no getting around him. 'Your father just needs to find out what Yaro wants. He's a powerful man in the human world. He could be in this one. And your father can't find any of that out if you're there. That's all it's about. That's all that's happening.'

She wanted to rail at Jay and push him away. Shout how unfair all this was. That Yaro just wanted his family to be accepted and included in the Atlantean world, but when she took in Jay's serious, unbending expression, she knew it would be useless. Her father would have discussed all this with Jay first and he would have agreed. They were infuriatingly close on most things. He would have taken the water-breathing princes with him and that was the only reason Jay was still there. He was assigned kid duty. All she could do was wait and see what the results of their stupid tests were.

CHAPTER 34

*Y*aro knew there was something wrong the moment he received the knock at 05:30 a.m. and a deep voice, 'Be ready at 6,' came through the door.

It wasn't as if he'd slept much, anyway, he'd been too wired. He rarely slept till early morning. He'd gone over and over the events of the previous day and knew it had gone too well. Something was coming.

To be invited to their hidden city after just one day was more than he could have dreamed. Too good to be true. Fairy tales did not happen for him. Only nightmares. It was the story of his family since they'd set out from Atlas all those millennia ago.

As he meticulously dressed, he knew the early hour was because of Alexia. She would be left behind and he was glad she would not witness what was to come. Her father was a shrewd ruler and would not simply let a stranger in their midst. Tests were certain to come. So in his heart he was glad. If he needed to fight, then he wanted her as far away from it as possible. Because he fully intended to marry her, whatever the outcome of today.

The dark-blue/green mottled robe covered his pale, blue-veined chest and the loose, matching pants hung low over his lean hips and legs. He had not chosen what they had laid out for him, opting for his own design handed down through generations of Ambragio that moved perfectly in the water – particularly at the speeds they travelled.

He knelt on the floor and breathed to centre himself. Whatever happened, he must bide his time and let them do their tests. If he lost his head, he could lose any headway that he'd made. He was convinced this was a result of Vionne's fear in holding his little part of the kingdom. He would do exactly the same thing if someone dangerous challenged him. However, he had no such designs. Not unless he was provoked.

He opened the door and two Santalini guards were waiting for him. He could tell by their auras that they were every bit as threatened as the Borge prince, Vionne. He bowed his head slightly and fell in formation with them down to the great hall.

The rest of the delegation were finishing up breakfast as they neared. Dante, the Florianna prince, Cesaré, the Santalini, Keenan and four Borge lieutenants appeared to make up the party.

Yaro recognised Alexia's other father, Jay. He remained at the table with Alfonzo and Sebastian Bonaci, Alexia's great-uncle and grandfather. The obvious stand-ins for the king when he was away. Vionne appeared to be absent. He would be forming the welcoming committee, of course.

Yaro's sonar senses were mapping the auras and mental signatures of the room furiously. He was impressed and a little amused at the effort they were making for him.

Dante got to his feet and stood directly in front of him.

He was a dull outline compared to the Ambragio, with an aura pulsing indigo and violet. A slightly elevated mood, but a strength and level of honesty he admired. It relaxed his senses slightly. 'Do you need anything before we leave?' Dante asked.

Referring to sustenance, he guessed, Yaro shook his head.

'You understand that I can't allow Alexia to accompany us today?'

He inclined his head. 'I think it would be wise under the circumstances.'

Dante absorbed his answer for a moment. 'You also understand that you will be submerged for many hours at a great depth. Are you OK with that?'

Yaro recognised it as the first test: whether he was confident in what lay ahead. He smiled inwardly as it was clever. While he wasn't about to spill family secrets immediately, to say yes would reveal a certain amount of experience, which he was forced to do. He smiled and nodded respectfully. 'I have confidence in my breeding.'

The king studied him a moment, absorbing his clever come back. Then he turned to those already on their feet, waiting. 'Come … I want to be away from here before my daughter wakes.'

Yaro removed his robe and left it on a chair next to the fountain. Then he followed the others over the wall, inching slowly to the centre in the shallows, where the water went dark and dropped away into the tunnel out of the palace. 'Get ready for the drop,' the king said when he was almost there.

Yaro's heart was already bashing the insides of his ribs. His whole clan had kept up their swimming abilities from birth, but his business dealings had kept him on land for most of the last hundred years and he couldn't remember the last time he went down to any real depth.

The king was watching his face closely. 'Ready?'

Yaro gave him a single nod and the king stepped back and dropped into the tunnel. He looked behind him and Keenan gave him a full-fanged smile to let him know there was no going back. He smiled sweetly back with just a hint of what was in his own mouth. He had machismo to prove today, but not while he was on land.

He copied the king. While he kept eye contact with Keenan, he took a single step backwards and dropped into the cool water that quickly engulfed and swallowed him. Drawing him down in its depth and surrounding him in bubbles.

His eyes began to clear immediately and his heart settled to its ultra-slow rhythm as the delicious salt-water entered his lungs. Every nerve ending tingled and came alive. He'd forgotten how exhilarating sea water was. He curled his body around and began to swim downwards. His heavy bone density allowing him to drop effectively with very little effort. Yaro followed the jagged rock tunnel as the gradient made a slow turn ninety degrees and swam towards the light in long, graceful strokes.

Just before the end, Dante was waiting and grabbed his wrist to stop him. *The craft is about twenty feet away,* he projected straight to his head.

He was still treating him as a blind man, which he allowed for the time being. He could already make out the small marine craft hovering a little way off.

They came out of the tunnel and the water was cool velvet, wrapping around his skin. He let out a contented moan at the feel of it. His skin temperature was so hard to regulate out of the water. In this part of the world it was a warm bath, particularly on Ambragio skin, whose body temperature was rumoured to run even colder than the Borge. He wished he could spend time to simply enjoy the feeling. To welcome that instinctual part of him he always had to hide. Now, there was no hiding it as soon as he exited the tunnel.

The sunlight that would have burned his skin on land, warmed him and every cell glowed in comfort. Instead of the stripes of the royal families, his took on a phosphorescent glow. His fear inspiring eyes cleared of blood to take on the colour of clear water and he was beginning to see with precision, as well as any other predator in the ocean.

It was another test. The whole party had waited to take a look at him.

Your skin ... magnificent. The king projected. And he really did seem in awe of it.

Yaro continued to swim and didn't explain himself. The king's clever mind was already whirring over the benefits of producing your own light at great depths and this was what the whole trip was about. Studying his differences and how much of a threat he was to have around them.

He didn't want to scare them. Not yet.

CHAPTER 35

*L*atitia barely slept. The clock now said 04:30 a.m.,
next to the soft glow of the lamp and JJ slept peacefully next to her. Only half an hour had passed
since she'd last checked. She felt hot. Her skin prickled and
her brain buzzed with everything that had happened in the
last twenty-four hours.

It was no good. She was forced to lean up on an elbow
and simply study him. His messy bed head was to the side on
the pillow, his perfect face smooth and relaxed, with his arm
resting above it to accommodate her lying next to him. His
heavily tattooed chest was bare, and the cool sheet was just
about covering his lower half. He looked breathtakingly
beautiful, like a magazine shoot.

She wondered for the hundredth time why they still
hadn't had sex. They were there, already bonded, semi-naked
in the same bed and he'd simply gone to sleep. She'd heard
what he'd shouted at Xavier and Alexia: *nothing should be
permanent at our age.* She hadn't intended to eavesdrop, but
he'd shouted it and she hadn't switched on the shower yet. It

wasn't her fault she'd been sucked into their whole conversation after.

She felt a little guilty that she hadn't let on and acted like nothing happened when she came out. Maybe she would have come clean had JJ not suggested they went straight to sleep. He'd still seemed preoccupied and it had been a hell of a day, so she'd gone along with it without saying anything. But she knew he was being cagey and hiding the turmoil he was clearly feeling. She wondered if he'd read and ignored something in her.

She didn't think so. Or he didn't care, because he'd got straight into bed and after falling asleep quickly, he'd turned and faced the other way. It was a cold shock that had really hurt and was what had kept her awake all night.

She hated that despite all that, she wanted to trace the line of his jaw. But she also didn't want to wake him. *Why was he such a contradiction? Why act like he couldn't resist her, bind her to him, then leave her emotionally alone like this? But wasn't this how he'd been from the start? Reeling her in with his overwhelming strength of attraction, then nudging her away and closing off. Using a lull to keep her waiting, aching, for the slightest bit of interest from him. He was reducing her to mush. Slowly but surely, he was draining her away like some energy-sucking vampire. And he would continue to do it until there was nothing of her left.* But she wouldn't allow it.

That was it. She got out of the bed, making him moan and turn into the warm, empty space she'd just left. 'Go back to sleep,' she whispered. 'Just going back to my old room for something I forgot.' His eyes opened for a second and closed again without saying anything. She dressed quickly and slipped out of the room.

. . .

THE MARINE CRAFT was outside of the docking area, hovering about three feet from the sandy seabed. The technology was beyond human imagination and of course, Yaro had never seen anything else. He swam with the others towards it and watched as Dante and then Cesaré dove underneath and disappeared up inside. He couldn't resist running a hand on the seemingly transparent surface. It rippled at his touch like Jelly, and he discovered that it wasn't see through at all, it simply reflected back. The only thing visible were small lights, running consecutively along it's sides like some deep-sea organism.

He looked over his shoulder in wonder only to see a wall of four Borge behind him. The threat was real. There was no going back now. They had no idea that he'd committed to this a very long time ago.

Go in the way of the others, one projected, pointing.

Yaro turned and dipped, seeing the hatch immediately, like the neck of a transparent balloon. He paused for a moment, then launched himself up into it. It felt like pulling a jelly sweater over his head.

Inside, he was disorientated for a moment. Several pairs of hands pulled him up. He swayed where his legs felt heavy. Then he understood. There was no air in the craft. Only a purified kind of water. The salt had gone and it felt silky around his skin.

OK? The king projected after a moment.

Yaro nodded and was immediately captivated by the completely transparent walls. Apart from a green hue, he could see everything outside. Then he took in the party around him. The four Borge had followed him inside and everyone had now transformed. Each one in varying degrees of Atlantean. The land dwellers were striped in grey but their markings distinctive to their individual families, but the ones that stuck out the most, were over a foot taller than on land.

The Borge had heavy black banding over every inch of their bodies, empty black eyes and their lower legs had grown, explaining the extra height. He couldn't help staring. They really were an underwater creature of fables. Murrs. Mermen.

The lights lowered and the craft smoothly moved off. The Murrs had not taken their eyes from him, either. It had been a very long time since he'd been this long under water. His family usually gathered somewhere in secret once a year, just to keep their abilities. Somewhere around the Mediterranean or Adriatic. But it had become like a holiday and was nothing as taxing as this.

Yaro knew what they were taking in. He had no stripes. His skin glistened and glowed and his aura became brighter, the deeper they went. Their minds were churning, working out that he was just like the creatures of the deep. The Ambragio were perfectly made for it.

It was Dante who seemed the most relaxed of them all. *I guess there was no need for camouflage for your ancestors,* Dante projected.

Yaro inclined his head, appreciating the intelligent deduction. *We had very few predators in the deep, and so we generated our own light.*

Appearing only in the darkness, Dante said, no doubt remembering the way he kept covered on land. He'd worked out that it wasn't just protection from the sun or to keep warm, but so that the humans didn't see his luminescence at night.

Dante came closer so they were almost nose to nose. Except Yaro had the advantage of a few inches taller. Those around them stiffened in readiness, but Yaro looked intently into his eyes, understanding right away that it was not an act of aggression. He was studying any changes in his face. *Your eyes are clear now, too. I guess you can see,* the king stated.

Perfectly, Yaro answered, also taking in the tribal markings that singled the king out as Dubonnetti. He recognised the analytical, scientist's mind. The curiosity, not trying to feed from any pre-conceived ideas.

The king stepped off just as quickly and everyone relaxed and took their seats. Yaro, right across a table from the king. He was surprised he wasn't blindfolded to protect their precious location. Unless they didn't expect him to return. He banked that thought.

Of course, any such precautions were useless as he had deep-sea senses for the dark, rather like sonar. He had already mapped where the land mass was behind him and that there was nothing immediately ahead, so they were taking him on a scenic route. They were unaware that he had an inbuilt sense of north, so it was virtually impossible for him to get lost. He inwardly chuckled at the meandering path they were taking. They were just around ten nautical miles from where they set off.

In the meantime, he contented himself with taking in the magnificence of the ocean, through the walls of the technological marvel they were travelling in. The water was clear and the swarms of fish became less and less as they hugged the sea bed.

Several minutes passed, until Dante tapped his shoulder and pointed.

At first, he couldn't see what he meant.

Then suddenly, he sensed a huge mass.

Then the huge dome, like an upturned glass bowl loomed ahead of them. He couldn't see through it as it reflected the blue/green of the sea.

The sheer size of it paralysed his gills and he swallowed down much stronger emotion than he anticipated. The grandeur, the technological know-how, and of course, that he was part of a people capable of building this. It was humbling because it was a step back in time. A glimpse of a home planet not seen for ten thousand years. His throat constricted and he felt deeply moved.

Dante hadn't missed a thing and squeezed his shoulder to steady him. Yaro looked into his sympathetic face, surprised for a moment at the king's genuine concern. He simply gave him a smile of encouragement. *Wait till you get inside,* the king said.

Yaro returned his gaze to the sight in wonder. The huge dome was almost upon them. He was captivated by its size and how it would allow them in.

They were there. Then the view became cloudy. Yaro's heart quickened a little in fear. Then they sped up as they were smoothly sucked inside as if absorbed by a bubble.

He blinked as his heart rate returned to normal and then everything came into view.

Blue and green glass was everywhere in every direction. The buildings were made from it. Gently curved architecture capped with soft domes like little hats. Reeds making fences and sea flowers made hanging gardens of all the eaves. Striped Murrs in their shimmering clothes were all over the place, going about their business. Some walking, some travelling around on small conveyances. There was something so cosy and normal about it and yet they were a people perfectly separate and untouched by humans. He couldn't remember the last time in his long life he was moved to tears. But he was then. Emotion simply overrode him and he couldn't help himself.

He felt the king's hand on his back, but he couldn't look at him. This was a snapshot of his home planet he'd envisaged only from the books he'd managed to collect. This was alive, living and vibrant.

Amazing, isn't it? the king said, now right next to him.

He hadn't realised he'd risen from his seat. His hands

were pushed to the jelly-like walls of the craft like a child at the aquarium. *It's the most stunning spectacle I've ever witnessed in my life,* he said more to himself.

Come ... we are docking soon, Dante said, patting his shoulder.

Yaro waited as the lieutenants and the king went through the hatch in the floor and he followed. He felt the Florianna and Santalini princes right behind him. When he came out from underneath the craft it was to see crowds of Murr people. Ashaya, Vionne and three males that had to be his brothers were waiting to greet them. The people immediately began to produce a strange clicking noise that reminded him of dolphins.

They are welcoming us, rather like clapping, Dante explained, whilst giving them a wave. The clicking increased in volume as if it had pleased them to be waved at by their king. It revealed how well thought of Dante was, even in Vionne's domain. *You are quite the celebrity,* Dante said, grinning, putting his hand around his shoulder.

Yaro recognised it right away as PR. Showing the masses he was nothing to fear. They were all here to marvel at the weird stranger, with clear eyes and bare skin emitting light. *Wave,* Dante prompted with a nudge.

Yaro, completely unused to being so conspicuous, put up a cautious hand. It delighted the crowd and the clicking went up like a roar.

A small boy rode right up to him on one of their small craft and looked up into his face. *Are you an angel from the caves?* The boy asked.

Yaro looked at Vionne startled, unsure what to say. The boy must have him confused with someone else.

Stories about your family have been told to the children for millennia.

It was hard to compute. He had to remember that Murrs

showed no expressions. Despite his calm words of explanation, animosity was pulsing off him in waves. And yet, what he said amazed and warmed him. It meant they hadn't been cut off from memory here. They'd just moved from reality to legend. Which he had to admit, was a whole lot better than on the surface, where they'd been relegated to the subject of nightmares. *Thank you for allowing me the honour of visiting your city.* Yaro bowed low, feeling genuinely grateful.

As he straightened, he saw clearly that Vionne was mapping his differences and noting the ease in which he moved in the water. The princes and even the king were still a little awkward, having to steady themselves to remain upright. His dense bones made standing easy. He saw the cogs working in Vionne's mind, that he was every bit as at home there and he was. Yaro shifted uneasily, knowing that was not the desired outcome of the visit.

Yaro did not miss the platoon of guards nearby that multiplied and joined the party the nearer the palace they got. Word spread and the growing crowd seemed to love the spectacle. But Yaro recognised it for what it was; precautions for the threat amongst them. He felt philosophical about the whole thing, deciding to shelve his disappointment for the time being. After all, he understood. He was a leader of a people, too.

Instead, he threw himself into the marvels of the palace he was approaching. The great domes and manicured sea gardens. The synchronised soldiers, swimming in formation, parting as he neared it.

Then after passing through a curious vault, the huge atrium rose up into infinity above him and he felt the curious feeling he was walking in air. However, he quickly recognised it wasn't air at all, but a strange, ironised water that somehow gave that impression. He inwardly smiled. He was already strong in the water, but with the drag taken away by their technology, he knew he was supremely powerful. Like the character, superman, he guessed. It was a real revelation and his eyes went straight to Vionne's, who'd guessed the same thing. His aura pulsed red with his simmering anger.

Dante saw the exchange and looked nervous too. It lightened his heart to see these pampered beings uncomfortable for a change.

They ventured deeper into the palace, through egg shaped corridors, as warren-like as the Filfla tunnels. Except these were smooth. All soft, sweeping curves like everything else in this place. Even the light panels were embedded in the walls so as not to ruin the aesthetics.

They eventually came to a stop and a waterfall appeared in front of them at a wave of Vionne's hand. Then he simply stepped through and disappeared. The solid seeming wall had morphed into liquid. Nothing was as he expected.

Dante held out an arm for him to do the same.

He paused for a moment, unsure. Then he bowed his head and slowly moved through the portal. It was very disorientating as he stepped out into another space and yet he was still under water. It took him a moment to acclimatise.

He felt the others coming in around him as he looked around at the room. It was a curious pale green conical shape that went way up to a point. The only furniture appeared to be a white pedestal right in the middle of the floor.

Everyone spread out and stood in a circle around the edge and Vionne made the waterfall portal disappear with a flick of his hand. Then he swept his arm to his forehead and bowed low. *Our lady Orb,* he said, and everyone copied him.

Yaro copied everyone else but kept his eye on Vionne and the pedestal everyone appeared to be focussing on. One word registered more than the others: *Orb.* As everyone else kept their eyes down, his heart raced and he looked around him. *Could it possibly be?* Just as he decided it was a prayer space, like a human church, green and red lights pulsed around the conical shell above him as if it was calculating or preparing for something. A loud buzz sounded and a shaft of light shot upwards from the pedestal to the centre of the ceiling. Then a hologram of a beautiful, white robed woman appeared in its beam, resembling a Greek goddess. Her skin was alabaster white, her eyes deepest blue and her lips rosebud pink.

She smiled and beckoned him with her hand. 'Come closer, son of Osman the 3rd, Ivan the 11th and Gregorian the 16th. Leader of all Ambragio. Yaro swallowed at her knowledge of the last three generations of his family, spanning a thousand years. His gut twisted as, to his knowledge, it had never been written in the tomes, and it was clear who the image must be, addressing him directly. He took a step closer and bowed his head. *Mighty Orb, I am humbled in your presence. Never in my wildest imaginings did I expect to meet you.*

He felt something tingling his feet and saw a circle of red light making its way up his body, while a blue one descended, scanning him for what? He could only guess.

'I can confirm the pure bloodline of Demidov. Family head of the Ambragio, elite guards of Atlas.'

The buzzing stopped and he felt the discord of those assembled around him. It wasn't the answer they wanted. He didn't care. His heart soared. Nothing could have spoken louder, with a more resounding endorsement of who he was, than from the Orb herself and they knew it. They feared him even more than before and he was glad, knowing he was vindicated today.

Vionne stepped forward and Yaro was forced to take his eyes from the miracle in front of him to look directly at him. *Permission to speak, all powerful highness.*

'Speak Lord Advocate of Murrtaine.'

I would ask the Ambragio prince what his true intentions are with regards the Atlantean and Borge peoples. What does he seek to accomplish for his own?

Yaro remained still, hoping that perhaps this was the test they had prepared for him today. After all, fear and ignorance were to be expected after his people had suffered over the millennia.

'How do you answer, leader of Ambragio, Yaro Demidov?'

Vionne's anger vibrated through the usually invisible water around them, without him needing to see his aura.

I seek only to be recognised as an equal and treated as such. As a pure race, with every right to be at court and in this great city.

Again, he felt the tingle of the Orb's scan. It was becoming more and more clear that this was why he was brought there. To be a subject for a living lie detector for all their questions. The real question would be if they could accept his answers, true or otherwise.

'The Demidov speaks honourably,' the Orb answered, making it very difficult for him not to grin in Vionne's face.

'Dante Dubonnetti. You have something to ask?' the Orb said.

He stepped forward next to Vionne, who seemed far from relaxed. *Was your interest in my daughter contrived to get close to me and where you stand today?*

Yaro admired that he thought of his daughter first, but his burning question was not asked, so he answered it for them anyway. *I am not here to take your kingdom. Either of you,* he said, switching his gaze to Vionne next to him.

'Answer the king's question,' the Orb prompted.

Yaro knew the Orb had a far deeper reason for wanting the answer to that. So he took a moment to phrase his words, then he turned to face Dante squarely. *I did not seek your daughter out. She came into my world. And I freely admit I knew exactly who she was. I was intrigued by her as a link to my lost world. I had long ago lost any will to take a mate, but she is very strong willed and persistent,* he said with a wry smile, knowing Dante knew his own daughter well. *So in short, I began to love all that was about her. The fact that she was daughter of a king seemed apt. As if the fates had come full circle and decided to repay me.*

He ignored the grumbles and gasps and watched Dante closely while he sifted through what he'd said. Then Dante fixed him with narrowed, shrewd eyes. *And yet you planted listening devices in my son's loft. Even in their human girlfriends' homes,* Dante projected. *Are you saying that is for my daughter's benefit?*

Yaro was not expecting that turn of questioning and became mildly perplexed, but he conceded that it was plausible from a character of his reputation. So he kept his tone soft and even out of respect for a king and future father-in-law. He would have much preferred that Dante had broached this earlier while they were alone. *I have no need to plant listening devices. Should I need to learn of your childrens' plans, you carry listening devices around with you all the time.*

It took only a moment for Dante to fall in with what he meant. *Phones,* he said, straightening with the realisation. *But we have guys who detect stuff like that.*

Yaro gave him his full-fanged smile. *As do I.* He finished bowing his head, slightly, closing the line of questioning adeptly.

The room grumbled.

Dante seemed sobered.

For a king's daughter, test him by divining ring, Cesaré Florianna called out, cutting through the escalating dissension. Yaro turned back to the Orb in exasperation. He did not possess a divining ring, seeing little point. Today was clear proof of that.

'Silence!' the Orb said. 'I am judge and my ruling is final. I find this prince acceptable as a mate for the Dubonnetti princess, who comes of age soon. I rule the petition honest and will indeed repay damages from the fates. Welcome, Prince Demidov, leader of Ambragio. Then she simply disappeared with the beam of light and the room seemed dull without her.

Yaro looked up to the Ether in thanks, not sure if the Orb was a god or not. Whether she dwelt in the heavens or below his feet. His heart felt ripped open. Exposed. But it was from sheer joy. Joy at finally being accepted. The day could not have gone any better.

But those around him were not happy. Not happy at all.

CHAPTER 36

*L*atitia had left JJ's room on a whim and now she was in the corridors, she realised it was still the middle of the night. Her old room was her best bet. She would sneak in and try not to wake up Paige, but she needed somewhere to think and maybe get some moral support or perspective on how she was feeling.

She followed the purple lights to the end of the royal corridor and was just about to join the main thoroughfare, when Tia, JJ's mother rounded the corner, coming the other way. 'Sorry,' they both said at the same time.

She immediately flushed, knowing it was a weird time to be out, when Tia answered before her. 'Sorry, I was in my own world after trying to talk sense into my husband.'

Latitia put up both hands. 'Couldn't sleep,' she said, simply.

JJ's mother smiled sympathetically. She was so beautiful. Effortless, even with her hair in a simple ponytail and no make-up.

Then her arms were around her neck and she crushed her in a tight hug. 'I know, sweetheart. It's all so overwhelming.

Forgive me. We haven't had a proper chat with everything else going on with Alexia.'

Latitia stood stiffly and listened, until Tia finally pulled apart, still holding the tops of her arms. All she could reply was, 'Mmm,' nodding and smiling like an idiot.

'Come with me,' Tia said, linking her arm through hers. 'Let's go get some coffee and have a chat at mine. It will be quiet there. Dante will be busy for ages.'

So Latitia allowed her to turn and lead her back the way she came. Past JJ's door and along the corridor, to the huge double oak doors at the end of the royal apartments.

Inside was huge, but as amazing and tasteful as the rest of the place. A window curved around like a huge aquarium; surprising, as it was the only one she'd seen outside of the great hall. The room was open plan, dotted with the familiar shiny oak furniture all the rooms seemed to have. There were oil paintings the size of cars, beautiful curtains and soft furnishings in pastel shades, making the place feel like an underwater castle of yellow sandstone. She stood, amazed and soaked it all in.

Tia was already talking into a phone, ordering coffee. Then she walked over to a cluster of beautiful, embroidered silk chairs next to the sea-window. 'Coffee won't be long. Have a seat,' Tia said, pointing, while she flopped into one with a huff.

Latitia walked over more slowly, gazing at the huge four-poster bed, hung with matching curtains in soft peach and beige. 'Wow,' came out, before she could stop herself. A real king and queen's bed.

Tia was smiling when she finally sat and tore her eyes away to look at her. 'Come in,' Tia called, before anyone knocked.

Latitia remained silent, while the young maid pushed in a trolley and left it next to them with a small curtsey.

'Thank you, Gabriella.' Tia poured the coffee and offered her a croissant from the pile. Latitia took one, breathing in the real coffee and freshly baked pastries that looked and smelled wonderful. She hadn't realised how hungry she was.

Tia picked up her coffee and sat back with it. 'So... new daughter...how do you feel? A bit strange...disorientated, I bet.'

Latitia chewed a huge mouthful of croissant and took a gulp of her coffee at the understatement of the century. 'Kind of,' she said, with a forced smile.

'I wanted to thank you,' Tia said.

Latitia couldn't help the frown of surprise that appeared immediately. Everyone else seemed to think they had ruined their lives.

'Not what you were expecting from me, eh? Guess not. But they don't know JJ like we do. Not even JJ knows JJ. What's good for him, anyway,' she finished, shaking her head, wistfully.

Latitia remembered what an enigma Tia had been to her. The stunning mother she had met on that fateful night in London, when JJ had taken her memory of the real him away. She'd been in awe of her then. And now, instead of warning her off, she was talking as though they were allies, as the closest people to him. 'He's not happy,' she found herself saying, before she could stop herself. 'I think if he could turn back the clock, he would.' She looked down and picked at her fingers in her lap.

'Nonsense,' Tia said, putting her coffee cup down in its saucer, loudly. 'You think the breath comes for anyone? I can tell you that it does not. It might not be aligned with what you're thinking or feeling at that moment, but it does align with someone who matches you perfectly, on a far deeper level.' She snatched a croissant from the pile and bit off an angry bite.

Tia's obvious anger about it fascinated her and warmed her insides. It was so much more than she could have ever hoped for. But she was studying her again. She pointed at her with the hand holding her croissant. 'But he's not the only one with cold feet, so spill!' Tia said, taking another bite, leaning forward and reaching for her coffee.

Latitia was taken aback by her direct and accurate read on her. She had to remember that JJ's family probably had similar powers and could sense far more than humans. Or she could see right through her, like her own mother could.

'Look, you can be honest with me. Like it or not, we're family now and you can't get rid of us even if you wanted to,' she said, laughter bubbling into her words.

Latitia couldn't help smiling along with her. She was so damn likeable, but she felt disloyal if she said what had really been running through her mind.

'JJ's not easy. I know that. He never has been. His start was hard and he's had a lot to deal with in his life,' Tia said, her expression conveying real heartfelt emotion. 'You can't get out of this, Latitia. Ever. But I promise, I will help you in any way I can.'

Every word felt like a punch. No one had been this straight with her, or as real, and she needed that. All her mother's threats of taking her away were pointless. She understood that part, but what she couldn't get her head around was where that left her as a person. As an individual. 'I had hopes and dreams, you know, before JJ came. I was going to be a dancer.' She half laughed and played with her fingers again. 'Silly, now… Just a dream.'

Tia was listening intensely and then she frowned. 'You can be that. We'll help you. See that you get every advantage.'

Tears filled her eyes and she looked out into the huge room as big as a movie set and it all seemed so hopeless. Pointless. 'How can I?' she said, resting bitter eyes on Tia again. 'I'm so out of control, I don't know what's me anymore. I couldn't love anyone more. He affects everything. I'm like some pathetic bird, waiting for him to throw me a crumb from his posh table. I don't want to feel like that. Do you know that I saw him once? That night at his dad's hotel. He took my memories. I was ill for weeks. Then he clicks his fingers and I'm back with him. And we're kissing. Not able to keep our hands off each other. And he knows what he did, and now I know, so I can't even escape the knowledge of how weak he made me. Even the breathing thing, I pushed him to do that. Just to see … Just to prove he's as hopelessly hooked as me.' By the time she got it all out, she was crying, tears streaming down her face. 'You asked me how I'm feeling.' She swallowed loudly while she framed her words. 'I'm physically stronger. I can hear better, see better, like I've changed. But I'm scared. All the time. I'm shrinking away, and pretty soon there'll be nothing of the old me left.' She finished with a knot in her throat and slumped back into her chair. She could make of that what she wanted. She didn't care. She was just glad that she'd finally got it out.

Tia didn't say a word. For so long, Latitia was forced to look at her and apologise. She didn't seem angry, she just studied her for a long moment. Like she was formulating her words. Until she eventually said, 'Did JJ ever talk about me and his dad?'

Latitia shook her head, relieved at the change of subject. 'Only that he, Xavier and Alexia had different dads.'

'Yeah, well, it might surprise you to learn that I know exactly how you're feeling. To feel pulled apart by love to the point where you just want it all to end.'

Latitia was shocked at the raw devastation in her eyes. It was hard to believe someone as beautiful and self-assured as Tia could ever feel like that, but it was written on her face. A queen and part of JJ's – she couldn't even form the word –

species, in her mind, let alone say it. 'What happened?' she prompted, when she seemed so lost in her own painful memories. 'You all seem so happy.'

The queen nodded and played with a loose thread on the arm of the chair. 'I am. The king is the greatest male I've ever known.' Then she looked her dead in the eye. 'But he is passionate, demanding, volatile, controlling and annoying as hell. Particularly when we were young.' She let out a heavy breath. 'What I'm trying to say is… I don't know what I'm trying to say, exactly. Look,' she said, as if she was clearing something up in her head. 'It's a very long and complicated story, but I met Jay, JJ's dad, before I met Dante. The fates had decided I would be with Dante, but it didn't stop how I felt about Jay, and he was human, like you are human, and we could only share a one-way bond. Just like you and JJ. So he knew how I felt, but I never ever knew if he loved me like I loved him, and to this day I will never know.'

It was then it started to sink in what Tia was saying.

'He has always been and will always be a deep and wonderful mystery, but I will love that man until the day I die. But I did get to understand him, finally. After much heartache, I might add,' she said with a sad smile.

'And you think it will be like that for me and JJ? What about the king?' Latitia felt desperately sad for her and couldn't imagine feeling like she did about JJ and being with someone else.

Tia frowned. 'Don't ever think I don't love Dante, because I do, desperately. They were best friends, brothers, and it tore me apart that we were trapped the way we were.'

Latitia began to understand. She was bonded to both of them. That must have been so much worse. How much of her that must have taken.

'So I completely get what it's like to feel like something's eating away at you. Loving so much that there is almost nothing of you left.'

'So what did you do?' Latitia asked, swallowing down a huge lump. If *she* couldn't work something out, what hope was there for her?

'I ran away…a lot,' she said, laughter breaking into her words. 'And was generally a pain in the arse, most of the time.'

Latitia grinned at that. She was such a cool mum. But the smile soon dropped from her face. 'But what can I do?' There didn't seem much hope in her doing anything so cool.

Tia's face hardened. 'What do you want to do? JJ would not have gone for any kind of wimp. I know London, I spent my youth close to where you live. You can't grow up there and not be tough.'

Latitia just stared at her and blinked. Overcome with admiration. She'd had no idea. She was right in everything she'd just said and had given her the biggest compliment. She'd been wallowing in self-pity for so long she'd lost sight of who she actually was. 'A dancer still, I guess.'

'You guess? Do you, or don't you?'

'Well yeah.'

'Then do it. JJ won't stop you. I won't let him. But I'm going to be honest with you, Latitia, you will only get your own life up to a point. If JJ wins his fight with Xavier, then he will eventually be king, and you will be his queen and you will have to give up your life to be with him, then.'

Latitia swallowed hard. She'd never thought about the prospect of that before. It filled her with butterflies.

'My advice to you is fight your battles early and become good at fighting, because they will always be your battles with an Atlantean male, especially JJ. He will always want to control you, it's in his DNA. It's now your job to always be his match. Do it quickly and draw your line in the sand of what you're willing to put up with. The battles will be glorious and many—especially in the early years, but do it, and he will be hopelessly yours. That's the secret, Latitia. By doing that, he will be as desperately into you as you are him.'

'And I won't disappear,' Latitia said, dreamily. She couldn't believe the queen had been so kind and understood her so completely. She burst into tears. 'Thank you,' she said, covering her face with her hands.

The queen's pulled her to her feet and soft arms wrapped around her. 'Don't cry, baby,' she said, kissing her hair. 'We have to stick together us girls.' Then she pulled apart and holding the tops of her arms, looking at her intently. 'But when you go back, you must be careful of who you trust. Trust nobody except who you've met here. Do you hear me? There are many who might try to get to us through you.'

Latitia nodded, a little scared, but feeling an over-whelming happiness with the ally she'd made in the queen.

'What about JJ? Should I say anything about this to him?'

Tia shook her head. 'No, he wouldn't understand. This is between us, OK?'

Latitia nodded again. 'So I just go back to normal at home?'

'Yes. Are you going to live with JJ?'

It felt flattering that Tia even thought that was a possibility, but she'd already sensed it was a hard no for JJ, even if her own mother allowed it. 'No.'

'Good. Keep some independence, even when JJ asks you to. I will give you my personal number and see to it that you get one of Dante's credit cards. You can call me any time, day or night, if you need anything. OK?'

'Won't Dante know then and tell JJ?' She swung from being deliriously grateful to absolutely terrified at what JJ would feel about all this going on behind his back.

'Don't worry about him. I'll smooth it over. He'll understand. The important thing is that you are happy and safe and you understand how important you are now, Latitia. Do you understand that?'

Latitia nodded, smiling, wanting to cry at the wonderful kindness she'd shown her. 'Thank you. Thank you, so much.'

Tia hugged her one last time. 'Now you'd better get along to wherever you were going. The palace will be waking up and JJ will want to know where you are.'

*Y*aro could clearly see that Dante looked troubled. Vionne and the rest of the Murrs were devoid of expression. But for he who could read auras, Vionne was pissed. Like it wasn't the answer they expected or wanted. Or more importantly, one they would respect.

For the first time, even in invisible water, he felt the water's pressure. Not from millions of gallons on top of him, but from the soft curves of the building itself, because he was convinced he would not be allowed to leave this place. If he wasn't careful, it would be his tomb.

After ducking through the fountain and a short walk along the corridor, they entered a vaulted great hall. This time, when the fountain opened for them, they were met by Vionne's wife, the enigmatic priestess, Ashaya.

He bowed over her hand with genuine pleasure to see her. She captivated him and he had to admit to a certain amount of relief that she hadn't been part of what happened before. She calmed some of the buzzing nerves beneath his skin, screaming at him to get the hell out of there, while he still could. Her aura's soft tones of the earth and sea, mesmerised and soothed him to see this out until the end. *Welcome, great prince,* she projected, pulling on the strings of his pride. *Please sit and take refreshment with us. I have something especially sourced for you.*

Intrigued, he studied her pool-like eyes until she averted them and turned and led him slowly into the room. It was huge, filled with rows of tables of striped Murrs already eating, with one long table at the opposite end, which was clearly for their party.

They all began to take their seats and Ashaya sat next to him with Dante on his other side and Vionne on hers. *I doubt you had much time before you left this morning,* Ashaya said, conveying something to a male youth waiting on their table.

Yaro inclined his head, fascinated by what she intended to give him and furiously trying to read if there was any ill intent. However, as expected, she had the strongest mental barriers he'd ever encountered and he had to give up. Her aura was soft and honest enough. *I am honoured to be a guest in your home,* he replied.

Yaro checked the other side of him. Dante was conversing with his Murr neighbour, while he was served spiced wine in a sealed flagon and helped himself to some kind of fish. He was at ease and seemed oblivious to what was about to happen. It was a relief, but he couldn't shake his unease. He hated the idea that he might have to hurt someone that Alexia loved.

His eyes travelled the length of the table to Cesaré and Keenan. They were hardly eating and keeping alert as if they were on guard. Their auras jagged and flashing as if ready for fight or flight. It was all the evidence he needed. In a place that should hold no threat, it could mean only one thing. That whatever Vionne had planned, those two were informed.

While Ashaya projected articulately about their great city

and all its many shrines to the five moons, his mind worked at lightning speed to find the most effective way out of this. He'd already mapped the room. The head count, those who could probably fight, exits, windows, weapons. And of course, apart from an excess of strong males, there were none. None that he could see, anyway. The structures were soft and formed at will by water and a matter composed of some kind of living organism. He saw it all now. No escape without knowing the commands.

His heart began to plummet. He was trapped. The plan was masterful. His eyes met Vionne's at exactly that moment. A certain glint meant he knew that he knew. He had him.

If he fought, he lost anyway, as even if he escaped, his entry into society would be irrevocably damaged. There would be injury or loss of life, the repercussions of which he could not recover from. Not in the eyes of the Murr people. For them, closed off from the human world, he would be a monster they wouldn't want around their children. Just like on land. If he wanted to safeguard that, then he would have to submit. All he could do was incline his head at the genius move he'd just pulled.

He sat dazed after that. He couldn't believe he'd been blindsided in this way. On land he was a criminal mastermind and he'd been bested by little more than a shrewd fish.

Vionne was watching him closely for his reaction. He obviously still expected him to kick off into action. He was clearly fascinated by him, not seeming to hide it like most of the Murrs. He was more expressive and didn't seem to freeze to absolute stillness when there was no reason to move. He gazed around at all the others engaged in a strange game of musical statues. Even the serving boys, who leaned over and froze sometimes for a full minute while food was taken from their trays. Only he and the Atlanteans seemed to play no part. An almost silent world of light music, like the type you heard in department store elevators, on land. What had begun as a homecoming now began to feel like a disturbing dream.

Great platters of shellfish and sea vegetables were being brought out and made a line down the centre of the tables. It reminded him of the human banquets of his youth.

Except for him. His section of the table was bare.

A single gold goblet appeared. It was sealed and came to a point like a genie's lamp.

It was brought in fresh for you this morning, Ashaya said next to him.

He searched her eyes curiously.

Never fear, it is human, she added, as if that was why he paused.

She smiled a radiant smile that seemed to spread through her honest aura. He didn't have the heart to squash the sweet gesture and tell her Ambragio never drank dead blood. When the spirit in it had gone, it had no nutrients and tasted something like sour milk. The moment it left the body it started dying. It was not only an insult to offer it to a guest, but it would undoubtedly make him sick.

He needed to think fast. He was sure she had no malintent. His eyes tracked to Vionne whose face was blank, but his aura was pulsing indigo in anticipation.

All he could do was incline his head at them both but had no intention to drink it and looked down at the goblet again.

Perhaps a little spiced water if that's not to your liking? Ashaya said. *We drink it all the time on our home planet. It is infused with essence of rose kelp. I cultivated it myself from the seeds I brought with me.*

In a single moment, the golden goblet was taken and a crystal one replaced it. This too had a spout, but he could see clearly the pale pink liquid.

Ashaya was looking at him with big honest eyes, so he

tracked his to Vionne again. They remained stern, proving he wasn't getting out of this without insulting his wife. Vionne had manoeuvred this well, as he knew he couldn't cause a scene in front of Dante, if he wanted to marry his daughter. He looked down at the goblet again and picked it up, turning and holding it up to Ashaya. *Good health to you, good lady.* Then to Vionne, *My gracious host.* Then with his heart turning somersaults, he sent up a silent prayer to Alexia and his brother, hoping they could hear it from where he was. Pavel was far away and his link with Alexia so small.

He put the crystal to his lips. *Dearest Alexia, help me. Because I am surely trapped. My family must come immediately, before it's too late. Contact Pavel. Do not delay.* Then he took a large swig of the water he knew was laced. His heart hardened and turned cold and black. And in that last moment he made a vow to the five moons, as soon as it was in his power, father or no father, king or no king, he would bind Alexia to him in every sense of the word.

He drained the glass and looked up at the ceiling and roared.

Shouting voices receded.

His eyes dimmed and the last sound was Ashaya's cry of anguish.

CHAPTER 38

*L*atitia found her way back to her old room with her head buzzing with everything JJ's mother had said to her. She loved her already and for the first time in a very long while she actually felt optimistic in a future with JJ. Excited even. She just needed to formulate a plan, or a way of being and JJ mustn't suspect.

She eventually slowed her steps and came up to the plain door in the guest corridor. She looked left and right, then turned the handle and found that it wouldn't budge. It was locked. *Damn, she whispered.* She gave it a quiet knock in case Paige was still asleep or having 'alone time' with Xavier.

'Who's there?' Paige's voice came from the other side.

'It's me, Latitia … can I come in?'

She waited, heard the rattle of the door handle and then a hefty thump that didn't sound right. 'I can't. Xavier has locked me in,' Page said, sounding on the verge of tears.

'Locked you in?' Latitia repeated, shocked.

Just then, Alexia came around the corner, her eyes red and fraught with worry. She was so preoccupied that Latitia had to call out, 'Alexia,' before she spotted her.

Latitia breathed in relief when she immediately diverted her steps and came over to her. 'What's the matter?' Alexia asked, frowning at Paige's door.

'Xavier has locked Paige in her room and we can't get her out. Do you know if there's a spare key anywhere?'

Alexia's unusually pale face clouded with anger. 'No need.' She looked at the lock with a frown and it clicked.

Latitia tried the handle and the door opened. Paige flew out and threw her arms around her neck in tears.

Alexia immediately ushered them both inside.

Paige's tears of relief meant she was still hanging onto her as they went in. Alexia brushed past and went straight over to Latitia's old bed. 'What the hell is Xavier playing at?' she said, flopping down with a huff.

'You can't treat a person like that. It's awful,' Latitia said, welcoming the distraction, brushing stray hairs out of Paige's pink, tear-stained face.

'Believe me, he can and he does. He used to do this kind of thing to me all the time.'

Paige was calming down as she listened to what Alexia was saying. Latitia pulled her with her to sit on the bed opposite and passed her the tissue box from the nightstand.

Paige plucked out some tissues. 'He's angry with me for spending time with Hunter.' She gave her nose a good blow, like a blast of anger. 'I thought he was following me in here to talk but he just tricked me and locked the door.'

'Bloody men,' Alexia said with a tut. 'I was supposed to go to Murrtaine with Yaro today and they all got up early and went without me.'

They all let out a tight-lipped sigh of solidarity and shook their heads.

'Well, I think JJ's regretting binding me to him,' Latitia said, feeling the weight of her turn to share. 'I heard him saying it to you earlier,' she said, looking sheepishly at Alexia. But the more she said it out loud, the more she was sure.

Alexia was already shaking her head. 'No, he's not … not that part anyway. It's easy to forget that he's just a teenage boy, Latitia.' She was looking at her with a regretful smile. 'They are absolute idiots at the best of times, powerful geniuses or not. I just think the responsibility of it all is sinking in.'

Latitia let out a long breath and looked around her a little exasperated. Tia understood. What Alexia was saying made sense but it went so much deeper than that. She was hurt and let down. 'Yeah, well, he's stuck with me for life now, apparently.' A hard lump came up into her throat and the fact she was getting upset just made her feel angrier.

Alexia bobbed her head. 'Well, yeah, that's true, but you also have to remember it's more than that for him. You know his childhood was much harder than ours because his father was bound to our mother and they had to separate. It caused loads of problems and heartache for us all.' She looked down at her fingers.

Latitia was waiting on her every word and comparing and adding it to what Tia had already told her. Even Paige had completely stopped crying to listen.

'There's this old prophecy, you see.' She shrugged, as if she'd dismissed something in her mind. 'I guess I can tell you now. You're like family and everything. You see Xavier and JJ do love each other and despite the constant fights and arguments, they are brothers. But there can only be one heir and the succession splits with those two.'

'What does that even mean?' Latitia asked, becoming frustrated. Tia had skated over that part, so she was thrown back to old conversations with JJ. Even then he only told her because he didn't want to be with her. He was always saying stuff like he had no future because he had to go into the family business. This was yet another new slant on it.

'They have to fight each other for it. JJ never wanted it … not really. It was Xavier that has always assumed it was his. But lately, since we came to London, it's all started to get worse. The competitiveness, I mean. And now this,' Alexia said, looking directly at her.

Her eyes went wide. 'What, me? What have I got to do with anything?'

Alexia became stern. 'He loves you, Latitia. Now he's not only got you to worry about, but your family and the school too. He would have realised that he not only has to fight, but now he has to win.'

Latitia's face flushed with heat. She was deeply shocked. She had no idea JJ was under so much pressure. Worse than that; bowing to such male-chauvinist bull-crap. It seemed so childish and unnecessary. She had an overwhelming urge to go and find him, tell him not to be silly and that she loved him. She was tough and could look after herself and her family just fine. They'd been alone for long enough before JJ came along. She was so glad she'd had that talk with Tia. It made so much difference how she looked at all this.

Thankfully, Alexia had already turned her attention to Paige and she didn't give herself away to further questioning.

'You must stick with us. Don't let Xavier push you around like this. I had to fight him all the time before I met Yaro.'

Then Alexia appeared to freeze and held her head with both hands as if she was in pain.

'What is it?' Latitia said, her heart spiking in fear. She wasn't sure if Alexia was in sudden pain, about to collapse or something.

'Yaro,' Alexia whispered. 'Oh my god, I'm coming.' She let go of her head. Her eyes were wide with panic and she was on her feet, running for the door. 'I need to get to a phone.'

She flung open the door and Latitia and Paige were soon following. They had to run to keep up with her down the corridor.

'What's wrong?' Latitia called.

'We can help you,' Paige said, running next to her.

Alexia couldn't think. All she knew was that she had to get to her father's study. It was the closest place with a landline down there. Phones with an outside line were scarce and mobiles were blocked for secrecy.

She slowed down as soon as she entered the corridor. Her breathing was shallow and her heart hammered against her ribs. No guard. Perfect. Her father was absent, so she guessed they didn't feel the need.

She went right up to the door and looked over her shoulder at the two girls still following, closely. 'Come on. I just need to use the phone.'

She was inside the room before she fully turned and stopped dead, with the girls bumping into the back of her.

She should have known.

No guard. Dad away. Jay was sitting behind the desk working. She sagged in disappointment.

'What is it?' Jay asked, immediately sensing something was wrong.

For a moment she warred with what to tell him, but she didn't have time to formulate a lie. She gathered herself to her full height and summoned her anger. 'Why did they leave me behind today? ... The real reason,' she asked, knowing he was unlikely to tell her much, but she needed the distraction and desperately tried not to give it away with her eyes.

Jay put down his pen and slipped immediately into business mode. He stood up and walked slowly around the desk to face her.

The phone was right there and for a moment she considered leaping for it, but Jay had already followed her line of vision and narrowed his eyes, quizzically. He moved in front of it to block her and force her to look right at him. 'I don't think it was decided until right at the last minute,' Jay said, in that infuriatingly reasonable tone of voice he used when he wanted to win someone over. All the while, searching her face with those earnest, amazingly blue eyes.

But it wasn't working on her today. She'd had enough and she ducked under his arm and went for the phone.

She screamed in frustration as his arm looped around her and swung her back around to face him. 'Let me go, Jay. I need the phone,' she said, struggling and starting to cry.

The other two girls shifted uncomfortably, unsure and wide-eyed with fright.

'Why do you need the phone?' Jay asked, not raising his voice at all.

'Don't act like you don't know,' she screamed in his face. 'They've done something to Yaro. He just called out to me in my head.'

'How did he?—doesn't matter,' Jay said, now not looking quite so calm. He led her closer to the desk, while he perched on the edge. 'Tell me exactly what he said?'

Alexia quickly weighed what she should tell him while he still held her arms and studied her intently. Her brain scrambled over the short message. Jay would not let her use the phone unless she gave him something and the clock was ticking. Her eyes began to fill with tears. 'They've trapped him. He asked me to bring Pavel to save him.' There. She'd said it. It was mildly gratifying to watch the shock and disbelief ripple across his face. At least it meant he didn't know everything. 'Please, Jay. I need to do something.'

He pulled a tissue from a box on the desk behind him and passed it to her. 'I'm afraid I can't let you do that.'

It was exactly what she expected him to say and sent her straight into tantrum mode. Stamping her foot and wanting to scream at him, but he threw up a sharp hand to silence her.

'What I will do is speak to one of the Murrs in the sick bay and get them to find out what's happening.' He walked purposefully back around his desk and picked up his headset, but he paused before he put it over his head. 'How does he have a link with you, Alexia?'

She sagged in frustration and for a moment she thought about lying, but she didn't have time for all this. They could be doing God knows what to him. 'Come on, Jay. I dunno. He took a tiny bit of my blood right at the beginning.' When he didn't move; 'Please, Jay!' she wailed, stamping her foot again.

He looked troubled, but it made him slip the headset on and speak into his mouth piece. 'Control? It's Jay. Can you get our Murr guy to contact Murrtaine and get Dante to contact me urgently? Yeah, thanks. Tell him that Yaro has managed to speak to Alexia … so who knows who else.'

Alexia's eyes went wide then fear and anger shot through her like a red-hot poker. 'Why did you say that? They could be torturing him down there.' She dissolved into tears of anguish and frustration. No one would help her and she was totally alone. Female arms came around her and she knew it was her friends. Their worries were forgotten as they tried to comfort her and she stared at Jay with all the hatred and betrayal she felt inside.

CHAPTER 39

JJ found Xavier lounging with a few of their cousins, after breakfast, around the fountain in the great hall. Rock and Flame were squabbling. Loki, Dannon, Ronnie and a couple of the human kids were with them. He put a hand up to Ronnie, son of one of his mother's Protectors, who must have only just arrived. A really good guy.

Xavier irritated him instantly with the grin he gave him. He knew he was going to needle him today, now he was taking this superior stance over him breathing with Latitia. The cousins were immune to it as he and Xavier had been arguing and fighting since they were small. 'Here comes the newly condemned man,' Xavier smirked.

JJ ignored it and slumped in a chair between Rock and Flame, opposite him.

Is it true you've taken a mate? Loki asked from his seat next to Xavier.

'Yeah, what's it like?' Rock said, turning in her chair to face him.

He looked stonily at Loki, flicking his eyes at Dannon,

busily playing games on a hand console, but still avidly listening. 'Why are you even here? Shouldn't you be on the big visit to Murrtaine?' JJ asked.

Loki shrugged in a very human-like way. *We were told not to come.*

Some no kids ruling. Dannon chimed in. *They wanted us away from the Ambragio while he is there.*

JJ's intense gaze shot straight to Xavier's, any rancour forgotten. 'That doesn't sound good,' Xavier said.

No it didn't. 'Did Alexia manage to go in the end?' JJ asked.

Loki shrugged again. *Don't think so ... they got up and went early.*

JJ was straight on his feet and walking briskly out of the hall. Xavier was quickly in step with him. The cousins knew even less than they did.

'What's the matter?' Rock called from behind them.

'They'll be back as soon as they've fought,' another dismissive voice said.

'What do you think is going on?' Xavier said, as soon as they marched into the tunnels.

JJ's thoughts were running wild. Mainly in fear for Alexia. This was far bigger than simply not letting her go. She would be frantic with worry and so would he in the circumstances. He fully suspected what was going on. 'I think they are doing what they couldn't do on land in front of everyone.' No kids at all, could mean only one thing: they were expecting trouble.

'No witnesses to blab to Alexia,' Xavier added, making JJ look sideways at him. Annoying, but right, Xavier's face was alight with excitement. 'They've finally taken him down. Way to go, Dad.'

JJ didn't feel so happy about it. Yes, Yaro was a danger. As king, it was probably the right thing to do. He'd just waited and seized the most opportune moment, instead of going in all guns blazing right at the beginning. *But at what cost?*

'Alexia,' JJ whispered to himself, feeling a pain in the centre of his chest for her.

But Xavier completely missed the point and let out a derisive blast of laughter. 'Yeah … as if Dad would actually allow her to marry him. Ridiculous.'

JJ wasn't sure how Xavier always managed to shock him with his selfishness, but he somehow had the flair. He wanted to smack him straight in his mouth, he was doing it so much lately. Instead, his mood hardened. 'Talking of ridiculous. Was that Paige I heard banging on the door to get out of her room earlier?'

It worked. Xavier's joy vanished and he immediately scowled. 'I can't trust her not to slope off to make 'chemistry' with Hunter,' he said with air quotes.

JJ didn't bother to answer. He didn't have the energy and they turned into the Royal corridor. His mood lifted as Latitia and Paige were coming the other way. He caught Latitia to him immediately and kissed her forehead and was a little surprised to feel her stiffen. But he couldn't examine it then. There was no time. 'Where is Alexia?' he asked, putting her away from him but keeping a hold on her hand.

'How did you get out?' Xavier asked Paige, looking irritated.

JJ was so amazed, he stopped mid-sentence to listen to Paige's answer.

'Your sister let me out,' she said with all her hurt and accusation in her eyes.

JJ felt sorry for her but didn't want to wait for the inevitable scene to come. Instead, he walked on with Latitia towards the study. 'Your dad is with her,' Latitia explained.

They walked in through the still open door and JJ said nothing. His father, Jay, was there hugging a distraught

Alexia. He let her go when she saw him and JJ took his place while she sobbed into his shoulder. 'How could he, JJ? How could he?'

JJ just answered, 'Shhh,' while he looked over her head at his father and rubbed her back. 'Everything will turn out fine.' But as he said the words, his own heart was aching because this would split them up forever. This was not one of his sister's petty dramas. Alexia would never forgive her father for this. Xavier was about to get dumped by the best thing that ever happened to him and Latitia was acting weird. There was only one thing for certain now, he would have to build even thicker walls around his emotions to do the job he had to do.

CHAPTER 40

Alexia revelled in the soft security of JJ's arms. After Yaro, it was the safest place in the world. The *only* other safe place, she thought bitterly. When she thought of her father, her heart hardened to granite.

'You go. Take Latitia and make sure Paige is OK. Your mother is coming,' she heard Jay say to him.

Alexia immediately pulled apart from JJ. Her eyes stinging with tears. 'I don't want to talk about this with Mum. She must have known.'

JJ backed away with a telepathic look from his father and reluctantly let her go. Then Jay picked up her hands. 'If she did, she didn't know any details. Only that they wanted to test him.'

'Test him,' Alexia repeated flatly, and stared into Jay's soulful eyes. 'Is that all you knew?'

He nodded, not taking his eyes from hers.

She sniffed, not sure if she believed him, just as she felt the scented breeze of her mother entering the study and closing the door.

Her mother looked stunning as always, blond lustrous

hair down and swathed in black and washed out denim. She kissed JJ, then Jay, her eyes staying a moment longer on his as if they swapped something only they understood. Then her arms came around her, bathing her in soft jasmine. 'Hey,' she said, her voice soft like warm rain, setting her tears off again. 'Please stop crying, baby … everything will be OK,' she said, stroking her hair.

'Stop it! Stop it!' Alexia shrieked, springing apart. 'I know they're hurting him because he called to me for help.'

Tia swapped a look with Jay, visibly alarmed. 'How. How did he speak to you, Alexia?' looking like everything had got a whole lot more serious.

She hated how they kept harping on about that. 'In my head,' she replied, in her best dumb voice.

Tia just tutted at her acting out. 'What did he say, exactly?'

Jay filled her in while she began to crumble.

'But he won't let me,' she screamed, trying to extricate herself from them both to get to the phone again.

Jay caught hold of her again as she attempted to sink to the floor, hating that his strong arms felt so good. She wanted to scratch and hit him, but he wouldn't allow it and she dissolved into great body-racking sobs.

Her mother was next to her whispering things to calm her like a child. Then she had to go and ask the question that made it all make sense. 'Does he have a bond with you, Alexia?'

Somehow the disappointment stopped her tears. There really didn't seem any point any longer. She dropped out of Jay's hold and took a step back from them. 'That's all you're bothered about, isn't it? Whether I breathed with him or not. Well, he didn't, OK? He's been a perfect gentleman.' The tears threatened to break through again when she thought of how tender and loving he'd been. Then her heart hardened to spite. 'I sleep in his bed every night,' she said, deliberately, hoping to injure them with every word. 'And he hasn't done anything yet.'

She should have known that Jay was impervious to her spiteful arrows. 'Then how does he speak to you like that?' Jay asked, lowering his tone, showing clearly he wasn't taking any more of her shit.

'I told you, he took a small amount of my blood, right at the beginning, for safety, so he always knew where I was.'

Jay swapped a meaningful look with her mother, then looked intensely at her again. 'Does your father know about this?'

'Of course not,' she shrugged. 'I'm not an idiot. Unless he got it from Yaro.' Her tears bubbled over at how that could be happening.

'Has anyone else taken a small sample of your blood, Alexia?' her mother asked in the same worried tone.

It was starting to get on her nerves, all the furtive looks between them and unsaid conversation. 'Of course not.' The idea she could get close to anyone else like that was ridiculous. Then she frowned, feeling suddenly uncomfortable. 'Except – ' her stomach rolled and fell away as the full memory slammed into her. 'Pavel.'

'Pavel?' both Tia and Jay repeated, flatly.

'Yaro's brother attacked and bit me just before we left. Yaro was furious with him.'

Her mother looked at Jay, horrified.

Jay didn't move, his face whitening as if he would kill someone. Then he was walking towards the door. 'I'll get a message to Dante right away.'

'Why? What's happening?' Alexia called after him, her voice cracking as panic started to rise in her. 'It's OK, I wasn't hurt.'

'What shall I do?' her mother asked as they both appeared to ignore her.

'Keep to the plan. Entertain everyone. Keep them busy,' Jay said, just before he disappeared into the corridor.

Alexia studied her mother's worried face and her heart was beating frantically. 'What is it, Mum? What's happening? I'm OK, I promise.' She wished she could take it back now and not have said anything. She hoped she hadn't made everything a whole lot worse.

Tia smiled and pushed back strands of her hair, but she knew it was just masking worry. 'It's OK, darling. It's just everything has got a whole lot more serious now.'

Alexia was confused. She wanted to rail at her for completely missing the point. No one seemed to be interested in helping Yaro. In the end her mother shook her shoulders. 'Stop this, Alexia. Don't you understand? Pavel bit you and just like Yaro, he will know where you are. That means he is coming.'

CHAPTER 41

JJ felt the weight Dante was under and it was daunting. They were all sworn to secrecy and told to carry on as if nothing had happened for the sake of everyone on Filfla. The last thing they wanted was panic. But it was becoming harder and harder to hide as more Santalini guards were flying in by helicopter all the time. The place was becoming a garrison. Fear and speculation were rife through the family and making everyone twitchy.

To make matters worse, no one actually knew where the best place for Alexia was. To send her somewhere else would make her vulnerable. To leave her there would reveal their location and endanger everyone. So Dante came to the unenviable decision for Tia to keep everyone occupied at the party while a covert team of Vionne's brothers collected Alexia and delivered her to Murrtaine. JJ guessed he hoped that with its superior technology, Pavel and the rest of the Ambragio still might not find them. Or if they did, with the Murrs guarding her, their underwater location was the strongest place to protect her. JJ couldn't remember a more serious threat since they were small kids.

It was evening and Tia started to DJ in the great hall. The lighting went down to a fairyland twinkle and the Murrs signalled they were ready from the fountain. JJ caught Alexia in a hug before she was spirited away. 'Be careful, Lexie. I don't think Father ever intended to hurt Yaro,' he said quietly before letting her go. She kissed his cheek without comment, which weighed heavy on his heart. She sloshed straight into the fountain without hesitation. Sinking beneath the water without a backwards glance. A huge hole gaped in his chest, like she'd gone for ever.

He took a ragged breath to gather himself and watched as the guards turned off the fountain and activated the steel cover that moved over it to seal the door to the sea. That had never happened in living memory. Then, as one marched past him, he heard the order go out for a complete lockdown and no more clearance for helicopters to land. 'Repeat! No more clearance to land until further notice.'

LATITIA STUDIED JJ, closely, knowing he was on edge and everything was not normal even for him. Something really big was going down, making her heart beat an irregular rhythm, ready to run. Tension dripped from the air, making her quiet and watchful for danger. Smiling for her mother, knowing her danger radar would be flashing red too.

'It's OK, don't worry.' JJ said, pulling her close and kissing her forehead. 'Hey, look,' he said, nodding towards his mother's DJ dais.

It was an obvious distraction and would have worked if she wasn't so preoccupied with so much more than Alexia's love-life. Although she did have to smile. Both her brothers were up there with JJ's mother, having the time of their lives and oblivious to everything. Dwayne was laughing with Richie and both had earphones on, helping to choose her next record. It was crowded as Rock and Flame were up there too. Everyone was noticing how much time the four of them were spending together. So adorable and simple. *If only.*

Her mind clouded just as they dropped a particularly laid-back, track, that everybody loved. 'Come on,' JJ said, attempting to pull her out of her mood and into the crowd, but he had no idea of the true extent of it. He was just worried everything was scaring her and it would spread to the rest of her family.

However, she allowed him to lead her. It was a mid-tempo song which meant they could dance together. It felt good and soothed her a little to have him close for a while. He moved well and was a natural, understated dancer. It gave her time to think about the last twenty-four hours. So much had changed. She'd changed. She still couldn't believe they were now an actual couple. A married couple, really, in the eyes of his family. She should be deliriously happy, but she wasn't. The reason, gut wrenchingly obvious – because *he* wasn't happy. And that made her feel clingy and weak. Something she had to resist and hide, just as he was trying to hide how he felt. But she knew in her bones that if he could turn back the clock and change it, he would. And that sliced her right through. No matter how she tried to reason on it and see it from his point of view, she couldn't shake the hurt or his mother's advice. It boiled down to the fact he thought so little of her. That he'd decided all on his own that she couldn't handle him. That she was weak. Forcing him to close off continually, and worse still, step up as some sort of white knight that he didn't want to be. Not only had he not had the decency to be honest about it, but it was hurtful and insulting. Especially with the depth of love she felt that was literally strangling her. She just couldn't stop thinking about it. They hadn't even had sex yet and he was acting like he'd got her pregnant and his life was over. With each thought, the pain cut deeper, making her heart heavier and sink lower, until it hit her gut like a stone. Rot was setting in and turning love to obsession and fear to panic, and she didn't know how to snap herself out of it. She loved everything about him, but the growing weight of it was crushing her. Everything. Him. All of this. She just couldn't allow it to consume her. She had to do something. She just didn't know how. Not yet. But Tia would help her. She held onto that like a drowning girl.

JJ WAS uneasy about how Latitia was reacting. She was so quiet. He cursed himself for the umpteenth time, how stupid he'd been to bring her there. Something was always going to happen to ruin things. The bond wasn't a gift it was a curse. For him, anyway. Because it could only be one-sided with Latitia. She could not return it. Which meant she would always be able to feel him and how he felt, but he would never be able to feel her in the same way. And that made him nervous. Her memories were now restored, and they'd come through the alien, different species, thing, and he'd been so happy. For a moment, he actually thought they had a chance. But now, with all that was happening with Yaro, right on top of their new bond, everything felt out of control. No wonder she was quiet. He'd been half-hearted at best. There was only one thing left to mend the rift and prove he was truly committed. To go all-in and seal the deal. The breath was ready, lying heavily on his chest, waiting. Shifting painfully as a reminder it was always there. She was probably feeling rejected, wondering why they hadn't. No wonder they'd fallen flat. It had hardly been a declaration of his love with her ending up in the infirmary.

His heart lightened with his new idea. The timing seemed perfect. Everyone was occupied. It would be easy to slip out.

Valarie was a little way off, dancing extremely closely with Reeve. He was supposed to be on duty and still wore his ear com. All the Santalinis were. JJ grabbed the opportunity and tapped Latitia's arm and pointed. 'They're definitely a couple,' JJ said, thinking it wasn't a bad thing. It certainly made their case easier.

Latitia nodded, thoughtfully, then looked up at him. 'I guess we're all-in now.'

Not quite. JJ became lost in the set of her jaw and directness of her large light brown eyes and nodded, a little shaken. Her aura was off. She was being honest, but there was something else there. A sharp edge he couldn't put his finger on. Like her straight-talking was becoming a wall between them. It was unnerving and made him study her for a long moment. She was right, though. It served no purpose to torture himself now. She and her family were in his world and there was no going back. There was no more walking away, hiding or lying. No more making excuses for who he was. When he really thought about it, it should be liberating.

He leaned down and brushed her lips with his, feeling the breath in his chest bubble and urge him on. He deepened the kiss and feeling her melt, became lost in the sense of relief it gave him. Like everything was right, and all the planets had aligned. However, it also threatened to take over in the middle of the crowd of dancing family and he was forced to pull apart, gasping. He rested his chin on her head to slow himself down and give him valuable time to think. To make sure he was doing the right thing.

Richie was now rapping over drill beats with Dwayne and he spotted Xavier arguing with Paige.

That clinched it.

'Come on. Let's get away from here.' He was already burning up as they moved through the crowds of cheering people intent on what was coming from the dais.

The welcome cooler air hit his face as soon as they walked into the tunnels. It was a blast of energy to his resolve and he sped up his steps, feeling instantly better.

They passed Keefa and Dannon coming the other way. One wolf whistled in his head and the other blasted, *You look very red, Cousin. Where might you be off to?*

JJ didn't bother with wisecrack comebacks or excuses. He simply steered Latitia past them and said over his shoulder, 'Cover for us.'

The two brothers stopped and stared at them. JJ smiled at Latitia, who despite kissing him earlier, looked blank and hard to read. The world knew what they were about to do and it was OK, because he was good with it. He wished he could shake off the feeling that maybe Latitia wasn't. Not as much as he would have liked, anyway.

They finally got into his room but it was him who was immediately slammed against the door. It took him a moment to catch up with Latitia's one-eighty. She'd completely taken him by surprise. And in the state he was in, now a slave to the breath, he wasn't about to argue. It was at that point he should have slowed things down, but she'd pressed the right buttons at exactly the right time, as if she'd known that he couldn't. He could barely breathe, or coordinate, he was so hot.

'Do you need the shower?' Latitia asked, catching her own breath and touching his hot face in concern.

He was simply relieved. Carried along with the fact that she was finally responding and not running away screaming. She was the one taking the lead. Pulling him into his own bathroom. Into the shower and moving the dial around to cold. Then, while he leaned back into the cool tile, she pulled up his t-shirt over his head and popped the button on his jeans. The sound of the water cleared the fog and brought him back to life. He didn't need help with the rest. 'Are you sure?' he asked, his voice gone to a rasp. 'I was starting to think you weren't that into it.' It surprised him how needy that sounded and just how much that scared him. He was being a sap.

She nodded, without making eye contact, and still with that same set to her jaw. This thing in her. Strength or what-ever, felt new. Different to when they'd bonded, and she didn't know what she was doing. Maybe it had always been there and he just hadn't seen it because he was too far up himself and busy in his own head. Either way, it was off-the-chart hot and he was into it. She was pulling him with her, under the spray, continuing to take the lead. Despite him almost killing her last time and never having done this before. She was fearless.

He turned up the dial slightly at her sharp intake of breath. He guessed it was then. Falling into those trusting but defiant eyes staring up at him. That very moment, that she'd won. She owned him. More than any one person on this sorry earth. Every last shattered piece of him fell into place. He closed his eyes and finally relaxed, feeling the soothing silk of the water slipping down, cooling his body, washing away the last of his barriers. His skin, already tingling. Coming alive with the very stripes that had terrified her all those months ago.

With only that as the last worrying reminder and the sound of tumbling water, he opened his eyes and was met not with her look of horror, but with one of wonder. Of unadulterated lust. There was no disguising it. She was raking her eyes all over him, taking in his whole body, including his changes. His heart stopped and time suspended, just in case it was a delayed reaction. But instead of eyes widening in fear, they softened with appreciation and she blew him away. 'Don't worry. I drank more of the medicine before the party.'

Strong, self-assured and premeditated. And he'd thought this had been his idea. He exhaled. His relief echoing around the tiled bathroom. He squeezed her to him, revelling in her beautiful smooth skin. His preconceived thoughts scattered, that she'd not only been aware this would happen, but she was completely on-board with it. He ran his hand over her slick wet back, wanting to span this feeling of complete acceptance out for ever, before he filled her with his essence in every way possible. His insecurities were obliterated. It felt perfect and he wanted to make it the same for her. It had to be. It was her first time and this was for keeps. If he was being truly honest, it was to bind her stronger to him. So she would never think of another man as long as she lived.

He dipped his head to trail a line of kisses to her mouth, but his heart stopped and he froze dead in his tracks. She gripped him by the hair and bit his lower lip hard, drawing blood.

He almost combusted it was so feral. Showing a roughness worthy of his own species. He was hanging by a thread already. He needed her now. In every way possible. But instead, he remained frozen. His breaths shallow. Waiting. Taut with anticipation at what she would do next. Then she spoke the words that hog-tied and enslaved him completely. 'If you ever tamper with my mind again, in any way, I will not only leave you, but I will hurt you in any way I can. Are we clear?'

He nodded and groaned into her neck at exactly the same time as she dissolved with the reaction from his blood. He caught her before she collapsed and held her while it surged and convulsed through her body. Such a small amount meant she quickly recovered, and worries, sane thought or anything outside of that small cave, no longer existed for either of them.

CHAPTER 42

Xavier had to drag Paige out of her room to go to the party. Thankfully, her mother had already left and a nanny, who knew how to keep quiet, was looking after her brother and sister for the evening. He wanted to scream in frustration that she'd complained he'd locked her in and now she refused to come out. She was so annoying. She was determined to see him as the villain, when she was the one talking to other boys. But what he hated most of all was that everything was out of his control. She was out of his control. That, he discovered, was something he couldn't abide. He cursed that he had promised he would not enter her head and make her. He was forced to admit that he had messed this up.

Him.

Partly JJ and his continuous competition with him. That's what was mostly behind this. Without JJ, he would have probably bonded first and thought later.

Now at the edge of his nerves, he pulled Paige with him into the throng of dancers and, for a moment, she relaxed into him to dance. The relief was like a boulder rolling off him. He felt tears behind his eyes and burrowed his nose into her hair and breathed. She was sending him crazy.

When he opened his eyes, they fell on Latitia and JJ, lost in their own little world. The kiss they shared, tucked into a shadow of a vine, was a shout to the world of what would inevitably come.

His heart screamed and he wanted to yell it wasn't fair. He wanted that with Paige. Why did no one believe that he did. He loved her and he hated what JJ had with Latitia. But with every cinder-tinged thought, he knew he wanted the kingdom more and he recognised in JJ his distraction. He couldn't take his eyes from the ultimate prize. Paige could be convinced later, when he'd won. Even now, he wanted to speak honestly to her, but he didn't want to affect the slight thawing he felt in his arms.

When the song blended seamlessly into another, he put his lips next to her ear. 'Can we talk, please?'

He felt her sigh and nod reluctantly.

He didn't risk taking her out of the great hall, so he chose the furthest point by the huge window. It was a bit quieter and provided its own light. He needed to see her reaction.

He turned her to face him but didn't let go of her arms. She was a flight risk, of that, he was sure. Her eyes accused him and the rest of her just seemed sad. Like everything he could ever say was pointless. He had an overwhelming urge to cry and smash things up. Why didn't she understand that she was the most important person to him. 'Why?' he demanded. 'Why have you changed on me?'

He took in her startled blue eyes, in that angelic face, and remembered the adoring trust she had in him back in London. Before Hunter. He'd never had a single doubt about her then. She was his and he could conquer the world.

But then she punched the wind out of his stomach. 'You

did, Xav. You changed. The minute we got here. It's like I don't know you at all.'

He glared at her and all he saw was honesty. He felt a rod of anger shoot through him and he must have shown it because her look turned fearful and she attempted to take a step back. 'Is it because of what I am?' he asked, clutching at the only thing he could and taking a step towards her.

She backed up again. 'No, of course not. I've always known you were different. It was part of why I loved you.'

'Loved?' The awful, jagged past tense lacerated his insides. 'And you don't now?'

She shrugged, looking exhausted. 'To be honest, I don't know. Do you?'

He recoiled, appalled. 'Of course I do. You're the only girl I've ever felt anything with.'

'But you could never bind me to you,' she stated flatly. 'Never is a very long time, Xav. Doesn't that kind of make me into the very thing you said I'd never be: a placeholder?'

Xavier stepped back, nonplussed, pushing his fingers through his knotted curls. 'Of course it doesn't.' His voice went up in pitch and volume. He wanted to shake her. They were getting strange looks from people and he wanted to scream at them to mind their own business. Instead, he stepped in closer again and moderated his tone. 'It doesn't mean I want anyone else. It's that I can't be weakened by it. You have to understand what's at stake here.' He could have bitten off his own tongue at the switch in her face to anger at being spoken down to.

'Oh, I understand what never is, Xavier. More time than I've got.' She snatched away her hands that he didn't realise he was holding, turned and bumped right into someone.

Not just anyone.

Hunter.

Xavier's heart dropped into his stomach and the two then

fell into his bowel. It weighed so much, it hardened to lead. 'You,' he said on a growl, jabbing a finger at him. 'You started all this.' He went to pull Paige to stand behind him out of harm's way. His Paige. But she stepped out of his range.

He wanted to scream at her. Instead, he launched himself at the boy he'd barely spoken to in his whole miserable life. Who never usually came out of his lab.

His fist almost connected with his jaw, but it was spun away with a force that threw him down to the floor, smashing a table flat. Paige was screaming.

Xavier scrambled to his feet and pointed. 'Fight me like a man, you bloody coward.'

'Why would I do that?' Hunter asked, not backing down an inch. 'That would infer you're an adult and you are clearly not.' Then it was Hunter's turn to point, making Xavier step back out of his reach. 'You have lost this girl because of your own stupidity… You!' he said, with a final jab of his finger.

Incensed, Xavier lost free thought and dropped under Hunter's arm and kicked out with a foot at his legs. They went from under him. Just like Jay had taught him. It was beautiful and he thanked the five moons for Jay, as Hunter landed heavily on the hard marble floor.

Then, while Hunter was still picking himself up from the shock of the manoeuvre, he switched his venomous gaze to Paige. She was cowering off to the side with Kali, Hunter's sister. Holding onto her like she was scared for her own safety. He cursed his million bloody cousins.

Hatred was coursing through his veins and he swore he would have combusted if it wasn't for his mother appearing and attempting to talk him down. But his eyes still bore into Paige. 'If you go with him, you're dead to me,' he said, his voice gone to gravel. Sweeping his gaze in disgust from her to Hunter, now brushing himself down. 'I guess you have a new protector now.'

He went to turn but changed his mind and stepped into Hunter one last time. He was numb now. Beyond anger. Strangely comfortable in his extra height because of his purer genes. It helped his injured soul. 'Don't mess with me again, Hunter. I'm the heir and I will crush you.'

Hunter narrowed his eyes, not intimidated at all. 'There lies the snag, Xavier Dubonnetti. There are many heirs.'

His mother was suddenly there at his shoulder. 'Xavier, come away. You will regret this in the morning.'

Xavier barely heard. He was processing what Hunter said. He always emphasised his family name like some sort of dig. Hunter was a Florianna and his stepfather was human. 'No one knows who the hell you are, Hunter.' Xavier grinned spitefully. Shooting a last, distasteful look at Paige, he allowed his mother to lead him off into the corridors. He felt more than dazed. Traumatised. He'd been running completely on nerves and now his heart felt like he'd pulled the scab off a raging sore. It was painfully weeping. Bleeding out into his chest cavity. His head throbbed an unsteady rhythm. A soft hand rubbed his back. 'Leave me alone, Mother!' he whirled around and screamed in her face.

She jumped back in horror.

'This is your fault. You and Jay.'

She went to take a step closer to soothe him again, but he pushed her off. 'You couldn't bloody keep your hands off each other, could you?' He hated himself as he saw the hurt register in her eyes. 'It's your fault there's another heir… It's all your fault.' He broke down crying.

'Xavier, please … let's talk. I know you wouldn't want a world without JJ.' She went to touch him again, but he shrugged off her hands.

'Leave me alone.' Xavier sobbed and staggered away, leaving her standing, gaping after him.

By the time he got near his room, he was crying tears of

anger and desolation. He went to bang on JJ's door. Ironic after the conversation he'd just had. He was the only other person he allowed close. But he remembered just in time what he'd be doing.

He was lost to him too.

Because of their mother and fathers.

Because of girls.

Because of time passing and growing up.

All the things that were robbing him of everything that was right and good in the world.

He got to his own room and found his mother standing there. She hadn't left him at all.

He stopped, never truly understanding love or loss or anything until then. She opened her arms and he stumbled into them. A lifetime of tears, falling like a great emptying. Until it was all gone. Thought, feeling, caring, and he had nothing left.

CHAPTER 43

Alexia's stomach churned with iron filings, pulled from pole to pole, now she was finally on her way to Murrtaine. She was desperate to get to Yaro but terrified of what she would find. She couldn't even entertain the thought he might be hurt. Her mind was soon flung to other terrors. *Would he still be there? Would he now hate her?*

She felt sick with worry and looked about her, trying to calm herself down. Darres and two of Vionne's strongest lieutenants were in serious mode, steering the craft escorting her to Murrtaine. She felt a sharp pang of guilt at the reason they'd allowed her to go. Filfla would be compromised if Pavel homed in on her there and her whole family would be vulnerable. But she quickly dispelled that as their own fault. They'd brought it upon themselves. They couldn't expect that Yaro would not defend himself. Now they would track her coordinates in the middle of the Mediterranean Sea. Maybe they would find nothing because of the sophisticated technology or maybe they would free Yaro and teach her father and Vionne a valuable lesson. You can't go around treating people like that. There was no need for it. *Couldn't they see Yaro was just happy to be here? To be accepted?*

She choked back her emotion as her eyes fell on Darres, watching her coldly. She was sure he'd read everything she'd just thought. That alone made her angry. She was allowed nothing of her own.

You love more than one person, Alexia. Yaro is one and we are many. Although he showed very little emotion, sadness was conveyed with his projected speech. They were able to do that. It made her feel a stab of shame. She wanted to argue, but he cut her off. *We are there now.*

One minute the sea appeared to go on endlessly in every direction, the next they were being sucked through the huge hazy bubble. The dome was always right on top of you before you knew it was there. The wonder of it still filled her with awe, but this time it made her heart sink. Pavel would not see it, either, or know to go through it.

She watched the green glass-like buildings pass, sullenly. What once filled her with excitement now filled her with dread. *Where are they holding him?* she asked, imagining him chained in some dark dungeon.

He has a room like everyone else, Darres said, shaking his head.

Alexia didn't believe him. He hadn't contacted her in her head again. That meant he'd been knocked out or cloaked in some way. She began to bite her nails while she thought of a way she could get to him. Her stomach was churning as they slowly traversed the Murr streets with everyone staring like statues as they passed.

JJ saw his mother sitting all alone in the great hall, staring out at the sea. He'd left Latitia sleeping and had come with the excuse of bringing back food for when she wakes. But if he was really being honest, it was to give himself the space to process what had happened last night. He still couldn't quite believe it.

He grabbed himself a coffee and came up behind his mother and kissed her cheek before he sat down opposite her.

She smiled immediately, but she looked pale and tired from worry. 'Your sister left last night,' she said simply, still staring out at the seascape.

He just nodded.

'I hope your father hasn't done anything stupid.'

He nodded again and didn't add anything. She was just thinking aloud and there was nothing anyone could do now but wait.

Then her eyes rested on him as if she only just noticed he was there and frowned. 'Is everything OK? Latitia OK?'

He sipped his coffee and raised his eyebrows, not sure what to say. Everything was OK. More than OK in some ways. But still confusing and unsettling, and for the first time in his life he felt unsure of himself. 'I left her asleep to get her some food,' he said as honestly as he could. It was weird because he could always normally talk to his mother. She was cool like that.

'I spoke to her yesterday.'

He blanched in surprise. 'What did you say?' It came out more harshly than he intended, but he was already calculating when it must have been in the timeline of how weird Latitia had been acting. She hadn't said a thing.

'Calm down, JJ. You'd just bonded with the girl and I bumped into her. I hadn't had a chance to speak with her.'

JJ relaxed down into his chair. 'Sorry, but this whole thing. She drives me mad,' he said, pinching the bridge of his nose.

When he opened his eyes, his mother started to smile. 'Got you on the back foot, has she?'

JJ scowled. 'Seriously, Mum, what did you say to her?' he asked again, grumpy that she'd got involved.

His mother started to laugh and put her hands up in surrender, annoying the hell out of him. 'Hey, JJ-bear, I'm on your side, remember.'

He shook his head and huffed. 'Don't ever call me that in front of her,' he said, knowing he sounded like Xavier and hating that even more.

'Look,' his mum said more reasonably. 'The girl is confused too. Not only has she found out that aliens exist, but that she's in love with one—'

'She actually said that?' JJ cut in, completely blown away.

'Yes, darling. She did. Of course she did. She loves you very much. But you have to understand something. Both you and Xavier. These girls might be human, but they are people, not belongings, and you can't go around controlling every aspect of their lives.'

'I'm nothing like Xavier,' JJ said, disgusted she would even think to compare them like that. 'And we're bonded. It's not the same at all.'

'Isn't it?' his mother said, looking at him with pained eyes. 'Life is never going to be easy for you two, you know that right? With a one-way bond, you are going to need a lot of love, communication and an awful lot of understanding between you. That takes time.'

JJ was more irritated the more she spoke. He knew all this. Of course he did. Last night—he didn't even finish the thought before his mother cut across it.

'I assumed if she's now in your bed, then you've … you know,' she said, waving a regal hand, watching him closely.

There was no point in pretending, so he nodded. 'Last night was the first time.'

She sat back, nodding to herself, sagely. Like something had slotted into place.

'What is it?'

'Nothing … you did well to last out that long, that's all. When the fates decide, it's only a matter of time.'

JJ frowned and thought about that for a moment. He'd barely considered the fates in all this. It was part of their religion, but it didn't feel like it belonged much in the real world. His world. But he guessed now everything was different. He knew his mother had been brought up in London, with humans, so she understood his life really well, and as a siren, and a very important creature to their species, the fates figured strongly in her choice of marrying Dante over his dad, Jay. It meant a lot to her and his people. 'You think it plays a part, even with humans?' he asked.

'Of course,' she said, her face fierce, like he was ridiculous feeling otherwise.

It was a sobering thought and a little comforting, because it meant no matter what problems they went through, he and Latitia would always find their way back together. As always, his mother had helped. 'Better get back before she wonders where I am.' He stood, leaned over and kissed her cheek.

She smiled and reached up and cupped his cheek, rubbing her thumb across it. 'My darling, darling, boy. Born out of pure love.'

A lump immediately came to his throat at the reminder so close to her mind. That she and his father, Jay, should never have been able to have kids. And yet here he was. With her being a siren, it should have been genetically impossible. The Darkly Begotten prophecy had always made him feel like a curse and here she was reminding him he was a gift. He hugged her to him tightly to hide his eyes misting over.

She held onto him for a full minute until she kissed his cheek loudly and let him go. 'Loving someone means giving them space to be themselves, too, JJ.' She looked off into the distance, then, and he knew he'd lost her to her own memories. A time she'd found desperately hard.

'Thank you, Mum … for everything.'

When she smiled up at him, it was radiant and her eyes were glazed with tears. 'Go … and allow yourself to be happy.'

He smiled and walked away, choked, she knew him so well.

YARO CAME to and sat up suddenly in a windowless room. At first, he had no idea where he was. Patches and strange flashes of memory speared through his head, making it thump and his mouth fill with saliva. He groaned and held it, while he slowly put the pieces together. The crystal jug of spiced water he'd been forced to drink after already turning down dead blood. Ashaya's innocent pleasure at finding something he could drink. Not wanting to insult her. Followed by the look in the Murr king's eyes. Triumph, that he finally had him. The exact moment he knew he'd been drugged. His cry to Alexia and Pavel. Then the descending mist, taking the blood from his face until he found himself here.

He had no idea how long he'd been out or even where he was. Only that he was still submerged. His heart pounded unnaturally. He waited for the dizziness to pass after a wave of nausea almost overcame him. Swallowing over and over, counting to calm himself down. Anger and frustration only made it worse.

'Welcome back, Yaro Demidov, son of Ambragio.'

He jumped and turned, suddenly, taking a minute to place the female voice. Then he remembered and slowly straightened in his narrow cot. *You! The Orb!* He was shocked. She had openly declared him honourable and now this. *What trickery?*

'Worry not, Yaro Demidov. My reach is far under this city. No one knows I'm here. I came to give you comfort and strengthen you for what lies ahead. Please do not mentally blast your power. Remember there are children and loved ones nearby.'

Her voice shook off the last of his lethargy. *Loved ones? Alexia. Pavel and my people?*

'Yes,' the Orb said. 'And also a people you profess to be a part of?' He narrowed his eyes while he absorbed that. *Was this a greater test of his intentions?*

'Alexia has arrived and your Ambragio will soon follow. We must conclude this so they can be welcomed.'

He frowned, listening keenly to the last part. Did she mean this was some initiation?

He felt the tell-tale tingle through his body as she read him. Then she answered; 'It is not I who needs to test you as I know your heart, as I do all hearts. You are a wily leader, but the rightful princes govern Atlantis and Murrtaine. You will not take it from them.'

Yaro relaxed down a little. It made sense for them to test his prowess under water, to see if he could take their kingdoms from them.

But I can't win either way. I am as strong in water as I am on land. That was why we were chosen for our destiny by our ancestors. They will condemn me anyway.

'I know,' the Orb said simply. 'You must come through the tests and trust in the fates. They need to test you to understand who you truly are. Your strengths. It is they who need to come to terms with that. That you are not simply base dwellers, but honourable knights of the first order. Have faith that I will not let any harm come to you or your family, if you trust in me.'

Yaro wanted to believe her. But he'd had a lifetime of dealing with ambitious, treacherous people and that was a devil on his shoulder. He could be being elaborately tricked, ensuring he submitted and his people rounded up easily. He could be quietly killed and a lie told to Alexia and no one would hear of him or the Demidovs again.

'Decide Yaro Demidov. Put your pride aside and let the tests begin.'

CHAPTER 44

The waterfall portal appeared in Yaro's room and he stood and braced himself, not knowing what would come through. The Orb's warning was still an echo in his mind. He was still undecided as to what he would do. He couldn't feel Alexia's presence or any of his family, so either his senses were blocked, or they were nowhere near.

The large, striped body stepped through. The formidable brother, Darres. He recognised him right away. Impressive. His aura was stark and unmoving. Showing an arctic, almost unmoving psyche. They had chosen well, as instinct told him he would be a worthy adversary.

Yaro straightened to show the male he was ready for whatever they'd planned to throw at him. *Where are you taking me?* he projected.

Darres didn't react right away. He simply stared at him with his dead-pool, black eyes, as if he was reading something there. His strong presence hovered on the edge of his consciousness.

Yaro slammed him down immediately.

Darres raised an eyebrow. The first test: mental blocks.

Yaro returned the favour and was squashed flat frighteningly fast. If all Murrs were as psychically strong as this one, there would be no breaching of minds. It made Yaro question what else they could do with it.

Darres' look was curious. Almost sardonic, as he held out a hand to exit through the portal. Strangely expressive. As if he'd followed his train of thought exactly. *No handcuffs?* Yaro asked with a smile, knowing this one was not a talker.

No need, was all he said back, with low-lidded eyes.

It was no empty threat. He decided he liked him. He seemed apart from the other Murrs. A story about him, he would one day like to know.

Yaro turned from Darres, a wall of muscle and bone behind him, and stepped through the portal. He could have disappeared in a breath but decided to wait it out. They soon fell in step, down the corridor to eventually reach steel double doors that opened to reveal a capsule.

Get in, Dares said, when he hadn't moved.

Yaro paused when it became obvious that Darres did not intend to follow. It didn't take a lot to work out that the only direction it went was down.

Just me? he said over his shoulder, stalling while his mind worked assessing the situation.

Just you.

Yaro felt his blood pressure increase slightly at the test to come. He sent up a silent prayer. *Mighty Orb, are you near?*

I am with you, son of Ambragio.

Is this the test where they intend to kill me? It was a quandary. He could easily escape the Murr if he did it now, but it would ruin his chance to prove he was no threat to them.

Trust in me, Yaro Demidov, the Orb whispered.

Yaro studied the curved walls of the capsule and the steel floor. It was a huge, steel egg. The strongest shape in the natural world. Then he understood. They thought they would win whatever he did. He stepped in.

The doors closed immediately and the capsule plummeted smoothly downwards. His stomach rolled until he became used to it. He had no idea how deep the shaft went. Whether it was natural, or whether they had made it.

Then it occurred to him in a bolt of inspiration. The Orb lay under their great city. The resting place of all their power. In the midst of their ridiculous tests, they had revealed staggering information.

He clenched his jaw with newfound determination. The speed they were travelling meant depth. Depth meant pressure. He smiled.

A voice crackled and he recognised it was Dante. *I apologise for this. Are you still comfortable? How do you feel?*

Peachy, Yaro said, looking around for a camera or speaker. He guessed their technology was way beyond that. *Was this your idea or the Prince of Murrtaine's?*

There was a pause where the king attempted to phrase his psychic words. *I can see the purpose of it,* Dante replied eventually.

Yaro continued to look around him. This had cold fish written all over it. He also knew he was already at a great depth but strangely not feeling the pressure yet.

You will soon start to feel the pressure to match the corresponding ocean depth. Please communicate when it starts to feel uncomfortable.

A simulation. Now it made sense. He looked up to the ceiling, imagining that was where they were watching but didn't respond. This whole thing was ridiculous, because if he got to the point where he couldn't handle the pressure, his lungs would compress and his blood vessels disintegrate, long before they could ever save him.

They had to be at a depth of at least 10,000 metres. He

smiled spitefully, exposing to the camera vicious fangs. The atmosphere in the capsule was slowly changing. The water lightening machine was being switched off and he floated up off the floor. He began to tread water. The structure around him groaned. The only thing in the whole of Murrtaine made of metal.

Yaro felt the swaddling water around him begin to constrict. Bearing down, feeling heavy and pushing on his muscles, like a huge blood pressure cuff. He could playact, to make them ease off before he got into any real trouble, but he felt angry and defiant and for the time being he waited, continuing to tread water. Looking at the ceiling with narrowed eyes, willing them to get the hell on with whatever they wanted to give him.

DANTE WATCHED the Ambragio prince with a heavy heart. This didn't feel right and not just because this was the male his daughter loved. However, he recognised it had to be done.

More! Vionne demanded.

Dante nodded at the Murr technician. He turned a heavy dial and they all watched the grainy screen.

Yaro appeared to be looking around him as if he was waiting for a lift to move. *Unbelievable,* Dante said in awe. *He's at the depth equivalent of the Mariana Trench.*

36,000 feet, Vionne said, confirming his thoughts. *More!* he said to the tech.

Come on, stop, Cousin. There is no advantage in giving him more. There is no place on earth at a greater depth. You will kill him. Dante felt something behind him and turned.

Ashaya was insisting she be let in.

It was just at the nick of time. Vionne relaxed, nodded to

allow it and sent a silent command to the tech, who turned back the dial slightly.

Ashaya entered the room quickly. *The Princess Alexia has arrived. Please stop this madness.*

Vionne gave Dante a stark look as if it was all he needed. *Very well. Your prince passes at depth, but we insist on a speed test before we let him go.* He gently touched the side of Ashaya's face to quell her fears. *Please welcome the princess in my place. We will be with you shortly. We have one more thing to do.*

Ashaya didn't look happy and agreed reluctantly, proving they were not a united front on this. She knew Vionne was up to something and so did he. He was not happy that Yaro appeared to be passing the tests with flying colours.

Dante checked the screen. Yaro was looking up at them, holding out his arms as if to say, 'come on'.

Dante agreed with him. *He has passed, bring him up,* Dante said to Vionne, over his shoulder.

One last thing. Vionne nodded at the tech. *Drain it.*

Dante frowned, his mind quickly catching up with what he intended to do. *What? Wait, you're creating a vacuum?*

Dante was furious that they hadn't discussed this first. He'd completely hijacked the tests. He hadn't been happy from the start. He'd gone along with it to a point out of sheer scientific interest. He wanted to see how Yaro handled it, physically and mentally, as a male intent on marrying his daughter. This felt wrong. A total disregard for a male's life.

Vionne remained hardened, riveted to the screen. He simply pointed as if he was missing a good show. All Dante could do was watch in morbid fascination as the water quickly drained from the pod and Yaro stood dripping.

At first he stumbled and shook his head. He doubled over and expelled his lungs of water in two efficient retches. Then he leaned with his hands on his knees as he appeared to be gulping air. But there was no air.

He didn't collapse.

That's enough, Dante said, becoming fearful that while Yaro was withstanding the trial, there had to be a time limit on it.

Astonishing! Vionne said more to himself.

Dante had to admit, he couldn't believe it either. His strength and resilience were immense. But they had no clue how long he could survive and he was not prepared to test it to the end. *Bring him out now, Vionne,* Dante said more forcefully. He'd had enough of Vionne's total disregard for his rank. *Stop this. It's gone too far. You could give him the bends if you have to oxygenate the pod too quickly.*

The look Vionne gave him was sardonic as if he was being soft.

I order you as your king. Think carefully. His family could be on their way here. A family with strength like that, Dante said, pointing at the screen. *They will arrive to find you have killed their brother without provocation.*

At last, Vionne appeared to relent, seeing the sense in what he was saying. *Very well. We will refill the capsule slowly and bring him up to a slightly higher depth, but I insist on the speed test before we conclude.*

Dante nodded, relieved to have finally gotten through to him. Although he had no idea how they would make a male like Yaro show them anything he didn't want to. Yaro was submitting now, but his concern was growing that Vionne was determined to push him until he'd had enough.

It took several minutes for the pod to refill and ascend to a higher level. Dante was glad of the breather more for himself than any real danger to Yaro. The pod had no air while it was empty, so decompression sickness was unlikely. Vionne was not acting objectively over all this. He had to question whether there was something else going on.

The next test is ready, Vionne said.

At least Yaro looked better now he was completely submerged. He thought he was coming up to seabed level, but Vionne stopped the pod and nodded at his lieutenant to open the doors.

The doors opened and the technician switched to a different camera view. Just a simple, plain grey corridor, with smooth flat walls and a dead end ahead.

Vionne's mental voice blasted, loudly. *Ambragio. Ahead of you is a maze. Find the way out and you are free.*

Yaro inched forward and looked around. He didn't trust them and Dante couldn't blame him. *There is no way out*, Yaro blasted back.

The exits come and they go quickly.

Dante understood the test immediately. If Yaro wanted out, he had to reach the exits before they closed again. A simple but effective concept.

Yaro stared up at the hidden camera with crow-like precision for a blind man. He'd had enough and he couldn't blame him.

And should you decide to slow down, you will not be alone, Vionne added.

Yaro rolled his eyes and sagged a little.

Dante whipped his head around to Vionne. *Have you lost your mind?* None of this was done on a whim. It had to have been prepared ahead of time and all without consultation with him.

Vionne was unrepentant and simply nodded his head towards the screen.

The lights in the maze went out to complete darkness.

CHAPTER 45

*Y*aro could feel his temper rising. He growled, showing a full set of fangs. Not because of their pathetic tests, but that he was being forced into the indignity of it. To perform like a circus animal for their entertainment.

To make matters worse, he wasn't even hidden by the dark. His involuntary luminescence was growing brighter. Lighting the corridor, for all to see. He was being poked and prodded like a lion, ready to jump through hoops, or, in this case, trapdoors.

He knew what this was. This was the speed underwater test. The subtext being 'the how much of a threat to them, was he', test. This would have to be negotiated carefully. Depth was one thing, survival was instinctual. But if they thought he could run rings around them, literally, it could be game over for him.

He inched forward along the corridor, not having a clue where an exit would appear and what form it would take.

The first was a waterfall like the ones he was accustomed

to. He stooped and it disappeared quickly, making him jump back, rubbing his head. He was lucky, they were just demonstrating. The portals would close fast and they could seriously hurt him.

OK, you wanna play, he muttered to himself.

It appeared again. He stood back and estimated with his hand that he had no more than two seconds before it slammed shut. Nothing taxing.

A short hop and he was on the other side.

It was an identical corridor.

This time, a section of the wall rose at an angle like a guillotine. Then crashed shut, just as deadly. It worked more quickly, proving they were upping the stakes.

Again, he calculated the timeframe with his hand. Then launched himself headfirst, landing in a roll, springing up on his feet the other side. Nothing remarkable. No extra speed required. He could keep this up all day, except he knew they were getting the measure of him. Just getting started.

The Murr prince's mental voice vibrated the water around him. *You have one minute to reach the lift pod in the centre of the maze. However, you will not be alone. Three full-grown Moray eels have been released into the tank with you.*

Yaro snarled. This was no longer a test. It was an assassination attempt. Those eels could grow to about three metres in size, operated perfectly in the dark and their bite was poisonous. Particularly to Atlanteans. He'd had enough playing around. They wanted to see what he could do, then he would show them.

Ah, I almost forgot. For this part, the water quantifier will be switched off. For this, you will need to swim.

WHAT THE HELL *are you doing?* Dante blasted. Vionne was out of control. *Alexia is here and you are about to kill the man I said she could marry.*

Vionne would not be swayed. He simply raised his eyebrows at the monitor. *Look!*

The lights were now fully extinguished to complete darkness and the true male was revealed. His luminescence exploded into what could only be described as an angel. The male he thought of as dark and soulless, with no aura at all, had the most spectacular one of all of them. It filled the space around him and would strike any creature with awe.

However, now Yaro looked angry.

A hatch had opened and a great spike-teethed eel slipped out into the maze, followed by another and another. Each seeming bigger and more dangerous than the last.

Please, Vionne. Think about this. He can't possibly win. He'll die or he'll... Then Dante fell into the extent of Vionne's plan. Vionne was forcing Yaro to prove him right. That he was dangerous to the people around him. That wasn't exactly playing fair when he was just fighting for his life. But, of course, no one except those in this room would ever know.

YARO DID NOT WANT to play their games any longer. No matter what he did, they would push him to the point where he had to defend himself, so they could declare him a threat to the state. Well, he was done messing around.

He centred himself and his aura charged and grew, lighting several feet ahead of him. A huge, ugly eel stalled ahead of him, in shock at his light. It whipped its head around and took a lunge at another coming up alongside him.

Yaro did a quick mental calculation and came to the conclusion that he had to be quick, even by his standards, to go over the top of them. Nevertheless, they left him little choice.

He took a step back, dropped his fangs to razor-sharp length and sprang. To him, it was slow motion. He flew. Twisting mid-water, curving around the wall, under, then over them, arriving on the other side. In reality, it lasted less than a second.

Sections of the ceiling were coming down to compartmentalise the maze. He dove dove dove, beating them one by one, positive the idea was to trap him with one of the eels. He beat three gaps consecutively until he halted suddenly, face to face with the biggest Moray he'd ever seen. Fortunately, it was just as surprised and scurried back in shock. However, it came up against a newly dropped wall. They were trapped together.

This was it. Not normally aggressive unless provoked, he knew it would attack in a confined space. It was unlikely he'd be unscathed even if he killed it. Its bite was toxic.

There was nothing left for him to do.

He closed his eyes and sent out a blast of his sonar senses far and wide. *Forgive me, great Orb.* It bounced back and told him the layout of the maze and the tunnel next to him. He concentrated all his kinetic energy to his hand and punched the wall next to him with every ounce of speed, power and strength in him.

Debris flew out the other side. He shot through lightning fast and did the same thing again and again. Wall after wall, until his senses told him he'd reached the perimeter of the maze. He ignored their pod in the centre. He had no interest in their game. He would no longer give them that control. Instead, he headed for a service corridor. The very last one before bedrock on the farthest side of the maze.

He smashed a hole large enough to swim through and

was away, just as the pulsing alarm sounded. He would need to escape fast. Pavel was nearby. He could feel him. And so was Alexia.

His heart thrashed with joy that they had both come to save him. However, he came to the cold decision to get to Pavel first. He must leave Alexia for another day.

CHAPTER 46

*D*ante watched the scene both fascinated and horrified. Yaro's strength and speed was immense. He glowed from within, lighting his own way with what must be some internal electricity. A power that was easily a match for the eels. But instead of destroying them and coming straight for his captors, he left them intact and obliterated Vionne's maze. He would have cheered him on had he not breached the outer walls and now posed a threat to his daughter.

Vionne took his eyes from the screen for the first time to look at him.

Dante just shook his head in disgust. *Nice one, Vionne. Now we have a pissed off Ambragio on the loose.*

We got what we wanted to see, Vionne said.

Ashaya was now next to him. *Yes, but he was only defending himself and has not harmed life.* She sounded dejected and disappointed, not able to look at either of them.

Not yet, Vionne said, already walking off. *Let's get back up to the city. There is no point in remaining here.*

Ashaya flashed her eyes at Dante as she turned to follow.

Dante swore to himself. He needed to smooth all this out with Alexia, while he still had the time.

WHEN YARO REACHED THE SHAFT, he swam upwards as fast as he could. He had no idea if that meant decompression sickness. He didn't care. He'd worry about that later. He had to get out.

He came to an abrupt stop at a blank wall. He waved his arms about manically like a mad male until a light panel appeared. Then, after Whac-A-Moling the buttons and thinking he'd have to smash through, a waterfall portal appeared. He swam through and landed in a heap as the water gravity sucked him to the floor.

A loud voice and a new alarm sounded overhead. *Unauthorised entry! Unauthorised entry! Service sector B.*

Shit! If he used any of the portals they'd know exactly where he was. His instinct was to fly through the building, at lightning speed. He would slip silently through any gaps as they appeared, until he was out of the palace.

His heart was beating harder and faster than any human. Hummingbird-fast. If he continued this pace at this depth he would give himself a heart attack. He needed to calm it down. He took a moment in an alcove, centring his thoughts and his body. Homing in on the driving pulses until they were heavier, louder and no more than twenty beats a minute. Then he sent out his senses around him once more.

Alexia was so near, but he couldn't give in to the urge to go to her. It was what the king would expect. He would have to bide his time.

Instead, he centred his energy again for speed and strength, then let himself fly.

Yaro's spirit soared at being able to give himself over completely to his genetic makeup. He so seldom got the chance. Maybe a handful of times in his three hundred years. He tore through wall after wall as if it were sugar glass. Nothing was brick or rock, but made from a crystallised coral, cultivated from their home planet. He no longer had to brace himself. He just bulldozed through, travelling almost at the speed of sound.

Yaro only took a breath when he reached the outside of the palace, where he took a beat to assess the situation.

He'd been right to come this way. An alarm had been sounded and all the Murrs were scurrying to their homes. The guards were rushing to protect the palace and the royal family. To Alexia.

He would go to Pavel, little more than a mile away.

He traversed the streets at lightning speed, so no one would see him. To them he was a streak of light. A passing comet, they would question was there at all. Until he got to the perimeter of the dome, where he finally came to a stop at the red blinking lights embedded in the sand. Up close, the wall looked smoky and opaque, but he sensed his brothers and several cousins were just on the other side.

Yaro hesitated, not knowing whether he could just go through like the marine craft. He tentatively put out his hand to test it. It felt weird. Silky and gooey, like froth. Nothing appeared to hurt, so he put his arm through to his elbow. A shoulder. Then walked through.

It was strange as it was not immediate. There was a thickness to it. Like smoke in a confined space that went on for about six feet. Then he was expelled on the other side and the cold hit him like an iced bucket of water. It was a shock that paralysed him for a moment, but then he opened his eyes and saw Pavel. Then his other four brothers and around ten cousins, standing there with him. Their stance, ready to fight, until their serious faces lit up with recognition. They rushed toward him and hugged him in one huddle.

Thank you ... thank you, Yaro projected over and over. He'd never been happier to see his family in his life, particularly his youngest brother, Pavel, who was openly crying.

Yaro roughed his hair in mock chastisement but pulled him close immediately after. They were all relieved and satisfied he was unharmed and eventually gave him the space to speak. He immediately relayed what happened directly to their minds.

Pavel swore. *Come, Brother, we are fifteen of the strongest race on earth. We can take this city.*

Yaro shook his head. *No, we must not.*

Pavel's face contorted with anger. *They have insulted you. Insulted us.*

Yaro held up his hands to halt his tirade. *No. I plan to force the king to keep his word. He promised me Alexia's hand.* He understood his brother's anger. He felt it keenly too, but this was far bigger than a personal insult. What he did now would set the path for the Ambragio family for ever. Whether they remained in the shadows, figments of nightmares, or finally taking their rightful place out in the light. Plus, something made him suspect that a lot of what had happened did not have the king's prior approval. His aura had been that of a straight shooter. Someone not able to completely hide something as underhand as this. No, this felt more like the prince of Murrtaine.

It made him feel a little better. Like everything the king had promised had not been all smoke screen and lies. He could work with that.

There was much arguing and disagreement among his family around him, until they reluctantly agreed to withdraw and regroup.

Come, Yaro said with a wave of his arm. *Before they widen their search and find us.* Then he and his fifteen swam east, towards Filfla, as fast as light.

CHAPTER 47

*A*lexia was distraught when her father told her that Yaro had broken out and gone. She blamed herself for not getting there fast enough, but, most of all, she blamed her father for letting it happen.

'How could you, Dad? Was any of what you said real?' She looked at him through angry tears, wondering if she ever really knew him at all.

Outwardly, he seemed upset and tried to pull her to him for comfort, but she threw off his hands. 'No!' she screamed. 'You don't get to smooth it all over. You tried to hurt him when you know I love him.'

'He abandoned you,' her father said, now looking exasperated, trying to gain some control of the situation.

'He escaped torture, Dad. That's not the same thing.'

Dante rolled his eyes and shook his head. Thankfully, giving up on his pathetic excuses of his treatment of Yaro.

Vionne approached and Alexia scowled at him too, but she wanted to hear what he had to say. *He is nowhere to be found.*

She grinned spitefully at him. She was glad their plans had failed but she was also filled with terror. He could be lying hurt somewhere, or, worse still, had given up on her. *He had to come for her. He just had to.*

Ashaya glided over and attempted to lead her away, but Alexia shook her off, determined to listen to what they had to say.

What the hell was that, Vionne? Eels ... really? Dante said, looking surprisingly angry.

He wasn't going to show us his speed without it. And he did, Vionne said, looking very pleased with himself. *He also showed us what a coward he is.*

Alexia went to cut in, but her father beat her to it.

No, Vionne, he didn't. With strengths like that, he could have done anything in his anger, but when we pushed him to his limit he chose to simply get out. That showed strength, not weakness. Now we have an angry Ambragio who thinks I lied to him. Who now knows where my seat of power is and your city. And he's pissed off, Vionne. Really pissed off. As I would be.

Vionne shuffled his feet uncomfortably.

Didn't it occur to you that we might have just asked what his abilities are? This is a diplomatic nightmare.

Vionne was now back to Murr stillness, but his jaw tightened and he straightened, obviously affronted by her father's mental tirade. *Any one of us Murrs could destroy his whole family with just one of our minds,* he said.

Yes, I expect you could. Darres could obliterate them single-handedly, but not around innocent people. You know as well as I do that to mentally blast like that would kill everyone around them. But by the time you even blinked, he could have slit all your throats. He's more than equal to any one of us, as you know full well. This is not the time for a pissing contest. All we can do now is hope that he is a wise-enough leader to take the time to think before he acts.

Alexia wanted to cheer. Vionne just blinked as if he'd been physically hit across the face. Even the ever-patient Ashaya looked exasperated with him. She simply said, *the Orb scanned him and proclaimed him honourable. I can't believe you, Vionne.* She shook her head and walked off.

It made Alexia feel slightly better that they hadn't all ganged up on Yaro. When Vionne looked directly at her, she shook her head and couldn't bring herself to even speak to him.

She was too busy reaching out with her mind in the hope of contacting Yaro. But there was no bond yet, and she was weak at it, so it was hopeless. He would go back to London, to his older, more sophisticated familiars and forget all about her.

JJ GOT BACK to his rooms after the chat with his mother, put the food down on the table, and just sat in an armchair and watched Latitia sleep. She was so beautiful in every way. Perfect for him. Maybe his mother was right and he hadn't given the fates enough credit for them finding each other. Still, he found it hard to believe. But when he thought about how she'd stood up to him when they first met, it made him melt inside. All that BS of taking her memories. Then making her almost lose her mind, because of it. No wonder she was angry when her memories were returned.

He chuckled at the stunt she'd pulled last night. She hadn't expected the punch to her nervous system from his blood though. He hadn't mentioned that part to his mother. Blood swapping outside of the Santalini family was forbidden and she would have been furious. But boy was it hot between them afterwards.

Latitia groaned onto her stomach and blinked blearily awake. Her facial expression was comical, when her eyes focused and she realised he was watching her. 'Hey, weirdo, what are you doing sitting over there?'

He grinned and without fully standing, he dove and stretched out next to her, leaning up on an elbow. 'You OK?' he asked, pushing the messy braids out of her face. Her eyes were soft and had lost their edge of accusation. They were still a little bloodshot and her cheeks a little flushed. He felt her forehead. She was no longer hot and had remained conscious, but he was still relieved she'd come through it.

JJ hated that he couldn't help himself with her, but at least he'd been able to keep more control this time. The elixir had worked, and her body had changed to accept him. After the shock of his blood, they'd gone the whole way and it had been a world of just the two of them. Ruled by instinct. Pleasure. Sensation. His stomach clenched just at the memory. He never knew it could be like that. The sense of completeness was overwhelming. It had only ever been a physical function with others before. His mother was right. This was everything to fight for. The fates had decided it. Now only time would tell if they'd decided the kingdom was his as well.

He must have betrayed his thoughts, because she ran a finger down the side of his face. 'Please don't worry about me, JJ. I'm fine. More than fine. It was amazing. You were amazing.' Her smile quickly dropped and her eyes narrowed in mock scorn. 'You could have told me about the blood thing, though. Not fair.'

They both laughed into a kiss and he loved that she was like this with him. It smoothed all his hard edges away. He hadn't hurt her and he'd managed to hold back his essence to no more than a couple of seconds. He only wished he could feel what it was like, just once. But he guessed that was the price of falling in love with a human. This was what it must be like for them all the time. Knowing her deepest feelings would have certainly helped decipher the strange mood he'd sensed in her before. A strong factor of what happened last night was to stop her pulling away. His mother's warning about control reverberated through his mind.

Then she blew away his fears with a devilish smile as he leaned his weight over her. It was a good sign and he had to be content with that.

'I never knew it could be like that,' she whispered, touching a finger to his lips.

'It's not...' he said, now mirroring her grin, feeling quite pleased with himself.

She smacked his shoulder playfully. 'I know it's different... Oh, you know what I mean.'

He did, but the amusement dropped away from him. 'You will never be able to compare... I won't allow it.' The rod of anger was strong and fast, bringing with it an image of his mother shaking her head in disappointment, which irritated him even more.

Latitia frowned, looking unsure whether he was joking or not. Then she gave him a hefty shove to get off and he immediately rolled onto his side to free her.

She was soon kneeling up and looking furious with him. 'Why did you have to say that? Of course not... I didn't mean that ... and anyway, you're the one that's been with loads of girls. How do I know it's not like that with all of them?'

He leaned on his elbow, exasperated that they'd gone from such closeness to this. He shook his head wearily. 'I told you. I've never breathed with anyone. I didn't know I could until you. But I don't think you *do* understand. This is as permanent as it gets. If you ever got with anyone else, I would kill them. That's not me mouthing off, I wouldn't be able to help myself.' The mental image of his mother was still shaking her head and he knew he was blowing it and should shut the hell up, but his cheeks burned to match hers and he began to shake from the elbow he was leaning on.

She drew back, shocked, and he had no idea if she was scared of him and would run. Then she completely took his breath by suddenly pulling him to her. Kissing his head and face, over and over. 'That's never going to happen, OK. Never.' She breathed the words with each kiss and he wished so badly he could feel one moment of what she was feeling. But warm breaths became a trail of nips down his neck. Interspersed soft murmurs of, 'Never … I promise … I will never do that with another living soul.'

He moved fast, pinned her beneath him and became lost to her. Sealing her oath with an all-consuming kiss. Problems gnawing at the edges of his mind were down the line and a very long way off. This was all that mattered. It was real.

PAIGE WAS in a dazed kind of shock. Once minute she was being comforted by Hunter's sister in the great hall and the next she was with them in Hunter's private rooms, where he was arguing with his brother and sister.

'I can't believe you got involved with the crown prince's girl. What were you thinking?' Kai said, pointing at his own head roughly. 'You know what he's like. He'll be coming for us, now, every chance he gets.'

Hunter sat down heavily on his bed, defeated. 'I didn't mean to.' He looked at her apologetically. 'It wasn't my intention.'

Paige nodded, vigorously. She was as shocked at the quickness of events as he was. One minute she was in love with Xavier, the next, he was fighting with Hunter, the handsome bad guy scientist who was saving her from the wicked, controlling prince. It was a fairy story made real. All she could say to Kai and Kali over and over was, 'Sorry.' She really was, for causing them all so much trouble.

'Well I think Xavier's a pig,' Kali said, flopping into an armchair. 'He can't go pushing people around like that – especially not humans,'

It still felt odd to be referred to like that. Another species. Even though she knew it was true. She'd entered an alternate reality that she now couldn't escape. She took a ragged breath. 'I really am sorry. I'll tell my family to get their bags together and we'll go home.'

Hunter was already shaking his head. 'You can't. The island is on lockdown for some security threat. No one is going in or out without the king's permission.' Hunter's look was sad, as if he was regretting having to say that to her very much. 'Can you give us some space?' he said, flicking his gaze to his brother and sister.

Kai was already walking towards the door, while Kali pulled herself to her feet lethargically. She went over and hugged Hunter.

Paige looked on, intrigued. She didn't know why she was surprised they were so close. They were brother and sister. She guessed it was because he was always so alone.

'Be careful,' Kali said.

Hunter nodded and quietly watched and waited until his brother and sister were out of the door. 'Call us,' Kai said, as they closed it.

They were now alone and Hunter switched his gaze to her. He seemed dazed.

'I can't believe what just happened,' Paige said, too shocked to even cry, 'He said I was dead to him. Does he mean it?'

Hunter looked around the room without seeing and shook his head.

She went over and sat next to him, on the bed.

'No. I dunno … maybe.'

'What about you?' she asked, turning to face him squarely. 'Are you hurt?'

Hunter smiled, but it didn't reach his eyes. 'It would take a lot more than a spoiled prince to hurt me.' Then he bobbed his head a little. 'Although he's learned some moves, I'll give him that,' he said, rubbing his shin.

'I'm not sure if it was lucky or not, but you arrived just as things were getting heated.'

Hunter scratched his head and looked bemused. As if he wasn't sure how to say something exactly. Then he looked directly at her with his strange, mesmerising eyes. 'I felt your pain.'

She stared at him, not sure how to answer that. 'Oh,' she answered eventually, but not understanding at all. 'That obvious, was it?' she said, dying at how pathetic she must have looked.

'No … I mean, I really felt it,' he said, angling his body to mirror hers. 'It was remarkable after such a small drop.'

She continued to stare at him while she slowly arrived at what he meant. 'What? Are you talking about the blood?'

Hunter smiled, looked away and back at her again. She couldn't help noticing how it transformed his face to devastatingly handsome. 'Evidently, it has more than trackable uses.'

He was making fun of her. 'What are you saying?' she asked, becoming irritated.

His body sagged a little, wearily. 'I told you at the time that blood is kind of like a bonding. A person's essence is in the blood. I guess I thought such a small amount wouldn't make much more of a difference than knowing when the other is near. It told me you were in distress.'

He was speaking honestly and directly, but he seemed very close to her by the time he'd finished speaking. She was completely aware of his presence. Heat coming off his body. Even his smell; some kind of warm, spiced cologne. Her heart was beating hard and she realised it had been like that the whole time since she'd tried his blood. She had no idea what it meant. It was just an experiment. 'Why? Why would you do that?' She felt open. Exposed. No wonder Xavier was angry.

Hunter smiled languidly. His eyelids low. 'It was a dumb experiment, remember?' He let out a sigh, registering her irritation. 'We wanted to see what would happen.'

She calmed a little. What he was saying was true, she guessed. Perhaps he had no more of an idea what would happen than she did. She was probably just taking out her situation on him. 'So have you done that ... experiment before?' she asked, having to avert her eyes. Confused whether it was a good or a bad thing. Not sure why it even mattered to her.

'No ... not with blood.' It was his turn to look irritated. He looked away as if he'd been taken to a dark place he didn't like to visit.

She felt it acutely. Devastation. Loss. Then it occurred to her. They were *his* feelings. She was experiencing them too, in real time. The blood. Just as he'd said. It was amazing. His sadness – no, his grief, was overwhelming. 'How then?' she asked, knowing it was really none of her business, but could no longer help herself. They were now kind of connected.

He let out a long breath and pushed his fingers up through his silky, almost black hair in the artificial light. 'A full bond ... A regular Atlantean girl, back in Cali ... she still had the ability.'

Paige widened her eyes in surprise. She wasn't expecting that. That level of closeness. He was so alone. So apart. 'Where is she now? Did you split up?'

His head dropped and he let his hand fall from his hair to

look at her angrily through his eyebrows. He looked like a different person; he was so hostile. She found herself instinctively leaning back out of his reach.

'No, we didn't split. I told you, there is no divorce from the bond. It is for life.' He shook his head, closed his eyes and pinched the bridge of his nose.

She was confused, but before she could ask what happened then, he cut right across her. 'She's dead. Wiped out on the rocks. Gone! Our bond severed. They didn't even find a body.' He laughed bitterly. 'Everyone said she'd just left town, but I knew. I couldn't feel her anymore. And I found this.' He pulled out a turquoise pendant from inside his shirt. 'I gave it to her. She never took it off.'

The weight of sadness coming off him was immense. She pieced together that he must be talking about surfing. His head was now in his hands as he covered up his emotion. She reached out a tentative hand to cover one of his and he jumped as if she'd burned him. Then he relaxed and allowed it, gripping hers back. 'I'm so sorry,' she said, fighting back tears of her own. 'I had no idea.' She felt a pang of longing for half the feelings he had for his lost girl to come her way, just once.

'No one has,' he said, looking away into space, desolate and lost. 'Except maybe my brother and sister.'

Paige swallowed, feeling a little braver now she had him talking. 'Was she nice? … What was her name?'

Hunter looked at her strangely. His eyes misty and reddened. As if he wasn't sure what to say. Weird, after such a logical question. Like he was gauging whether she really wanted to know. Then he seemed to relax and sink into his skin, as if none of that really mattered.

He laughed, mirthlessly. 'No, she wasn't nice.' He shook his head as if there was something he didn't fully understand himself. 'She was tough, sarcastic and cutting. Brutal, in fact.'

He was laughing genuinely at that. 'I don't think she liked people very much, let alone me.'

The more he spoke about her, the more Paige frowned and didn't understand. But she was intrigued by the emerging dynamic between them. Hunter so rarely talked about himself and his life outside his lab. Especially anything as intimate as this. 'So tell me about her. Who was she? She sounds interesting,' she finished with a half-smile.

He looked sideways at her to check for sarcasm, then relaxed, leaning forward with his elbows on his knees. 'She was a surfer. Like everyone. Ave, her name was. Avalon.' He laughed and looked sideways at her again. 'Imagine that. Me … the Merlin of the West Coast meets an Atlantean girl called Avalon. The Fates. It had to be.'

Paige watched his face soften with all the little tells of love. Deep love. The kind you never really get over. 'What else?' she asked, coughing. Her voice gone to a croak.

'Like I said. A surfer. A free spirit. Worked in the local surf shop. Lived for the swell, you know.'

She didn't know, but she nodded and 'ah-ha'd,' as if she did. 'Did she like science?' she asked.

He laughed loudly, screwing his face up as if she'd said something preposterous. 'No … she was the furthest person from a nerd. She was a badass with attitude. Everyone knew her on our surf-break.' He rolled his eyes at her mystified look. 'Our regular surfing spot.' He shook his head and looked at her again. 'But she was smart. Frighteningly so. More tuned into the natural world than anyone I ever knew.'

She seemed a complete contradiction to how he'd first described her. 'And you loved her.'

Envy gnawed at the insides of her abdomen. She tried to imagine Xavier talking like that about her and it shocked her that she couldn't. She couldn't visualise him ever being that deep. This girl never knew how lucky she was.

'Love her,' Hunter corrected.

Paige had lost the thread of what he'd been saying, she was so lost in her own daydream. She studied Hunter for a long moment, taking in his reddened cheeks where he was annoyed. 'Do you think she's in Heaven?' She wasn't being tactless. She was genuinely interested in whether Atlanteans had the same belief system.

She was relieved when he just shook his head. 'We believe in the ether. The energy leaves our bodies and communes with the universe. That's where she is. She would have totally got on board with that. Riding the cosmos,' he finished with a private smile. A tear rolled down his cheek.

It brought a lump to her own throat. 'So, are people sentient there?' she asked, coughing it away.

He flashed his eyes at her sharply. 'I'd like to think so,' he said, narrowing them on her.

She just couldn't shut the hell up, even though his look was warning her. 'Do you feel like she's with you?'

'She comes to me in my dreams,' he said in the same flat tone.

Paige wanted to ask how he squared all that away with his scientific mind, but his look dared her and she had the sense to keep that one to herself.

He simply smouldered at her and eventually looked away.

'Well, at least you got to experience a great love like that. My nan always used to say, 'better to have loved and lost than never loved at all.'

'And have you loved and lost?' Hunter shot right back at her.

Paige studied the spite evident on Hunter's face or felt it through the blood, she wasn't entirely sure. But she felt it. Like he deliberately wanted to hurt her. 'Not fair, Hunter,' she said, getting to her feet. This conversation wasn't going anywhere good. 'I think I should go.' She wanted to cry. The thought of going back to her room now that Latitia had moved out, filled her with dread.

Hunter was on his feet in a second and pulled her into his body. It happened so fast, she was stiff in his arms. 'Sorry,' Hunter said into her hair. He sounded so broken, she relaxed. Wondering how they'd gone from almost arguing to this. Then it dawned on her that maybe tonight wasn't solely about her heartbreak. 'Tonight brought up things I try not to think about.'

She nodded, enjoying the feel of his arms around her and instantly feeling guilty. 'Can we make a pact not to hurt each other, wherever possible?'

He didn't answer right away, but pulled back to study her eyes. He had a strange, growing smile.

'What?' she asked, half laughing herself.

'It's nothing … just ironic, that's all.'

After what just happened, she didn't feel like she could ask him to explain, although she was dying to. Instead, she blurted, 'I don't want to go back to my empty room.' She didn't. She didn't want to ever go back there again. It made her think of Latitia and JJ. So in love that they couldn't help themselves and how Xavier had disappointed her so badly.

Hunter was studying her again, like he often did when he was making up his mind about something. 'OK,' he said, letting out a slow breath and nodding.

'OK, what?'

'You can stay here.'

She wasn't sure why she was so shocked. She guessed she expected him to come up with excuses to protect his privacy and loner lifestyle.

He smiled haplessly. 'I'm not sure what I can offer you exactly … except maybe, great science?'

She laughed at that. It completely relieved the tension. 'Sounds perfect,' she said, pulling him close for another hug.

In that moment, it *was* perfect. *He* was perfect. They were friends. Two hurt souls. But as she held him, despite what Xavier had put her through, she wasn't as injured as this boy she held now in her arms. And Xavier would have to get used to it.

CHAPTER 48

*A*lexia went immediately to her room in Filfla and flopped face down on the bed. There was soon a soft knock on her door. She wanted to scream for everyone to leave her alone. There was nothing anyone could say that could make her feel better.

She recognised the presence immediately: *her mother*. 'Go away, Mum!' came out muffled into her pillow.

'Please let me in, sweetheart.'

Alexia leaned up on an elbow and clicked the lock with her mind. Her mother came in cautiously, looking fresh from the party, still with her earphones draped around her neck.

Any energy left her and she flopped back down on the bed. 'I suppose you were in on it,' she mumbled into the bedding.

She felt her mother's hand gently rub her back. 'I'm not going to lie to you, Alexia. I did know your father was going to take Yaro without you, but you have to understand that your father is king. Yaro is relatively unknown to us. He's a dangerous man on land and your father has a huge responsibility to those who look up to him to lead.'

'And that's a reason to torture someone, is it? The man I love and intend to marry,' she said fiercely, at her mother's concerned expression. Then she fell back down sobbing all over again, as it was unlikely to happen now. Everything was hopeless.

'Oh, darling. It wasn't torture. They wanted to introduce him to the Orb so she could scan him and back up what he'd told them.'

'Check him for lies, you mean.'

Her mother bobbed her head. 'Well, yeah. But you're probably too young to remember the last real threat we had and how bad it got then.'

Alexia leaned up to look at her mother again. 'Hunter's dad, you mean? I do. Some things. I know we were all separated and I was scared.'

'Then you know your father loves you and would not let anything like that happen again.'

She wanted to argue. She didn't want to put herself in her father's shoes. There was no excuse that would cover what he did. 'What did the Orb say?' she asked, moodily.

Her mother seemed to gather herself as if she found it difficult saying what she knew she had to. 'Well, she said that Yaro was honest and that Ashaya's commander had downloaded Yaro's family tree into her memory all those years ago, when they visited. We were just never aware of it.'

'So no one thought to check that Yaro was telling the truth,' Alexia said, flatly. Her heart rose only to be slammed down again. 'So explain to me why Yaro ran away then, Mum? He contacted me for help and then disappeared.' She hitched a breath. 'They must have done something to him.' Alexia got louder and louder, the angrier and more terrified she got.

Her mother put up both hands to calm her down. 'Things got a little out of hand, I'll grant you.'

Alexia's heart was beating harder. 'Like what?'

'They may have put something into his drink.'

'They what? They drugged him? Oh my god, Mum, he doesn't even drink.'

Her mother was shaking her head before she finished speaking. 'I know. It sounds terrible, but your father had no idea they were going to do that. Apparently, it was only to confine him.'

'So you're saying, they drugged him so they could lock him up.' It got worse by the minute. She looked Heavenward after her mother's look of guilt. 'Then what?'

Her mother averted her eyes. 'They took him down below the seabed to test his abilities at depth.'

Alexia's heart was now thrashing. 'Then what?' Knowing there must be more.

'Then in some sort of maze, I think. I don't fully understand it. To test his speed under water.'

Alexia shook her head. 'I don't get it. Why did he run?'

Her mother looked decidedly uncomfortable.

'You'd better tell me. I'm going to find out one way or another.'

'You have to understand that your father had no idea about any of this beforehand.'

'What? What did he have no idea about?'

'Your father said that they put something in with him because he wasn't showing them anything.'

Alexia dreaded the answer but had to know. She closed her eyes and then opened them again. 'Put what, Mum? Tell me.'

'Your dad didn't know.'

'For god's sake!' she screamed.

'Eels … they put eels in there.'

Alexia frowned while she tried to picture squiggly black worms. 'Why?' They didn't seem so bad.

'Moray eels. Three, I think.'

The light went on suddenly in Alexia's mind when she remembered an old biology class. 'What, three Giant Moray Eels? The ones that look like something from *Jurassic Park*?'

Her mother looked startled and guilty and began rambling fast. 'All he had to do was go through a few doors before they closed.'

'Oh my god, Mum. No wonder he'd had enough and wasn't willing to play any more of their games. Get out! Get out!'

Her mother got up and quickly walked towards the door. Before she left, she stopped and turned to say something. But Alexia picked up a can of spray next to the bed and threw it before she had time to speak. 'Get out! I hate you!'

Her mother darted out the door.

Xavier felt drunk and irritable.

Rock and Flame had smuggled booze, along with Richie and Dwayne, into his private rooms and they were all giggling and play fighting like kids.

Xavier sneered at them, not knowing what he was doing there. They were behaving like idiots and annoying the hell out of him. In fact, everyone did at the moment.

He was hit by an overwhelming wave of sadness. He didn't have a single person to go to when he felt like this. It had always been JJ or Alexia. Maybe, at a push, his younger brothers, Roman and Zander, but they were too young and wouldn't understand what he was going through. JJ had become his opponent and Alexia, his enemy. It had been him and Paige since he'd been to London and he was good with that. They'd been so close, there had been no need for anyone else. Now all he felt was loss.

It had always been a game between him and JJ. At every

school. Every trip. Every sport. One always trying to score over the other. What really hurt this time was that JJ wasn't even playing. He, Xavier, didn't even factor into his decision to be with Latitia. He hadn't mattered. He guessed it had been the same for him and Paige to an extent.

Why had he messed that up? Why did he have to open his big mouth? Was binding her to him so bad? At least she would have been tied to him for life. No playing around with Hunter then. Maybe binding wasn't such a bad option.

Then he thought of JJ and how preoccupied he'd been since it had happened.

Xavier shuddered. No, Paige had been unreasonable to expect that from him. He needed to concentrate on the kingdom. His birthright. A king's mate would have to understand that she had to come second. Paige would come around in the end. She had to.

'So, what you gonna do?'

Xavier looked up from his thoughts to Rock's expectant face, waiting for an answer.

'You gonna challenge him?'

Dwayne sat up to listen from his lounging position with Flame on his bed. 'What, like a duel or something?'

'Boy, you people are mad,' Richie said laughing, scratching the back of his head as he shook it.

Xavier let out an exhausted breath. He'd had enough of their company. But it was a good question. *What was he going to do?*

'You told her she was dead to you,' Flame reminded him quietly. Knowing full well how foolish that had been.

Xavier gave her a dead look as if to say, 'like I don't know that'.

'You'll win her around,' Dwayne said. 'Who is this Hunter character, anyway?'

'He's OK. A bit weird. Quiet,' Rock said.

'Can you all leave?' Xavier said, suddenly getting to his feet. He didn't shout. He didn't look at them. Just pointed at the door. He felt devoid of emotion. All he knew was he needed them to go.

They looked at each other, stunned.

'Please,' he prompted. Sweeping his arms to scoot them towards the door.

They got up slowly, still not knowing whether he was serious.

'Go!' he was forced to shout.

They filed towards the door. Rock was last. 'We'll be in Richie and Dwayne's room if you need us?'

He nodded. Registering that she was being nice but not trusting himself to speak and lose patience with the last allies he had.

The door clicked shut and he was alone at last. He picked up the phone by his bed and pressed zero. It went straight to the control office that was the centre of everything at Filfla, including the phone lines. His eyes darted around the room while he went through his options. His first thought was Paige's room. Then he shifted immediately to Hunter's. His blood sizzled at that. He calmed himself, knowing that he had to be cleverer than that. A fight would not win Paige away from him. Nor would apologies or pleading. He had to think outside the box. Craftily, like something his father or Jay would do.

'Hello, your highness. Can we help you with anything?' the female voice answered.

He came to a quick decision. 'Can you put me through to one of the guest rooms? Linda Hopkins' room, please.' His heart thrashed in his chest as his call was connected, at what he was about to do.

It rang for several rings before an uncertain female voice answered at the other end. 'Hello?'

'Hi, Linda. It's only me, Xavier. I don't want to worry you, but we need to talk.'

CHAPTER 49

*Y*aro and his family had gathered in the catacombs below Filfla. They avoided the upper levels as the loading dock was there and it was monitored by CCTV. Instead, they dove down through narrow inlets, to uncharted caves. The one they settled on had an air pocket that must have been from a time when the landmass of Malta was much larger.

Despite his trials, Yaro felt surprisingly good. Instead of skulking in the shadows of south London, he was living the life his family were born for. They expelled their lungs and sat, catching their breath and getting their bearings. Then gradually began to speak in quiet, husky voices. 'We should have crushed them while we had the chance,' Pavel said, throwing a pebble into the water nearby. 'You don't think we could beat them?'

Yaro let out a sigh. 'Yes, we could beat them. But you didn't see it, Brother. Murrtaine was astonishing. A glimpse of home and a time we can only dream about. Didn't we strive to be recognised? Vindicated? A part of? Not to crush.'

His brothers looked at each other. Pavel opened his

mouth to argue, but Yaro cut across him. 'The king gave me Alexia's hand.'

He looked up when he got no response. They all stared back at him with stunned or suspicious faces. 'I know what you're thinking. That it's easy to offer that which you have no intention to give.'

'That's right,' a few of them murmured.

'Why did you need to escape if they were treating you with respect?'

'Don't worry … the Murr will face my revenge. The king, I am yet to decide. I'm not sure how much he knew beyond seeing what I could do.'

'What is your plan then, Brother?' Pavel asked.

Yaro looked out over the water of the cave, as if there were a horizon. 'What is our greatest strength since we have lived on this planet?'

There was silence for a beat.

'Speed,' someone said.

'The same abilities on land and in sea,' said another.

'The very things they tried to trap you into showing them,' Pavel said, venomously.

Yaro inclined his head towards his brother. 'All those things are true, but none of them are our greatest. The things that have made us great are stealth, cunning and, above all, the ability to instil fear. In the words of the great sages that came millennia ago, "As above, so below". Look where we are. Right under the Atlanteans' noses and no one knows we are here.'

'Are we taking the kingdom?' Pavel asked, with a fervent light burning in his eyes.

Yaro shook his head and smiled ruefully. He had little doubt that he could. 'No … today I met the great Orb of this planet and she declared the Dubonnetti king, rightful, and the Borge, leader of the Murrs.'

'What then, Brother?'

'At the moment, we have a kingdom of the sea that shows fealty to the Atlantean king of the land, who straddles both. I will make myself the unseen king of the sky. The Osprey king. The one who flies high above the law and dives deeply below it. Taking all he wants with great accuracy. I will marry the king's daughter, then no one can argue my family's place in this world.'

Everyone cheered, then immediately hushed. It was what they'd always wanted. What each of them had prayed for their whole lives.

Yaro's fervour simmered on Alexia. She would be his first revenge. He would let them think he had abandoned her. Then he would swoop in and take what was his. He would bind her to him in every way. That would suffice as revenge on the Dubonnetti king. The Borge king would take more thought and planning. All he knew was that it would be swift and he wouldn't see it coming.

CHAPTER 50

*I*n spite of all the drama of the last few days, Latitia woke up on Christmas Day, draped over JJ, the happiest and strongest she'd ever felt in her whole life, and the feeling only grew every day. She could only put that down to JJ's constant breathing with her, strengthening the bond that grew inside her. Not only was it the most unbelievable pleasure she'd ever experienced, but she was able to think more clearly than she ever had as well. Like she could achieve anything she wanted. They couldn't keep their hands off each other and breathing was a regular part of it. JJ couldn't help doing it and she couldn't get enough. It was a potent drug, but it was changing her. Day by day, little by little, until the whole thing amounted to a lot. She wasn't comfortable talking to Tia about something so personal, so she kept her strange feelings to herself and hoped that JJ remained unaware. She didn't want to alarm him and he was super intuitive.

It had started from the moment she'd come out of her fever in the infirmary, with the strange alien doctor hovering over her. It was as though her real life had started from then.

It was more than an abundance of energy. She felt more alive. She sensed things more. It was hard to explain. Like everything had become clearer. Tia had helped her clarify a few things. Who she had been in the past and who she was determined to be in the future. It certainly wasn't the silly, inexperienced girl who moped around waiting for JJ to make up his mind whether he wanted a girlfriend.

It seemed laughable now. She'd been terrified of the strength of her feelings for him. That once she gave herself to him completely, she'd be left just an empty shell. The most confusing thing about it all was that even though he'd chosen her, bonded with her and they'd gone the whole way; despite bringing them together as a couple, it had made her feel much stronger and self-assured. The complete opposite to what she'd expected. She loved him and fancied the hell out of him, of course, but she recognised that the last piece of the intimacy puzzle was still missing. Even though JJ was as addicted as she was, he was still covering up his misgivings. The bond never lied and gave her a window to his fears, his emotions and his deepest intentions. They seemed honest enough and she knew he did love her, but with it came a huge weight of fear and dread, and that she found unbelievably hurtful, considering he had instigated it all. The worst thing in the world was to feel like a burden. So from the moment she'd spoken to Tia, a deep resolve began to creep over her. She wasn't sure how she would do it yet but by the time they got back to London, JJ would be in for a surprise.

For now, she kept quiet. Smiling, as he groaned into her neck. She didn't want to ruin Christmas. There was enough trouble going on around them.

JJ began to kiss a trail from her neck, down her body and she sighed, feeling safe and happy. This was definitely the best Christmas ever. Richie and Dwayne were getting closer to Rock and Flame and her mother was definitely up to something with Reeve.

She threw her head back and groaned at JJ's expert mouth electrifying her skin. She liked the idea that they were all getting tied to this new life, because she had no intention of leaving it. No matter what happened in the future. JJ would not be able to get rid of her, not even if he tired of her.

Sane thought exploded into shock waves through her body and she closed her eyes and gave herself to JJ. To this new her. This life of absolute pleasure. Until everything else disappeared. His mouth was on hers, and she was soaring. Never-ending bliss. Floating, coming back to a whole new world of delights and pleasure. Now hers. All hers.

AFTER THEIR LONG SHOWER, Latitia spent the rest of the morning with her family where they swapped presents in her mother's room. Joseph and Marcus were beyond excited, so there was no sleeping in for anyone. She was grateful she was now firmly ensconced in JJ's room as she wasn't sure what grand customs JJ's family had and wanted to be awake for that. But she had to admit, it was quite nice to preserve a little of what they had at home.

JJ joined them later and looked on indulgently. Laughing at the whoops of joy from the little ones, ripping off wrapping paper like tornadoes, then squealing with delight when they got the action figures they'd been hoping for.

Latitia kissed her mum, not missing the new inner glow she was radiating, while thanking her for a new sweater. It was soon brushed over by big hugs from her brothers for new, gleaming white trainers.

JJ seemed genuinely touched when her mother gave him a flat, painting-size present. He opened it cautiously as if he didn't trust what it was. Her little brothers were bouncing to help, he was taking so long. He eventually turned it in his hands to reveal a collage of ancient-looking photos of Latitia at all different ages. From goofy to gangly, with questionable fashion sense. She inwardly cringed. 'You could have given him at least one decent photo of me, Mum.'

'Not possible, Sis,' Dwayne said. 'Believe me, we helped choose.'

'We felt it was a good representation of you through the years.' Richie said, rubbing his chin.

Latitia punched him in the arm, in mock outrage. It was good to feel a little bit like her old self.

JJ laughed. 'I love it.' He leaned in and her mother offered her cheek stiffly. The only clue she hadn't fully forgiven him yet.

Then they finally left their bubble and boisterously trouped off to the great hall for brunch. Her heart light and optimistic.

JJ THOUGHT it was a sombre gathering for Christmas Day. The usual loud banter between families was reduced to mild chatter in whispers. News had travelled that the new prince had absconded and Alexia refused to come out of her room.

JJ sat with his arm around Latitia in a group of Xavier, his closest cousins and the Johnson boys, who seemed to have formed a cosy foursome with Rock and Flame. Loki, Keefa and Dannon joined them after checking all was OK back in Murrtaine.

He scanned the room and was just about to whisper in Latitia's ear that Paige was not there, when in she walked with Hunter. Since the bond, he and Latitia had reached a new level of understanding in their relationship and every-thing felt easier in her company. Without a word, she followed his line of vision and saw what had taken his attention. It looked as though they were a couple.

JJ watched them skirt the edge of the room to find their place with Kali and Kai and the Florianna family.

He glanced at Xavier, who'd done the same and remained fixated on their place. He wanted to say something, but everything seemed inadequate. Particularly when Keefa projected loudly, *Isn't that your human, Xavier?*

Xavier didn't answer. His jaw was clenched, his eyes dark, as he continued to stare at the group where Paige sat. JJ felt sorry for him, but he had pushed her away with his own stupidity, like he always did, trying to control the people he loved. Alexia, the case in point. Deep down, he would know it was his fault.

Looks as though Hunter is finally moving on from his mourning, Dannon projected.

JJ flashed him a look, wanting to tell him to shut the hell up, but he wasn't making fun, merely airing a fact. He stiffened as Xavier got up. He went to stop him, but, Latitia held his arm. Instead of causing a scene, Xavier went and sat with Linda, Paige's mother. It was the last thing he expected him to do. It didn't make sense. Punching Dannon or Hunter, yes. He had no idea he had gotten so close to the family. Especially when Linda hugged him, got to her feet and marched around the outside of the room to where Paige was sitting.

PAIGE DIED A THOUSAND DEATHS, walking in with Hunter. She knew heads would turn and all eyes would be on her, curious and judging. Hunter said she shouldn't let Xavier dictate anything anymore and promised her she'd be safe with him. But she never imagined it would feel as bad as this. She sat on a beanbag, so she was as low and unobtrusive as possible.

Hunter shook his head as if she was hopeless and passed

her a glass of cola. 'Your mother is on her way over,' he said, discreetly.

Paige closed her eyes and her stomach sank. When she opened them, it was Hunter's mother watching her from her seat with his stepfather. She was beautiful, but wild and strange, like there was definitely something different about her. *How will you handle this, little mouse, now that you have my son's attention? Don't you hurt him.*

It was in her head, but she knew it was sent telepathically. Her cheeks burned at being called out so directly. She was so embarrassed, she wanted to run from the room. The pressure of her stare was so great. The question was rhetorical, but she felt she needed to say something. At least introduce herself, but there wasn't time. Her mother's jean-covered legs appeared in front of her. She kept her eyeline on the floor, not sure how she deserved all of this.

'Paige!' her mother hissed in a loud whisper. 'Can I have a word with you in private, please?' It was in the tone her mother reserved for when one of her children were misbehaving.

Paige nodded, without looking up, and scrambled out of the beanbag, onto her feet. She caught Hunter's eye with an unsaid apology.

He simply smiled. *Do what you have to do. Don't worry about me,* drifted into her mind.

It affected her deeply, making a pain stab right through her heart. 'Thank you,' she said, feeling tears prickle behind her eyes. She stooped and kissed him on the cheek. Then feeling his whole family's eyes on her, she followed her mother around the outside of the room to the corridor, out of sight, behind the pyramid.

Her mother immediately whirled around on her. 'What are you doing, Paige? You're being so rude. Xavier brought you here and you're with that other boy now? He's heartbroken. Your room hasn't been slept in and Xavier's really worried about you. He said that boy is dangerous and you could really get hurt by him.'

With every word her mother said, Paige's blood rose higher and her heart sank lower. She wanted to scream at how unfair her mother was being. She wanted to defend Hunter, who was only looking after her, and kill Xavier for stirring her up like this. She could hardly mention bonds that lasted for ever and crazy blood pacts. Or, basically, explain anything that justified her actions. All she could say in a monotone, which just sounded like stroppiness, 'Xavier is just jealous and controlling. Hunter is a friend.' As the words left her mouth, she felt a huge weight of sadness. Strangely, not for Xavier's obvious hurt, which she was sure came mainly from damaged pride, but for Hunter, who was getting blamed yet again and for the love he lost that made him so unavailable. If only they knew how wasted their words were. Her mother was so wrong about him. He was broken. Unable to be fixed and very definitely not by her.

Her mother was still talking in a blah-blah; she mostly tuned out: 'I want you to come and sit with me and your own family. I can't believe you've behaved like this. Xavier brought you home and you're making him look terrible in front of his whole family. I'm ashamed of you right now.'

Paige felt like she would explode with the injustice of it all. Instead, it just came out as a long sigh. Arguing was futile.

Her mother picked up her hand and pulled her along with her roughly, back into the great hall and in the direction of her seat with the Johnsons and Xavier.

Paige's eyes went to his immediately. He didn't look hurt, just satisfied, with a hint of curiosity at what she would do.

'Sit!' her mother ordered, while she dropped heavily into her own seat.

Xavier moved over, leaving the only available seat next to him.

She sat slowly, trying to leave as much gap as possible between them. She shrank inside as she felt his arm go around her shoulders and his breath next to her ear. 'Can we talk? I forgive you, OK.'

She turned sharply with an intake of breath and he was right there, his lips an inch from hers. His eyes looked sad and bloodshot, like he'd been crying. In fact, he looked terrible. She wanted to shout at him that it was her that needed to forgive him, but it was useless. Xavier's mind was set and she knew him well enough already, that it couldn't be changed by anything. She gritted her teeth and spoke quietly through them. 'Do not get to me through my mother again.'

His face lit up with a dazzling smile. 'Deal!'

Her eyes fell on JJ, who was watching them closely.

CHAPTER 51

The day wore on to evening and presents were passed out from under the biggest Christmas tree Latitia had ever seen. All the kids ripped off the paper with laughter and squeals.

Jay, JJ's father, came over and ruffled JJ's hair. 'Here,' he said, dropping a heavy black key fob in his lap.

JJ caught it with lightning-fast reflexes and looked at the key.

'Merry Christmas.'

'What's it for?' JJ said, looking more closely at it. 'A car?'

'It's nothing flash. It's in your car park for when you get back. Hopefully, not up on bricks.'

JJ laughed. 'Thanks, Dad.'

Latitia smiled up at Jay. What a lovely dad he was. She'd settle for anything from her own father. A glimpse of him once in a while would be nice. She guessed Jay was kind of her dad too, now. It was a nice feeling.

Jay put his hand in his pocket and pulled out something else and passed it to her. She took the small box from him gingerly and fumbling a little, took off the lid. Inside was a stunning silver charm bracelet. Each segment had a hanging charm in a blue stone. Strange symbols on each one.

'Dante asked me to give it to you.' She looked up into his intensely blue eyes. Then across to JJ, who was watching her closely.

'Each one represents the five royal families. JJ belongs to them all.'

Latitia was suddenly filled with an overwhelming wave of emotion at this new world she now belonged to. She loved it and she loved the gift. She remembered his many tattoos and looked back at JJ. He gave her a small smile as if he followed her thought process. 'It will protect you.'

'Like a Saint Christopher,' Jay added.

Valarie came over and peered at it. 'Aw, how beautiful, Jay. Thank you.'

He tipped his head. 'You're welcome. It's from all of us. Mainly Dante.' Then he pulled something else out of another pocket. Four black cards. At first Latitia thought they were store vouchers. Then she remembered that JJ had one exactly the same. They had a big gold A on one side, in the motif of an eye. 'This one is yours,' Jay said, holding one out to Valarie. 'These are for Latitia and the older boys.'

'I can't.' Valarie was already shaking her head.

'You can. Dante insists. You are family now.'

Latitia's heart swelled with joy. Jay had said out loud what she already knew inside. They were family. She wanted to shout at her mother to just take it. This was real and they deserved it.

Her mother was crying when Jay pulled her in for a hug. He put her away from him and she was saying, 'Thank you,' over and over.

'Look, while Dante won't be moving you out of your current living situation, he wanted you to be comfortably off.

You'll have a monthly allowance and he will be talking to you about a new job at the school.'

Valarie seemed bewildered and threw her arms around his neck again. Her brothers were swapping baffled looks, not sure what to make of it.

Latitia thought her heart would burst. She didn't think she'd ever been happier. 'Welcome to the family,' Jay said, pulling apart from her mother and giving Latitia a wink, like he knew what it meant to her.

Suddenly Reeve was right there and Jay laughed and moved off. Latitia didn't miss the strange look Reeve gave him. He was acting territorial over her mother. It felt strange seeing her mother as the object of a man's desire, but she was glad for her. Her mother certainly didn't mind with the adoring look she gave him.

Latitia locked knowing eyes with Richie, who raised his eyebrows. No one was going to fight against it. They were all tied in now, one way or another.

The unspoken conversation was broken by Dante, the king, entering the great hall and making his way over to them with JJ's beautiful mother. She was carrying two wrapped square boxes. 'From the tree,' she said, smiling. 'I'm not sure who they're for. One says Marcus and the other says Joseph. Do we have anyone here called that?'

'Me, me, me, me!' both her brothers shouted, jumping up and down.

Tia laughed and gave them each a gift.

They tore off the wrapping paper in about two seconds to reveal two brand-new, pristine, children's laptops.

Her own mother looked more shocked than happy.

'It's OK, they're specially for little ones. They won't break them,' Tia said, immediately, taking in the look on her mother's face.

Dante pulled her into a hug. She was crying. 'It's too much, Dante.'

'It's nothin', you're family now.'

Latitia was looking on, trying not to cry. An endorsement by the king himself. Nothing would ever beat this. Ever.

Then her mother was hugging Tia. Richie and Dwayne were hugging everyone. It was turning into one big love fest.

Latitia looked at JJ, bewildered and deliriously happy. 'I love you,' she said, before she could stop herself. 'I really do.'

He'd been quietly watching her the whole time.

CHAPTER 52

Paige had been stunned with the presents the whole of her family received. Her little brother and sister had received expensive spelling consoles and her mother a new phone. There was also a promise of a new job at the school. Her mother didn't know what to say to Xavier's mother and father. All she managed was a solemn, 'Thank you.'

Xavier waited till last and passed her a large, flat box. His eyes glittered as she gingerly took it from him. It felt weird, considering where they were in their relationship. For him, it was like their bust-up hadn't happened. 'Open it, then,' he prompted.

She pulled off the last of the wrapping paper and put her hand to her mouth. 'Oh my god.' It was a top of the range Litebook, Pro. Only the richest kids at school had them as they were the best laptops that money could buy. She was stunned. It made the book of motivational quotes and geek repellent air freshener for his car look ridiculous in comparison. 'It's too much,' she said, trying to pass it back to him. It felt wrong on so many levels, especially as she wasn't even sure they had a future together.

Everyone seemed to take a step towards her at the same time as Xavier and all said, 'No!' Xavier pushed the box right back at her.

Her mother said, 'Don't be rude, Paige.'

Strangely, it was Dante who held her attention. 'It's from all of us, to help with your studies. Xavier tells me you want to be a doctor. Do well this year in your exams and we'll see if we can get you a summer job at The Royal College Hospital, just down the road from you. It will support your application to study medicine at university. Have you decided where you want to go?'

No one had ever talked to her seriously about her wish of becoming a doctor. It was so pie in the sky that she'd barely ever told anyone. She felt the biggest lump in her throat, so she couldn't speak. It was a dream, particularly as it was very unlikely that she would get the grades. She just looked at him with eyes filling with tears.

Xavier cut in. 'She's still undecided, Dad. Maybe Imperial or Kings College,' he said, putting his arm around her and giving her a squeeze.

'Excellent,' Dante said, nodding at her appreciatively. 'I'll have a chat with the head when you get back, see if we can't get you into some kind of intensive tutoring programme after school to make sure you're on track.'

All she could do was swallow and nod like an imbecile, but the tears still came. She just couldn't help it. The kindness was just overwhelming.

Several pairs of arms came around her, but she was aware of Xavier's the most. As if he wanted to take the lead even in consoling her. His mouth was next to her ear. 'I'm sorry, Paige. Please let me make it up to you. We'll talk, I promise, OK? It's forever, you and I. Forever.'

She drew back to look deeply into his eyes to see if he meant it. They looked misty and intense. But not before she felt the heavy shadow of Hunter passing like an eclipse. She didn't turn but she felt him and instinctively knew he'd left the room. Leaving her feeling the worst kind of imposter all round.

Thankfully, after many hugs and good wishes, her cloud dispersed and so did the crowd around her. The lights dimmed to candlelight and she felt Christmassy for the first time that year. Finally, she could relax and enjoy what turned into a magical evening. The strange angelic woman from the underwater city was introduced as the High Priestess of the Five Moons. Xavier explained that their official religion was known as The Way of the Five Moons. She led the prayer of thanks to something they referred to as the Orb and then everyone sang a song with a haunting melody and unfamiliar words. It was hypnotic and strange, as all the tall ones from her undersea family sang from their minds and yet they could hear them all. Then, when they built to a huge crescendo, everyone clapped as if they'd achieved a marvellous thing.

The king held up his glass, looking as moved as she was. 'To family and friends. Long may we continue to gather like this. Appreciating and supporting each other. Grateful that we prosper in this beautiful world.'

Everyone clapped and cheered.

'Now let's dance, and ring in the Orbstice.'

The young children took turns in ringing a huge bell and then went off single file with the nanny. Each one smiling and waving as they went to 'ahs' and clapping from the onlookers. The music went up to full as Xavier's mother slipped behind her decks. Chairs and tables were pushed aside and everyone began to dance. Waiting staff rushed here and there, clearing space and carrying off the remnants of supper.

Xavier pulled her to him. 'I really do love you,' he whispered next to her ear.

The flutter in her heart was immediately stabbed through with a painful reminder. 'You hurt me,' she said, coldly back. He looked so wounded that holding onto her anger felt churlish, especially after all the wonderful presents and speech from his father. A king. A real, bona fide king. She had to concentrate on not getting swept up in it.

She searched Xavier's unbelievably handsome face that looked back at her with curiosity – a small smile now playing on his lips as if he sensed her thawing. 'Please say you're still mine, Paige. I made a terrible mistake. I know that now. If I could go back and change what I said, I would.'

'But did you mean it though, Xav? Binding seems a pretty big deal to your family. And never is a pretty long time.'

He let out a long sigh and pulled her off to the side where the music wasn't quite so loud. They both leaned against the stone wall. 'Look, I'm not going to lie how important inheriting my father's kingdom is to me, but please don't forget that I love JJ too. Even though he is my opponent in it. When I said what I said, I did mean it in a way.'

Her eyebrows rose in shock and she turned to walk away, but he pulled her back. 'Hear me out, please, Paige. What I was going to say was that I can't have that kind of distraction right now. When I win and there is no doubt of the succession, if we go the distance, then yes, of course I will bind you to me.'

Paige took the hand he placed over his heart as a solemn promise. It was everything she'd wanted to hear and her heart ached at the strength of it. But despite his frank words, she couldn't help thinking of Hunter now alone in his lab. So beautiful and sad, with no one but his grief to keep him company.

The next thing she knew, Xavier's lips were on hers, branding her as his with a searing kiss. She felt stiff at first, not able to shift from the mental image of Hunter. Her mind seemed clogged with 'what ifs', and 'maybes'. Hunter was right, Xavier did always get what he wanted. But then she remembered what he'd been like back in London. How she'd loved him then. How he was around her family. How brilliant he was about everything. There was no place for Hunter back there. Nor would he ever want to be. Hunter was all about magic and the sea. Something so far out of her realm of experience. Xavier was real. He operated in her ordinary, everyday life. Then Xavier's father's offer of generous support of her career and it was easy. So easy to give in.

She was kissing Xavier back. Fully. Deeply. From the depths of her soul. She was a fool to ever think she could pull away. 'OK,' she said, breathing heavily next to his lips.

His forehead rested against hers. 'Don't ever scare me like that again,' he said, huskily. 'I thought I'd lost you.'

'Don't be a complete arse again, then.' She grinned.

He laughed and kissed her. 'It's the best Christmas ever. Let's get out of here.' He went to walk off and pull her with him, but she stood her ground. 'I just need to go somewhere first.'

Xavier's face immediately clouded. 'To him.'

'No ... yes. Don't say it like that. He's a friend, Xav. I just need to let him know I'm OK. Please trust me.' As she said the word, trust, a pain pinched her heart as she knew she wasn't being totally honest. The truth was, she needed to check on Hunter. To check they were OK. It confused the hell out of her.

Xavier was studying her for lies and eventually nodded. Then tried to lead the way. 'But I'm coming.'

She shook herself out of his grip. 'No you're not. The least you can do is give me the space to see that my friend doesn't worry.' She watched the small flinch register on his face and knew she had the upper hand. She immediately softened. 'Please, Xav. I promise that's all it is.'

Xavier reluctantly took a step back out of her way.

She walked away quickly, without looking him in the eye. Her stomach became filled with a mixture of gurgling acid and butterflies. *Was this normal? Was she normal thinking like this?* All she knew was that after kissing Xavier like that, she had to go to Hunter. To explain. To check he was OK with it. Excited. She felt terrible. Totally confused.

ALEXIA REFUSED to come out of her room for the whole of Christmas Day. It was only really celebrated to acknowledge the host planet. In reality, it was Orbstice Eve, or Night of the hallowed Orb, as it was known in the old language. It celebrated the night the Orb chose and landed on the Earth, 10,500 years ago. It brought it out of the last ice age and made it the habitable world it was now.

She sent her food away, even though it was her favourite: clam fettuccini and a huge slab of chocolate cake. She had it every year and loved this holiday, but this year, everything was ruined. It was supposed to be the best one ever. Instead, she could only languish in her bed alone, listless, crying and praying that Yaro would not give up on her in is hatred of what her family had done to him.

There was another quiet knock at her door. She knew the powerful presence immediately. She glanced at her clock. 9.30 p.m. The time for gifts and prayers of thanks must be over and it was bedtime for the children.

'Go away, Dad!' she shouted.

Please, darlin' came directly into her head. *Let's talk.*

'I don't want to talk to you ever again. You broke my heart.'

Oh please don't say that. All is not lost.

She thought about that. Did he mean it, or was he just trying to smooth it all over so that they could go on as normal? Her father was definitely crafty enough. However, curiosity got the better of her and she unlocked the door with her mind. He could have barged in, but he didn't.

She flashed angry eyes at him as he came and sat on the bed next to her. She remained lying on her side, with her hands pressed together under her cheek. 'I don't know what you think you can say to make me feel better,' she said, refusing to look at him.

He put out a hand and touched her back, looking at her intently. 'Please come and join us or at least eat something.'

'Why would I do that?' she snapped. 'You ruined my life.' It all welled up in her again and her face crumpled as she attempted to hold back her tears. All her plans of being with Yaro, had been so close and were now in tatters.

'I thought you believed in your male,' her father said in his thick Irish brogue, gently giving her arm a squeeze.

'Of course I do,' she said, sniffing. 'I love him. More than anyone,' she added, flashing a spiteful glare at her father.

His eyebrows rose a little in surprise. 'Well, you're acting as though everyone was right and he was only after what he could get.'

She sat up sharply, shrugging his hand off her. 'That's a lie. He loves me, I know he does.'

'Then why do you think he would give up on you so easily?'

She scowled, hating that her father had a point. *Deep down, did she think Yaro had decided she was not worth the effort?*

'Look,' her father said, reaching out and gently waggling her chin. 'Do you know what I think?'

Her eyes remained on his as she weakly shook her head.

'I don't think he's gone far.'

'What makes you say that?' Her voice sounded small and pathetic, just like she felt inside.

'Well, there's only one airport in Malta. They could have swum to Sicily, but none of my sources say anyone fitting their description has flown from there. They are kind of conspicuous,' he said with a wry smile. 'I don't think he's finished here.' He sat back and nodded as if he were talking to himself. 'Now if I were you, I'd be more worried about what his next move will be. Does he plan on exertin' his revenge on us all? I don't think this is over, Alexia.'

Her heart hammered. He was right. She'd been acting like a silly little girl. 'Well, you do deserve it. Why did you have to do that to him, Dad?'

Her father sensed her thawing and pulled her into his arms. She allowed it, needing time to think. To plan. She had to be ready. *What kind of daring rescue would Yaro hatch?*

'Ahh, it all got out of control. I will be having serious words with Vionne, you can be sure about that.'

She couldn't help hugging into her father. He had made her feel better.

He kissed the top of her head and kept his face there, smelling her skin, as he'd done since she was small. 'For what it's worth, your male handled himself very well, I thought, and would be a formidable enemy.'

'What makes you say that?' she said, drawing back, completely intrigued.

'Well … despite his bad reputation on land with the humans, he escaped without hurting a soul while causing quite a bit of damage,' he chuckled.

She breathed easier and looked at him earnestly. 'I still want to marry him, Dad.'

'I know you do,' he said, stroking her hair.

CHAPTER 53

*A*lexia only agreed to go for the remainder of the Orbstice celebrations just to show her face. To the humans, it was Christmas Day night. The twenty-fifth. Just as the world's celebrations were slowing down after eating and drinking too much and slobbing out in front of the TV, theirs were only just beginning. A great party went into the night, giving thanks for the bounty the Orb had always given them. Only there were no celebrations in her heart this year. Nor would there ever be again. Not for the Orb, her family, or anyone. Not until she was reunited with Yaro. Until he was truly accepted, given his rightful place and she was married to him.

Her father cajoled her into coming down to be amongst family, even if she didn't want to join in. He settled her on a sofa next to her Aunt Lacy, her mother's favourite sister and her Uncle Keenan's wife. Their kids, Rock and Flame, were off somewhere with all the other teenagers.

After a big smothering hug from Lacy, she curled into a ball on the sofa and people watched. How easy it was for everyone else. They weren't forced to fit into the human world. To go to school with strange people and strange customs.

She spotted Rock and Flame flirting outrageously with Latitia's brothers. *With Dwayne.* They were laughing and falling about as if they were drunk. How childish it all seemed now. Yet only a few months ago, she'd have given her right arm to be one of them.

Her gaze fell on her Murr cousins next, looking on with wonder, already wishing for human girls of their own.

Her attention was caught when Paige walked across the room to the exit. She tracked back and saw Xavier watching her walk away. He didn't seem upset. More worried and agitated. He'd come up against something he couldn't control. Feelings were like that. She could only imagine how hard he was to deal with. Still, she wished them luck. Paige was good for him. He would be impossible without her. If only she knew how much he cared. *What a lug head.*

It took a while sifting the crowd before she spotted JJ and Latitia. The ones she envied most of all. They'd found a darkened corner. She could only just make them out, totally lost in each other's worlds. She was so happy for JJ. All the angst of last term seemed forgotten now everything was out in the open. It made her well up with emotion. She never thought it would happen for him. He was always such an intense, disconnected boy. But Latitia had reached him in a way that no one else could. So even though they were far too young, she was optimistic for them. If anyone was going to make it as a couple, it would be those two.

Her aunt sat on Keenan's lap and kissed him. They'd been together since they were children. Her gaze shot to her mother, being pulled from her dais by her father to dance. Even Valarie was dancing with Reeve, the strong and handsome guard. Everyone had their lives. Their loves. Everyone was allowed to love the person they wanted, except her.

'Hey!' a familiar voice said.

And one other. She looked up sharply and saw Jay standing there, holding out his hand.

JJ COULDN'T KEEP his hands off Latitia. So much so that Xavier was smiling smugly every time he looked over at him like he was turning soft. He hated it and wanted to punch the look right off his face, even though a small part of him knew he was probably right. He'd pulled Latitia into a dark corner just to be this with her. Alone, dancing so close, it was barely legal in present company. And she responded so perfectly. Her body moulded to his, moving effortlessly to an old reggae tune he knew was one of his dad's favourites.

The bond shifted in his chest and he moved his mouth next to her ear. 'Let me know when we can get out of here.'

She giggled and simply looked up at him. She didn't say anything. She didn't need to. The look she gave him said it all. 'Stop teasing, I'm hanging by a thread here,' he said, trying to look serious.

She laughed playfully. How lovely it was to see her like this. Carefree. Happy. Such a different person to just a few days ago.

'Whatever will you do when we go back to London?' she asked. 'I'll be back at mine and we'll be at school all day. You'll be off doing all your dodgy schemes with Xavier.'

She was toying with him, watching his reaction, but she had a point. He hadn't given much thought to when they went back. He must have given himself away, because she kissed him on the lips and said, 'Don't worry, I'm not trying to move in with you or anything.' She visibly shuddered. 'I'd end up doing something I'd regret to Xavier.'

He smiled at her, but it troubled him. *What was he going to do when they got back?* They were a very different couple to the one they were when they left. He could barely keep his hands off her. The bond demanded feeding every day. That could make her very sick if it began to starve. And she would need protection. How could he do that if she was streets away?

'What's the matter?' she said. 'You look like you've seen a ghost.'

He tightened his grip around her as if she would be spirited away right then.

'Tell me, JJ. You're scaring me.'

Her little face looked so cute and concerned that the words just slipped out. 'I love you.'

Her face transformed into the most beautiful smile and she kissed him solemnly. 'I know you do, silly,' she said, pulling away. 'I know everything about you now.'

He searched her face so full of wonder. Of course, he did know that, but now she understood how little he knew of her. He could only guess by her actions and maybe sense a bit more from her aura, but a huge gap of how she felt was missing. 'Maybe we *should* live together when we go back to London.'

Her look of surprise was not exactly what he was going for.

'Not with Xavier, but a place of our own, where I can look after you.'

Her face slowly transformed from surprise to anger. 'I don't need looking after,' she said, shoving him away from her in the chest.

He immediately let her go, but he couldn't understand why she was acting like this. He thought she'd be happy. This was huge for him. 'What?' he said, nonplussed. 'That's not what I meant at all.'

'Yes you did. You think I'm a silly little human who can't think for herself. Well, news for you, buddy, I don't want to live with you.'

Buddy? His eyes widened in shock, still hoping she was joking. All he could say was, 'What?' he was so blindsided. How did they go from him telling her he loved her to this. 'I thought you'd be into the idea.'

She tutted and went to push past him and leave him standing there like an idiot, but he caught her by the arm and swung her around. 'You don't get to swan off like that, Latitia.' She was driving him to the point of temper and that rarely happened and wasn't pretty. 'You'd better start talking … Now!' he demanded, through a clenched jaw so tight, he felt his teeth creaking. His mind zeroed to perfect clarity, waiting for the answer that was a long time coming. It was gratifying to see she was finally taking him seriously in the large swallow she took.

But she didn't cower. Instead, her hands went to her hips, her face creased in anger and her head tilted to the side. Then she jabbed a finger at him. 'You don't get to speak to me like that, JJ. And you don't order me around or pull me about, either.'

His arms flopped to his sides in exasperation, he was so completely at a loss. *Where had all this come from?* She'd never spoken to him like this, and for a moment he couldn't speak. Her aura, normally weak, was flashing colours of fire, proving she meant every word.

It was a hard knock to his ego that he managed to pull together into one razor-sharp point. 'What do you want then?' His voice was now several octaves lower as he tightened his jaw and unclenched his fists. He clearly didn't know the girl that stood in front of him now.

She shifted her weight uncomfortably, but his anger was a

stalking animal that would not let her get away with an outburst like that. 'Well? What's your plan?'

It was mildly gratifying to see her deflate under pressure. She was already wishing she hadn't taken them into such unchartered territory. It was all over her startled face.

'Well?' he prompted, eyebrows raised in a question. In that moment, they weren't in a huge room full of revellers. It was just the two of them with the world on mute. 'You've got something to say. Let's hear it.' He didn't know why he was pushing her like this. She was clearly out of her depth. But he was beyond furious, in a way he'd never felt with a girl before. He'd done everything for her. Even laid himself open and admitted he loved her, and she'd taken it like it was nothing and stamped all over it.

Her eyelids dropped to narrow slits, like everything drained down to pure hate. 'So that's how it's going to be, is it? You don't have to be such an arse, JJ. I only picked you up on the way you think you can push me around. I love you. I *am* in love with you, but I don't want to be reduced to an accessory. I'm my own person and I want my own things. And if you don't know that then you're not the person I thought you were.' She kissed her teeth, turned and said viciously over her shoulder. 'Don't speak to me until you can behave like a grown up … Xavier.'

Xavier? How dare she. He and Xavier were poles apart in who they were. He stood there blinking as if she'd slapped him across the face. She'd managed to do it again. Just when he thought they had some kind of even footing, she threw him a curve ball he never saw coming to hit him round the side of the head. He had no idea what she meant, whether they were still together, or even if she planned on seeing him when they went back to London.

. . .

'CARE TO DANCE?' Jay said, with the most irresistible wink and smile Alexia had ever known.

Alexia rolled her eyes, not helping the smile that stole across her face. She really tried her best to hold onto her bad mood but still put her hand in his. 'I'm supposed to be angry, Jay. I don't want to pretend I'm not.'

With the smallest flick of his hand, she was on her feet and dancing with him to a slower song. He held her gently, but his arms always felt strong. Safe. Home. She nestled into his warmth and they were quiet for a long moment.

Jay seemed on his own a lot. His wife, Ruby, would be there somewhere. Usually with her own family, the Santalinis and their only child together, Persephone, who was only about seven or eight. Ruby had never been particularly close to any of them growing up. Civil, that was about it. Everyone knew that Jay's heart had never really left her mother. That must be hard for a second wife to bear, even though her mum had chosen her father in the end.

She felt desperately sorry for him then and hugged him to her. She felt his chin rest on her head. 'You *are* like my dad, Jay.' she said into his shoulder.

He drew back slightly, smiling at her. 'I'm honoured, but what brought this on?'

She shook her head and hugged into him again. She didn't want him to see her tears. 'Even when I'm angry, I wanted you to know that I do know that.'

He strengthened his grip around her and she wanted to let it all out and cry. He was probably the only person in the whole room who got what it was to love someone you couldn't have. Maybe she'd been kidding herself all along. Her father was never going to accept Yaro. He was probably right. She was just a silly young girl and someone like Yaro would never really be interested in her. Someone who'd never lived or had anything interesting to say. Maybe her brothers were right, too, and she should be the one laughing in the group of teenagers, with Dwayne. All she'd been to Yaro was the perfect link in the golden chain to the power of the kingdom. That was all. What a stupid, stupid fool she'd been.

Then, in a gust of wind, every light and sound went off and they were plunged into darkness.

CHAPTER 54

*A*lexia went totally blind to the cause of the screams and gasps all around her. Then, before she could adjust, a white light ignited, just as blinding. Halogen bright. Jay's rough hands pushed her behind him. Her nose was pressed against his back and she could smell his warm scent coming through his shirt.

Before she knew what was happening, the males had herded them together, forming a wall of strength around them on the outside, all in no more than a few seconds. There was a moment of quiet, where they all jostled and groaned in shock. She turned her head, making sure she kept her body in contact with Jay. Several sources of bright light shone equally spaced around the room. She managed a clear view when a guard quickly stooped to grab someone still outside the circle. Her heart was beating so hard in her chest, she could barely breathe. She was beginning to focus and the source of the lights started to take shape. Masculine shape. She had to squint, as if she were looking at the sun. If she tried to look away, she couldn't see anything but their outline printed on her retinas.

Then, in a heart-stopping bolt, she understood. Like the weight of a huge boulder crushing her chest.

Ambragio. Lots of them. Like a fanfare, or a proclamation of power. Their inner light exposed in the aura of angels, revealed in the darkness for the whole assembly to see. She forgot her fears. Her heart exploded with pleasure. Exhilarated. Honoured. So proud of who they were, she felt she'd burst.

She heard Keenan behind her. 'What the hell are they?'

Her heart was beating so hard. 'It's Yaro,' she whispered, next to Jay's back.

Jay attempted to keep her behind him, but she ducked under his arm to stand next to him. 'I'm here, Yaro.' It came out high-pitched and broken, as she looked along the line of males. Until one turned his phosphorescent face towards her and held out his arms. His smile was as dazzling as it was beautiful. He was beautiful. 'Come to me.'

She went to run, but Jay caught her arm. She struggled and Keenan stepped forward to help, but Yaro put up a warning hand to him that stopped him in his tracks. Then shifted it to Darres, who also went to help. His reflexes were unbelievably fast. 'Stop!' Yaro said, still holding up his hand. 'I want no violence. I have come for Alexia and I will leave.'

'It's OK, Jay,' her father's voice came from behind her. 'Let her go.'

Jay's hand loosened on her arm and she ran to Yaro's glowing form. His arm immediately went around her and she was surprised to feel he irradiated heat. He kissed her forehead. 'Moya Lyubov.' Her heart fluttered at him calling her his love. She hugged into him fiercely.

Yaro's keen, seeking eyes rested on her father, Dante. He walked forward with her mother and Jay on her other side.

Pavel stepped in to bar their way, but Yaro put up his free hand to stop him. 'It's OK. Let them approach.'

'It appears you are king in my great hall,' her father said, but he was not joking today.

'I have no wish to take your kingdom. Only that which I was given in front of this very room of witnesses,' Yaro replied.

Alexia looked up at his taut jaw and knew he was suppressing intense emotion.

Her father normally so tall and imposing, seemed to shrink with weariness. 'Please, Yaro. As the father, I know you must be, after living such a long and successful life … she is so young.'

Alexia blinked as she watched her father's mouth move and then up as Yaro's did the same. She recognised only that what he was saying was tight and clipped. She was stuck on her father's referring to common ground with Yaro being a father too. That couldn't be right. She'd seen no children. He never spoke of passed wives. Dead wives. *Oh my god!* Current wives. *Could he be ... married to someone else?*

She was in such shock; all she could do was burrow her nose into the bare skin of Yaro's chest. She smelled the salt-water. They had come straight from the sea. Salt was already drying in crystals.

Strangely, it was her father who cut through her nose-dive. 'What do you want, Alexia? I'm not saying you can't see him. Only that you live at home and go to school, like any other teenager your age.'

She could hear the distress in her father's voice. Despite his strength as a king, he was pleading with her. She could also feel the tension running through Yaro's body, like piano wires. She could feel him containing it, perfectly, as he always did. She knew she could do what her father wanted. Be around her family, with all her loved ones. But she also remembered what it was like in the beginning, back in London. When even JJ thought he could rule her life. How she'd only met Yaro in the first place because of her need to escape them. She could feel the tightness under Yaro's skin. His apprehension. His worry at what she would decide. That wasn't a sign of a male in love with somebody else. In the whole time she'd lived with him, there had never been a slip or mention of anyone.

Children. That was another matter. A subject that had never come up in conversation before. A question she would need answering. However, she had always known, as with any older male, that he could not reach his great age without having some sort of past.

In that moment she made up her mind. That despite loving every single person in this room, she would never know a day's happiness again unless she went with Yaro. She needed to find out for herself if they could make it as a couple. 'I want to go with you,' she said quietly, looking up at Yaro.

His sharp eyes softened and he nodded once. 'You have your answer,' he said, facing her mother and father again.

She wanted to burrow into Yaro's body at the look of disappointment and anguish burning in her mother and father's eyes. Her mother went to come forward to plead with her, but her father held her back. 'We wronged you. I know that,' her father said, addressing Yaro, rather than her. 'But I spoke honestly in all my promises to you and your family. All your requests have been met. Please think of Alexia. Don't take her away like this, from everything she knows and loves … because of pride.'

She let out a squeal as a whirlwind spun her around and Pavel caught her. Yaro moved so fast, out of her arms and into her father's space, she hadn't even seen him move. Guards shouted and stepped forward, way too slowly. Her father stopped them with a hand. 'The children,' he said as a sharp reminder, flicking his eyes at her.

A deep resignation sank like a stone at how he saw her. How he would always see her.

Yaro, however, didn't bat an eyelid. 'You think I ended your pathetic tests out of pride?' Annunciating every word, slowly and distinctly. They were toe to toe, eyes locked, taking the measure of each other.

Alexia's initial shock and fear that one of them would get hurt was displaced by a strange sense of pride. This was the only man on this earth who could stand up to her father. At that moment she couldn't even call who would win. Despite the trappings of power and kingdoms. As men, Yaro was not afraid of her father and she exulted in it. He was undoubtedly the man for her.

'Yes, I am proud. Proud of my family. My heritage. That we survived in the most harsh and unforgiving conditions for aeons. That we are strong even though we have been hated and reviled for centuries, despite founding this world that you now stand in and enjoy. A pompous, spoiled nation, that has no clue what sacrifices were made. So yes, I guess I did leave your tests out of pride. Morey eels and a few trapdoors are an insult to me. I sought to be a part of this great nation, but you proved we will never be seen as such. We will forever be despised. It is clear to me now that it is nothing more than a whale's graveyard. Empty bones that were once animated by a great, majestic creature.'

'Then why do you take my daughter?' her father asked, through tight lips and narrowed eyes.

Alexia held her breath to take in every nuance of Yaro's response.

'I take her as the only promise I hold you to. We will leave as silently as we came. It will be as if we had never been. You will never find us. Never know where we are. Only that we are out there. Somewhere. Alexia and I will marry on her eighteenth birthday. This is enough. We were accepted by the mighty Orb. Our great history is in her memory. She told me this herself. That, and with Alexia, I have all that I need.'

By the time Yaro finished speaking, her heart was beating out of her chest. There was no waiting for a response from her father. Her breath was taken and she entered a vortex of wind, of light and of darkness. Until all she felt were the air bubbles and the searing cold of the sea. She was travelling so fast; she couldn't even expel her lungs to breathe the water.

DANTE BLINKED. In a gust of wind, Yaro, all his men and Alexia were gone. Even the lights and music whirred back on, as if someone had stopped and released the turntable with their hand. Dante looked around him, startled. Everyone appeared to be doing the same and began to whisper their surprise to their neighbour. Tia fell into him in tears.

'The fountain seal has been broken,' one of the guards said. 'That was their way in and out.'

'They were too fast to stop them,' said another.

Dante faced his old friend, Jay, looking stonily back at him. He was as speechless as they all were. All he could think was, his daughter had gone, and there wasn't a damn thing he could do to stop him.

That was the true answer to the tests, right there. His eyes locked with Vionne, thinking the same thing. *He could have taken everything, but he didn't.*

Yet, Vionne replied.

CHAPTER 55

$\mathcal{P}$aige knocked on Hunter's lab door amazed that she'd even found it. Maybe it was that she'd been there a few times. Or maybe she'd been guided by instinct. *His blood.* Her heart kicked at the thought of that.

It clicked open as if by magic and she pushed it and went inside. It took her a moment to get used to the low lighting and find Hunter sitting eating on his sofa. Then the lights went off, throwing them both into darkness. She drew in a sharp breath. 'Not funny, Hunter.'

'It's not me. Stay where you are. I'll find you.'

She stood rigid, listening to the slightest sound, until she heard the tisk and saw the burst of light from a match. Hunter took something from a shelf and lit the wick of an old lantern. 'Come in,' Hunter said. His face looked dark and creepy, from the soft glow underneath. He lit another three candles on petri dishes and flopped back down into the sofa. 'Power outages aren't unusual here.' He held out an arm for her to sit at the opposite end. 'What are you doing here? Thought you'd be loved up with the brat prince, now you're cosy with the family.'

She frowned at his snark. 'I am… Well, kind of. I just wanted to come and see if you're OK. To explain.'

He laughed and shook his head. 'And why would you feel the need to do that?'

He was annoying her now. 'You don't have to be a prick, Hunter. I'll just go.' She went to get up, but he leaned forward and stilled her arm.

'Don't go. You're right. I am being a prick.'

They both eased back into their seats.

'I guess I just hate these gatherings … and I have to admit, I hate that Xavier always gets his way.'

She frowned, processing that.

'Well, the lights have gone off, so the party will break up. So, there is that,' he said, grinning.

She couldn't help grinning back, not sure if she should be agreeing with him. He was such a grinch.

He looked puzzled.

She hoped he hadn't just read her mind. It was hard to keep up with what everyone could do.

'Weird the emergency lighting hasn't kicked in though.' He shook his head, thoughtfully, and she relaxed with relief at the change of subject. 'So, what did you come here to talk about?' he asked, absently. He reached over and picked his plate back up from the coffee table and resumed eating.

'Oh, nothing particularly.'

His eyebrow went up at that.

'I dunno, I was just worried about you.' Then, realising how lame that sounded, 'I wanted to come here.'

He let out a short breath and shook his head as he put a forkful of food in his mouth, chewing and looking at her deadpan. 'Pet project, am I?' He rolled his eyes and continued to chew.

It was coming out all wrong. 'No … no, of course not.' It wasn't why she was there at all. *Why was she there?* He was right. She was kind of back with Xavier. 'They got me an expensive laptop for Christmas – all my family expensive gifts, in fact. The king said he could get me a summer job to support my university application. And my mum a job at the school, so she doesn't have to work three cleaning jobs… She loves Xavier,' she threw in, knowing how it all sounded.

Hunter was watching her closely. Calculating. Judging her. 'So, he bought you,' he said, like a matter of fact, taking a large gulp of his soda.

Paige jumped to her feet. 'That's not fair, Hunter. You don't know what he's like when we're alone. How well we get on in London.' She wanted to cry. A surge of anger felt like it was strangling her. Hating that there could be a grain of truth in what he was saying.

Then he was there in front of her and she was looking up into his brown face. His eyes were so dark, they were black pools of oil, aflame with the reflection of the candle. 'And do you love him?' Hunter asked, his head at a slight angle. 'Because there is a world of difference between a deep love that constricts your soul so tight you can't breathe and simple flattery from some prince who made you feel special for once in your life, with a few gifts.'

She narrowed her eyes at his unrepentant expression, after verbally slapping her. There was no nice way this conversation was going but she was caught in his words. 'Is that how you felt about Avalon?'

As intended, his attack retreated immediately. He scowled and flopped back down on the sofa. 'That was different.'

Now she had him on the run, she couldn't help herself. 'Why was it different? You were still a boy and girl, weren't you? Atlantean or not.'

He laughed at her derisively, then dipped his head as if she had played a great counterattack.

'Well, weren't you? You've got so much to say about me

and Xavier.' It felt like she was going for the kill. She just couldn't stop herself.

He narrowed his eyes, playfulness gone. 'You and Xavier,' he said, laughing bitterly again. 'There is no real you and Xavier. No comparison.'

Now he was really getting on her nerves. 'What do you mean by that?'

'You haven't slept together. He hasn't bound you.'

Paige couldn't believe he was being so spiteful. 'He told me he will bind me when he's king. He just needs to concentrate on that first. I think that's sensible.'

Hunter really laughed at that, like another slap. 'You think JJ thought about anything when he bound your friend? Or me with Avalon? It's passion, Paige. It comes over you and takes over everything. Your body. Every sane thought. You can't help yourself … Even if your life depended on it,' he finished, trailing off, averting his eyes.

Paige knew he wasn't saying everything. A painful memory had taken him to somewhere dark. Nevertheless, his blow landed. If Xavier was making a conscious decision about her, then he was either very strong, or simply didn't feel it. It was a low blow that hit her hard. It hurt and made her want to lash back. But most of all she felt confused. Disappointed. In Xavier. In Hunter. She turned on her heel and went to walk towards the door. 'You don't have to be an arse all the time, Hunter.'

'Maybe that's all I know how to be,' he said, in a quiet voice.

It made her stop and turn around to look at him.

'It was our thing: arguing, Avalon and me. We did it constantly … I mean, I didn't want to, but she lived off it. Like she needed it to feel. It wasn't exactly healthy, our relationship. But I was an addict for it. The fights … The passion that followed.'

Paige wandered back over to where Hunter was sitting. He looked devastated. As if it only happened yesterday. 'It must have been terrible losing someone you loved like that?'

Hunter flashed his eyes at her angrily. 'Try losing someone with unfinished business. A relationship that was one long argument, that ended badly. Leaving questions that I'll never get answered,' he said on a bitter huff of laughter. 'And she knew... Yeah, she sure did. That I'd never get over it.' His face was contorted with rage, tears glittering in his eyes, making her reach out a tentative hand to touch his shoulder.

He jumped, making her snatch it back. His look was pure hatred. 'You don't understand. No one ever will. I loved her *and* I hated her. She had no love in her, but I loved her in spite of it... Because of it... I dunno. All I know is, she was cold. But for some reason she wanted only me. Needed me. And I clung to that. Oh boy, did I. Couldn't get enough of her... I guess, in the end, we were the only ones who could give each other what we needed.' He was lost in his tirade, his face crumpled with anger and disgust. 'We didn't talk, only fought. I'm a living scar, Paige. Broken by her. And every cut she made never heals. It festers and it's the way I want it. I never want to heal, because then she'll be truly gone.'

Paige felt the tears run down her own face, crying for him. His wretched pain that felt like a demon attached to his soul. 'Stop, Hunter!' she pleaded as a sob escaped her. She couldn't stand any more.

'Then she went and left me for her watery grave and had the last laugh. I dream of it every time I close my eyes. I see her drowning face in mirrors, glass and especially when I do the one perfect thing we shared. The only place I can be free: when I surf. She whispers from beneath the waves: "You couldn't save me. You're nothing. Nobody. Useless. A pathetic excuse for a male. You need me to live. You'll never be free of me ... never."'

Paige was sobbing by the time he finished. His face was ashen and lost in his nightmare. She took in his hunched-over body, utterly beaten down by his heartbreak. She didn't know whether to leave him or go to him to give him comfort. Instead, she took a breath and just said the only thing she could think of: the truth; 'You were in an abusive relationship, Hunter.' She'd read about it and seen it in films, but she never truly understood the horror of it until now. The way he mourned her. Shut himself away. Making no connections with other people. To think she had envied it. She'd simply believed it was too beautiful for him to let go. But it wasn't that at all. He just clung to it. A warped idea of love he depended on, as the only thing he knew.

When he finally looked up at her, blinking, as if he'd just woken up, he was stricken. For a moment, she couldn't tell what he was thinking. What he would do. Strike her or run. Her heart beat a hard, uneven, rhythm in her chest. 'Surely, you can see that a love like that would either burn itself out or kill one of you? That is the answer to your unanswered question.' Her feet felt frozen to the floor and she whimpered as he slowly rose from the chair, glaring at her.

'Why are you looking at me like that?' he asked, stalking closer to her.

She leaned back as her feet wouldn't move. He was trying to scare her and it was working. 'Because I like you, Hunter,' she whispered, swallowing a gulp of air. 'Someone's got to say this to you. I've just realised that I didn't know you at all.'

He remained staring at her in shock as if she'd punched him.

'You're this insanely good-looking, cool scientist, oxymoron of a person, who's strong and clever. Brooding over a lost love, like every girl's dream and the truth is, you're mourning someone who treated you appallingly. I can't believe that.' She wished she could just shut up because Hunter's face was becoming redder and angrier the more she spoke and the closer he got, until his face was mere inches from hers. He was so close; she could feel his Cherry Coke breath. She was barely breathing by the time his mouth was almost touching hers.

For the first time in knowing him, she felt a real quake of fear. But along with it was something building in her abdomen. A growing, gnawing need, unfurling. She'd never felt it before. Not even with Xavier.

'You wanna know why I loved her, little page-turner? Because I recognised something in her that was a mirror of me. She was irrevocably broken. And, unlike me, I admired that she never questioned it. She didn't analyse it. She just lived it. Taking what she wanted with no apology to the world. That is perfect strength, little girl.'

Paige was blinking with every word, as his mouth was so close to hers it grazed it a few times. He was deliberately belittling her to something small and insignificant in his temper, but her temper was rising too. She smiled spitefully back. 'Don't you dare try to put me down. You ... you're a fraud. You've memorialised a drowning girl, and I don't mean drowning in the literal sense,' she said, her own face creasing with disgust as she poked him in the chest to get him to step off.

His eyes widened as if she'd slapped him back. It gave her the confidence to keep going. She poked him again. 'She was drowning long before the sea took her. She was pushing you under just to keep her head above the water. Can't you see that? She admired you. She must have done. A prince, as clever and accomplished as you are. She knew who you were and got off on diminishing you.'

He snapped out of his shock and anger returned to his

face. He stepped into her again. 'You didn't even know her,' he spluttered, but with nowhere near as much venom. More, with exasperation.

Paige knew he was beaten. The cogs were clicking away in his brain as he sieved through what she'd said. Her words had hit him and taken his legs of argument away. Words that no one had dared say to him before. 'You're a fraud, Hunter, but you're not as bad as she was.'

For the first time, he frowned and took a step back in his uncertainty. She took her opportunity and began to walk towards the door. 'Don't you dare look down on me for getting back with Xavier,' she said over her shoulder. 'Avalon trod you down consistently just to function.'

She was at the door and just about to put her hand on the handle.

'Some of us need a love like that to make them feel something … anything,' Hunter said quietly. His voice sounded husky and deep.

She turned and looked at his dark, ghostly form in the candlelight. 'You've got a wonderful family who loves you. You need to step out of her shadow and into the light.' She turned back and pulled the door open a little.

'Everyone hates me because of my father. He didn't just disgrace himself, but me as well.'

Paige thought about that for a moment, her hand still on the door handle. She didn't know what to say, she knew so little about it. 'Then prove you're nothing like him.' With that, she snatched open the door and walked out into the bright corridor. The lights had come on and she could breathe cool air. She hadn't realised how hot and stuffy it had become in there. She closed her eyes and felt it lift her spirits. Suddenly she wanted to be with her family. Her friends. Xavier. She wanted his arms around her, whispering everything was going to be OK.

CHAPTER 56

*L*atitia was already asleep when JJ finally got into bed much later that night. Peaceful. Oblivious. Facing away from him, like she didn't give a damn.

He lay on his back and stared up at the carved rock ceiling. At least she was still there in his room, he guessed. She was such a contradiction nightmare. He couldn't remember anyone he'd spent time with ever being this hard.

Alexia had left an aching hole in his chest and taken the last of his fears of being all-in with Latitia with her. Like a wake-up call, that they weren't kids anymore and there was no turning back the clock. Typical, that Latitia would choose this night of all nights to decide that she wasn't so sure. Just when he needed her.

His arm slipped over his eyes as his heart sank lower. This was exactly what Xavier was talking about. Latitia was making him lose his mind. He had to pull himself together, otherwise he'd lose her and his fight for the kingdom.

His mother and father were distraught and had closed themselves off in their apartments. There was no bothering them now. Cesaré and Keenan had gone to talk with their grandfather and uncles of waging war to get her back. But it was clear where she wanted to be. They just had to come to terms with it. And despite Yaro's questionable lifestyle, there was no one better to look after her.

JJ just felt sad. Probably because on top of everything going on with Latitia, he knew Alexia had gone forever this time. That fierce little girl who always stood up for him, braided his hair and told him bedtime stories, was no more. She would have advised him on what to do if she was there. It tore him up that he'd taken her so for granted. She was the one person with her own mind who could always be relied upon. Now the strong girl had grown into a formidable young woman, who'd chosen to marry a dangerous prince, but he was a prince and a purebred, nonetheless. No one could deny he was eligible. Instead, the whole palace was in mourning because, deep down, they had all come to realise the same thing as him.

He wondered how Xavier felt about Alexia leaving. Whether he felt any guilt for his part in pushing her away. He doubted that. He was back with Paige, maybe a little more sobered now he knew she wasn't a pushover. JJ was glad about that, because she would need that strength if she was ever going to hold her own with Xavier.

He let out a deep sigh and turned his head to look at Latitia still sleeping obliviously next to him. Her tight braids were fanned out all over the pillow where she hadn't bothered tying them into a tight knot. At least they were going back to London early. He didn't think he could stand the strain for much longer. He needed to know where he stood and what life would be like between them.

He envied her ignorance. She had no idea what trouble lay ahead for them. He guessed there was no need prolonging it. The celebrations had fallen flat and there seemed little point trying to revive them now. His mother and father needed space to process it all.

Latitia stirred and turned towards him after an enviable good night's sleep. JJ didn't give her time to fully wake before he kissed her, pulled her up with him and led her dozily towards the shower. He needed to know just how deep this new resolve went. She padded along with him, adorably half asleep, but allowed him to lead her. After all, it was nothing new. Since the bond, they showered together every morning. It was their routine. He was merely carrying on as normal what had become natural for them as a pair. She understood he needed the water to remain cool, but today, it gave her time to fully wake and the opportunity to stop what would inevitably happen if they got in the water.

She wasn't terrified of his changes, she now looked for them and seemed to like them. It was liberating and hot to see the interest in her eyes. More than he could ever have imagined. He never knew a human girl could hold this kind of power over him. She never had ambition for power and riches like Atlantean girls. He'd always thought she was purely into him for who he was.

Until the revelation of last night.

The water hit her skin and she sucked in a breath. There was no warming the water for her today. He wanted her fully awake. No room for sentiment. Today, just a cold; 'Do you want me?'

She frowned. 'Of course I—'

He cut off the last of her words with an all-consuming kiss that turned into a frantic tangle that pinned her to the wall. Kissing, breathing, lost in her completely, till there was nothing of them left. Falling to hard tile, rolling, bruising, scratching. On and on. Till every part of him exploded into pieces with her and they landed on the soft bed. Soaking wet and exhausted. With no concept of time or any idea how they got there.

JJ still had her in his grip, laying over her. Studying the hot blush form so beautifully in her cheeks. Despite the passion and the best sex of his life, he regarded her coldly. Watching for the slightest expression of love. He didn't speak. He'd already had his answer. The moment she succumbed in the shower he knew he had her. She couldn't resist him. She still wanted him as much as he wanted her. No amount of discussion or argument would ever outweigh that.

She frowned. 'You're angry.' She stated the words in a higher pitch, like she was upset and didn't understand why.

His anger was on a slow burn. She wanted space. He'd give her space. *We'll see what will happen then.* 'Not now,' he said, springing off her. 'Come on, we'd better get ready.'

Latitia got to her feet more slowly, thoughtful, furtively watching him while they dried and dressed. Then while they silently packed the rest of their things. 'Why does your father need us in his study?' she asked, finally breaking the silence, putting the last of her toiletries in her bag.

JJ shrugged, taking a last look around for anything left behind. 'Probably just wants a last word with us before we go.' He was not willing to let her off and make things easier. She wanted distance and he did distance well. He held out his hand for her to take. 'Leave the bags. Someone will take them,' he said with a cold smile.

She smiled nervously and took his hand like a timid fawn. He tried not to crush it during the short walk through the royal corridor to the king's study. The Johnsons and Paige's family were already there with Xavier, Cesaré, his grandfather Sebastian and great-uncle and statesman Alfonzo, Keenan and, so, he noticed, was Reeve. It was revealing that his position with Valarie had now progressed. He was glad.

At least it would keep her off his back. Only his dad, Jay, was missing.

Dante sat behind his desk, looking grim, like he hadn't had a wink of sleep. 'Perch somewhere, JJ. I won't keep you long.'

Valarie made room for Latitia, and JJ sat on the arm of the orange sofa next to her. The gravity of the atmosphere was a palpable weight in the air.

Dwayne raised his eyebrows at him, acknowledging that none of them knew what was happening. Xavier just shook his head, irritated with the whole thing already, having little patience for it.

'Thanks for coming,' Dante said, eventually. 'I wanted to apologise for cutting your stay short. As you can imagine, my wife and I are very upset with what has happened and have much to sort out for you in London. Living arrangements will remain the same … for now,' he said, fixing a hard glare on JJ and then Xavier. 'Girls with their parents, please.'

Xavier tutted and JJ stared at his father, blankly. It made no difference to him. However, he felt the heat of embarrassment from Latitia next to him. He didn't look at her. She'd made her decision.

Dante switched his gaze to the big guard standing at the back. 'Reeve, you are natural bodyguard to Val. Linda, I will assign someone for you.'

JJ looked across and thought she looked a little shaken, but she still nodded, albeit a little nervously. Paige gave her hand a squeeze. 'Your security will be increased, but please be on the lookout for anything unusual. We don't know yet whether we can trust Yaro Demidov's word. He is a powerful man in London … any last questions?'

'What about school?' Dwayne asked. 'Do we go as normal?' he asked, giving his brother a sideways grin.

Dante smiled and nodded. Probably just pleased he wasn't

freaking out. 'Yes. Act like nothing has happened. Go to school like always, except I've put some changes in place for the new term.' Dante looked directly at Valarie and Linda. 'Both of you will report to the head's office on the first day of term for your new jobs and give notice for your old ones. Everything will be fully explained when you get there.'

'What if we don't want a new job?' Valarie asked, but she was smiling and not annoyed at all.

Dante grinned at her menacingly. 'It will be an offer you can't refuse.'

Valarie locked eyes with Linda in mock surprise. She seemed to be taking it all really well. So much so, he wondered what had gone on without his knowledge.

JJ and Xavier swapped a glance too, both raising their eyebrows. Few got to see this side of Dante. He was always so light and charming. This was his no-nonsense king side, that JJ admired. 'What about us?' JJ asked, now a little unsure about more than just Latitia.

Dante looked at him and shrugged. 'Go on as normal. Except I want to know any interactions with Yaro or the Ambragio, right away … are we clear?'

He looked over at Xavier and they both nodded cautiously. 'What about the bugs?' Xavier asked. JJ had completely forgotten and noticed several swapped looks of confusion among the other youngsters. No one bothered to elaborate for them.

'That is no longer an issue,' Dante said and continued as if it had never come up. 'There will be a much stronger Atlantean presence at the school.'

JJ wasn't satisfied with Dante's whitewash and liked the sound of that even less. Xavier looked equally startled and unsure what that meant. 'Like what?' JJ asked. The last thing they wanted was interference in the new lives they'd painstakingly created. As if he didn't have enough problems.

'You won't be the only Atlanteans there,' the king said, already putting papers away in his desk.

Everyone was starting to get up, like the meeting was over. 'Like, who?' both he and Xavier said together. 'Teachers, guards, kids?' JJ persisted. Determined not to let the meeting break up before they knew.

'All three!' Dante said, getting to his feet. 'Several of your cousins will be starting.'

JJ sat up straighter. Everything was going too fast. People were leaving the room, but for him and Xavier the meeting was only just starting.

'Who, Dad?' Xavier asked, flatly. His face hardened, not liking the sound of it any more than JJ did.

Dante shook his head as if it was of little importance, or he couldn't be bothered to remember. 'Er, Keenan and Lacy's kids, Lily and Lance's ... and a couple of others. I'll let you know the full list when I know,' he said, dismissing it with a hand.

Xavier continued to stare at his father.

JJ didn't think it was so bad. Rock and Flame would be fun. Then JJ fell in. That meant Kali, Kai and Hunter. Hunter was coming to the school.

CHAPTER 57

Xavier turned on his heel with a huff and marched out, shouting, 'This is bloody ridiculous!' as he went. The rest of the room filtered out, quietly, after him, taking a wide-eyed Latitia with them. JJ stayed rooted to the spot.

Dante, now on his feet, frowned at him. 'What is it, JJ?'

'Can I have a minute?'

Dante regarded him closely in that eerie way that saw right through him. Then he relaxed, put his leather satchel down on the desk and perched on the edge of it. 'OK … shoot,' he said, pointing for him to sit down on the orange sofa.

JJ sat and leaned forward with his elbows on his knees and looked up through his eyebrows at his second father.

Dante grinned, suddenly back to his playful self. 'God, you look like your dad sometimes. The spittin' image … Go on,' he said, with a wave from his wrist.

JJ looked down at his hands clasped in front of him, not quite sure where to start. Or even if Dante was the right person to be having this conversation with. He was just the first of his parents he'd seen and it seemed an opportune moment.

Dante remained silent, so he was forced to look up at him again. 'I've got myself into a bit of a mess,' JJ said, looking down again after.

'Well, that's the truth,' Dante said, leaving a gap of silence for him to fill again.

JJ shook his head wearily. 'Not that … well, it is that. Connected to it … I don't bloody know.' He pushed his hand up through his hair and flopped back into the sofa. 'I bound her and just got my head around it and now she wants space. What the hell do I do with information like that? How does it even work?'

Dante's grin widened with every sentence, until he wanted to swear at him, give up and just walk out.

However, Dante seemed to relent, and his smile softened. 'Welcome to the adult and fickle world of women and relationships, Son.'

JJ scowled, not able to help himself. This wasn't helping and he didn't need his father making fun of him.

'Calm down about it all,' Dante said, patting the air with a hand. 'These things have a habit of working themselves out… Do you love her?'

JJ felt his cheeks heat. 'Well, yeah.'

Dante chuckled, which was as disconcerting as hell. 'And she loves you?'

'I think so,' JJ said, shuffling uncomfortably in his seat. 'She can't resist me.'

Dante laughed loudly at that. 'Oh, she can't can she?' He schooled his features and regarded him more seriously. Even looking a little sad. 'I'm afraid it's the curse of the one-way bond. Your dad felt it keenly,' he said, looking like he'd been transported to a distant time.

The dynamic between his dad and his father was fascinating. His dad, Jay, spoke of it so little. Probably because it was too painful or disloyal to his wife, Ruby. Or maybe just because he didn't talk much at all about stuff like that. It made him decide that Dante was the right person to talk to.

'How did dad get through it?' he asked, cautiously, not wanting to remind Dante of painful memories and clam up.

Dante let out a long sigh while he thought about it. 'Well, yer dad was the human, so it was your mother that never knew where she stood with him. But your dad was never one for shows of emotion anyway, as you know. Latitia isn't like that. I've seen the way she looks at you.'

JJ conceded that with a bob of his head. But fancying someone and love were two different things. 'Supposing she wants to split up. What happens then?' his hand dropping like a lead weight from his hair, in frustration. 'There's the bond … what if she wants to date someone else.'

'Hey … Hey!' Dante said, cutting him off. 'Stop getting ahead of yourself.'

JJ looked into his father's concerned eyes, in absolute misery. The more he talked, the more he realised he had no idea how to navigate any of this.

Dante leaned a little closer. 'Listen to me JJ. You are strong. Mentally and physically. You always have been from the moment you could walk. You got the obstinate trait from yer dad,' he said smiling, to lighten him up. 'Relationships are hard at the best of times; without everything you've got on yer plate. Let her do her thing and know she will not go far. You have nothing to worry about. Human boys won't even come close.'

It did make him feel a little better. He took guilty pride in the fact he'd ruined Latitia for other boys. But then he half frowned and half smiled in confusion. 'But how does that work? My dad's human.'

Dante laughed loudly and wagged his finger at him in

reproof. 'You cheeky bugger, get off with yer. You'll be fine. You have the strength of yer dad and the devil of yer mother. No one can resist that; I know first-hand.'

JJ got up from his seat and Dante pulled him into a tight hug, smacking his back loudly before releasing him and keeping hold of his shoulders. His face immediately switched back to serious mode. 'The bond … that's the important thing. That needs to be fed, whatever happens.'

'I know,' JJ said, already trying to turn towards the door, but Dante held him fast.

'No, you don't know, JJ. I've seen what starvation does. It ravages the body till you can't function.'

JJ stared into Dante's desolate eyes. He couldn't tell if he meant from his own experience, his dad's or his mother's. Only that there was devastation there. He nodded, sobered, receiving the message loud and clear.

'If she continues getting in the water with you on a regular basis then you have nothing to worry about. But if she stops doing that, then you need to contact me or your dad immediately, because more drastic measures will need to be taken.'

'Like what?' JJ asked, now more worried than ever.

But Dante gave him a gentle nudge. 'Go! It won't come to that. She's clearly yours. Go be with your girl.'

JJ walked slowly towards the door, trying to make sense of the advice Dante had given him that wasn't really advice at all. Yet he always seemed to make everything feel better, in his weird, dysfunctional parenting kind of way.

He took one last look over his shoulder at him before he left the room. He had big shoes to fill. Then he remembered, 'And the bugs, thing. Did you get to the bottom of why Yaro needed to listen in to the girls?' It had never made sense why Yaro needed to do that.'

Dante was no longer looking at him, busy collecting the

last of his stuff. 'I did.' He stopped what he was doing and looked at him flatly. 'He said it wasn't him and I believed him.'

JJ frowned, completely thrown. 'But that means—'

'Someone else.' He continued to close his briefcase. 'Leave the worrying to me. Just stay vigilant,' he finished with a genuine smile. 'Now go be a teenager. Think yourself lucky you don't have Xavier's problems.'

JJ scoffed, finding that very hard to believe. Xavier had a big mouth, but he'd managed to get Paige back. *What problems did he have?*

Dante was now walking quickly towards him, his mind already on other things. He rested his hand on his shoulder as he passed and marched off down the corridor, leaving him alone. He wished he could have questioned him more. He was so strong and knew so many things. About all kinds of people and what they thought and felt.

What did he know about Xavier that he didn't? He hadn't bonded with Paige. But without a bond, he guessed, girlfriend or not, she was fair game. *That could be it.* But all he had to do was bond with her and she'd never want a human boy again.

Then his heart dropped like a stone in his chest. *But what about another Atlantean?*

Hunter. That's all it could be.

He looked down the corridor in the direction his father had gone and slowly closed the door to the study after him. He wandered back to his room in deep thought and came to the conclusion that Dante was right. This could work out perfectly for him. He could have his freedom secure in the knowledge that Latitia was not really going anywhere.

Xavier, on the other hand, will be driven to distraction.

Without even realising, his father had given him a valuable clue. Xavier had far bigger problems on the horizon than his own.

CONTACT T

To receive your two, free, 21st Century Sirens Novellas, and be the first to know anything relating to T's books, leave your details here: https://mailchi.mp/d18c89c14f50/tstedmannovellas

Want to get reading something new right away?
Try The Blackwood Curse, Book 1 in the **Night Shades Series where you can download it from you favourite platform** or browse all T's books.

And please don't forget to leave a review wherever you bought your book, I really appreciate the feedback.
Much love,
T
www.tstedman.com
Facebook
TikTok

ALSO BY T STEDMAN

Young Atlanteans

Cross Heirs

Two Tribes

The Night Shade Novels

Demon in the Attic

The Blackwood Curse

(18+ books)

21st Century Sirens

Soul Breather

Blood Sister

Shield Maiden

Tiger Lily

Night Goddess

Darkly Begotten

Dark Valentines Collection

Star Child

The Watchers

Diablo

The Novellas (Part of the Sirens' Storyworld)

Protector

Lost Moon

Non-Fiction

My Migraine Story

ACKNOWLEDGEMENTS

A special thank you to my readers, who, I'm sure, are some of the best in the world. And as always, my team, Nicky Lovick, Daniela Orwegoor and Jane Harrison.

GLOSSARY

Characters

Principal Royal Children

Xavier – Son of Dante and Tia
Alexia – Daughter of Dante and Tia
JJ – Son of Jay and Tia
Rock – Daughter of Keenan and Lacy
Flame - Daughter of Keenan and Lacy
Keefa – Son of Darres and Isla
Dannon – Son of Darres and Isla
Loki – Adopted son of Vionne and Ashaya
Hunter – Son of Lily - stepson of Lance
Kai - Son of Lily and Lance
Kali – Daughter of Lily and Lance

Principal Human Children

Latitia Johnson
Dwayne Johnson

Richie Johnson
Paige Hopkins

The Dubonnettis

Dante Dubonnetti – King and married to Tia Storm -
Biological father to Xavier and Alexia
Tia Storm – Queen - Mother to Alexia, Xavier, JJ, Roman
and Zander

The Humans

Jay Gardiner – Biological father to JJ and bonded to Tia
Storm
Valarie Johnson – Mother to Latitia, Dwayne and Richie
Linda Hopkins – Mother to Paige
Lance McCabe – Married to Lily – Step father/Father and
mother to Hunter, Kali and Kai

The Demidovs (Ambragio)

Yaro Demidov (Rasputin) – Alexia's chosen lover
Pavel Demidov – Yaro's brother

The Bonacis

Alfonzo Bonaci – Head of the Bonaci royal family and great
uncle to the Royal Children
Sebastian Bonaci – Brother to Alfonzo and grandfather to
the Royal children
Drew Stone – Children's uncle – Coach to the basketball
team

The Borge (Murrs)

Vionne Borge – Lord Advocate of Murrtaine - Adoptive father to Loki

Ashaya Borge - Wife to Vionne - Adoptive mother to Loki

Darres Borge – Married to Isla – Father and mother to Keefa and Dannon

Naomi – Grandmother to all the royal children

The Florianna

Cesaré Florianna – Head of the Florianna royal family

Santalini Guards

Keenan Santalini – Married to children's aunt Lacy – Father to Rock and Flame

Reeve Santalini – Fellow guard and lover to Valarie Johnson

Terms particular to the Atlanteans

Elixir – Potion taken by humans to prevent an extreme reaction, or even death, in the event of breathing an Atlantean's essence.

The Breath/bond – The essence of an Atlantean, passed to their lover.

Filfla – Royal palace and island hideaway

Murrtaine – Underwater city

Atlas – Atlanteans' home planet

www.ingramcontent.com/pod-product-compliance
Lightning Source LLC
Chambersburg PA
CBHW050604170726
48283CB00001B/105